Diamonds Are Forever

Vogue

Crown Jewelz Publishing

Diamonds Are Forever
Part II of The Diamond Collection
Third Edition
Copyright ©2013 Vogue

Cover Design by Vogue

ISBN: 978-0-9888004-3-4

This book is a work of fiction. References to real people, events, establishments, organizations, or locales are intended only to provide a sense of authenticity and are used fictitiously. All other characters and all incidents and dialogue are drawn from the author's imagination and are not to be construed as "real."

Acknowledgements

I give all praise and honor to your name, dear Lord! Thank you for answering every single prayer that I've had. You are the reason I breathe! You are the reason I write!

Mama, you nicknamed me, "Starchild." You knew from the day I was born, my capabilities. I live to make you proud. I miss you! I love you! Daddy, thanks for instilling so much wisdom in me! One of the greatest moments of my life is hearing you say that you were proud of me! I love you!

To Eldrena, you are the inspiration for Flame, Inc. The world is waiting to see your talent. I can't wait until they do. I speak your success into existence!

This book is dedicated to Sherise and Madison Jones. Sherise, you dealt with my ramblings all night and day. Thank you for always listening to me and helping me to figure things out. *Diamonds Are Forever* wouldn't be the same without you!

To the Blanding and Simpson families, I am truly blessed to have such a wonderful support system! I love you all.

It is imperative that I thank the following individuals and businesses who have shown me immense support. I would not be where I am without you all: Shannon and Hair Essentials (Rock Hill, SC), Marcel Thorton and the staff of The Marcel Show (Hot 96.3 WMAR FM), Cristina d'Erizans, Stacy Brice, Jose White, Carol Battle, Gwendolyn Spurlock, Marie Dickerson, Alisha Campbell, Alberta Falls and Beauty of Color Hair Studio (Rock Hill, SC), Michael Burris, Keidra Hardin, Janie Steele, Mandy Haney, Rachelle Orange, Miranda Williams, Kyvia Crisco, Ashley Gary-Roper, Theresa Gary, Crystal Starkes, Michele Brock, Jessica Banks, and Kelly Stratoti.

In addition, Tyler Young, Dominque Grisby, Stacey Hope-Lindsay (Stills by Stacey), Jessica Lucas, Lakia Barr, Sabrina Hammond, Shandy Manigault, Ursa Hawkins, Willie and Toya Graham, Nick McClain, Cindy and Dean Bowens, Tiffany Sanders, Shawn Damon, Lisa Orr and Nu Cuts Salon, Niki Behr, Sharon Wallace, Mary Roddey, Felicia Robinson, Trenton Jackson, Sedrick Singletary, Dominique Elease, Desiree Brecheisen, Kayauna Wiggins, Good Ole Boys, Michael Kirk, Barry Thompson, Levitate Magazine, Lisa

Howard, Charles Graham, Sharieka Wade, Rashawn Mccombs, Gabrielle Price, Jennifer Steele, Betty Thorne, Michael and Alicia Smith, Tiffany McMullen, Sharlene Williams, Bradley Suber and Ann Glenn.

To Jonathan Cruse and Eartha Montgomery, you two have always supported me even when *The Morning Talk* was nothing, but a note on Facebook. Thank you from the bottom of my heart. Your encouragement and support does not go unnoticed.

To all the authors who have shown me love and given me encouragement, thank you!

To the Transfers, thank you for writing, "Get 'Em," it was my inspiration to be on the grind.

To the women of Sigma Gamma Rho Sorority, Inc., thank you for exhibiting true sisterhood. You have supported me since 2005 when I introduced myself to the world as a Sigma woman. EEE-YIP!

To all my readers, you are the true diamonds! I would not be where I am without you! Do not ever give up on your dreams! Stay on the grind!

Contact

Author Blog: www.simplyvogue.net
Instagram: iam_carmendavenport

Prologue | *May*

The pale grey door opened slowly, allowing Carmen to take a step outside her 8x5 cell. She told herself when this day came; she wasn't going to look back. She was going to put one foot in front of the other, leaving behind the stale smell of the wing, the loud yelling of the inmates and the memory of being locked up.

Now, after a total of six months, she kept her promise.

When the guard led her out her cell, she took her into a small room to change into regular clothes. Carmen was accustomed to the lack of privacy and nudity no longer fazed her. Therefore, she was quick to let the jumpsuit fall at her ankles. A coral sundress was on the table, which she slid over her undergarments. It stopped about two inches above her knees, fitting her frame perfectly. Once her shoes were on, she followed the guard to the releasing department.

"Are you going home?" an inmate asked as she walked by.

"Yes, ma'am," Carmen answered. She took a quick peek at the inmate, realizing she was new to the facility. After giving her a small smile, she gazed forward, continuing the trek to the administrative wing of the prison. When she reached her destination, she collected her belongings as well as the money her parents had put in her account.

"Are you having a girl or boy?" the clerk asked, peering at her belly.

"A boy," Carmen replied, drumming her fingers on the counter. She touched her head, feeling the tight cornrows she got the night before. Due to the vitamins and pills she took for the baby; her hair had grown down her back.

"Are you ready?" the guard asked.

"I've been ready for six months," Carmen responded. Tears formed in the corner of her eyes and fell down her face as it hit her. Her prison days were over. While the memory would remain, at least it would be on the outside of the facility. The thought made her remember her first night in prison. She even saw a flashback of Kane, an undercover federal agent, as he played a tape of her confession in court.

A damn Triad agent, Carmen thought. She remembered her father, Harold Davenport, shaking his head as her sentence was read. As for her, she nearly blacked out. The outcome of her trial seemed to be the biggest thing to hit Brookstone. The news couldn't stop talking about how Harold Davenport, the owner of Davenport Realty, was now the father of a convicted felon. In addition, she was reporting to prison nearly four months' pregnant.

Carmen signed her final release papers and watched as the door opened, leading her back into the outside world. She searched the parking lot for a familiar face until she saw her best friend, Tiara, standing out front. Her hair was now a medium auburn color and she had gained a couple of pounds. Carmen didn't know whether to smile or frown. Tiara was by her side during the trial, but once she turned herself in, her friend went ghost. She placed Tiara's name on her visitation list, however, her friend never showed.

"You are fat," Tiara greeted, patting her stomach. She was about to say more until she noticed the solemn expression on Carmen's face. "I know we have plenty to talk about, let me get this from you." Tiara grabbed Carmen's bag and led her to her car. Still driving the same Bentley Brooklands her ex, Carlos, had given her, she placed Carmen's bag in the backseat before opening her door. "Don't expect this kind of courtesy every day. You're lucky this is a special occasion," she joked.

Carmen didn't reply. She got inside and put on her seatbelt. In less than six seconds, Tiara started the car and was pulling out the prison's parking lot. Silence filled the car as she drove. Carmen could see Tiara staring at her every now and then. They hadn't spoken in almost six months, so she didn't sweat the twenty minutes of silence.

"I know you're wondering what's been going on with me."

"You took the words right out my mouth," Carmen replied as they neared the interstate.

"I've been taking care of you."

Carmen needed an explanation. "You've been taking care of me?"

"I've been trying to get things in order. When the shit went down with Jay, I couldn't leave you hanging. I had to step up," Tiara told her. "I got you a fully furnished apartment downtown, which is only a couple of blocks away from headquarters."

When Carmen didn't respond, Tiara kept talking, updating her on everything that occurred during her six month prison stint. "Since you confided in me about working for Carlos, I knew there was money somewhere. After you were taken to the hospital, I made it my duty to find it. Luckily, your diary wasn't hard to find. You wrote an excellent account of where everything was and all I had to do was collect. I took all your valuables from Jay's house, the money from the Bentley, and your check from the Diamond Exchange. I had your accountant help me take control over your funds and I worked on your dream. I got the building for headquarters and opened two stores. There is one in Times Square and one in the Brookstone

Galleria. Of course, the first location is still open and probably has the most sales."

Carmen faced the window and closed her eyes.

"I found the designs that were in your drawer, too. I guess you weren't sitting in your office doing nothing like I thought. I took the liberty of getting those manufactured. The white suit, the one with the cubic zirconia cufflinks; it took you to the top. I mean, it's not every day a woman gets out of prison and is already a self-made multi-millionaire."

Carmen opened her eyes, allowing the tears to fall down her face. She then turned in Tiara's direction so she could get a visual picture of her appreciation.

"You may have thought I had forgotten about you," Tiara continued, "but I didn't. I was taking care of business. I dropped out of college so I could make sure you and your son were set for life. I knew no one else was going to do it. Flame went through a lot after you got arrested. Thankfully, your employees remained faithful, and the doors stayed open. Now, you have a whole new set of executives who you need to meet."

Carmen hung on to every word, feeling ashamed for the hatred she formed for Tiara. Her friend hadn't abandoned her like she thought. She was too busy to visit because she was running her company. In silence, Carmen praised God for the blessing.

"Say something, Carm," Tiara urged, looking at her.

"Thank you isn't enough," Carmen muttered. She stared at Tiara as she drove, talking a mile a minute. "Why did you do this? After all I've done to you? You know I slept with Carlos behind your back. You know I was working for him."

"Girl, let me tell you this. It was either help you or kill you and the last thing I want is to be sitting in prison." Tiara laughed at the thought. "We don't have to talk about it, though. Your parents are flying back in this weekend. They want to be here before the baby is due." Tiara paused. A moment of silence was needed for her next question. "Have you heard anything from Jay?"

Carmen shook her head. While she did have an update, all she could think about was how things had turned out for her ex-boyfriend. He was currently being held in the men's division of the Metropolitan Correctional Facility under maximum security. She heard about the fights he was in and even the guards he assaulted. His mouth was bound shut because he started biting other inmates, too. Carmen kept up with him via the news and learned he was given a life sentence. He also was diagnosed with bipolar disorder.

"Malik went and saw him yesterday," Carmen told her, remembering the conversation they shared. One of Jay's right-hands and a mutual friend, Malik was a regular visitor of the prison. When he came to see her, she told him she was having a baby boy. She also gave him permission to tell Jay, the father of her child. In return, he gave her an update on Jay's condition. From what Malik said, the rumors were true. Jay was in confinement and kept away from general population. Somehow, Malik was able to hold a conversation with him. When he asked him about a future with his son, Jay's response was ice cold. He told him he didn't want it. The words hurt Carmen to her core, and she learned to accept that her son wouldn't have a relationship with his father. "He doesn't want him," she shared, taking a deep breath.

"For some reason, I already knew that." Tiara rubbed her lips together, trying to decide if she should bring up Kane. When they first met him, he pretended to own a clothing store named Production. Now, they knew him as a federal agent who received praise for taking down one of the country's biggest drug lords. "I know someone who wants him. You know him as Kane. He used to—" Carmen interrupted her.

"No, I know him as Michael," she blurted. "His name is Michael Antonio Kane, and he is the Triad agent who went undercover as a store owner to take down my boyfriend. He then pretended to fall in love with me and arrested me during a raid at Jay's warehouse. I did six months of an eight-year term because of him."

Tiara swallowed at the brashness in Carmen's words. "He wrote you when you were locked up. He gave me every single letter because he knew he couldn't mail it to you. If you read the letters, it will clear up everything. Give him a chance."

"I don't want to read anything he's written. I refused his visits, phone calls and even vomited all over my cell the day they tried to make me see him. He wouldn't leave me alone." Carmen remembered the day vividly when Kane arrested her. He stared her down, asking her repeatedly if she was pregnant. She told him yes and he proceeded to put a set of handcuffs around her wrists. The next time she saw him, they were in court, and he was playing a tape of her confessing to theft.

Tiara shared her thoughts. "He didn't know he was going to fall in love with you, Carm. He was doing his job. Your parents were able to forgive him, why can't you? I've spoken to him, and I know he loves you. He wants to make it right, but you won't let him."

"How do his actions prove he loves me? He testified against me."

Tiara wasn't going to argue about the issue any longer. She encouraged her to read the letters, which she stashed at Carmen's apartment.

Her friend only huffed in response before turning away from her. Tiara allowed her to have her moment because she knew Carmen had been through a lot. If anything, her friend needed peace. She couldn't make her read Kane's letters like she couldn't make Jay have a relationship with his son. All she could do was pray for them and allow God to lead their paths.

***

Carmen dumped the envelopes onto her bed so she could start sorting through Kane's letters. If she did her math correctly then there should have been roughly a hundred and eighty or so. She put the letters in order based off the date written in the far right corner of the envelope. She then picked up the first one, almost scared to open it. As if he was egging her on, her son started kicking. "Damn, Jayceon," she said, touching her stomach, "I'll open it." She slid out the letter and her son's kicking ceased.

I guess I should start off by introducing myself. My name is Michael Antonio Kane. There it is. You finally got my real name after that night on the boat. I work for the International Triad Intelligence Agency. Right now, I am a detective at the Brookstone Police Department. There were a lot of problems with the way I handled the Santiago case. I did not remain professional and because of that, I was put on temporary leave. It worked in my best interest. After what happened, I wanted to remain in the area because I wanted to be there whenever you were released or gave birth. I planned on returning to the Triad once my leave was up.

I am now 29 years old and am still living in your parents' house. I really did buy it, but of course, I never had a store called Production. That was the worst cover-up I think I ever had. I guess this is the right time for me to tell you how I got started on the case. The Triad has been following Jay's father, Hector Santiago, for a long time. However, he was way too brilliant. Due to his ties to the government, it was hard to find substantial evidence to put him away. However, it was different with Jay. Although he had ties to the government, it wasn't anything like the ties his father had. I watched him for a long time, even visiting Sapphire on several occasions. When I started the case initially, I went undercover as a modeling agent. I planned on getting close to Tricia to get to Jay. When they broke up, the investigation was halted. I kept at it for a few more weeks, but the case was going nowhere.

I sat back in the cut until word came through that there was a new girl on Jay's arm. The captain had pictures of you and told me to watch you for a couple of days. I did and it wasn't long before I started falling for you. I even went to the captain, telling him I couldn't finish out the case. I knew I would mess up, which I did. When your parents put their house up for sale; I knew it was God's way of telling me it was time. I used my meetings with your parents as a chance to learn more about you and decided to go undercover as a clothing store owner.

However, things didn't go like I thought. I was attracted to you, but I never thought I would fall in love. I don't know if you remember, but I told you on the plane I couldn't have feelings for you. I was contemplating telling you the truth then. It never was my intention to put you in prison or to testify against you. I didn't have a choice. Agents could hear everything I said, you said, and others around us. I wanted desperately for you to tell me you didn't know about the diamond. When you admitted to stealing it; I knew it was over. I knew what they were going to force me to do.

I don't care anymore about you sleeping with Carlos. I don't care you're pregnant by Jay. I will love your baby as if it were my own. I love you, and I'm not going to stop working on your case until you've been released.

Carmen rubbed her stomach, closing the letter. While she thought it would soften the hate she had for him, she still felt the same. However, she knew her feelings could potentially change. Carmen went to the second envelope, opened it, and kept reading until she fell asleep.

***

It took Carmen four days to get through all of Kane's letters. Within the first twenty, Kane explained the entire operation up until the day he raided Jay's warehouse. The letters, thereafter, detailed his life and how she came to be released. Due to her confession that the pink diamond was located underneath a floorboard at the Santiago estate, the Triad began an extensive search of the mansion. Nevertheless, the pink diamond was never found. Since he was placed on temporary leave, Kane could no longer be hands on with the case. He still believed in the validity of Carmen's confession and convinced another agent to take over.

When the diamond wasn't located, Kane took matters into his own hands. He secretly met up with Tiara only to learn the diamond was in her possession. She refused to turn it in; although he informed her there could possibly be a retrial. Tiara wouldn't give up the diamond, so Kane brainstormed a new idea. He even brought Tiara and Malik in to help him execute it.

As far as Carmen knew, in early April, news reports surfaced, stating that the Pink Sunrise diamond was found underneath a floorboard in the attic of Jay Santiago's mansion. Days later, it was revealed the diamond was a fake and Carmen Davenport was wrongfully imprisoned. However, the real Pink Sunrise diamond was still missing.

Carmen remembered the day to a T. Her lawyer came to visit her, telling her he was starting her release process. It was the best news she ever received. To know Kane was behind her getting out, it made her more sympathetic about their relationship. She didn't know when she was going to see him, but she knew it would be soon.

Saturday morning, her parents arrived, spending the night at her apartment. After devoting herself to them for the weekend, she returned to work on Monday morning. She had barely drawn while she was in prison and wanted to know what her company was selling. There were about ten drawings left in her office drawer and every single design was now being modeled in an ad overlooking her receptionist's desk.

"This came for you today," her receptionist said as soon as Carmen walked up to her.

Carmen greeted her, noticing her nameplate read Cathy Devoe. While she wanted to socialize, the note was from Malik, and she needed to read the contents. For the first time, she went in her office, taking only a quick peek around before reading Malik's letter.

Carmen, we need to talk. I'll go ahead and let you know this is about the baby. I want to see you tomorrow. You can meet me downtown at Flame at about ten o'clock.

Carmen folded the letter, wondering why Malik wanted to meet with her. They had already spoken rather recently. She wondered if their conversation was going to be centered on Jay. Malik was the only person who was still in contact with him. While many of Jay's men faced prison sentences, Malik was never arrested and got away scot-free. Carmen knew he was handling Jay's business affairs and this impromptu meeting sparked her curiosity. Carmen pondered on the matter until she grew tired of thinking about it. She could spend hours on end trying to figure things out or she could wait until she met with Malik.

Carmen decided on the latter and proceeded to check out her office. In six months, she had gone to prison, became the CEO of a multi-million dollar brand and now was about to become a mother. While it seemed everything was perfect, Carmen had one more task to take care of. Before the day ended, she had to visit Michael Kane.

***

Carmen spent a good five minutes trying to locate the Narcotics division of the Brookstone Police Department. Police were running amuck, making it hard for her to focus on anything. It was bad enough she randomly dropped by. Carmen looked around the department until her eyes landed on Kane's bald head. He was writing on a notepad and by the time she reached him, he sensed her presence.

Kane sat there frozen as he noticed Carmen at his desk. His eyes darted all over her, starting at her protruding belly then at her hair, which had grown past her shoulders. Her skin was still the dark mocha he remembered; smooth with a glow to it. The mere sight of her made him drop his ink pen and stand up. He dreamed countless nights of what he would say to her, but now, he was at a loss for words.

Unlike him, Carmen wasn't tongue-tied and greeted him with a soft hello. Automatically, he said the words back, rubbing his hands over her stomach. "Be careful with him," she warned. "He's a little aggressive today." Carmen gave him a warm smile before asking how he was.

"I'm doing better now that you're here," he replied. "I was…" Kane moved towards his desk, picking up the letter he was writing. "I guess you can read this now." He handed her the letter and watched as she folded it in two. She then slid it inside her purse.

"I'll read it tonight. I've already read all the other ones, all one hundred and eighty-three." Carmen watched as his lips parted and when he apologized, she pressed her finger on his lips like he did the first day they met. "You don't need to say anything about what happened. I've heard it a billion times," she said, rolling her eyes. "I hated you for a long time. Well, it was six months to be exact. After reading the letters, I understood the position I put you in. You are a good man and I still believe we may be soulmates."

Her words made Kane drop his head. He wanted her to say that. His purpose in writing the letters was to convince her to forgive him. "What did Jay say about the baby?" Carmen's face fell and Kane knew the outcome wasn't good.

"He doesn't want him," she answered.

Kane's eyes glanced at her stomach as he realized her predicament. She was bound to be a single mother since Jay received a life sentence, but now, it was official. Jay refused to have any kind of relationship with his son. While the chances were slim of him ever being released, Kane was aware Jay's lawyers were working night and day on an appeal. "He doesn't deserve him," he told her. "I want him, Carm. I'll take care of him. Can I have him?" He didn't wait for her response, continuing to speak. "We'll get married. I'll formally adopt him, and you won't have to worry about him ever knowing about Jay."

Carmen wasn't quick to agree. "I don't know about this. I know this situation isn't good, but I want my son to know who he is. I spent twenty-one years of my life not knowing my father's real identity. He changed his name to separate himself from the Santiago cartel. I don't want my son to experience that. Besides, I've already picked out his name. I want to name him Jayceon King Santiago."

"He doesn't need to know about Jay," Kane shot back. "He doesn't even want him. We can name him Jayceon Santiago Kane and we'll call him King."

"I haven't agreed to this yet," Carmen replied with a nervous chuckle. "We're talking about telling my son that you're his father. My name has been plastered all over newspapers and magazines because of my relationship with Jay. It's no secret that Jay Santiago is the father of my child. The whole world knows about us."

"Why should it matter if Jay doesn't want to be in his life?"

Carmen didn't have a response. She heard out Malik's own mouth that Jay didn't want King. In addition, her mother already reprimanded her about giving her son Jay's last name. She told her the right thing to do was to make him a Davenport since she wasn't married. They went back and forth on the issue until Carmen put her foot down. Now, she felt as if Kane was convincing her to change her mind. *If I start a relationship with Kane, and we get married, my last name will be Kane. If it happens within the next year, King will still be a baby. He will only know about Kane. He'll be his father regardless.*

Carmen pondered on the thought a minute or so longer until she became satisfied with the decision. Kane was willing to make an honest woman out of her while also giving her son the two-parent household he rightfully deserved. "Okay," she agreed, "we'll name him Jayceon Santiago Kane and we'll call him King."

Kane's mouth formed a large grin and he grabbed Carmen's hand, planting a kiss on top. He made a killing off the Santiago case, and his earnings were going to be well spent. As soon as he could get to a jewelry store, he was purchasing an engagement ring and getting down on one knee. Within the next two months, if all went well, he planned on becoming a husband and was going to welcome his first child.

***

The following morning, Carmen walked in the parking lot of Flame towards Malik's car. She wasn't quite sure what they were set to discuss and at the same time, she had to inform Malik she was engaged. In addition, she had to break the news that Kane would be officially adopting King. Unsure of how he would take the announcement, she got inside Malik's car without saying hello. He didn't seem to notice, greeting her, happily.

"Dang, shorty, you're big," he yelled, looking at her stomach. "You're about to drop that little boy any day now."

Carmen patted her stomach. "So what's up?" she asked, wanting to get to the bottom of everything. "I know you spoke with Jay about the baby."

"I lied to you," Malik admitted. "I can't see Jay, but there's a guard who's been giving me some leeway. Jay is talking to him and he's talking to me. He still doesn't want the baby, but he wants to take responsibility for his actions. So here," he continued, handing her an envelope.

Carmen grabbed the envelope, feeling how flat it was and opened it. Inside was a check written to her for ten thousand dollars.

"Each week, I'll be handing you a check for the baby. It's gonna take me a while to get Sapphire back, but Jay had a lot of money hidden in various places. He wants me to use the funds to take care of his son and his businesses."

"Malik, I don't need this money. Kane and I are getting married and—" Malik cut her off.

"I don't give a fuck what you and Kane are doing. If Jay wants to take care of his child then I'm going to let him. Look, I've been working with Jay's lawyer, Gomez, on a plan to get him out. He's gonna be there a while, but hopefully not for life. If he does what his psychiatrist says then getting him out can work a whole lot faster."

"So what's the plan?" Carmen asked. Her life would change drastically if Jay was released. He wouldn't be pleased to learn she married Kane or that he adopted his son.

"The plan is to reopen his case," Malik replied. "The jury didn't buy the story of him fighting in self-defense. They completely ignored the scar on his face or the fact that Domino fired a shot at him. If Jay is good and making progress, we can get the case reopened with a new jury. If you're concerned or scared, rest easy, it's not like he's getting out tomorrow."

Carmen stared at the check. She wanted to tear it up because it was a move she expected Jay to make. In the past, he always showered her with purses, diamonds, and clothes, when all she really wanted was him. It made her question if he would ever learn there wasn't a price tag on love. Since their current situation wouldn't allow her to find out, she decided to collect the checks and create a trust fund for King. He wouldn't be able to touch the money until he was eighteen and hopefully, when the time came, he would use it to start his own business.

"Carmen," Malik began, interrupting her thoughts. "Jay is sick. He's not talking straight, and he looks a mess. He did the right thing, making sure he gave you money. Don't look at him like he's the only guilty party. You did some foul shit to him."

Carmen was aware of what she did and didn't need the reminder. "I never said I was innocent. I know what I did to him, and I know what he did to me."

Malik studied Carmen's face. A part of her did sound apologetic while another part sounded like she blamed all her problems on Jay. In his opinion, she was the one in the wrong. The only reason he was helping her was because he knew how much his brother, Rakim, loved her. He would've wanted him to look out for her. "Every week we'll be meeting up for me to give you a check. When the baby is born, I need one picture to show Jay. That's all he wants," Malik stated. "Is that a deal?"

Carmen agreed. "I'll give him a picture. I do want to let you know I'm getting married. Kane is going to officially adopt the baby. His name will be Jayceon Santiago Kane, but we're going to call him King."

"I'm not telling Jay any of that. I wish I didn't know. All you need to do is give him his picture and take the money. Other than that, you don't need to communicate with him."

"Fine," Carmen blurted, opening the door. She got out the car and slammed the door shut.

"Carmen," Malik yelled as she headed towards her Lexus. He waited for her to turn around and when she did, he gave her another word of advice. "Don't put a name on the back of the picture. You can keep your face in the news all you want, but don't put the kid. I know you gotta do press for Flame, but it's only going to mess Jay up mentally if he sees his son with Kane. It was only a matter of time before he was gonna get him, too. Carlos told him about the affair. He knows you and Kane were together."

Carmen bit her lip at his words. She never wanted Jay to know about Kane. In fact, she had every intention to be with Jay once she learned Kane skipped town. Her plan was to devote herself to him and eventually become his wife. Nevertheless, things took a turn.

"Believe it or not," Malik continued. "Jay still loves you. He just has a hard time believing the good girl he fell for deceived him. Once his broken heart heals, so will his mind."

1| *Like Father, Like Son*

"Get his money."

Kristian turned her head, not wanting to see what her brother, King, was about to do. For the past six minutes, she and her best friend, Coco, watched him give one of their peers, Darnell, a classic Brookstone beatdown. Now, King and his friends were getting ready to rob him.

"Get his shoes, too, those are some nice shoes," King was saying as his friend, Jerome, dug in the guy's pockets.

"King, you settled it, let's go," Kristian said, grabbing his arm. Her brother looked at her, giving her one of his, 'you're next,' type of looks. The expression alone made her shut up.

"That's all the money?" King asked, looking at the cash.

"Yeah, he only had three hundred dollars." Jerome held out the money for King to see.

It wasn't enough to settle the debt and King needed every penny owed to him. He took the money from Jerome's hands, counting each dollar himself. "How much y'all think those shoes are worth? It might be able to cover somethin'."

"Man, at least ninety bucks," Jerome guessed, taking one of Darnell's shoes off.

"Don't take his shoes, Jerome," Coco yelled. She covered her face, still in shock at how the afternoon panned out. A few minutes after the bell, she and Kristian headed to the school's parking lot, only to see King, jumping one of their classmates.

"Girl, shut up, we're taking what we can get. He's in debt to me. He's lucky I let him live." King hated that Coco and Kristian were witnesses. His brawl with Darnell was supposed to be a private matter.

"She's right, King," Kristian agreed. She wrinkled her face. Darnell's face was bloody, and he was trying to catch his breath. King had proven his point and it was time to move on.

"Get in the car, Kris." King approached his sister because he didn't want her in his business either. Although he and Kristian were close, she was going to mess up his plan.

Kristian didn't budge. "I'm not. You have your money, now leave him alone."

"Man, his ass is short on the money," King argued, stuffing the cash into his pocket. King flipped Darnell over, so he was lying on his back. "Look at me," he ordered, punching Darnell in his chest. "Open your eyes." Darnell squinted. "What else you got on you?"

"King, let's go, people are starting to notice." Kristian saw some of their peers pointing in their direction.

"Didn't I tell you to get in the car?" King was agitated. "You want a ride home or what?"

Kristian backed away from her brother and folded her arms across her chest. She didn't necessarily need a ride home, but she couldn't call her parents otherwise King would be in trouble for not picking her up. Unsure of what to do, she looked at Coco.

"My mama is coming in a few minutes if you want to ride with me," her friend said, shrugging her shoulders.

"Nah, I'm going to call our father," Kristian announced, pulling out her cell phone. She knew their father was the only one to calm King down.

"Don't do that," she heard King say as she walked away.

"Well, come on, then," she yelled back. Kristian walked up to King's black Mustang. She knew their father was either at the precinct or patrolling around Brookstone.

"Man, y'all hold up, let me get this chick squared away," King growled. He was growing irritated with Kristian since she kept interrupting his business. "Come here," he shouted, grabbing her arm. He pushed her onto the hood of the car so she would understand he wasn't playing. "You need to stop runnin' your damn mouth," he said through gritted teeth. "I'm taking care of business."

"Get off me, King."

"Shut up," he yelled, holding her wrists. "Darnell owes me money." King let her go and walked towards his latest victim. "How am I gonna get my money?" He watched as the boy struggled to speak. King had loosened a few teeth in his mouth, which was evident from the blood on his face.

"We need to roll out, rent-a-cop is coming," Jerome announced, walking towards King's Mustang.

King looked up, seeing the school's security guard. "This is your lucky day," he barked. He had no choice but to let Darnell go. "You better have my money the next time I see you."

"Let's go, King," he heard his sister yell.

"I'm coming," he shouted. He looked across the street, seeing the security guard sprinting. He punched Darnell several more times in the face. "You better get my money." With a final glance in Darnell's direction, he ran towards his Mustang. His friends were piled in the car, and he noticed Coco was the only one left behind. She bore the same features as his sister except her hair was silky and jet black. Despite her undeniable beauty, he still gave her a warning. "You better not say shit," he told her, sliding in the driver's seat, "or you'll be my next assignment."

Kristian sucked her teeth in response as King pulled off. Due to traffic, the security guard hadn't made it across the street, but eventually, he would. Coco would be forced to talk since she was a witness to the brawl. Unlike them, she couldn't jump in a car and roll out.

"You know he saw us, King." The words were spoken by King's other friend, Rico, who was sitting in the backseat next to Kristian. He was growing nervous by the second because he was just released from juvie. In addition, his cousin, Jerome, was released only days earlier.

"Man, whatever, he isn't going to do anything. He'll let my dad handle the situation."

Kristian knew her brother expected their father to bail him out. Sometimes it worked, sometimes it didn't. She also knew the cops at the Brookstone Police Department were fed up with him. It seemed like every month King would get into something. The only time he wasn't getting into trouble was when he was spending a couple of months at the juvenile detention center downtown.

"Your little sister better not rat on us," she heard Jerome say.

"Shut up, it ain't like you did anything," Kristian shot back.

Jerome turned around at her comment. "I was the one who caught him. I laid his ass down first."

"Who even cares about that shit, Kris?" King replied.

"Whatever," she yelled back.

Kristian sat lower in her seat as King headed towards West Brookstone. He was dropping Rico and Jerome off since they stayed over on the Westside. After several absences and run-ins with the law; they were like King, high school dropouts. They ran with her brother all week long until one of them ended up in juvie. Then, once they got out, the cycle would start over.

"So, what do you want me to do with his shoes?" Jerome asked.

"Wear 'em, what do you think?" Rico answered with a chuckle. "Hand me one of them bad boys."

Jerome tossed one of the shoes to Rico and watched as he smelt it.

"That's some foul shit right there," Rico said, laughing. He handed the shoe back to Jerome who did the same.

"This mug has some athlete foot type shit going on." Jerome made a face, taking the shoe away from his nose.

"He probably does," King chimed in. He glanced at the shoes, knowing he had taken a loss. Now, he was going to be short for his own dealer. The last thing King wanted was to be ducking and diving from Lil' Noc. He had until Friday to come up with the money and if he was a dollar short, there would be repercussions. The idea of being in another fight made him think of his sister. She was upset, and she had every right to be. At the current moment, he couldn't handle another run-in with the law. A judge already told him if he saw him again he was going to jail.

"Man, drop me off right here," Jerome ordered, interrupting King's thoughts.

They were passing by a diner. King figured Jerome wanted a bite to eat. He wasn't getting a cut of what he took from Darnell, so he hoped he had some loot. "I'll check y'all later," King said, once he parked. King stared at Jerome, seeing a look of surprise on his friend's face. For a brief second, he was unsure of what it meant. Then, he remembered. Jerome was expecting a cut of the money. In King's opinion, the shoes were good enough. Jerome didn't owe any money to a drug dealer so he could easily sell the shoes and eat for a good week. Since his friend wouldn't want that suggestion, King decided not to say anything. He simply got out the driver's seat so he could let Rico out.

"Well, what about—" King cut Jerome off.

"I said I'll check y'all later," he repeated. King put some thunder in his voice so Jerome would know the discussion was over. In reply, Jerome turned towards the backseat where Kristian sat. Automatically, King knew what his friend was thinking. Jerome had been feeling his sister for a hot minute. King was overprotective of her and didn't want her rolling with someone like Jerome. Besides, his friend only wanted to fuck. "Get out of here," King muttered, getting back inside his car. He didn't owe Jerome anything and he wasn't going to make Kristian go out with him.

Thankfully, Jerome didn't press the issue. He got out the car without another word and walked in the diner with Rico. Once they were inside, King glanced in the rearview mirror to stare at his sister. He knew why Jerome wanted her. Kristian had a smooth chocolate complexion and a shape fit for modeling. A lot of dudes wanted to get with her. Kristian was a good girl and an excellent student who never put their parents through anything. As for him, he was the exact opposite, even physically.

He was light-skinned while everyone else was dark-skinned. Even his grandparents were dark. King remembered being around six-years-old when he started to wonder why Kristian was so much darker than him. He thought she was dirty. He filled the tub up with hot water and put tons of bubble bath in it. He undressed her, sat her inside, and then started to scrub her. He didn't even know the water was too hot for her skin until her cries caught their mother's attention. That was when she sat down and explained to him his little sister wasn't dirty. She told him Kristian was made in the image of God, which meant she was perfection. Ever since the conversation, King never felt like he belonged. In his opinion, he was the oddball.

"I don't know why you're looking back here. You know I'm not getting with Jerome," Kristian fussed.

King rolled his eyes as he proceeded to leave the diner. "I don't need a reminder," he shot back.

"Officer Rogers saw you. You know he's going to tell Daddy."

"Shut up," King yelled.

Kristian sat further in her seat. It was obvious her brother didn't care. Sometimes she wondered if her brother even knew what he was doing. If Darnell pressed charges, King was going straight to jail. The concept was simple, yet King acted as if he didn't grasp it. If he wanted attention, he got plenty of it. He had seen a psychiatrist, but the lady said she couldn't break him. He refused to talk to her no matter what angle or trick she used. Kristian tried to talk to her brother, but he would only push her away.

She was fed up and looking forward to getting a break from him. When he pulled into their driveway, she noticed that neither one of their parents were home. Their mother, Carmen, was a fashion designer and CEO of Flame, Inc. She arrived home at about five or six, depending on how things were going at the office. Her days were usually spent designing clothes, approving ads, and sometimes on the weekends, attending fashion shows. This year, her mother was starting a juniors' line entitled *Peaches*, which she had become the face for.

Kristian tried to focus her mind on the modeling campaign versus her brother since he was upsetting her. Nonetheless, King had other plans. Once they were in the kitchen, he talked about how she didn't know the full story of what happened with Darnell. In true sibling fashion, she argued with him, trying to get him to see the error of his ways. It didn't work and soon, she was sitting there in silence as her brother fixed a sandwich.

"Do you know Lil' Noc?" he asked, starting another conversation. "I work for him."

Kristian chuckled at the idea. "Yeah, right," she muttered. "You don't work for him."

"I do work for him. All that paper I've been having, I got it from him. Those new rims on my Mustang, the money came from him. He didn't get at Jerome or Rico, though, just me."

"So what, King, do you really think you're royalty now? Noc is like one of the biggest drug dealers over there on the Westside. You're destined to go to jail for messing with him."

King ignored her comment, continuing to fix his sandwich.

"You know about Mama's past. She already told you she doesn't want you to end up like her. Do this for Mama, King."

"The shit is done. If Darnell doesn't have my money by Friday then it's over for him."

"Are you going to kill him?"

King grabbed a knife, sliding globs of mayonnaise on both sides of his bread. He wasn't supposed to reveal anything about his first murder. He wished he hadn't spoken of it. "Darnell owes me money. I owe Lil' Noc money. If Darnell doesn't give me my money then I can't give Lil' Noc his."

"I guess you're shit out of luck then."

King noticed she used a curse word. "You're never going to understand."

"You're right," Kristian agreed. "I'm not. I don't understand you, King. I don't understand what your problem is. Why do you have to hustle anyway? We're rich kids. Our parents have more money than they can spend. You're living the good life."

"Maybe I don't want to live the good life. Maybe I don't want to be some damn rich kid."

"Whatever, King, you have some major issues." Kristian slid off her stool and was about to leave the kitchen until she heard a door open.

"Sit down," King ordered, taking several bites of his sandwich.

Kristian ignored him, heading in the den. She stopped in her tracks when King gave her a look that scared her. She went back to the stool, praying her parents didn't know about Darnell. When her mother came in the kitchen, Kristian knew her mind was elsewhere based off her conversation.

"I said the same thing," her mother was saying. "That shirt was terrible. She wasn't putting that in my store."

Kristian watched as her mother headed for King. She planted a quick kiss on his cheek before giving her the same treatment.

"It was a hot mess, but I have to go, the kids are here," she said, walking to the sink. "I might cook. It depends on how Kane feels. Sometimes he wants takeout, and sometimes he wants a home-cooked meal."

Kristian watched as her brother raised his knife to her. She made a face at him but stopped when her mother turned around.

"Okay, Tiara, I'm gonna let you go," her mother said, hanging up the phone.

"Hi," Kristian greeted, trying to appear joyful.

"What happened?" her mother asked, seeing through her façade.

"Nothing," Kristian said.

"So, why was your brother pointing a knife at you?"

Kristian realized their mother had seen him through his reflection in the window, which was over the kitchen sink.

"We were just messing," King explained, piling the rest of his sandwich in his mouth.

"Just messing?" Carmen asked. She raised her eyebrow at King, knowing he was up to something. Kristian always knew what her brother had done before anyone else. "Don't be pointing weapons at your sister. Besides, you're the one who looks like you've been stabbed."

King didn't see any stains on his shirt until he felt his mother's hands on him. It was then he saw a blood stain from when he was beating up Darnell.

"So, who's going to tell me what happened? Or should I wait for the cops to arrive?"

Carmen stood there with her hands on her hips. The one thing she hated was having the cops come to her house to pick up her son. The whole neighborhood would be in their business as well as the press.

To keep from being the bearer of bad news, Kristian headed towards her room. Unfortunately, she wasn't off the hook. Carmen demanded for her to stay until she got to the bottom of everything.

"Someone better tell me why there's blood on his shirt," Carmen ordered.

King was quick with a response. "I got into it with a dude, that's all."

"Who," Carmen probed. "I want a name. The last dude you got into a fight with was the governor's grandson."

King chuckled, thinking about how easy the fight had been. It landed him a long time in juvie, but he didn't care. He taught the governor's grandson a very important lesson. About to express the thought, he was interrupted by the doorbell.

"You better pray there's a Jehovah's Witness on the other side of that door." Carmen placed her hand around her son's neck. She gave it a slight squeeze before heading to the foyer. She wasn't gone for two minutes before the kitchen became filled with police officers. Kane wasn't with them, but it didn't matter. They pushed King onto the floor, laying him on his stomach as they handcuffed him. In the meantime, Carmen stood behind them as they read King his rights.

"I haven't done shit," King yelled as they cuffed him. "Where's my Daddy?"

Kristian watched as the officers brought King to his feet.

"We'll be right behind you," Carmen announced, grabbing her keys out her purse. "Come on, Kristian, you have some talking to do."

Alongside her mother, Kristian followed behind the police officers. King usually tried to fight them, which was why so many had come. She could hear King cursing, but his words went ignored. The rule of thumb when dealing with King was to let him talk until he got tired.

"Go ahead," her mother ordered as soon as they were in the car.

Kristian didn't speak right off, which prompted Carmen to look at her. "From what one of the officers told me, King rearranged some guy's face. Who is this kid and how did he end up on King's bad side?"

Kristian grunted only because she hated the interrogation process. Since she was the only one who knew the story, she had to snitch. "His name is Darnell, and he goes to Brookstone High. King let him borrow some money and he reneged."

Carmen's suspicion was that the whole ordeal was over drugs. She knew her son was hustling because he got caught before. Not to mention, he had a new set of rims on his car and tons of new clothes. She stopped giving him money a long time ago, so she knew he was doing something illegal. She thought when she told him about her days as a hustler, he would straighten up. In the end, it only drove him to go harder. His new mantra was that hustling was in his blood. Every day, she hated he was right. More and more, he was becoming like Jay. She married Kane to protect him, but it didn't matter. King was a Santiago, and he was going to go the Santiago way. Now, here they were again, following him to the police department. Carmen couldn't take much more. "Call your father," she ordered.

Kristian did as she was told. She dialed her father's number and waited, hoping he would pick up. When he didn't, she left him a voicemail hoping he would call her back.

"He didn't answer?" Carmen asked. Kane had to know about their son's arrest. "I don't know where he is. He called me this morning at work, but he didn't call me on my lunch break. That's unlike him," she said, pulling in the parking lot of the precinct. She parked the car, looking at King who was giving the officers a hard time. "Just look at him, steady mouthing off, I don't know what to do with him."

"Man, y'all ain't shit, ain't never going to be shit, probably can't even shit," King was saying.

"Just listen to him. He's already in enough trouble." Carmen followed them inside and went straight to her husband's office, which was empty. She sat at his desk while Kristian took a seat in one of the visitor chairs. "He's not even here and our son is about to go to jail."

Kristian rubbed her eye, watching with the other one as her mother went through her father's things. "What are you doing?"

"Being nosy," Carmen replied. She didn't see anything but a bunch of cop stuff. "Are they booking him?"

"I don't know, Mama," Kristian answered. "They probably are. He got arrested." Kristian didn't know why her mother asked her that. Booking was in another part of the precinct.

Carmen ignored her daughter, clicking the mouse on her husband's computer screen. The portal for the police department came up and she minimized the window. "I wish he would hurry up. The sooner we can see what the charges are, the quicker we can get to this bail hearing. Shit, I should've stopped paying by now." Carmen heard a beep come from the computer. Her husband's instant messenger popped up.

Hey, a message read on the screen.

Carmen raised her brow when she noticed the sender wasn't another police officer. "Lady8721," she said under her breath. She shot a glance at Kristian to see if her daughter was paying her any attention. Kristian was busy digging in her tote bag. Carmen quickly replied.

Last night was great, the sender wrote back.

Carmen thought back to the night before. She cooked dinner and after spending some time with Kristian, she went to bed. Shortly after returning to her room, she and Kane made love. She knew for sure he hadn't left the house. However, she decided to play along.

It was great, she typed back, *when can we do it again?*

Whenever your wife isn't home, the sender wrote.

Carmen froze. She thought about what to say. Should she tell the woman she was Kane's wife, or should she go find her husband? Carmen knew the woman couldn't have been with Kane. He had been with her all night.

Are you still there, Kane?

Carmen typed back yes. She decided to let the woman know who she was talking to. *Just to let you know, I don't appreciate you sleeping with my husband,* she wrote back. Carmen knew after the woman responded she was going to be in jail right along with King. The minute she saw Kane she was going to choke him.

Well, I don't appreciate you going through my things, the woman typed back.

Carmen became confused until the lady sent another message.

Look downstairs to the left of the stairwell, the lady typed.

Carmen stood up, looking out her husband's office window. Her eyes darted across the Narcotics division until she saw her husband standing in front of a desk. He waved to her, and she realized it was all a joke.

You're wrong for that, she typed to him after she sat down.

He typed, *Why are you going through my stuff?*

You know I'm curious about what you do. You're lucky this was a joke. I was about to go to prison. Carmen wondered how he knew she looked at the things on his desk. She figured he could see her through the window.

I have confidential stuff on my desk. Some things you can't see. I'm still employed with the Triad, remember?

Yeah, I remember, but, you were about to get hurt, she typed back.

Carmen watched as her husband sent her a smiley face.

"What are you typing over there?" Kristian asked, realizing her mother stopped talking to her.

"I'm talking to your father. He's on his way up." Carmen smiled, now finding the joke humorous. Her smile broadened even more when Kane appeared in the doorway.

"Did you know your mother was going through my stuff?" he asked Kristian, planting a small kiss on her cheek.

"Did you know your father was playing pranks?" Carmen shot back.

Kane grinned, knowing he got her good. Carmen loved to be nosy when it came to police business. "Where's King?"

"I guess in booking. They should be done fingerprinting him if he hasn't tried to fight them yet," Carmen replied. "Speaking of King, he's right at the door." Carmen narrowed her eyes as an officer pushed King in the room. His hands and feet were both handcuffed.

"When is the bail hearing?" Kane asked Officer Tucker.

"I don't know. Darnell's parents want to press charges. He might be in for tonight."

Carmen held her head down before looking at King. Her son had a blank expression on his face like nothing fazed him. "Are those handcuffs tight enough?" she asked him. He shrugged his shoulders.

"I read the report, so I don't need to ask you anything about the fight," Kane stated, speaking to King. "Are you still selling drugs? Do you have anything stashed at the house?"

"I'm not going to hide any fuckin' drugs at the house," King yelled. "I'm not fuckin' stupid."

Kane was determined to keep his composure. "You're—"

"Is there any way you can speed up this process," Carmen interrupted. "Can we just pay Darnell so this thing can be over?"

"Carmen," Kane began. He paused, knowing she didn't understand. Every time King got in trouble; all she wanted to do was write a check. "It isn't going to work like that, baby," he said, cautious of his tone. "He's gonna be here for tonight. He may even be transported to the county jail."

Carmen directed her next question to King. "Who were you with when you beat up Darnell?"

King chuckled. His mother knew he wasn't a snitch. He wasn't going to bring down his friends because he had to spend a night in jail. He could handle one night. He probably could even handle federal prison. "Can I take these things off?" he asked, ignoring her question.

Kane told him no. King was being charged with attempted murder. He didn't want to voice it, but his son was probably going to be in jail all week before bail was set. He also knew they would be spending a nice chunk of change to get him out.

"Man, fuck this shit. Go ahead and show me where I'm sleeping at tonight. Hurry up and pay these motherfuckers so I can be out." King caught his father's expression. He could see it in his face he was holding back. They stared at each other until King figured it out.

Kane spoke. "You know I don't want to do this, right?"

King turned his gaze to the floor. He couldn't look at his mother because he knew what her face looked like. She told him countless times she didn't want him ending up like her.

Seventeen years ago, she got arrested for stealing a diamond from another jewelry thief. His father even testified against her. Most of her pregnancy was spent in prison and every time he got in trouble, she would tell him the story.

"How long," Carmen asked, figuring out King's situation.

"I don't know," Kane replied.

"Can I make my phone call?" King asked.

"Who are you going to call?" Kane questioned.

"Let me get my phone call."

Kane watched as King stood up, walking towards the door. "Don't go out there without a police escort."

"Well, come on then," King shot back. There was only one lifeline out there for him. He had to get in contact with Lil' Noc. Noc would round some dudes together to go looking for Darnell. Once they found him, they would force him to drop the charges. The only downfall was that Lil' Noc had his eye on Kristian. He would want a date with her if he was able to get the charges dropped.

"Go with him, Kane," Carmen said, walking over to him. She touched her husband's face, kissing him. She didn't want King to spend any time in jail, but there was nothing she could do. When Kane led him out the room, she sat beside Kristian. Minutes later, Kane returned, however, King wasn't with him. "How long?" she asked him again.

Kane's eyes shifted from his wife to the police report. He held it up, so the images of Darnell were visible. Rather disturbing, Darnell had a bloody face, which was caused mostly from his missing teeth. He probably didn't look half as bad now since he'd been cleaned up. Unsure of what else he needed to say, he handed the papers over to her and left the room. He didn't go far, walking to his son's holding cell. King's back was towards him, and he waited for him to sense his presence. For the time being, his son was staring out the window as if he was thinking about his freedom.

"It's time for me to be a man," King said, moving towards his cot. He stretched out on the small bed. "I need to take responsibility for my actions."

"Sometimes I wonder where I went wrong."

"There's no need to wonder." King turned over onto his side. He did it as a sign he wanted to be alone. He already contacted Lil' Noc and in the morning he would know the status of the charges. Lil' Noc was giving Darnell a few hours to get everything overturned. Since Darnell was a weak individual, he would have it done in record time.

Once he was released, he had to get back on the block. He currently owed Lil' Noc three thousand dollars and he only had three hundred of it. He wouldn't have been worried if Lil' Noc wasn't a second generation gangster. Word on the street was that his father use to work for one of the biggest drug cartels in America. King couldn't compare himself to him. Therefore, he had to get his money and he had to get it fast.

2 | *Like Mother, Like Daughter*

Carmen was sitting in bed when Kane came through the door. She stared at him before focusing her eyes on the scripture she was reading. He was being rather noisy, and his movements caught her attention. She watched as he removed his gun holster and shoes before undressing. In the last couple of months, he had started a new workout routine, which showed in his muscle tone. She admired his new physique until she noticed his facial expression. He appeared troubled and she knew it was because of their son's latest brawl. "Do you want to talk about it?" she asked him, closing her Bible.

"No," he answered.

Carmen laid her Bible on the nightstand. She sunk down further in the bed, turning away from him. It wasn't long before he turned off the lights and knelt on the floor. Kane always prayed on his knees and Carmen respected him for it. She said her prayers as well, praying for King, her daughter, and for her husband. She even prayed for her parents, knowing in the morning she would have to call them. By the time she was finished, Kane slid in beside her. Every night she slept on his chest, but tonight, she was scared to touch him. Something was bothering him, and she could tell he needed space. Instead of pestering him, she closed her eyes. His movements prevented her from drifting off and after a few minutes, he got out the bed. When she sat up, she saw him with his head in his hands. "Baby," she whispered.

"Can you give me a moment?"

Carmen bit her lip. She waited a couple of seconds before moving closer to him. She touched his back, kissing his right shoulder blade. She wanted him to know she was there for him. "We can talk about it," she coaxed. She kissed him again until she felt his hands wrap around her.

"I don't want to. Come here," he said, sliding her in his lap.

Her husband wanted to be comforted, but she would have preferred to know what was bothering him. If it was the situation with King, the feeling was mutual.

"I love you," he said into her ear, taking his lips off hers.

"I love you, too, baby." She kissed his forehead, hoping she was making him feel better. To ease his worries even more, Carmen reached in his lap, tugging at the waistband of his boxers. Their bedroom door was locked so she went ahead and pulled the boxers down to his ankles. Kane licked his lips as she did it, making Carmen pause to stare at him. Every time she saw him, she got butterflies. She had been with him for almost twenty years and each day, she loved him even more.

He moved on top of her, sliding underneath the covers. She knew what was to come yet his body was frozen on hers. Minutes passed by, yet he didn't move. Then, without warning, he laid his head on her stomach. "Kane," Carmen whispered. When she saw his tears, she put two and two together.

The drama with King reminded him they hadn't had any more children. Although he had given her Kristian; it was only because of in vitro fertilization. It took a long time to get him to agree to the procedure because he refused to see a doctor. Carmen knew something was wrong when King was turning two and she still hadn't gotten pregnant. They weren't using protection and she checked out fine. After Kristian's birth, Carmen begged him to try in vitro again. The suggestion only stirred up an argument. What hurt her was not that he didn't tell her he couldn't have kids, but that he wasn't willing to do everything possible to make one.

She learned to live with it, but moments like this, angered her. He wanted to be comforted over the issue, yet it was a problem, which could easily be solved. However, instead of voicing her opinion, she massaged his back. After a few minutes, his tears had ceased, and he was sleeping peacefully. Since it was obvious they weren't going to make love, Carmen closed her eyes, and eventually drifted off.

The following morning, for the first time in ages, they both were in the bathroom, preparing for work. She was combing her hair while Kane was next to her, shaving his head. They hadn't said two words to each other aside from good morning and the tension made Carmen nervous.

"What time do you have to be there?" he asked, finally speaking.

Carmen gave him a quick and simple, "Ten."

"Do you have some time to spare?"

Carmen checked the clock in the bathroom, and saw it was going on 9:30. "Traffic is always crazy downtown. I really should be leaving now."

"You need to make time."

His words were stern, and Carmen felt him as he pushed his body up against hers. The move was unexpected, and she grabbed the countertop to keep her composure. When she felt his growing erection, she knew what he was hinting at. "Do you have time now?" he whispered.

"I do," she moaned, feeling his hands unbuckling her pants. Carmen closed her eyes as Kane's lips pressed hard onto hers. Aware he dropped Kristian off at school; their lovemaking wouldn't have any interruptions. At the thought, she slid her hands underneath his shirt, feeling the muscles in his abdomen. At the rate they were going, she was bound to be late for her weekly board meeting.

Since a quickie was all she had time for, she unbuttoned his jeans. In an instant, their bodies became intertwined, meeting each other in the place they connected best. The sensations were strong as he pumped inside of her, and Carmen wondered if it was because they were standing up. He wanted to make up for last night and he was doing a hell of a job. He plunged deeper with each stroke, almost making the sex painful.

"Shit," she heard him moan in her ear.

Kane wasn't one to curse, but when he did; she loved it. That was when she knew he had become vulnerable to whatever she put on him. This time, she came first, nearly screaming as her body became tense. Kane wasn't quite there yet, and it took a few seconds before she felt his juices sliding down her inner thigh. When she was finally able to see his face, he appeared to be in a daze. Even if he didn't agree, Carmen knew this time was their absolute best.

"I don't even want to move," he said in her ear.

Carmen stifled a giggle, smelling their lovemaking.

"What time is it?" he asked her.

"I can't even think of time," she replied. Carmen knew she was going to be late to the board meeting. Although she needed to get a move on, she knew her executives were busy discussing her son's latest fiasco. His brawl had made the evening news along with his brand new mugshot. She could already see the board, sitting in the conference room, discussing whether he was going to do serious time. The topic would keep them occupied until she walked in the door, demanding for the meeting to start.

"That was good," Kane said, pulling out.

Carmen chuckled at his comment before placing another kiss on his lips. "I love you."

"Are you saying that because I just banged the shit out of you?"

"Nah, baby, I love you." Carmen kissed his lips once more before heading to the shower. While they did need to clean off their lovemaking, she also was ready for round two. Not bothering to look at the clock, she spoke her mind. "We have a few more minutes. Why don't you come inside?"

***

While Carmen and Kane were both running late to work, Kristian was doing the same, except with school. Upon arriving, she was bombarded with question after question regarding King's fight with Darnell. To get away from the gossip, she skipped first period and was standing behind an abandoned building across from her school. Coco joined her, and they went unspotted for most of the morning until a candy apple red Cadillac pulled in front of them. Freshly painted, the car belonged to Lil' Noc, a nineteen year-old drug dealer from West Brookstone.

"What do you think he wants?" Coco asked.

Kristian shrugged her shoulders. King was working for him, but she didn't know what Lil' Noc wanted with her. If he wanted to know about the charge, he could've watched the news. Her brother was the top story because he was the son of a fashion designer.

"Can I holler at you for a minute?" Lil' Noc asked, after rolling his window down.

Kristian replied with a quick no. Lil' Noc gave her a slight chuckle before repeating his question. "I said no," she retorted.

"You know your brother called me yesterday," Lil' Noc began, forcing her into the conversation. "He wanted me to pull some strings for him. We kind of made a deal with each other. You know he owes me money, right?"

"You need to leave my brother alone. You're the reason he's in so much trouble."

Lil' Noc laughed, seeing how bold Kristian was. "For real, I'm the reason he's in so much trouble? Please, your brother was catching cases way before I signed him to my team."

"Just tell me what you want. Second period is about to start."

"Hop in," he told her, unlocking the Cadillac's doors.

Kristian shot a glance at Coco. She knew what her friend was thinking. Almost every girl at Brookstone High wanted to be cruising around in Lil' Noc's car. If the shoe was on the other foot, Coco would've hopped in without another thought. The only reason Kristian didn't is because there was a nasty rumor he had a domestic violence problem. Most girls didn't care, but she did.

"He might have some information about King," Coco whispered.

Kristian stared at her friend and then at Lil' Noc. He was giving her a devilish grin, which made her hesitate even more. Coco continued to coax her and eventually she gave in, telling her friend to give her five. When she got inside, she barely had the door closed before the Cadillac took off down the street. "Can you hold up a minute? Let me get my seatbelt on."

"Girl, you're fine," Lil' Noc snapped. "Your brother owes me three G's. If he doesn't have it on Friday, you know what that means."

"My brother is in jail. How do you expect him to be in the streets, hustling for you? Why don't you give him an extension?"

"Do I look like a punk to you?"

"No," Kristian said, as the car came to a smooth stop at a dead end.

"He has until Friday to get the money. More than likely, he's gonna be out by this afternoon. If he doesn't have it, well, I'm gonna be getting into something."

Kristian felt Lil' Noc's finger as it slid down the left side of her face. She knew exactly what the move implied. She also knew King would never make a deal like that. He was too protective of her. The last thing her brother wanted was for her to be giving her goodies away.

Kristian looked in the rearview mirror as Lil' Noc continued to touch her. The affection made her nervous. Lil' Noc was one of the finest men she'd ever seen, brown-skinned with big muscles, dimples in both cheeks and he stayed rocking skull and baseball caps. He was known to be dangerous and the idea of walking on the wild side was tempting.

"You understand what I mean, don't you?" he asked, moving his finger down her neck.

Lil' Noc's finger stopped at the top of her left breast. He was testing her. He wanted to see how far she would let him go. Before she could move his finger, he grabbed her breast with his hand. Suddenly uncomfortable, Kristian brushed his hand away as a smile flew across his face.

"Why are you trippin', Kris? Oh, I see. You're still trying to get with that A-I wannabe."

"Dijuan is not an A-I wannabe, he has game," Kristian explained. Dijuan Harrison was the star basketball player at Brookstone High and her best friend. She had been crushing on him since his family moved to Brookstone, which was about five years ago. About five-ten in height, the same complexion and build as Chris Brown, he caught her eye the moment she saw him. "Do you know how many points he scored last season?"

"I don't care about that shit," Lil' Noc snapped.

"Because you know he got game." Kristian reached in her tote bag and pulled out her cell phone. Only fifteen minutes were left in first period, which meant she needed to head back to campus.

"Whatever, Kris, make sure your brother has my money."

"Do you really think you're going to get some of this?"

"I'm gonna get some regardless. I see how you stare at me when I drive by. You want me like I want you."

"Please, no one wants you," Kristian griped. "You think you're somebody because you have a fly car and some money in your pocket. Please, my parents have more money than you."

Lil' Noc laughed at her antics, knowing he had her right where he wanted her. She was steady talking junk to him. She loved his Cadillac, and he knew she wanted to get with him. "What do I have to do to get with you, Kris?"

Kristian leaned in closer to him so he could hear her words crystal clear. "Nothing, you'll never get with me. You're not worth my time."

Lil' Noc saw an open opportunity, which he decided to take. He got in her face, watching as Kristian backed down. "It ain't so fun, is it?" he said, leaning over her. "You think this is a game, don't you?" Lil' Noc saw a flash of fear appear in her eyes. "Your brother owes me three thousand dollars, which he has less than four days to get. If he doesn't get that money, your pussy is mine."

Kristian pushed him away, but he only grabbed her arm. She unlocked the door with her free hand, and he locked it back with his.

"Why are you running? You can be all up in my face, but I can't be in yours? I guess I've scared you now. I'm taking you back, don't worry."

Kristian felt disgusted. She knew in her heart King hadn't made a deal like that. He was way too protective of her. Lil' Noc was trying to play her for a fool. If she listened to everything he said, he would have her eating out the palm of his hand.

"Are you okay?" she heard him ask as he pulled up in front of Coco. She didn't reply and her silence only made him talk more. "Look, shorty, business is business; you know I'm not gonna hurt you."

"Whatever," she said under her breath. She grabbed a hold of the door handle, feeling Lil' Noc's hand on her arm.

"I'm not gonna hurt you, you know that, right?"

Kristian saw a slight hint of sympathy. She didn't let it faze her, getting out the car without another word. Just her luck, Coco wasn't alone. Dijuan was with her behind the abandoned building. She saw the concerned look on his face, and she knew she had questions to answer.

"What were you doing with him?" Dijuan asked as Lil' Noc drove off. "He's a drug dealer, Kris."

"It was nothing," Kristian replied, looking at Coco. She wanted to tell her friend everything that happened. However, she couldn't do it with Dijuan standing there. Still shocked that Lil' Noc grabbed her breast; she tried not to think of the incident. "We need to get to class," she announced, heading towards campus. "I missed one class because of my brother, I can't miss two." She took baby steps towards the school, allowing Dijuan to walk ahead of her and Coco. As expected, her friend demanded she give up the dirt once Dijuan was out of earshot.

"Lil' Noc is supposed to be getting King out of jail. If King doesn't have his money by Friday, Lil' Noc gets my goodies."

"How is King going to give your virginity away?"

"He didn't make that deal. He's way too protective of me to do that. He's gonna have Noc's money by Friday. I know he will."

Coco frowned at the thought. Although she had known him all her life, she really didn't know much about King. He was the neighborhood bad ass who got in trouble all the time and a person her mother warned her not to hang around. On the other hand, he was also the boy she was secretly crushing on. Sadly enough, he never paid her any attention. Still, she knew she would catch his eye one day. She had grown into a woman over the summer, and it showed in her figure. If he didn't see her maturity now, she didn't know when he would. "If he doesn't have the money, it's going down at the block party."

"Block party," Kristian questioned.

"Yeah, Dijuan told me about it when I was waiting on you to come back. Nobody misses the Harrisons' block parties. Lil' Noc is gonna be there and so is Darnell."

Kristian grunted. She already knew what was going to happen. If Darnell's path crossed with King's, her brother would be back in jail in no time. "I don't think I like this idea."

"I don't, either. I know one thing, though," Coco admitted. "No one is missing that block party."

Kristian couldn't agree more. About to share her thoughts, she stopped in her tracks when she noticed Akaila DeGonzaza, her only known enemy at Brookstone High, approaching Dijuan. They had been against each other since elementary school and Kristian couldn't even remember why she didn't like her. She only knew Akaila did things, such as talking to Dijuan, which got under her skin. To keep from starting an argument, she focused her mind on the block party. Once Akaila walked away, she gave Coco a quick glance. "Everyone is going to be at the block party," she stated, "with a bucket of popcorn." The block party would be the highlight of the school year. With King, Lil' Noc, and her arch nemesis in attendance, Kristian wasn't going to miss it for the world.

3 | *Surprise, Surprise*

The block party on Friday was the least of King's concerns. For the past minute or so, he was sitting in front of a telephone, waiting for his visitor to show. His patience was running low and so was the amount of time he had to get Lil' Noc's money. It was bad enough he was transported to county just like his father predicted. Since he was still in jail, it was obvious his charges hadn't been dropped.

When Malik walked in the room, King became agitated. Malik, or Uncle Malik, as he was affectionately called, was an ear to the streets. It didn't matter whose crew you ran with; Malik always knew what was going on. In addition, he was a good friend of his parents. His mother met him in college although he wasn't a student at Brookstone University. From what he was told, Malik's twin brother, Rakim, attended college with her. In a sad turn of events, he was murdered during a shootout at a local convenience store.

Despite his ear to the streets, Malik never encouraged him to hustle. He simply gave him pointers on the game. In fact, he was doing it now. "These bars don't look good on you," he told him, after they picked up the telephone. "Word on the street is that you got a deadline. I need you to dust your shoulders off, playboy. You need to hit the ground runnin'."

"My cell phone bill is three G's."

"I don't pay another man's debt. You need to Noc on another door."

King scowled at Malik. His uncle was sitting on money, but he never offered a helping hand. He always popped up here and there, trying to school him, but when things got rough, he wouldn't do anything for him.

"So when are you going to be released?"

"Soon," King answered. He kept his answers short because Malik was trying to get information. If he wasn't, then he was looking for confirmation.

"How is your sister? I haven't seen her in a few weeks."

"She's good. Mama is going to let her model for Flame."

"I heard she's been hanging with Lil' Noc."

"No she hasn't. Who made up that rumor?" King asked.

"That's word on the street," Malik voiced, throwing his hands up. "I heard she was with him this morning. Someone saw them talking."

King's jaw tightened as he thought about the crush Noc had on his sister. If Kristian was with him, he knew Noc made a move. "He knows she's off limits. He wanted a little tease."

"Of course, he did. He also knows you can't do anything about it." Malik placed his palm on the glass. "You have to get out of here first."

"Oh, I'm getting out, don't worry about that." King's words were cold and stern. If he didn't get out of jail soon, he didn't know what was to come of anything.

"I'll be waiting, hit me up when you get released."

Malik hung up the phone. His uncle didn't even give him any advice on how to get Lil' Noc's money. While he knew what Noc wanted, he wasn't giving up his sister. Kristian was his heart. It was his job to protect her. As soon as he was released, he was putting the mark of death on her predator.

***

The board meeting was reconvening after a short recess and Carmen still hadn't received an update on King's charge. She was thinking the worse and if it wasn't for the meeting getting underway, she would've worried herself sick. "All I'm asking is for you to take another look at where our highest sales were this year," she began, pointing at a chart on the projector screen. "As you can see, it was in the summer months. If we release *Peaches* in June, will we have the same success?"

"The product will sell, but how over the top do we want to be?"

The question came from Jerry, the Senior Marketing Director of Flame. He was the only one who talked as if the company was doing too much. He was scared Flame's image would become tainted because of the new juniors' line. His vision for the company was for it to start manufacturing couture-styled clothing.

"Very," Carmen answered. "How many designers have heard of Flame from a logo in a movie or through one of our joint ventures? Why do you think we have a multi-million dollar company? This line is going to put us over the top and that's where we want to be. Plus, this kind of fashion is perfect for the summer."

Carmen paused, letting the board take in what she showed them. She knew she was right about putting the line out during the summer. They wanted her to start manufacturing some of the clothes now, but she knew it wasn't time.

"We've got to clothe the Tarantino movie and add a new stylist to the set. Do you think it'll be too much?" Jerry probed.

Carmen got ready to answer until the sound of a door opening caught her attention. She turned towards the doorway to see Cathy standing there with a cordless phone in her hand.

"Mr. Malik Washington is on the phone," she announced. "He says it's an emergency."

Carmen's head turned to Tiara. When her friend shrugged her shoulders, Carmen knew she needed to take the call. "Can you take over the debriefing?"

Tiara grabbed Carmen's notes, ready to take over. As Vice President of Flame, Tiara knew the company in and out. She taught Carmen the ropes and was majorly responsible for the company's success. If it wasn't for her, Flame wouldn't be a household name.

"Let's review last year's sales one more time and our goals for this year," Tiara said, starting to debrief.

Carmen walked out the conference room and into her office. She clicked the button labeled line one to get Malik off hold and said, "Every time you call, you cost me money. I walked out of a very important meeting."

Malik chuckled on the other end. "This is important, Carm. Are you sitting down?"

"No, but I will," she said, taking a seat. Carmen moved her mouse, bringing up her desktop. She checked her email, seeing she received a few fashion show invitations.

"I didn't tell you, but a couple of months ago I got a call from Gomez, Jay's lawyer."

"I don't want to talk about him, Malik," Carmen muttered, twirling around in her chair.

"We were able to get Jay's case reopened."

Carmen froze. "What do you mean reopened?"

"They opened his case back up. He had a new trial, and—"

"Are you saying Jay is out?"

There was immediate silence and Carmen grew nervous. Something big and hard dropped in her stomach. "What are you saying, Malik?" The silence came back. Her friend was stalling.

"Jay was released this morning."

Carmen closed her eyes as Malik explained.

"I didn't know it was going to be this soon. I didn't know they would overturn his sentence like this. I would have said something, but I thought the trial was going to be longer. I thought the jury would want more evidence to prove self-defense. I didn't know it was going to be like this."

The only thing Carmen could think about was King. Her son was in jail and his father was just released. Carmen grabbed the armrest, seeing an image of Kane. He hated Jay. He never wanted her to talk about him. Although he was a Christian man, he would kill Jay on the spot if he saw him. Her husband longed for the day when he received the news Jay Santiago was somewhere bleeding to death.

"He's not the same, Carm. He's kind of mysterious in a way. I know he's been through a lot. I'm always wondering what he's thinking. He doesn't really say too much. He did give me a few orders though."

"Like what?" Carmen asked, finally speaking.

"He wants to see you."

"Hell no," Carmen yelled. The door to her office flew open. When Tiara stepped in, Carmen waved her away.

"Carm, please, that was the first thing he asked for. He wants to talk to you. Just one time, in private, you and him, he won't hurt you."

"You don't know that."

Malik sighed. "Either you agree to this arranged meeting or he's gonna find you."

"He doesn't have the guts."

"Are you saying no?"

"I'm saying hell fuckin' no," Carmen mumbled. She hung up the phone as rage roared within her. *What in the world do I have to say to Jay? Hi, Mr. Santiago, I married Kane and gave him your son. Or it could be, hey, Jay, how was seventeen years in prison?*

Carmen paced the floor. *Jay, Jay, Jay,* the name rung in her mind as she tried to remember what he looked like. Some of it was blurry, but she remembered his eyes. She remembered those beautiful hazel eyes she used to stare into every night. She remembered how he used to hold her and the way he would say I love you. She also remembered his tantrums. Carmen exhaled. She didn't know where Jay was, but it didn't matter. He was free. She wanted to call her husband, but she couldn't. She wasn't allowed to say anything about Jay around him. Kane only had to tell her once to forget about him. When he gave the order, he meant business.

***

Unbeknownst to Carmen, King was receiving his release papers. "I guess I'll see you in a week," the releasing officer said, putting the documents in his hand.

"What's that supposed to mean?" King shot back.

"You'll be back in a week," the officer replied.

King stopped himself from punching the guy in the face. He had three G's to make and a limited amount of product to make it with. The decision to ignore the officer's snide remark was an easy one as he made his way out the county jail. He checked his surroundings as he went, waiting for a taxi to pass him.

"Over here," a voice called out to him. "I know you need a ride."

King turned to his left, seeing Lil' Noc's Cadillac in the parking lot. He didn't expect for him to pick him up. His presence reminded him of the money he owed him and his rumored encounter with Kristian. If anything, it was the perfect time for him to give Lil' Noc a piece of his mind. Therefore, he got inside, closing the door. He didn't speak yet he gave Noc a look, which told him there was bad blood between them.

"Why you look so uptight? You should be straight. I got you out."

"I heard you were with my sister."

Lil' Noc set back in his seat. "I already told you about that."

King was stern. "I told your ass no."

"You can't say no when there's three G's on the table. You can't say shit. I got you out of jail. Do you think I take no for an answer?"

"Look, I'm good on the money. Don't be fuckin' with my sister."

Lil' Noc narrowed his eyes. He pulled strings to get King out and he wasn't seeing any appreciation. All he was getting was a warning to stay away from Kristian. "Tell me something, King, what makes you think your sister doesn't want me? She might want me to put something on her."

"Kristian doesn't know shit about that kind of stuff."

"It didn't seem like it today."

King opened the door to save himself from a first degree murder charge. Two seconds after Noc made his statement, he remembered where he was. The last thing he needed to do was commit a crime in front of the county jail. To keep himself out of trouble, he headed down the street.

"Don't sweat the shit," Lil' Noc yelled, driving beside him. "You got a fine little sister. A lot of dudes have their eyes on her and Coco."

King ignored him as he thought about Kristian's encounter with Lil' Noc. Since he wasn't available to take her to school, she was dropped off by their father. To spend any time with Noc, she had to skip. If she did, King was putting his foot down her throat.

"She's young, but she has the body of a grown woman," Lil' Noc was saying, still riding by him.

King knew he was being tested. If he was strapped; he would've taken Lil' Noc out right then and there. *Fuck the three G's and fuck being in front of the county,* King thought. *After I get that money to him, I'm taking his ass out. I'm gonna put his money in his hand, pull out a glock, and blast him right in the chest.*

"Get in this car," Lil' Noc ordered, swerving the car close to King.

King turned around to see a taxi coming up behind him. He waved down the driver and when the cab stopped in front of him, he got inside.

"Don't do that, we need to talk."

Lil' Noc's words went ignored. "134 Bradford Court," King told the driver. "I need you to get there as soon as possible."

King closed his eyes, knowing he had a long night ahead of him. As soon as he got to his car, he had to start making sales. Then, he had to find out what happened between Kristian and Lil' Noc.

4 | *Confrontation*

Coco watched as Kristian came up the ramp with Dijuan not too far behind. When she caught Kristian's attention, she signaled for her to friend to look behind her. Kristian only smiled in return, which led Coco to turn her attention to Dijuan. Once he caught up to Kristian, they made small talk until they came in her vicinity. "The conversation doesn't have to stop," she joked.

"Oh, I was telling Kristian about the block party. You know my parents aren't going to be there," Dijuan explained.

"True, but your uncle will be," Coco replied. "Your parents aren't going to leave you at a neighborhood block party without supervision."

"My uncle is cool, though. We can get away with a lot."

"Yeah, right," Coco said, rolling her eyes. "Like what?"

"Like, booty butt dancing, grinding," Dijuan stopped, hearing Coco's laughter.

"First of all, you shouldn't be looking forward to any booty butt dancing or grinding because in case you haven't noticed, you can't dance."

"Oh, so you're trying to clown me now?"

"You can't dance, Dijuan, and let's be for..." Coco's voice trailed off when she noticed an all too familiar car approaching the front of the school. "King," she said under her breath.

Kristian noticed her brother's Mustang in the school parking lot. It shocked her to see him because she thought her father was picking her up. In addition, she thought he was in jail.

"He's out?" Dijuan asked.

"Yeah," Kristian said, knowing Lil' Noc had come through for him. She expected her brother to be in a pleasant mood, but when he marched up to her, he was ready to attack.

"Get in the fuckin' car, Kris," he yelled, only a few feet away.

"Don't be talking to me like that."

"I'm not playin' with you, get in the car."

"I'm not going anywhere with you." Kristian took a step back, trying to figure out why King was angry. When he grabbed her arm, she jerked it out his grasp, causing her textbooks to hit the ground.

"I told you to get in the fuckin' car," King repeated, picking up her books. "I don't have time for this bullshit."

"King, you need to calm down," Coco said, intervening.

"And you need to stay out my fuckin' business," King growled. "How many times do I have to tell you that?" He stared Coco down before looking at his sister. "Get in the fuckin' car."

"No," Kristian shouted, "What's up with you?"

"King, let's talk about this, what's wrong?" Dijuan asked, hoping he could diffuse the situation.

"You want to get in my business, too?"

"You need to calm down," Coco repeated. She put her hand on King's arm, but the move was the wrong one. It seemed to set off a grenade and before she knew it, he pushed her into a stone pillar. Too shocked to respond, she watched as Dijuan and Kristian pulled him away from her.

"I told her to mind her fuckin' business," King barked, "I don't give a fuck about hittin' a female."

Kristian directed her brother towards his Mustang to put distance between him and Coco. At the same time, she could hear Dijuan asking if Coco was okay. With no time to discuss the incident, she signaled to Coco she would call her before getting in her brother's car. He hadn't even started it up before he fired a question at her.

"You better give me a good reason why you were in that motherfucker's car."

Kristian bit her lip. King's anger stemmed from her conversation with Lil' Noc.

"That shit is all over the streets," he continued. "He spent five minutes with your ass and went back and told everyone. Malik even knows y'all were together. I told you, I don't want you hanging around him."

"I can take care of myself."

"You can take care of yourself? Lil' Noc keeps a total of six guns or more in his car. You say the wrong thing, he takes your head off. You can't take care of yourself."

"I did today." An image of Lil' Noc's hand on her breast came in her mind. She couldn't tell King the truth. He was already furious and if he knew she was violated, it would start another brawl. Therefore, she threw him a curve ball. "What if I like him?"

"What if you like him? Do you really think I'm going to let you talk to Lil' Noc? I'm going to tell Daddy."

"You're going to tell Daddy? How childish does that sound?" Kristian muttered. She broke into a smile, hearing his words all over again. She knew he had done the same when his mouth formed a grin. Then, as suddenly as it appeared, it went away.

"Look, Lil' Noc beat up one of his girlfriends a while back. I don't want any girl getting with him, especially not my sister."

"You say that like you didn't push Coco into a pillar. Wait a minute, weren't you the one who said you didn't have a problem hitting a female?"

"I didn't hurt her. I barely touched her. She's too sensitive."

"You hurt her feelings, King. You need to apologize."

King cracked a smile, knowing he did probably hurt Coco's feelings. He was just tired of her always making little comments when he came around. He wished she would stay in her place. "I'll apologize," he said, starting up the car. King exhaled as he pulled away from Brookstone High. "I'm protective of you because I know what men do. I've seen it. I wouldn't be able to live with myself if something happened to you."

Kristian heard her brother loud and clear, but she didn't respond.

"Promise me you're not going to mess up."

Kristian heard the sincerity in his voice. "I'm not going to mess up. I promise." When King glanced at her, she gave him another smile. However, it wasn't until he was pulling onto their street, she told him a small part of her conversation with Lil' Noc. "You can calm your nerves, you know. Nothing happened in the car. He only told me he was working on getting you out."

King pulled into their driveway, which was empty. "Good to know. You're still not off the hook," he joked, "I'm still telling Daddy." They shared a quick laugh before he unlocked the doors. While she went inside the house, he backed out the driveway, heading back to the streets.

***

Kane ignored the sound of his office door opening. For most of the morning and afternoon, he was visited by several of his colleagues at the Triad and the Brookstone PD as they coaxed him into taking a case in California. Although he wanted to go back undercover, he couldn't. He hadn't received an update on his son's case, which meant he had to stay in Brookstone. In addition, he promised Carmen he would never take another case at the Triad. Ready to voice his decision again, he watched as a stack of papers landed on his desk.

"Do you see that?" he heard someone ask. The voice belonged to Lieutenant Harris and Kane grinded his teeth as he stared at King's mugshot. "I mean that," Harris continued, flipping the page to reveal King's release papers. "Those bitches dropped the charges."

Kane picked the papers up, examining each document.

"Tell me how he got them to drop the charges. You've seen the photos of their son. Why would they drop the charges?"

Kane laid the papers on his desk. He figured his son got one of his friends to pick him up since his Mustang was still at home. If he was back in the streets, Kane had to find him. It was only a matter of time before King would get into even more devilment.

"You know what this means, don't you?" Harris said, sitting down.

"What?" Kane asked, putting the papers back in order.

"There's nothing stopping you from going to California."

Kane expected the response. "Y'all will say and do anything to get me out there."

"Well, why not? Your kids are grown. You don't have that hanging over you. Your son is out of jail."

"I have a wife, who has needs. I also have needs and going back to the Triad for six months isn't going to be easy. That's why I took a break in the first place. I can't go six months without my wife."

"We'll get you some videotapes and magazines."

Kane chuckled. "I can't even have this discussion with Carmen. She tenses up every time I say Triad."

Harris ignored his comment, changing the conversation to another pending case. "Why don't you flip those papers over some more?"

Kane did as Harris suggested. He watched as a picture of a woman came up.

"You don't remember her?"

Kane shook his head, trying to identify the woman. He could tell she was Hispanic from her skin color and the texture of her hair. She was also makeup-less and looked as if she'd been through a hard time.

"That is Tricia DeGonzaza, a former model, and Jay Santiago's ex-girlfriend. You're staring at a recent picture of her taken last week."

"Dang, what happened to her?" Kane asked.

"Drugs," Harris said. "She has two kids, a son, and a daughter. She got booked last week for possession. She begged for Social Services not to be called. One of the rookies gave her a freebie. You don't want to go to California? Then, deal with this."

"This isn't a case."

"I know. It's a counseling session," Harris explained. "She needs help and since you're a familiar face, I think you can help her. This woman is on the verge of having her kids taken away."

"I'm not a social worker and I'm not a counselor. I'm a Triad agent. The only reason I'm here is because I have a family."

"Then go to California and be a damn Triad agent."

Kane sensed Harris' attitude. "Where's their father?"

"Dead, his name was Consuelo DeGonzaza. Tell me how you feel about this." Harris showed him a picture of the man. "He was arrested when you took down Jay. What do you know; she was fuckin' the ringleader and the help. Two years ago, he shot himself, one bullet to the head. See, after he got out, he had a hard time finding work. He tried his hand at hustling, failed, got frustrated, and took himself out."

"Who are the kids?"

"I don't have pictures of them, but Akaila goes to school with your daughter. I believe she's fifteen, and her little brother, Malachi, is in middle school. He's twelve. I know you're not a counselor, but this family needs some help."

Kane studied the photo. Tricia was a pretty woman, but the drugs ruined her appearance. Her eyes had black rings around them, and she had whittled down to almost nothing. "So you want me to go to her house and say what?"

"Watch her for a few days and bump into her. Make sure you tell her you're an agent and trying to help." Harris paused for a few seconds before asking a question he desperately wanted an answer to. "Tell me something, why didn't you marry her?"

Kane was taken aback. He never had a romantic relationship with Tricia. Of course, he thought she was beautiful, and she had a great figure, but he never liked her. He voiced his thoughts to Harris.

"You liked Carmen, though."

"I love Carmen," Kane said, stressing his words.

"Why did you marry her?"

"What do you mean—" Harris cut him off, raising his voice.

"It almost ruined the case. You could've lost your job."

"I did my job. Triad wanted Jay, they got him. That was my job."

"You took your wife down, too."

"I had fuckin' bugs on me," Kane yelled. He wasn't one to curse, but Harris' comment made his temper flare. He was tired of explaining his relationship with Carmen.

"Even with the bugs, y'all still don't know who killed that man on the ship," Harris muttered. "You and your wife were both on that boat."

"He's been dead for seventeen years, let him rest in peace."

"Maybe one day we will," Harris replied. He pointed at the picture of Tricia. "Deal with that," he said, going out the door.

Kane knew the case was punishment for not going to California. Harris could deny it all he wanted, but the truth was there. The common denominator between Jay and Carmen, Tricia made the case delicate. If he pursued the case like Harris wanted, he couldn't let Carmen know. He would have to keep it a secret so his marriage would stay intact. If he didn't, there would be hell to pay.

***

Tiara watched as Carmen came in the break room. "Coke?" she asked, offering the can in her hand. Carmen shook her head, grabbing a bottle of water. "The meeting went well. At least they agreed to do the line during the summer." Tiara waited for a response and when she didn't get one, she became concerned. "Are you okay?" Carmen nodded her head, but Tiara read right through her. She knew her friend was lying. "What did Malik want?"

"Nothing," Carmen answered, setting the bottled water on the table.

"You don't have to lie to me, Carm. It's Tiara Smith, remember? Your best friend since middle school, the girl who ran this multi-million dollar company while you were getting your hair braided in D-Block."

"I don't want to talk about it, Tee."

"That's all you had to say, don't play that secret shit with me."

Carmen grabbed the bottled water from the table. "I'm going back to my office. I'll catch you later." With a small wave of her hand, Carmen left the break room. She wanted to tell Tiara what was going on, but in a way, she didn't. The last thing she wanted was for the news to get out. She checked the local Brookstone newspapers to see if a story leaked, but nothing was there. She did a search for Jay, but most of the articles written on him had been deleted. No one cared about him now.

Carmen stared at the ceiling after hitting the button for the elevator. She texted Kane shortly after her conversation with Malik, but he hadn't returned her message. It was unlike him, but he was probably out in the field. She saw a vision of him patrolling Brookstone until she heard the elevator doors open. She stepped inside, feeling a bit of queasiness in her stomach. She knew it was because she hadn't eaten anything. She was too antsy over the news of Jay's release to think of food. *Hopefully, work will clear my mind*, she thought.

A minute later, the elevator doors reopened. She stepped onto her floor where most of the executive offices were. Almost to her own office, she noticed Cathy, standing at her door. "I'm right here," she called, getting her attention. Cathy started to speak but stammered her words. Too impatient to wait on the news, she opened her door and went inside. She chuckled over her antics until she saw the reason Cathy was shook. In less than two seconds, a ton of bricks had landed on her chest.

Jay was standing in front of her. His hair had been cut low and he was dressed in one of her designs. It was a black pinstripe suit with a pink tie, which he paired with Stacey Adams shoes of the same color. His expression was blank as they met eyes. After hearing about his behavior in prison, she had every reason to be scared. It also didn't help he had a scar running down his face.

Suddenly, he moved his head, looking out the window. He then loosened his tie as if he was going to say something.

"Damn, I'm not going to hurt you."

Carmen didn't know whether to believe him or not. She was guilty of so many things and he had every reason to want revenge.

"You're holding onto the wall like I'm about to charge at you. I haven't moved an inch since you walked in."

Carmen remained quiet. His words were accurate. Both her hands were holding onto the wall for support.

"Damn, Peaches, I said I'm not going to hurt you." He called her by her childhood nickname.

Carmen watched as he took a step forward and she took a step back, hitting the wall.

He then paused, seeing she wasn't comfortable. "Tell me something. How do you expect for me to leave your office if you're guarding the door? Do you want to move that way while I move this way?" He pointed left and right. "Tell me so I can leave. There's no need to be here if you don't feel comfortable around me."

Jay took another step forward. Her nerves got the best of her, and she moved as well, hitting the back of her head on the wall. A loud thud sounded at the impact and the pain was instant. Automatically, she slid onto the floor, holding her head in her hands. As if the pain wasn't enough, Jay was now standing over her. She could feel his hands in her hair, touching her scalp as if he was feeling for a knot. Carmen hoped she didn't have one, although her head was starting to throb. Although she didn't want to, she allowed him to help her to her feet.

"Come over here," he said, leading her to the brown leather couch in her office.

Carmen sat down, feeling his hands massaging the back of her head. His touch was gentle and reminded her of what Malik said. After a seventeen-year prison stint, her ex wasn't the same. "My head," Carmen whispered, feeling the throb worsening.

"Do you have some Aleve?"

"Top drawer, over there," she told him, pointing at her desk. He went to it, opening a drawer. He rummaged around for a bit until he found the bottle. "Micro Fridge is over there," she said, pointing towards the left corner of the room. He went to the fridge, opening the door to display several bottles of orange juice. He grabbed one before going back to her side.

"Here," he said, handing her the Aleve and orange juice.

Carmen took the items from his hands.

"You really need water, but I guess that will do," he told her.

Carmen popped the tablets in her mouth, gulping down the orange juice. In the meantime, Jay walked away from her, heading towards her desk. Something caught his eye and she wondered what it was. Her question was answered when he picked up a picture of her and Kane. Not quite sure how he was going to react, she gulped the orange juice down faster.

"Are you okay now?" he asked, facing her.

Carmen shrugged her shoulders. "It takes a second or two for these things to work." His expression changed to one of agitation and Carmen apologized.

"You don't make this easy."

"It isn't going to be," she responded.

"Do you think you're the only one who had something done to you? I think you forgot I went to prison for both of us."

"How is that?" Carmen shot back.

"If it wasn't for you cheating on me with Carlos, what reason would I have to kill him? If it wasn't for me trying to kill him then I would've never found out about his father murdering my dad."

"I didn't send you on a killing spree, Jay."

"It might as well have been you. Did you know I was going to propose when you got back from the Bahamas?"

"Carlos may have mentioned it," Carmen shared.

"You didn't care?"

"I had mixed emotions, Jay. I was falling for Kane. I was selling drugs. I was lost. I didn't know what I wanted."

"You knew you wanted him," Jay said, raising his voice.

Carmen watched as his left index finger pointed at the picture frame on her desk. "He's my soulmate," she told him, speaking a little over a whisper. He walked past her. He was about to leave until he stopped in his tracks.

"How's my son?" he asked, not turning around.

"He's in jail. He beat some kid up at school. That's not where his trouble started, though. He's been in juvie, group homes, psychiatric centers, and every other agency for behavioral youth since he was six. Why do you care to know?"

"Did you just ask me why?"

Carmen became confused. She thought he would be more shocked to know his son was in jail. "I'm asking you why because you were the one who told Malik you didn't want him when I was nine months pregnant."

"I did want him," he yelled.

Carmen glared at him. "Malik told me you said you didn't want him. Now, you're trying to tell me you said you did."

"No, I said I didn't want him, but I did. Did you really think I wanted my son coming to see me in prison? My arms and legs were chained up; I had a mask on my face like I was Hannibal Lector. I couldn't talk to anyone. I was so far gone. I didn't want him seeing me like that, so I said I didn't want him. I do want him, Carm."

Jay reached in his pocket and took out a picture. It was the same picture she gave him when King was first born.

"He is mine, isn't he?" he asked, walking towards her.

"He's very much yours," Carmen replied.

"Does he know about me?"

"What do you think?" Carmen wished she caught herself. She knew Jay was thinking she didn't have any empathy. "I'm sorry," she said, feeling guilty.

"Forget it, I shouldn't have come here," he said, turning away. "It was a mistake."

"Jay, wait," she said, getting off the couch.

"I said forget it, Carm. I don't even want to talk about it. Keep things the way you have them. You've got your life already figured out."

"No, wait," she told him, grabbing his arm. He turned around to face her. "Please," she begged. "I'm sorry, Jay, I'm going to try, I promise."

"I can't remember if you were one to keep your promises."

"I'll keep this one," she told him, letting go of his arm. "Do you want to meet him?" She could tell he was thinking of his answer, however, he told her no. After saying the word, he walked out her office, leaving her confused about his visit. Carmen didn't understand. He said he wanted his son but refused to meet him. *What does he want then?*

"I'm sorry I let him in. He said he was here on business, and he had all these documents," Cathy said, appearing in the doorway.

"Documents," Carmen said, knowing Jay was in her office empty-handed.

"Yes, he set them here," Cathy stated, pointing towards her desk.

Carmen put her finger up, signaling for Cathy to be quiet. She saw a manila folder, which hadn't been there before. She opened it, displaying the contents. Inside was a business proposal for a restaurant that was going to be in downtown Brookstone. It explained why Jay wanted to see her. He wanted her to go into business with him. She saw her name listed as one of his funding sources and partners. Carmen wondered if Jay said anything to Cathy. "What did he say when he came to your desk?"

"He said he was an old friend who missed you. He wanted to talk to you about something."

"Yeah," Carmen said, seeing how professional his proposal was.

"He also left this," Cathy told her, holding out a box. "He said you deserved to have it. He wanted me to give it to you after he left."

Carmen saw the white box, wondering what it was. It was the size of a jewelry box, and she took it from Cathy's hands, flipping it over a couple of times. "Can you excuse me for a minute?"

"Sure," Cathy told her, heading out the office.

Carmen opened the box the exact moment she was alone. A piece of notebook paper was folded inside, and she removed it to see a nineteen-carat diamond ring. At the sight of it, her attention went back to the notebook paper, which she opened.

I got you pregnant on purpose. I kept my promise. I said if you got pregnant I would make you my wife. You were the one who made me break my promise.

Carmen realized it was her engagement ring. She slid it on, seeing it fit perfectly. However, she didn't like having it on the same finger as her wedding ring. She slid it off, putting it back in the box. She planned on storing it at her apartment where she kept her journals. It was the one place her husband didn't know about.

5 | *Pay It Forward*

Kane juggled his car keys in his hand as he headed up the walkway to Tricia's house. The house was small and rundown. Although there wasn't a car in the driveway, he still knocked on the door. When the door opened, Tricia appeared. He almost turned away, seeing the dark circles around her eyes. The glow from her skin had faded and she had lost her curves. "Hey," he said, wondering if she remembered him. "Do you remember me?" He took another step, hoping she would allow him to come in.

"Who could forget you? The whole city knows you're 5-0," she told him. "You're a snake."

Kane stepped in the doorway. "I need to talk to you," he told her as he held up a warrant. He hadn't come to search her house, but he had got one so he could go in without a problem.

"I don't have any drugs in here. Are you trying to take me to prison, too? I guess you want to come and take my kids."

"I'm not trying to take your kids—" Kane caught on to what she said. "So you think that's what I do? You think I take men to prison so I can take their kids?"

"Isn't that what you did to Jay? You sent him to prison and the minute his sentence was read you adopted his son. Shit, you didn't even adopt him. You put your name on his birth certificate."

"I married his son's mother," Kane clarified.

"You sure did, after you put her in prison. You knew she was pregnant by Jay."

"You know, that isn't any of your business. What's your business is the needles you've been running up and down your arm. If you don't clean up your act then your kids probably will be living with me." Kane watched as her facial expression changed. She pulled the sleeves down on her shirt so he couldn't see the marks.

"I'm not doing that anymore," she told him, trying to appear confident.

"Are you sure? Looks like you have everything laid out on the table." A needle was sitting on the table next to a mirror, which had a white substance on it. Her kids were still at school, so she had enough time to get high before they got home.

"I said I'm not doing that anymore. My babies want me to get clean," she told him, blocking his view.

"Why don't we sit down and talk?"

"I don't think so, I have things to do."

"I have things to do, too. This is one of them." Kane held up the warrant and listened as she sighed. "Come on, Tricia, you need some help, don't you?"

Tears came in her eyes. She then nodded her head. He grabbed her arm, stepping inside and closed the door behind him. "We have to get this place cleaned up," he said, seeing the dirty dishes in the sink. The house smelled stale and he could see dirt on the walls. The furniture was falling apart, and he could tell she didn't have a working air conditioner. "Why don't we sit down and talk for a minute," he suggested. He saw a decent-looking couch in the living room. He felt comfortable sitting on it, which he did. He patted the space next to him. "What's wrong?" he asked her.

"Can't you see?" she told him, crying. "I don't have any money. I can't get a job because I have a habit. I tried a twelve-step program a couple of months ago. It backfired on me."

"Where were your kids at this time?"

"They were here. Akaila's old enough to take care of her brother. She can cook and make sure he's in school. She's a good girl." Tricia's cries turned to sniffles. "I can't get any kind of public assistance. We both know I can't work at a fast food joint or a mini mart."

"You need money, don't you?"

"I dated Jay Santiago and Consuelo DeGonzaza. Do you think I want people to know they left me with nothing? Jay used to take care of me. Whenever I got in a bind, he would slide some money my way."

Kane cringed, hearing the name Jay. About to respond, he listened as the front door opened and Tricia's daughter came in the house. He could tell she was shocked to see him.

"What's going on?" she asked, not taking her eyes off him.

"I'm Kane," he greeted, extending his hand, "I'm going to be around for a few days helping your mother out."

"Oh," she said under her breath. "You work for a ministry or something?"

"No, I'm a cop, a Triad agent to be exact," he told her. She didn't shake his hand.

"Oh," she said again, "I'm Akaila."

"It's very nice to meet you." Kane directed his attention back to Tricia until Akaila's voice sounded once again.

"You're King's father, aren't you?"

Kane realized Akaila knew who he was. "Yeah, I have a daughter, too. Kristian is your age," he told her, confirming her belief. He noticed

Akaila hadn't spoken to her mother. He waited until she left the living room before he questioned Tricia about it. "Does that happen a lot? Your daughter ignored you."

"I really don't bring men around my kids," she replied.

"Your daughter ignored you."

"No, she didn't," Tricia disagreed, "she was trying to figure out who you were. Her mind was elsewhere."

Kane realized Tricia was in denial. "I wish one of my kids would walk in the house and not speak to me." He heard Akaila's footsteps once again. She came back in the living room, heading straight for him.

"So, you're going to be helping my mom out?"

"Well, I'll be helping the whole family. You know, making sure your mother stays clean, food is on the table, that kind of thing." Kane stood up, spotting a pile of garbage, which needed to be taken out. He grabbed the bags and headed for the front door. He figured he would help them clean up before heading to the nearest grocery store.

"Look, Mr. Kane, I don't mean to be disrespectful, but the last cop who came around here only left my mama with one thing, an STI."

Kane dropped the bags at the girl's comment. Tricia appeared to be shocked as well. "Well, I'm married," was all he could muster out. He then picked up the bags and headed to the dumpster. As he went, he could hear Tricia in the background.

"So that's what you think I do, huh? You think I'm sleeping with him?" she was saying.

It was obvious they didn't get along. Tricia had a habit that was keeping her from taking care of the household and Akaila felt trapped. At her age, the girl was already under immense pressure.

"That's a nice earring in your ear," he heard a voice say.

Kane saw a young boy coming towards him.

"You're shining all the way over here."

Kane realized the boy was Malachi, Tricia's son. Kane had forgotten about the diamond stud in his left ear. He got it when he was younger as a way of rebelling against his parents. Still wearing it, he knew he wasn't the traditional forty-five year-old father. He didn't look like half the men his age. He kept himself in shape and he hardly ever wore suits. T-shirts and jeans were more his style. "I guess I am," he replied.

"Do you hustle or something?"

"I work at the Brookstone PD," Kane told him, walking towards the dumpster.

"So you got a lot of weapons and shit?"

"Aren't you a little young to be cursing?"

The boy pulled up his shirt sleeve, revealing a deep cut on his arm. "I'm not too young for anything."

Kane dumped the trash bags inside the dumpster before giving Malachi his attention once again. "So you're in a gang or something?"

"Someone gotta help my sister keep food on the table. I already know you're here to help us. You won't snitch on me. You won't put my mother through any more bullshit than she's already going through."

Malachi had him figured out. He wouldn't have arrested him even though he confessed to being in a gang. "So since you know I'm here to help you, how come your mother and sister don't get along? I can smell the tension from a mile away."

Malachi looked at his house, thinking about his sister. They were both fed up with their mama, but there was nothing they could do. With the man looking out for them, there would be some peace for a while. "There's tension," he admitted. "What's your name?"

"You can call me Kane, its spelled K-A-N-E, not like in the Bible. My real name is Michael, but everyone calls me Kane." When Malachi asked why, Kane shrugged his shoulders. He knew the reason why, but it wasn't an explanation he felt like sharing. If he wanted to break Malachi's ties to his gang, he didn't want him to know about his days as an undercover drug dealer.

"Our first names are kind of similar," Malachi said, thinking of the spelling.

Kane agreed. "Are you ready to head in? I'm treating y'all to dinner."

Malachi's eyes darted across the street where he'd been standing. He was trying to hustle the last little bit of weight he had, but business was slow. He had homework to do, and it would only be a matter of time before Akaila came outside bugging him about it. "I guess," he said, waving at his friends across the street.

Kane opened the door, seeing Tricia inside throwing expired food in a trash bag. Akaila was in the living room, starting on her homework and Malachi joined her. "Why don't we get something to eat?" he asked Tricia. "I know the kids are hungry."

"We need to go grocery shopping. You can treat us tonight, but what are we gonna do tomorrow?"

"Why don't you let me worry about that?" Kane told her. He already had a plan in motion since he saw how much work needed to be done.

"Maybe I will," she said, giving him a smile.

Kane returned the gesture before telling her he was grabbing some takeout. He left the house and got inside his Jeep, ready to complete the task he was handed.

***

Over on the Westside, King was doing the same. However, his task was interrupted when Malik pulled up beside him. He didn't mind his presence; he simply wished he hadn't made an appearance when he was trying to hustle.

"I guess Noc got Darnell to drop the charges," Malik voiced.

"I don't know how he did it, but ya boy, Noc, is a genius," King said, pretending his relationship with Lil' Noc wasn't on the rocks.

"Does your mama know you're out?"

King shrugged his shoulders. "I don't know. Mama is always wrapped up in Flame. What are you doing over here?"

"Watching the streets, what about you?"

King chuckled. Malik's comment was only a hint he was trying to keep an eye on him. "You said there was money to be made."

"There is money to be made, but not like this. Let me holler at you for a minute. I have a proposition for you."

King tightened his grip on the steering wheel. Malik was always trying to play daddy with him, but he figured it was because he didn't have any kids of his own. "You're making me lose business," he told him, starting his car.

"Please," Malik grumbled, taking his foot off the brake, "there's no business over here." He sped down the road, checking in his rearview mirror to see if King was following. He planned on taking him to the diner where he first met Carmen and Tiara.

Malik pulled in a parking space and waited as King came around the corner. Once King pulled in beside him, Malik got out, walking towards the diner. He went over in his head how he was going to talk King into working for Jay. Malik knew Jay wanted to keep his nose clean, but they also needed to stack some money. With the skills King had, he would be the right addition to Jay's crew.

"You know you're paying, right?" King asked.

"I got you." Malik opened the door to the diner. He gave the manager a quick nod before sliding in his regular booth. Seconds later, a waitress came, setting two menus on the table. Malik noticed the diner was empty. It worked in his favor because the last thing he wanted was for someone to be eavesdropping on his conversation. He didn't want anyone to know Jay was back in town. The raid on Jay's warehouse seventeen years ago sent a lot of men to prison and their families weren't happy. In addition, all his businesses went under, leaving about a third of the city out of work. Jay needed to rebuild, and Malik figured they could start the process with King. "I know a guy who needs some help."

King was curious. "What kind of help?"

"He needs someone who can be his right-hand man. He has a few businesses he wants to start, but he needs someone who can help him raise the money." Malik was halfway lying because Jay wasn't looking for anyone. The only person Jay was concerned about was Carmen.

King scanned the menu. "How much is he paying? Shit, fuck that, what do I have to do?"

"I don't know the details yet. There is something I want you to do."

"What's that?" King asked.

"Keep your nose clean. I don't need you going back to jail any time soon. I know about this block party on Friday. I want you to stay with me for a little while. I can't help you with this money if you're locked up."

"So, if I work for this dude, I can get the three G's before Friday."

Malik was honest. "Probably not, but I can get you an extension with Lil' Noc."

King chuckled, not seeing how Malik was going to work that out. King didn't think he had any pull. He didn't even know what Malik did for a living. Whatever it was, he did the job well since he lived lavishly. "How long will the extension be?" he asked as the waitress came to take their drink orders. They both ordered iced teas and the waitress left the table.

"Maybe a week," Malik replied. "I'll see what Noc says."

King was satisfied with the answer. He could do three G's in a week and four days easily. "So, are you going to tell me who he is?"

"Nope, it's not important. If anything, I'm gonna try and find Lil' Noc. I need to speak to some people before I leave the Westside so hopefully I'll run in to him."

"And if you don't?"

"I'll see him sometime this week."

King wondered if Malik would keep his promise. He didn't like the idea of having to wait for confirmation. He needed to know if he had an extension right now. King quickly changed his thought when he snuck a peek at Malik. Instead of worrying about the extension, he needed to find out who Malik wanted him to work for. Certain he didn't know him; he made a mental note to keep his ears to the streets as well.

When Malik drove by Sapphire, the last thing he expected was to find a Rolls Royce parked outside. The club had been closed for fifteen years and no one had been inside since. Malik thought he had done well since he was able to keep two of Jay's houses, but in the process, Sapphire closed and so did Jay's laundromats. It was a small price to pay to get the money for Jay's legal fees. Now, Jay was out and needed to rebuild.

When he walked inside, the place smelled musty, and dust was everywhere. He heard movement above his head and when he peered up, he saw Jay in his office. He headed in that direction; ready to give Jay an update on his cartel. Throughout most of the day, he tried to contact every man who used to be on Jay's payroll who wasn't incarcerated, dead, or on the run from the government. None of them wanted to come back to the Santiago cartel. They knew it would be work. However, there were a few young dudes who had heart and dedication. The main one was Jay's own son.

King was perfect for their operation. He had Santiago blood and was a king in his own right. He just had to convince Jay to get back in the game to build his money up.

"Zero," Jay said, seeing Malik in the doorway. He chuckled as he thought of the number. "You need one man, and you can't find any."

Malik knew what Jay was talking about. He had the same number for him. "I got an idea," he announced, coming further in the room. He took a second or two to get his thoughts together before telling Jay his plan. He wanted the words to come out so good Jay wouldn't have a choice but to say yes. "There's this young dude who's kind of running the streets now. He has a real smooth swagger about him. He dropped out of school, but he has brains. We can let him take over, help us generate some money and then we bring in Carmen. All we need is her name. She signs the paperwork, becomes the face of the whole thing, and we take everything to the bank."

Jay thought hard about Malik's proposal. He was ready to retire although Malik didn't want him to. His right-hand wanted him to give the business to someone else who could bring others in. He couldn't do it because many of his connects refused to work with him. They knew the Triad was on his back and feared for their own operations.

"Think about it, Jay. You're sitting in the cut, letting him run everything. He's bringing in about thirty dudes who are ready to take the Santiago cartel back to where it was. We start there till we got like five hundred on payroll. We take over New York, New Jersey, and eventually, the whole East coast."

Jay scratched his chin at the game plan. Malik was adamant about him continuing in the drug game. He didn't want to go that route, but Malik made it seem like he had to. "Who is this dude?" Jay asked, raising his brow.

"He's from the Eastside," Malik answered, not giving a name.

Jay thought the matter over. He couldn't give his father's empire to anyone. It had to be someone who was a warrior and could think outside the box. For a long time, he thought it would be his son. The idea was now impossible. "Tell me about him," Jay said, wanting more information. "What kind of skills does he have? I need a businessman, Malik. See, me and you, we're businessmen. I need men like me and you. If I want someone selling my shit on the streets, I got that. I need someone who can put on a suit and blend in with CEOs and stockbrokers."

"He can do that," Malik said, remaining confident. "He's the one."

"Who is he?" Jay asked, wanting a name.

Malik could tell Jay was pushing him. He wasn't going to let him leave without getting a name. Therefore, he decided to be honest. "They call him King." Malik watched as Jay narrowed his eyes.

"Do you really think I'm going to let someone name King run my shit? Let's go back to the drawing board."

Due to Jay's response, Malik became desperate to change his mind. "Look, Jay, things are totally different from before. You gotta—"

"Why didn't you tell me my son was in jail?"

Malik gulped at the question. Jay's visit with Carmen had completely slipped his mind. There was a fifty-fifty chance Jay knew who his son was. "I didn't want you to be bothered with that right now."

"Smart move," Jay responded, opening a drawer. "Carmen asked me if I wanted to meet him. I told her no. I can't handle that shit right now. I'm doing good staying sane knowing she married Kane." Jay paused so he could shoot an evil look at Malik. "The Triad agent who took me down is also your new best friend. It's a very small world."

Malik never mentioned anything about his friendship with Kane. Somehow, Jay managed to find out. "I won't lie to you," he stated. "We are friends. We've been friends for several years."

"I know how to put two and two together. If you were coming around Carmen for seventeen years, you had to run into her husband. On to bigger things, though, when can I meet King?"

"I'll arrange something for Saturday morning."

"So we're going back to six a.m. interviews?"

"Something kind of like that," Malik said, standing up. "I've already spoken to him, and he's interested. Hopefully, this meeting will run smooth."

"Well, on Saturday, we'll see if it does," Jay muttered. "For the time being, I'm out."

***

Way past midnight, King spent the wee hours of the morning driving around Brookstone until he came to Coco's house. He didn't know what led him there other than the apology he was supposed to give her. Since it was obvious she wasn't up, King knew he needed to leave. For some reason, he couldn't find the urge to. Part of the reason was because he didn't have anywhere else to go. He couldn't go home because he would only be subject to his parents' rules. His only option was to stay in the streets.

King stared at Coco's house, seeing a light come on. It was almost six o'clock in the morning, which meant her parents were probably up preparing for work. Their blinds were open, so he expected to see a figure at any moment. When Coco approached the windowsill, he didn't know what to think. He stared at her and she appeared to be staring at him. To see if she was, he motioned for her to come to him. It took her a few minutes, but she came out the front door, dressed in a bathrobe, which covered her pajamas. As she walked towards him, he took a good look at her. She had grown up over the years, but he was just now able to see it. For the longest, she was simply Kristian's best friend, the nerdy, yet beautiful young girl who his sister liked to shop and gossip with. Now, he was seeing a young lady who wasn't anything short of a goddess.

"What are you doing here?" she asked once she was at his side.

"I came to say I'm sorry," King explained. "Get inside, it's chilly out here." He noticed Coco's hesitation and when she got inside, he continued his apology. "You know I've been stressed and I kind of took it out on you. I'm sorry. It shouldn't have happened. I own up to my actions."

Coco's face was blank, yet she wore a smile on the inside. She accepted King's apology when he stated the reason he was there. Now, she was gushing over the fact she was alone with him. "I accept," she said, remembering to answer.

"Cool, now that we've cleared the air, tell me this. Did something go down between Kristian and Noc? I want you to be honest with me."

"King, you can't ask me questions like that. It goes against the Best Friend code. I can't reveal information about Kristian's personal life to her brother. Besides, even if he was trying to get with her, Kristian isn't having sex. Intercourse is painful."

King became confused. He could've sworn Coco was a virgin, but based off her reply, she could've given it up. "Are you a virgin?"

"Of course, you don't have to have sex to know about it. Have you taken the plunge?"

King mumbled a small yes. He lost his virginity two years ago to a girl who went to Brookstone High. Since then, he hadn't done anything aside from a small sexual encounter with an older woman. His first time was something he barely remembered. He was at a party with some friends, had too much to drink and ended up in a room with a fellow classmate. There was a bed and somehow he ended up on top of the girl and inside her. He didn't remember much, but he did remember not having a condom. Thankfully, she didn't get pregnant.

"Oh," he heard Coco mumble. "What are you doing at my house so early? You couldn't wait until school got out for an apology?"

"I was trying to figure that one out myself." King drummed his fingers on the dashboard. "I didn't have anywhere else to go. I figured I would swing by here. You were the one trying to calm me down today. Everyone wants to know what's going on and what's wrong with me. Maybe, it's time I find the right person to tell my thoughts to." King paused so he could catch her facial expression. Her eyes told him she wanted to know more. "I look at myself and I don't see anyone who looks like me. I feel out of place. I try to deal with the emptiness by wilding out. When I do, my mother always comes running. She gives me the world then. Once I straighten up, she's back to her normal routine, running Flame and chasing after Kristian. Do you know she made her the face of her new line?"

"Of course, I do," Coco admitted. "From what I'm hearing, you're upset because your mother only pays attention to you when you're in trouble. Maybe you should tell her how you feel. You're her firstborn, King. Your mother was in prison when she was pregnant with you. If something was to happen, your mother would go off the deep end. I hope you don't think she doesn't love you."

"I know she does," King said. "I just want her to talk to me regardless of what I have going on. There have been times when I've been good, and I won't hear anything from her."

"Then take the initiative and talk to her."

"Maybe I will," he said, starting up the car.

Coco didn't want to leave, but she needed to get back inside. School started in less than three hours, and she wanted to go back to sleep. On the other hand, she loved her alone time with King. "Do it tomorrow and let me know how it goes."

King told her he would before pointing towards her house. He saw her mother walk past the window and Coco needed to make it inside before she was caught. She took the hint and in a flash, she was out the car and running towards the house. King chuckled as she went before pulling out her driveway. *I was wrong about you, Coco,* he thought, *you've grown up overnight.*

6 | *Phoenix Rising*

Carmen turned over in bed, feeling for Kane's body. She fell asleep before he got in and from what she was feeling; he wasn't there. Her eyes opened, allowing her to see that his side of the bed was still intact. More than surprised, she looked at the alarm clock. It was 6:04 in the morning. Carmen wondered where he was.

Maybe, he needed to clear his head. There's a lot going on right now. I wish he called to say he was working late. He didn't call me all day.

Carmen moved to the center of the bed. Despite her longing to have her husband's arms around her, she drifted into a deep sleep. She started to dream, admiring her husband's chocolate skin, and perfectly toned physique. She also saw an image of her husband undercover without her knowledge. The last thing she wanted was a call from the Brookstone PD with the news he gotten shot or stabbed to death. Carmen got worried, and her eyes reopened. She hadn't seen or spoken to her husband since the previous morning. Something told her he found out about Jay. If he did, he would turn over hell if he knew Jay paid her a visit. Carmen told herself not to think the worst. To calm her nerves, she grabbed Kane's pillow, and held on to it. Until he was there, she would pretend it was him.

Hours later, Carmen was no longer on pins and needles. She was heated. It was eight o'clock and Kane hadn't called or came home. She called him, checked the house, the garage, and even called the precinct. No one had seen him. A part of her didn't want to go to work for fear he would come home, and she wouldn't be there. She wanted an argument, and she needed an explanation.

Busy combing her hair, Carmen wanted to throw the comb at the mirror. She didn't, continuing to style her hair so she could kill time. She was in mid-stroke when their bedroom door opened. Seconds later, Kane's reflection appeared in the mirror. He was undressing and once he was nude, he came in the bathroom. She waited for an explanation, but he didn't say anything. *He knows about Jay. It's the only reason he isn't speaking to me.* Kane went straight for the shower, not even acknowledging her presence.

"Where were you?" she asked.

"Can we talk later? I'm tired," he replied, moving underneath the showerhead.

"You didn't come home last night; we need to talk now."

"Baby, I'm tired. Can we talk about this later?"

Carmen stretched her eyes at how he was brushing her off. "You didn't come home last night. You walked in here not saying a single word and you still don't want to talk? I would've at least appreciated it if you came home and said, 'Honey, I was out all night, I want to say hi, I love you, and we'll talk later,' but no, you didn't say anything. You took your clothes off and jumped in the shower."

"Carm, I've been up all night. Can we not do this right now?"

"So you don't think I'm tired? You don't think I was up all night worried about you?"

"I really don't want to hear this."

Carmen couldn't believe what he was saying. She was more heated than when she got up that morning. All she could do was stare at him. Kane had never acted like that towards her. "You don't want to hear this? You know what, Kane. I'm tired of you. I'm tired of you standing here, telling me about how tired you are. Why didn't you call last night? We wouldn't be having this conversation if you made a phone call."

"Carm, I'm tired. Can we talk about this later?" Kane asked. He raised his voice a little so she would get the point. He should've called, but he couldn't. Shortly after dinner, Tricia started experiencing withdrawals. It went from bad to worse and before he knew it, it was midnight. While he should've called backup and sent her to rehab, he didn't want Akaila and Malachi in the system. They were already halfway there, and they didn't even know it.

"You can't give me an explanation or anything," Carmen fussed.

Kane felt his temper rising. He was wrong, but the last thing he wanted to hear was what he should've done.

"Walk in the house, can't say hi to his wife, and then don't want to talk," Carmen said. "What kind of man did I marry?"

Kane tried to remain calm, but it was getting harder to do with her screaming in his ear.

"I can't believe this, Kane; you have the nerve to—"

"I said I'm fuckin' tired."

Kane yelled before he could catch himself. For the first time in twenty years, Carmen drove him to curse. He watched in agony as she walked away from him. Not bothering to finish, he turned off the shower and followed her in their bedroom. "Carm, I'm sorry," he began. He grabbed her, but she pushed him away. "Baby, come here," he urged.

"Fuck you," she bellowed.

Kane's face fell at the language they were using towards each other. Aware they weren't going to make up in the next five minutes, he watched as she slid on her suit jacket. She then grabbed her purse, heading for the door. "Don't leave like—" He was too late. His wife walked out the room, slamming the door behind her.

***

Carmen was on her way to Flame, not knowing her son, King, beat her there. Currently stretched out on the sofa in her office, Cathy let him in when she arrived that morning. Since his mother wasn't there, King got a little shut eye while he waited on her. Automatically an image of Coco appeared. Vulgar thoughts filled his mind until he heard his mother's voice.

"I said fuck you and left. Can you believe he came home and didn't say one word to me? Do you think I should have stayed? I gave him the chance to talk to me, Tee. He didn't want to. I left him there, buck naked, dripping water all over the damn carpet."

King cracked a smile, realizing his parents were arguing.

"I don't give him any when I'm mad at him. He already knows there will be no sex tonight. I don't even look at his dick when I'm upset."

King scrunched up his face, hearing his mother talk about her sex life. The conversation made him open his eyes and he noticed his mother's shadow reflecting on the wall opposite of him.

"A part of me doesn't even want to go home tonight. Is that doing evil for evil?"

King saw his mother move. He closed his eyes, pretending he was asleep. When he heard her sigh, he knew she noticed him.

"Big surprise, King's here, asleep in my office, yep, that's another man I've been worried about, I'll catch you when you come in."

A few seconds passed before King felt his mother's presence. She sat on the edge of the couch and touched his chest. He opened his eyes as if he was waking up.

"Morning," she greeted. "How did you get in here?"

King faked a small yawn before replying with, "Cathy."

"So you were only pretending to be asleep? Cathy doesn't come in until eight o'clock and it's a little after eight-thirty."

King cracked a smile, knowing he couldn't fool his mother. "You're right, I was pretending, and I also know that Daddy isn't getting any."

Carmen blushed because he caught the tail-end of her conversation with Tiara. Embarrassed, she changed the subject. "I'm glad to see you're out of jail. Was this your way of telling me?"

"I wanted to talk to you about something."

The first thought in Carmen's mind was Jay. Her son didn't look like his biological father, but they shared the same complexion and persona. Ready to face the music and deal with the issue, she replied with, "What?"

"Can you not say that?" King caught a slight attitude but calmed down when he realized his mother didn't mean any harm. Instead of apologizing, he started the discussion. "Have you noticed, I mean, how do you..." King stopped. He took a few seconds to collect his thoughts before trying again. "How come you only pay attention to me when I'm in trouble?"

"King, I'm paying attention to you now. You were the one who was tongue-tied."

King grunted. "When I'm at home, you don't talk to me. As soon as I have cops trailing my ass, you want to come around like you're a psychologist. Why can't you talk to me when I'm being good?" His mother tried to interrupt him, but he was on a roll. "You pay attention to Kristian. You take her to the movies and shit. You're letting her do this juniors' line. Why can't I model? I'm fine, I look good."

"I'm sorry you feel this way, King, but the only time I know where you are and can talk to you is when you're locked up."

"Why are you acting like I'm never there?"

"Because you're not and you know you're not."

King stood up. "Why did I even try?"

"See, I'm trying to listen, but you're giving up and running away." Carmen stood up as well. "I want to know what's going on with you. The only time I can sit down and talk to you is when you're in trouble."

"That's why I get in trouble."

King felt like a boulder was lifted off his shoulders. It felt good to reveal the truth. Now, he had to see what she was going to do with it.

"You get in trouble because you want my attention? You don't know how much I love you, do you?"

King knew she loved him, but he wanted her to show it.

"King, when I was in prison, all I had to keep me sane was you. You gave me hope. All I wanted was to be a good mother to you. You are my heart. I want to spend time with you. I've tried, King, but you gotta make yourself available, too."

"Are you saying it's my fault?"

"It's not anyone's fault, baby. I don't want you mad at me or hating me because you feel this way."

"I don't hate you," King said, sitting on the couch. "I don't know, Mama. Sometimes, I wonder who I am."

"Well, have you ever Googled yourself?" Carmen joked. She giggled for a bit before quieting down. "Look, King, any time you have a problem, come talk to me. I want you to," she told him. "Hopefully, we can start rebuilding our relationship. I don't want you mad at me."

"I'm not mad at you. I'm mad at myself. I should've said all this a long time ago. It probably would've stopped me from fighting and getting all those charges." King gave her a crooked smile. "I'm gonna be staying at Malik's for a while. I need some time to think about things. So, if you want to find me, I'll be there."

Carmen leaned down, giving him a hug. "If that's what you need," she told him. She kissed his cheek and watched as he pulled away. When he stood up to leave, she thought long and hard about what he said. He mentioned he was going to be staying at Malik's. In the past, she wouldn't have cared, but now, Jay was back in Brookstone. It was only a matter of time before their paths would meet. *Hot damn*, Carmen thought, *here we go again.*

***

Both Carmen and Kane were busy having heart to hearts. While King visited his mother, Kristian came to her parents' bedroom, banging on the door right when Kane was about to head to sleep. She demanded a ride to school, and Kane had to stop himself from giving her twenty dollars for a cab. He tried to come up with other alternatives, but since he didn't know where King was, he had to get out of bed and take her. Now, she was heated, and it showed in her expression. "You want to talk about it?" he asked.

Kristian was aggravated. "I'm going to get my license," she announced. "Y'all know I need a ride to school. If King isn't at home then you gotta take me. It's a very easy concept. School starts at eight-thirty, not nine and not nine-thirty."

"Kristian, I'm sorry."

"Who's going to pick me up?" she barked, overlooking his apology.

Kane scratched his chin until he remembered Akaila. "From now on, I'm gonna pick you up and take you." He needed to tell Kristian about Akaila, but he didn't want to put the girl's business out there. He decided to feed Kristian a little bit at a time "Did you hear the arguing this morning?"

"Of course," Kristian replied. "I heard the door slamming, too."

"I'm working on a new assignment, and I didn't come home last night. Your mother was mad because I didn't call so we got into it. I'm going to give her a little time to calm down. Everything should be fine."

"Whatever," Kristian said, unlocking the door.

"Can you wait a minute? Hold up for a sec."

Kristian decided to trash the attitude.

"Look, I'm going to be helping this lady out for a while. She has a drug problem and I'm trying to get her some help. She's in danger of losing her kids. There may be times when I might have to bring my work home. I want you to keep everything confidential, okay?"

"Okay," Kristian said, confused. "I got to go. Class starts in ten." She gave him a quick peck on the cheek and jumped out the car.

Kane watched as she headed towards her friends. He was trying to warn her about Akaila, but it was too late. She would find out when he came to pick them up from school that afternoon. While his heart was set on going to bed, he couldn't. Carmen was mad at him, and it was eating him up inside. A part of him couldn't stomach what they said to each other. They never talked like that. He wondered what was making it happen now.

7 | *Throwback*

Carmen flipped through the business proposal one more time, sticking her ink pen in her mouth. She read over it ten times and every time she did, she got an even better idea. She commended Jay on the structure of his proposal, but several details needed to be tweaked before he took it to banks and other loan companies. He wouldn't be able to get anything in his name, but she figured that was where she came in. She didn't know how to reach him, but she figured he wouldn't be hard to find.

Carmen wondered if she should call Malik. She could get Jay's number from him, and they could meet to discuss the proposal. She was taking a chance, but if anything, Kane was asleep in bed.

Not thinking about it further, Carmen picked up the phone and dialed Malik's number. When he answered, she didn't say hello, but gave her request. "I need Jay's number," she told him, standing up. "I read his proposal and I want in."

"Ahh, so you're kind of feeling it a little?"

"Look, Malik, get me the number. I don't want to hear any jokes about me and Jay."

"Alright, ma, hold on, let me check with the boss to see if he wants me to give out his new number."

Carmen waited, realizing she'd been put on hold. Malik knew Jay wanted her to have the number otherwise he wouldn't have left a copy of his business proposal on her desk. When Malik came back on the line, she wanted to voice her opinion, but he was talking a mile a minute.

"I spoke to Jay. He wants to meet with you if you're interested in the proposal. He wants you to meet him at twelve-thirty for lunch at Old Town Bistro downtown."

"Malik, that restaurant is outside." Carmen closed her eyes. She didn't want to be sitting downtown with Jay. Anyone could see her and tell her husband she was eating lunch with him. They were already on the warpath and being spotted with Jay would only make the situation worse. Carmen bit her lip until she realized it was twelve-fifteen. She needed to be leaving now. "I'm on my way," she blurted, hanging up the phone. Carmen grabbed her purse along with the proposal and headed to Cathy's desk. "I'm going out for lunch, direct all my calls to my voicemail, or have them e-mail me. If one of my kids call, tell them to text me," she told her, rummaging through the mail that had come.

"Christian Monroe called about the collaboration."

"Tell him wintertime. Right now the board doesn't want a new line. I barely got them to okay *Peaches*."

"Tiara wants to know if you've approved the official ad for *King*."

"Nope," Carmen replied. "Tell her to use her best judgment. She ran this company before me," she joked. She walked away from her receptionist's desk, not wanting to answer any more questions. If she was lucky, she and Jay could get to the restaurant before the lunchtime rush. In her opinion, Jay only picked the restaurant to announce his return to the city. People would also see they still communicated.

Carmen's nerves may have been on edge, but the drive to the restaurant was even more stressful. However, she wasn't in this by herself. Malik was also in a difficult situation. Both Jay and Kane were his best friends. Carmen didn't know how he was separating his relationship with the two.

She glanced at her speedometer, seeing she was speeding. With Jay picking the restaurant, he would be there before her. Like she thought, she found him at a table in front of the restaurant.

He was dressed in a blue pinstriped collared shirt with a multi-colored tie and suspenders. His attire changed over the years, and she thanked herself for it. He was decked out in one of her designs. "Well, hello," she greeted, giving him a smile.

"Hello to you, too, Mrs. Davenport. I hope this is better than yesterday." Jay picked up his glass of water as Carmen laid her copy of the proposal on the table. His eyes widened when he saw the red marks. "What's wrong with it? I didn't need an editor."

"There are some things I think you should think about. Before we get into it, let me order, I'm hungry as hell."

"I already ordered for you."

Carmen raised her brow. He mimicked her. "What did you order for me?"

"It had to be your favorite, Carm," he told her, grinning. "I got you the number twenty-one with a side of dumplings."

Carmen held her tongue not wanting to hurt his feelings. That had been her favorite when they were younger, but it changed. Kane turned her on to their honey barbecue ribs, which was now her favorite. "Good job," she lied.

"I knew I was good," he said, taking out his copy of the proposal.

"Where's my drink?" she asked, noticing there was only one glass on the table.

"I got a bottle of wine coming, Alice White Chardonnay. It's one of the cheapest, but for some reason, it's your favorite. I keep on impressing you, huh? I remember a lot."

Carmen had to agree. Alice White was still her favorite. "Okay, let's get past favorites and on to business. I only have an hour for lunch."

"Only an hour, I cleared the whole day," he joked. "Well, I have a building I think I want. It has two floors. I figured the restaurant could be two levels. There are some rooms in the back, which can be used as offices and there are bathrooms on each floor. There are also some nice-sized spaces for kitchens. I had Malik meet with the owner, but she is only looking for renters."

"I wonder why," Carmen voiced. "Do you think you can get her to change her mind?"

"No, but you can. I figured you could meet with her."

"Jay, look, I want to help and I'm excited about this, but I have a job to do. In addition, I'm a parent, which is a full-time job."

Jay scrunched up his face. "I'm a parent, too."

Carmen didn't want to argue. "What do you want?"

Jay licked his lips and leaned in closer to her. "I need you to put everything in your name. These people aren't going to give me anything. I have two murders and an assault charge on my back. Not to mention, they got me for selling narcotics, and the weapons and diamond shit. Everything I got now is in Malik's name and I can't use him for everything. I need this building and I need licenses. I need you to pretend like you're starting this. I can take care of the money part. I only need you to be the face."

Carmen set back in her seat. "I thought I was going to be a partner."

"Things changed."

Carmen flipped the proposal closed. She expected to lend Jay money, not be the face of his operation. "How are you going to get the money for this?"

"Here it is," she heard a voice say.

Their waitress placed their food in front of them. When Jay requested they have privacy, Carmen took her attention off her food. He was bowing his head and she did the same, praying for God to lead her in the right direction. Once she said, amen, she opened her eyes and picked up her fork. It had been a long time since she had the number twenty-one and a part of her was glad he ordered it for her. Catfish was still one of her favorite things to eat.

"I would be lying if I told you there wasn't going to be some hustling involved. I don't want to do it, but my money is looking funny. Once I shelve out the dough for the restaurant, I'm going to be in the red."

"You can't afford to get locked up."

"Neither can you."

Carmen stuck her fork in her catfish fillet. "I'll donate some of the money. I don't want you selling anything."

"I'm not trying to have any major part in it, Carmen. In fact, I'm enlisting a new guy to handle my shit. I'm going to get my money up and then I'm out. The only reason I'm going back to the cartel is because I need some money to start my businesses. Once this restaurant takes off, Sapphire is open, and Iceland is available to the public, I'm out. I promise."

Carmen wondered who Jay found to do his dirty work. Seventeen years ago, men would've died to work for him. At one point, she felt like Jay couldn't be touched. Times were good. Then, Rakim passed, and both of their worlds came crashing down.

The memories came flooding back in her mind. Carmen stopped eating. Since time was of the essence, she picked up her fork again right as her phone started to ring. She pulled it from her purse seeing a text message from Kane. *I love you*, the message read. Chills ran through her body, and she set her phone down, not wanting to think of her husband. "I need some wine," she whispered. She searched the table for the bottle of Alice White until Jay signaled for their waitress to come to their table. He reminded her to bring it while Carmen went back to her food. She also glanced over the proposal, taking note of the things they needed to discuss.

"What did your message say?"

Carmen didn't reply and the silence led Jay to pick up her phone. She tried to grab it from him, but he was quick.

"I love you. I love you. I love you. Let's do lunch. I love you. I miss you. Last night was great, I love you. Did you check the mail? I love you. I love you. I love you. I love you. I love you. I miss you." Jay paused, becoming disgusted. "This is who you left me for?" He slammed the phone on the table. He then reached in his pocket, pulling out his prescription. He stuffed a tablet in his mouth and chased it with water.

"I know that isn't easy to see," Carmen admitted. "I know I did you wrong. That is one of the reasons why I want to see you win. People will think I'm stupid because I'm helping you, but I've always been indebted to you."

"You need to clean out your closet."

Carmen blinked her eyes. "I need to clean out my closet. What are you talking about?"

"You left all your shit in my house, Carm. You never came back after they took you to the hospital. Since you've moved on, you need to clean out your closet. What if I get married? Where is my wife going to put her things? Do you think she wants to share a closet with you?"

Carmen never thought about Jay being with another woman. In fact, he hadn't been with one in seventeen years. "Are you seeing someone?" she asked, not ready for the answer.

"Are you worried about who's going to be around my son?"

"No, I'm worried about her. Not every woman can handle you."

Jay agreed. "True, I need a woman who knows me in and out."

"You're right. What woman knows you in and out?"

Carmen knew she had Jay right where she wanted him with her question. There wasn't anyone on the face of the earth who knew him in and out aside from her. Unfortunately, she was already spoken for.

"Tell me, why are you so concerned about who I'm dating?"

"I'm not. I want to make sure the next woman who gets in your bed knows what kind of fire she's dealing with."

"Does your husband know the kind of fire he's dealing with? Come on, Peaches, we both know I have you wrapped around my finger. If you were scared, you wouldn't be here. If you were worried about what your husband would say, you wouldn't be here. All I gotta do is look you in the eye; snap my fingers and I have you under control. You're vulnerable, you've always been weak, and that's the reason Carlos was able to fuck you. You were a good girl who discovered she loved gangsters and a quick thrill. You go crazy when a man demands control of you. All I have to say is, 'Carm, come jump on this dick,' and you're already there, riding away."

Carmen grabbed her napkin, covering her food. The last thing she needed was Jay trying to make it seem like he controlled her. She knew there was a trick to her being a part of his proposal. He wanted her to run back in his arms. Although she was mad at Kane, there was no way she was going to cheat.

Carmen ignored his spiel and opened the proposal. She started at the first page. "First off, you don't need to open a seafood restaurant. There are too many in the area already. What Brookstone needs is a high class soul food restaurant. It needs to be a restaurant that offers breakfast, lunch, dinner, and is open real late on the weekends. If you change the menu, your restaurant has a greater chance of being a success."

"Is there anything else," Jay asked as she turned the page.

"It's all about location. There's a building a couple of blocks from here. It is in Davenport Realty's listings so you can buy it from my father. If I coax him the right way, he'll sell it to me. Besides, everything will be in my name anyway. It fits the description of what you want and the only reason I know is because I checked it out. How do you feel about that?"

"I don't want your father involved. He's out to get me, too."

"I think you tend to forget you're Hector Santiago's son. My father may hate you, but he loved your father, meaning he'll spare your life." Carmen continued to look over the details of the proposal. "That's all," she told him. "I can contact my father this evening about the building. He'll put one of his agents on it and I'll give you a call about the price."

Jay smiled as she slid her copy of the proposal over to him. He figured she wanted him to keep it so he could review her notes. "Why don't you come to the house after lunch?"

"I have work to do," she told him, pushing her plate away. "My daughter is going to—" Carmen paused when Jay's eyes got big.

"You have a daughter? You had another baby?"

"Kane and I have a daughter together. She's fifteen and she goes to Brookstone High. She's going to be the face of my new collection. I want more kids, but unfortunately, I didn't learn Kane was sterile until after we were married. We used in vitro to conceive."

Jay grabbed the wine, twisting off the cap. He poured Carmen a glass and slid it over to her. In the process, he took the opportunity to give her a good look. Her face was fuller, and she was about twenty pounds heavier than when they dated. The weight went in the right spot directly to her hips. "How about dessert?" he asked. "I have your favorite coming. You always loved the peanut butter pie. I used to stop and pick it up for you all the time." Jay snuck Carmen another smile. "I remember everything about you, Carmen Denise Davenport."

"Hmm, so you think you do. Why don't we take a little quiz? Tell me, Jay, why do my parents call me, Peaches? You love to say my nickname."

"That's an easy one. When you were born, you came out the color of a peach."

"Good answer, Mr. Santiago. Now, why is my name Carmen?"

"You were named after Dorothy Dandridge's character in *Carmen Jones*. I'm not going to lose, Carm. I know everything about you."

"We'll see. Let's see if you know the answer to this one. Well, this isn't about me. How do you spell your son's name? It isn't pronounced like its spelled."

Jay's face tightened. He didn't know his son's name. No one told him, and she hadn't written it on the picture she gave him.

"What's wrong?" she asked, seeing his frown.

"I don't know his name."

Carmen didn't understand how he didn't know King's name. "You don't know his name?"

"I don't know his fuckin' name, Carm."

Carmen sighed. "His name's Jayceon. It's spelled J-A-Y-C-E-O-N. You pronounce it just like Jason; however, most people love to say Jay-see-on. That's his name. Every time I say it, I have to say yours."

8 | *Caught Out There*

Kane picked up his phone, noticing Carmen hadn't texted him back. He was trying to calm things down, but she was making it hard. He knew she got his messages. He texted her every day, sometimes multiple times, and she always got the messages. She was trying to be evil. To be the bigger person, he sent another text message, saying I love you.

"Who do you keep messaging?" Tricia asked as he drove to the store.

"Carmen," he replied.

"Oh," she mouthed. Tricia turned away, still slightly dazed. They had just left the outpatient treatment program Kane put her in. "Why don't you call her?"

"I could, but if she isn't answering my texts then she isn't going to answer my calls. Besides, texting is a normal routine for us." Kane merged into the right lane. "We had a little argument this morning because of last night."

"Sorry about that," Tricia apologized.

"Don't worry about it, we'll be fine. I'm going to make sure I get home tonight before she gets off so I can fix dinner. We'll have a romantic evening and it'll put everything back on track."

"Look, I know you and Carmen are married. You don't have to come here every day. Once a week is fine. I don't want to get in the middle."

"You're not getting in the middle. We're fine. We had a little argument, that was it. She doesn't even know about you." Kane turned into the parking lot of Publix.

"Are you going to tell her?" Tricia asked as he parked.

"The situation is too uncomfortable." While he did plan to tell Carmen one day, he knew she wouldn't jump head over heels. He did, though, expect her to accept his new assignment.

"She shouldn't have a problem with me. I should have a problem with her. She was the one messing around with my boyfriend." Tricia took her grocery list out her purse. She realized they hadn't discussed who was paying. She figured Kane knew she didn't have money. "Um, are you paying for this?" She opened her door.

"I'm paying," he said, as if she should've known. "I said let me worry about this, remember?"

"Yeah, I remember," she told him, starting to walk towards the store. She grabbed a buggy while Kane was about six steps behind her. When she turned to look at him, she noticed he was still texting. *She better return those messages*, Tricia thought. If Tricia was Carmen, she would've been texting back with, *I love you, too*. Since she wasn't, she hoped he received a response. "I'm going to the bread aisle," she announced.

"Cool," he said, following behind her. Kane watched as a text message came to his phone. He prayed it was Carmen, but the sender was Lieutenant Harris. He wanted to know how everything was going. Kane didn't bother to text him back, stuffing his phone in his pocket. "I know you need a lot, but I have to pick Kristian and Akaila up at three-thirty."

"Oh, we'll be done," she said, grabbing a loaf of wheat bread.

Kane followed her down the aisle, hoping she knew she had no spending limit. He wanted her to get enough because she had two growing kids. He saw the way Malachi ate and the boy could eat someone out of house and home.

"What kind of snacks do you like?"

Kane snapped back to reality, seeing Tricia dumping Little Debbie cakes in the buggy. "You don't have to buy anything for me, get what you want," he told her.

"You mean you don't have to buy anything for you," she joked.

"Yeah, something like that," he told her as she continued walking down the aisle. He studied her for a bit, seeing she tried to style her hair. If she got herself together she would be one of the finest women in Brookstone. She reached up to grab a bag of chips and he checked out her figure. The Tricia he remembered was thick, but the one in front of him lost a lot of weight.

"Stop staring at me," she blurted.

Kane covered his eyes. "Sorry," he told her as she put the chips in the buggy. "I didn't realize I was staring."

"You were, but it's not a big deal. You can stare for as long as you want."

Her tone was somewhat seductive, and Kane smiled in response. He felt bad for looking at her. Carmen was the only woman for him. He could never leave her for someone else. Love and seventeen years of marriage made it hard for him to.

***

Both Carmen and Kane had feelings of guilt regarding the people they were spending the afternoon with. Carmen was supposed to be at work while instead she was at the park feeding ducks with Jay.

"It's peaceful out here," he was saying. "I came out here one night and just wanted to sleep. I cleared my head of everything. It felt so good to finally be free. I guess you feel like that after you've been locked up for so long." Jay threw more bread in the lake, which ran through the middle of Brookstone Park. The ducks immediately swam to where he was, eating like they hadn't been fed all day. "I'm about to be fifty. I'm an old man."

"You look good, though." Carmen walked around the lake, hearing Jay's footsteps behind her. She was about to speak until her phone vibrated again. She took it out her pocket and read another *I love you* message from Kane. He was trying, but those three words weren't going to cut it this time. They needed to have a serious discussion.

"Why don't we go to my house? You can start cleaning out the closet. You obviously have some free time."

"How about I go to work, and you check up on Malik? You need to tell him to stop looking for chefs that specialize in seafood, don't you?"

Jay smiled. She still didn't want to come to the house. He didn't know how long it was going to take to get her there. "I do need to do that. I guess you want us to go our separate ways, huh?"

"We need to," Carmen replied. "You're going to disappoint the ducks, though. They like you."

"Man, those ducks are eating me out of house and home. I've already given them two loaves of bread." *Shit*, Jay thought, *they know when they see me it's feeding time.*

"I need to get back to the office." Carmen walked in the direction of their cars. She stopped, not hearing Jay's footsteps. "Are you coming? We can at least walk back to our cars together."

"Nah, I'll catch you later," he said, staring at the ducks.

"Alright, well, I'll see you around." Carmen walked to her car. Quite naturally, she thought of Jay and their past relationship. The short amount of time they spent together reminded her of why she fell for him the first place. While he did have a temper, most of the time he was a gentle giant.

Carmen drove to Flame anxious to get back to work. Upon arriving on her floor, Cathy approached her first with a notepad and ink pen.

"I'm glad you're back," Cathy yelled, nearly out of breath. "Monroe's people keep calling about the collaboration. They really want you to sign off on this. They said the payout could be millions."

Carmen exhaled. "I don't have the time or the energy for a new line. Tell them we're releasing a new collection in the summer. If they call the office again, I'll personally tell them no."

"Done," Cathy belted, returning to her desk.

Carmen went inside her office and closed the door. Tiara was seated at her desk with her feet propped up. A bottle of wine was in her friend's hand and the image made Carmen giggle.

"Girl, I needed this," Tiara mumbled, holding up the bottle. "Where were you? Did Kane make you take a three hour lunch for makeup sex?"

Carmen frowned, realizing she hadn't told Tiara about Jay. Her friend didn't even know he had been released. "Can you keep a secret?"

"I answered that question yesterday in the break room."

Carmen walked to her desk and sat down. "There's no easy way to say this, but to say it. Jay is out of prison. His case was reopened. The self-defense plea worked. He is strolling through the park as we speak."

"What the fuck?" Tiara stood up, dropping the bottle of wine on the desk. "Who let that piece of shit out? Does he have something to do with you not being here?" Tiara became suspicious, giving Carmen the once-over.

"He's opening up a restaurant and I agreed to let him use my name."

"Whoa, hold up here, wait a minute, you've been meeting with him?"

"We met yesterday, and we met for lunch today."

"Are you out of your fuckin' mind," Tiara yelled. She stared at Carmen, trying to figure out how she could let Jay be in her presence. *Did she not remember this was the man who dragged her down a flight of steps?* "You know, what they say about domestic violence is true. The cycle of abuse is real. So what, you want him to beat your ass again?"

"Tiara, I need your support right now. I don't need you judging me."

"You don't get it, do you? This man left you for dead. He was gonna kill you. I saw him beating you. I saw the way he was. He wasn't thinking about you, Carmen. He wanted you dead. He hit you like you were a punching bag. Do not throw away what you've built. You have a good husband, two beautiful kids. You need to stay away from Jay. He's only going to do it again." Tiara couldn't stress her words enough. She couldn't believe Carmen was about to jump headfirst into a business relationship with Jay. She thought her friend learned her lesson years ago.

"Tee, he's changed. We went to the park today and he was so gentle. I mean, he fed the ducks. I mean, come on, Tee, did you ever think you would see Jay feeding ducks?"

"Does it look like I fuckin' care about him feeding some damn ducks? I eat duck."

Carmen closed her eyes. She expected Tiara to react like that, but she hoped her friend would understand. "He's changed. He's on medication. He's doing well and he needs a second chance."

"He got his second chance after he nearly pushed you down the steps the first time. Do you remember that? It was the night your parents were out of town. He tried to kill you then, Carm."

"I thought you would understand, Tee." Carmen grabbed the bottle off her desk. She took a long sip, allowing the bitter taste to go down her throat. She swallowed as Tiara looked at her in disappointment.

"I would understand if I didn't have to hit him with a baseball bat so he would take his hands off your damn throat. I can't believe..." Tiara paused, thinking of King. "Does King know? Does your son know Kane isn't his father?"

Carmen shook her head. "Jay's not ready to meet him."

"Does Kane know Jay is out?"

"I don't think so," Carmen said, setting the bottle down.

"You know what, I can't take this. I really can't. Give me this damn bottle." Tiara snatched the bottle from Carmen's hands. "I'm going home. I need to drink this shit off."

Carmen watched as her friend left her office. Tiara was disappointed, but she would understand her decision in a few days. Once she saw how Jay changed, she would understand completely. All she needed was a little time.

***

The bell rung precisely at three-thirty and Akaila dreaded the sound. Her mother mentioned Kane would be picking her up from school, which meant she would be in the car with Kristian. While she had known her since first grade, they were complete and total enemies. Kristian represented the lifestyle she perpetrated, and Akaila was envious of her for it. Once Kristian saw the way she really lived, she would blab it to the whole school.

To soften the blow, Akaila walked towards Kristian and her friends who were standing at the front entrance of the school. She wanted to tell her what was going on before she got in Kane's car. "Can I talk to you?" she asked, interrupting their conversation.

"Yeah," Kristian said. She noticed the looks on her friends' faces. They appeared to be suspicious and so was she.

Akaila started talking as soon as they were out of earshot. "Look, I'm gonna be riding with you from now on. Don't act surprise when you see me get in the car."

Kristian narrowed her eyes. Her father told her he was bringing his work home, but she didn't think like this. "You don't even live near us."

"Why don't you let your father explain things to you? Do me a favor, though. Don't make me out to be a charity case. I can take care of myself and my family. You also need to tell your father about us. I don't want him thinking we're best friends when we aren't. He needs to know we don't like each other. Just because he's helping us out doesn't mean we have to be buddies."

"Fine with me," Kristian agreed. "Speaking of my father, there he is. Let me say goodbye to my crew." Kristian walked away, thinking Akaila had some nerve. She approached her out of nowhere, barking orders like she was the blabbermouth. Akaila was the one who had been running her name through the mud since elementary school. She even tried to holler at Dijuan, knowing she liked him. Since she was talking about being a charity case, Kristian assumed Akaila wasn't rich like she thought.

"My father is here," she announced to Coco and Dijuan.

"When did Akaila ever want to talk to you?" Dijuan pointed in Akaila's direction, shocked at their interaction.

"Don't point, Dijuan. She moved in our neighborhood and her mother wanted my parents to look out for her," Kristian lied. "She's going to be riding to school with me. It's no biggie. We still don't like each other."

"Dang, her mother finally caught up with her."

"Yeah," Kristian said. Akaila was standing outside her father's car as if she was waiting on her. "I guess I better get going. I'll see y'all later." Kristian waved at her friends. She knew they were going to dissect her story.

"Hey, Daddy," she greeted as she got inside her father's Jeep. He gave her a warm smile before peeking at Akaila. The girl's arms were folded across her chest as if she didn't want to be there. Kristian rolled her eyes, sensing her attitude. She wanted to say something, but she kept her words to herself. "How was your day?" she asked her father, taking his attention off Akaila.

"Other than the fact your mother isn't speaking to me," he began.

Kristian exhaled, knowing it was only a matter of time before her mother would call him. Her mother simply needed a few hours to calm down. Once she did, they would be back in their lovey dovey state. She didn't express her thought, remaining silent as they drove Akaila home.

The girl lived in West Brookstone, which shocked her. From the way the girl dressed, she thought she lived in East Brookstone. When they pulled up to a small yellow house, Kristian tried to keep her facial expressions together. *She can't live here. She wears name brand clothes every day.*

"Tell your mother I'll be over in the morning after I drop y'all off."

"Yes, sir," Akaila said, getting out the car. "Thanks."

Kristian listened as the girl closed the door. She couldn't believe she discovered Akaila's secret. The girl wasn't rich like she pretended to be. It didn't matter to Kristian, but she knew it would be the talk of the school if anyone found out. She watched as a skinny woman walked out the house and waved at her father. Kristian knew it was time to ask her father what was going on. She was eager to know. "Is this where Akaila lives?"

"Yeah," Kane replied, pulling into the street.

"She told me to ask you for all the details."

Kane sighed, seeing he had to be the one to tell Kristian the truth. "Well, her father is deceased. He killed himself about two years ago and her mother has a drug problem. She and her brother are in danger of being put in the system. This assignment is supposed to be my punishment for not taking a case in California. The Triad begged the Brookstone PD to put me on leave so I could go. I told them no and Harris gave me this. I didn't take the case because I would've been gone for at least six months. Don't tell your mother, though. I don't want her to know anything about California."

Kristian's mouth dropped wide open. "You mean she's poor?"

"Dirt poor," Kane replied, looking at his daughter. "Half of the food in their house was expired. Her little brother, Malachi, hustles to help pay the rent and light bill."

"I had no idea."

Kristian sat back in her seat not believing what her father told her. Akaila was fronting all along. It made her wonder why she was really in all those boys' cars. *Was she selling herself to help her mother out?* She closed her eyes as her dad drove home, thinking of what she found out. Kristian didn't understand. The girl was always wearing the latest fashions. She was on top of every trend. *Of course, she was, Akaila was trying to protect her image.*

Several minutes passed before her father pulled into their empty driveway. A black Mustang was nowhere in sight, and it reminded Kristian she hadn't heard from King all day. It wasn't a surprise because she knew he was trying to get Lil' Noc's money. She just hoped he got it before Friday. If he didn't, Kristian could only imagine the consequences.

"I have a special evening prepared for your Mom. I figured I'll be nice and let you drive my old car to church. What do you say?"

Kristian wrinkled her face, knowing what that meant. Her parents wanted to do the nasty. Her father knew she didn't have a license, so he desperately wanted her out the house.

"Come on, I'm giving you a car," he told her as they got out.

"Daddy, I have homework to do. Where do you expect for me to go on a Wednesday night? Aren't you coming to bible study?"

"Nah, I want tonight to be special. You can take notes for me."

"Eew, y'all are some freaks," she joked.

"Don't start that," he told her, opening the front door.

Kristian went inside, dropping her tote bag on the floor. "Maybe, I'll go to Coco's and do my homework there. Then, we can go to bible study. You and Mama should be coming, too, with the way y'all slam doors."

"I didn't slam any doors," Kane corrected. He walked out the house, going to the mailbox. Between the stuff he got from Triad and his wife's fashion show invitations, their mailbox stayed full. He opened it, growling at how much stuff was inside. He went through the mail seeing most of it was Carmen's until he came to an envelope from *Girlfriend Magazine*. It was addressed to the Kanes, which meant he could open it. He waited until he got inside, coming in the kitchen where Kristian was.

"Is that yours?" she asked him as he tore into the letter.

"Mind your beeswax," he told her, jokingly. "Pour me a glass," he ordered, pointing to the pitcher of orange juice. He slid out the letter, opening it up. "Dear Mr. and Mrs. Kane, it is our great pleasure to write to you inquiring your participation in our November issue of *Girlfriend Magazine*. Over the years—" He stopped, hearing Kristian's voice.

"Please don't read word for word," she said, sliding him his glass.

Kane rolled his eyes, reading the letter silently. "*Girlfriend Magazine* wants to do a spread on the family. They want to do it next month," he announced.

Kristian swallowed, taking the letter out his hands. "Cool beans," she said, reading over it. "Just make sure King isn't in jail."

Kane cracked a smile. This was the kind of news Carmen needed to come home to. He could tell her about the spread over dinner. It would make the evening even more special. "Why don't you go ahead and take the car? You want some money for pizza or something?"

"No, I'm fine. I got money. Besides, Coco can cook. That's practically her chore in her house."

"Okay, well, I'm going to get started on dinner. I have lots to do."

Kristian set her empty glass in the sink. She had a flashback of her parents' argument, which led her to take another shot at her father. "You sure do," she joked. "I wish you the best."

9 | *Temptation*

Carmen held her head down, unsure of what she was doing. She didn't even know why she was there. A part of her wanted to turn around and get back in her car, but she couldn't. She prayed to God, asking Him to lead her in the right direction and somehow, she ended up at Jay's house. Her presence was the only evidence he needed to prove he was right. She was vulnerable when it came to him.

"Couldn't resist it, could you?" he asked.

Carmen took a deep breath as he let her in.

"I had dinner cooking," he said as she walked in the foyer. She stared at the walls, seeing everything was the same. The house smelled stuffy, but she knew it was because it had been shut up for a long time. She walked down the hall, getting goosebumps. It was like everything was coming back to her. She even stopped in the living room to see the portrait of his father, which was still above the fireplace.

"Come on, let's eat," he told her, pulling her towards the kitchen. "I got baked chicken, green beans, macaroni and cheese, black eyed peas, and a beautiful pan of cornbread," he said, showing her the spread.

"Who taught you how to cook?" Carmen asked, admiring the food.

"I read a lot of cookbooks when I left confinement."

"Oh," Carmen mouthed, eyeing the rest of the food.

"Let me get you a plate," he said, slapping his hands together.

Carmen sat on a stool, watching as he rinsed off two plates. He then grabbed two glasses, before opening the fridge.

"Alice White," he said, showing her the chardonnay she loved. He brought the items to the kitchen's island. He then handed her an empty plate before saying, "Bon appetite." It was a hint she was serving herself.

Carmen took the plate from his hands, sliding off the stool. "Did you know I was coming over?"

"Nope, I figured I would cook a little something to celebrate my release. It wasn't like I had a welcome home party waiting on me."

"Well, if I knew you were being released, I could have set something up," Carmen responded.

"Please, you were about to pee on yourself when you saw me."

"How did you expect me to react?" Carmen scooped up a spoonful of macaroni and cheese as she waited on his reply.

"I don't know. Jump on my dick or something."

He had been saying that phrase a lot and Carmen knew it was because he was horny. "Do you want me to sleep with you?"

"You're married, Carm."

"So what's with all these sexual comments?"

"It's a joke, ha, ha, ha, don't take it serious," he said, taking the spoon out her hands. "Please don't," he said, scooping some macaroni and cheese on his plate. He headed in the dining room, sitting at the head of the table.

Carmen knew Jay hadn't rejected her. Even though she had no intention of sleeping with him, if she wanted to, he wouldn't say no.

Carmen picked up a pair of tongs, grabbing a chicken thigh. She then went for some of the green beans, black eyed peas, and cut herself a big piece of cornbread before heading in the dining room to join him.

"Jayceon Santiago, that's my son's name."

"Um, it's actually Jayceon Santiago Kane," she corrected.

Jay shot her a look, grinding his teeth. He was about to curse, but he told himself to stay calm. "I should go down to the police station and see his mug shot. Shit, the police would handcuff me before I got to the door."

Carmen started to eat and in the process, she felt Jay's eyes burning onto hers. When she returned his gaze, she noticed he was staring at her. To keep from saying anything, she continued eating.

"Who knows you're here? Does anyone know we've been meeting?"

"Tiara knows," she told him, setting her fork down. "She wasn't too happy. You know she had to go down memory lane."

"Of course, everyone is," he agreed. "Everyone is going to remember what I did to you like I'm going to remember what you did to me." Jay swallowed. "What I hate the most is that no one asked me what my intentions were. My actions were about more than killing you. I wanted us to die together. I wanted you to belong to me eternally. If I couldn't have you in life, I wanted to have you in death."

Carmen stopped eating since they were about to have a serious conversation. "You tried to commit suicide before. You were going to do it again? Is this something you think about often?"

"I was on some Romeo and Juliet type shit, Carm. If that's what it took to make you mine then that's what I was going to do. What else did I have to live for?"

"How do you feel now?"

"You got all these how-do-you-feel questions, Carm," he said, laughing. "You sound like my fuckin' psychiatrist. I feel like I can handle it. You're married. You got your life and now it's time for me to have mine. I need to find a companion, start my family, but of course before that, I need to get my money together. I need to get this restaurant started and I need to get Sapphire back to where it's supposed to be."

"So you want more kids?"

"I want a family, Carm. I've always wanted a family. Did you get my note and the ring? I told you I got you pregnant on purpose. I wanted you to be my wife. I wanted you to have my kids. I can make a baby."

Carmen sighed, hearing his words. She knew he could make a baby. That was one of the reasons she felt she had come to his house. She wasn't about to jump in the bed with him, but a part of her wanted to. She could've cared less about the sexual pleasure. She only wanted the baby. If her husband was willing to try in vitro again, she wouldn't even be having those thoughts. Since she was, Carmen ate quickly, knowing she needed to get out his presence. They ate in silence until he stood up to dump his plate. She was pouring herself a glass of wine when he brought up the closet again.

"Why don't you come upstairs so you can see what's in there?"

"I will in a minute," she told him, "I'm relaxing."

"Okay, well, I'm gonna grab some boxes for you."

Carmen watched him until he was out her sight. She didn't have time to clean out the closet, but she could at least see what she had left behind. She finished her wine and headed up the steps to their old bedroom. When she walked inside, she placed her cell phone and purse on a dresser, heading for the walk-in closet. Jay was inside with several boxes at his feet. "I really don't have time to go through this. Maybe, I can come back on Saturday and go through everything."

"That's fine; I can keep the boxes out."

Carmen browsed through some of the items, taking a trip down memory lane. "I remember this dress," she told him, pulling out a tube dress. She held it out in front of her and looked at the tag. It was a size ten. She wasn't a ten anymore. The dress would be one of the items going to Goodwill. She hung the dress back up, going to a few other things. Most of the items weren't even fashionable. She knew history repeated itself, but she couldn't see herself wearing those designs. Carmen scanned through her things, making a note of things there. Most of the stuff she planned to donate, but she knew Kristian would want her stuffed animals.

"I'm going to take a shower. You can let yourself out when you're done. Just pull the door up."

"Okay," she told him as he threw a towel over his shoulder. Carmen spent a few more minutes browsing through the closet before she left. She wanted to say goodbye, but she could already hear the shower going. She grabbed her purse and headed downstairs, taking another peek at the portrait of Hector Santiago before she left. She got ready to get in her car until she realized her hands were empty. She forgot to grab her cell phone.

Carmen went back in the house. She went upstairs, taking the steps two at a time, and pushed the door open to Jay's bedroom. Her cell phone was on the dresser, and she snatched it up right when Jay's voice caught her attention. He was singing a song by Maxwell, and she noticed the bathroom door was cracked. She shouldn't have been peeping, but a part of her wanted to see him. She held her breath as she looked through the glass doors of the shower. Carmen outlined his body with her eyes, starting at the top of his head, until her eyes focused on his penis. She hadn't seen him in so long she forgot how big he was.

She watched him as he bathed himself, wishing his hand was hers. His skin was like pure golden honey. Carmen could see herself walking up behind him, slipping off her clothes, and joining him. She could see herself letting go like the day she gave him her virginity.

Suddenly, she heard silence and it hit her. She was starting to lust after him. Carmen backed away, ashamed. She left the house, hurrying to her car. She knew Jay didn't see her, but it didn't matter. The seed was planted.

10 | *Derailed*

It was going on nine o'clock and Kane stared at the empty table. He covered his mouth, seeing the untouched honey barbecue ribs, the fried corn, potato salad, and Carmen's favorite dessert, lying in front of him. There was even a bottle of Alice White to commemorate the evening. Still, his wife hadn't come home. He called the office at seven and all he got was her voicemail. Kristian had gone to bible study and called to say she was going over to Coco's for an hour or two. From the looks of things, he didn't need the privacy. Carmen was doing the one thing he thought she wouldn't do.

Kane got up from the table, staring at the meal he took three hours preparing. He got ready to push everything off the table until he realized the whole thing could be one misunderstanding. There was a strong possibility she hadn't gotten his texts. He also knew she was working on a new collection and had to put in extra hours. The thought calmed him leading him to fix himself a plate so he could get to bed. It took him seven minutes to eat and twenty to put the food away before he made his way up the steps. On the way up, his phone vibrated. When he saw Tricia's name, he prayed she hadn't relapsed. "Hello," he answered.

"Can you come pick me up?"

He recognized Akaila's voice on the other end. "What happened?"

"I want to get away for a while. Can I come to your house?"

"Akaila, it's been a long day. Why don't I give you Kristian's cell?"

"We don't like each other, Mr. Kane. She didn't tell you?"

"Then tell me what's wrong and I'll send an officer. I'm in the middle of something right now," Kane lied.

"I don't want another officer. Just give me Kristian's number."

Kane gave her the number and listened as Akaila hung up. He knew if her mother was having withdrawals she would've told him. Since she didn't, he wasn't concerned. His attention needed to be focused on finding his wife.

Kane let out a loud sigh as he thought of Carmen. He remembered the first time he saw her. Her picture joined the lineup of more than a hundred associates of Jay Santiago. He couldn't deny his attraction. He told the captain he couldn't take the case, but he got assigned it anyway. Kane knew once the case was over; he was going to try and get with Carmen. Thankfully, things worked in his favor. The minute Carmen saw him; they had an instant connection. It was the same when they first made love. He had gone in perfectly. He had waited a long time to have her and on their wedding night, he went crazy. The only thing he asked of her was a baby. Two months later, he learned he couldn't give her one.

Now in their bedroom, Kane stared at their bed. About to fall on it, he felt his phone vibrate. Somewhat agitated, he answered the phone with a resounding, "Yeah."

"Akaila wants to spend the night at our house. She said you told her to call me. Why did you do that? Daddy, I don't want her there. I can't stand her."

Kane rubbed his face, knowing he wasn't about to get in the middle of some teenage drama. "I'll deal with her. Can you call your mother?"

"Isn't she with you?" Kristian shot back.

"No, Kris, she's not, can you call her?"

"Sure, I'll let you know what I find out," Kristian replied, hanging up.

Kane ran out his bedroom and down the steps. Akaila hadn't said anything about spending the night at his house, so something major was going on. Ready to find out what it was, he sped the whole way to West Brookstone. When he pulled in front of her house, he saw a few knuckleheads in the front yard. "What's up?" he called to them, getting out the car.

"Are you here for Akaila, too?" one of them asked. "She won't come out the house. Tell her, we have cash." The boy reached in his pocket, pulling out two large stacks. "Are you her new pimp?"

Kane flashed both his badges. "We can make this easy or we can make this hard." The guys dispersed, cursing under their breath. He stayed outside until they were gone to make sure they left the property. When the coast was clear, he headed towards the house, seeing Akaila peeking through the blinds. "Open the door," he barked, not bothering to knock. Akaila opened the door with a duffle bag in her hand and a book bag on her back. "Where's your mother?" he snapped. "Where's Malachi?"

"I don't know," she said, stepping on the porch.

Kane stared at her as she walked past him. "Where are you going?"

"To your house," she told him, turning around. "I told Kristian I wanted to spend the night. She didn't tell you?"

Kane followed her to the car. "She did tell me," he whispered. He got inside his Jeep and backed out the driveway. During the drive, he checked his phone, noticing Kristian hadn't called him. Ten minutes away from home, he prayed Carmen had made it in. In the meantime, he needed to use the time to counsel Akaila. "Do you want to tell me about those guys in your front yard?"

"No," she answered.

"I think you need to."

"I think you need to mind your fuckin' business," she snapped. "Besides, they're not coming back. Those niggas are scared of the Triad."

"Please don't use that word around me." Kane let out a sigh, knowing he had to be real with her. "Have you been selling yourself? I'm asking because I need to know. You know your mother is in danger of losing you and Malachi. If something happens and you two get taken away from her, you're gonna have people asking you a lot. I know the system. I suggest you tell me now before you end up telling a social worker."

"I did what I had to do."

Kane noticed she was close to tears. "You can tell me, Akaila. I won't tell Kristian. I won't tell anybody. I need to know. I don't want your mother to lose you. I don't want you and your brother separated. It'll be between me and you." Kane sped up. He was in a rush to get home, although he needed to finish his conversation with Akaila.

"I was selling myself for money."

"Do you think you're pregnant?"

Akaila mumbled a low no. "I've had too many abortions. The doctor said there's a possibility I can't have kids."

She was only fifteen-years-old, the same age as his daughter. "When did this start?" Kane probed.

"Three years ago," she replied. "My father was having a hard time finding work and I wanted to help. There were these guys in West Brookstone who had money. A girl told me all I needed to do was get with one. I did and he gave me money on a regular basis. We dated for a long time until I started aborting his babies. He found out what was I doing..." Akaila didn't finish the sentence.

Kane didn't notice at first because he was pulling into an empty driveway. Carmen still wasn't home. About to curse, he didn't when he noticed Akaila's face. It was a reminder he needed to put aside his personal problems. "What happened when he found out?"

"He beat me," she whimpered. "I left him after that. I couldn't get any more money from him, so I had to do all the guys. It became my job."

Kane took a deep breath. "I know your mother's habit and your father's suicide forced you to grow up. You wanted to take care of the household, but that isn't your responsibility. It isn't fair for you to wear the household on your shoulders. Since you did, you lost yourself in the process. Hopefully, I can help you. From now on, your past is your past. Today, this moment, it begins your future." She wiped her face until his old Corolla pulled in beside him.

"Did you call your mother?" Kane asked, getting out.

"She didn't answer," Kristian told him. She stared at Akaila who was in the passenger seat. A duffle bag was also in the girl's lap. *Dang it, she really is spending the night*. She didn't know how long Akaila was staying, but Kristian didn't know if she liked her trying to get close to her father. She was the daddy's girl, and she wasn't going to share him because Ms. DeGonzaza couldn't get her act together.

"Let Akaila in the house. I'm going to find your mother. Give me your cell phone, too," he ordered, reaching out his hand.

"No, what if Dijuan calls me?" Kristian asked, frowning.

"I don't care, give me your phone," he barked.

Kristian pouted, but still handed her cell phone over. She didn't know why her father wanted it, but she gave it to him. Once it was in his hands, he said a few words to Akaila.

"I have something to take care of. There's food in the fridge. Kristian will show you where the guestroom is. Call your mother when you get in and find out where Malachi is."

"Yes, sir," Akaila replied, getting out the car. She knew Kristian was uncomfortable with her being there. However, she didn't show any signs of it. She directed her in the house, making her feel at home.

***

Carmen walked in her apartment, staring at the walls. She hadn't been there in so long. "Home sweet home," she mumbled.

She lived there for less than six months before moving back into her parents' home, which Kane purchased. While she had a home with him, she maintained the lease on the apartment out of fear he would leave her. The news of their engagement brought negativity not only from the press, but also from his family.

Kane's mother made it known she didn't like her and didn't show up for their wedding. Kane had a lot of pressure on him, and Carmen wanted to make sure she and King had a place to stay if Kane backed out. Luckily, he didn't and when Kristian was born, two years later, his mother accepted her.

Carmen closed her eyes at the memory and decided not to think about it. Since it was going on almost ten, she retreated to her bedroom, lying on the bed. Her original intent was to stay at the apartment for the night to teach Kane a lesson. Now, she was staying there because she felt guilty for lusting after Jay. His nakedness intrigued her to the point she wanted to get naked with him. All at once, memories of their relationship came rushing back. She even asked herself if she still loved him.

The question brought tears to her eyes. If it wasn't for her phone ringing, she would've bawled. Kristian was calling, but she didn't answer fast enough to keep the call from going to voicemail. Instead of calling her back, she called the home phone. Kristian answered with a quick hello and Carmen replied the same.

"Why weren't you answering my calls? Daddy is looking for you," Kristian shouted.

"I know, baby, I needed some time to myself. I'm going through something right now," Carmen told her, wiping her face. "Did you get something to eat?"

"Yeah, Daddy cooked, but I don't think it's edible. I'm going to make Akaila try it out."

"Who, baby?"

"Akaila goes to school with me. Daddy has been helping her family out because her mother has a lot of problems. He says it's his punishment for not going to California. He was at their house last night."

"What are you talking about, Kris? What's going on in California?"

Carmen listened as her daughter sighed.

"I wasn't supposed to say anything, Mama. I'm in big trouble now."

"Kristian, what is going on?"

Kristian let out another sigh. "There's a case in California the Triad wants Daddy on. It's for six months and because he won't take it they gave him another assignment."

"Continue," Carmen urged.

"Mama, I told Daddy I wouldn't talk about it with you."

"Fine then, don't tell him we talked." Carmen hung up the phone. She wasn't mad at Kane for not going to California. He made the right choice. She was mad because he spent the night at another woman's house. The news was all she needed to convince her to spend the night at her apartment. *Let me give him a taste of his own medicine*, she thought. *Two can play this game.*

***

It was two o'clock in the morning and Kane was sitting on the steps, watching the front door. For a quick second, he thought Carmen had gone off the deep end. He was ready to put out a missing person's report, but it was pointless. She was staying away to make him angry. Evil for evil was her game and he was merely a pawn in it.

Every hour he waited for her, he found it harder to fight sleep. His body was shutting down and his eyes could no longer stay open. He put up a fight, but in the end, sleep won. Right there, on the cold hard steps, he fell into a deep slumber.

11 | *Curve Ball*

Six minutes away from the Kane residence, Malik was wide awake in his living room. With King next in line to take over the Santiago cartel, he had to keep better tabs on him than what he was. He expected King to come home around twelve and when his godson showed closer to three, Malik jumped down his throat. "Where were you?" he growled. "I told you about coming in my house late."

"You also told me I needed to be making this money," King replied. "Is my room ready?" King dropped his duffle bag on the floor before plopping on a loveseat.

"Your room was ready the day you were born."

King closed his eyes, aware he needed to be getting to bed. The three hours of sleep he would receive would be more like a nap because he needed to be back in the streets at six a.m. Though he ran out of product, he needed to find a way to hustle a G. "Did you get the extension?" he asked, opening his eyes.

"Noc doesn't want to talk to me."

"That's bad news, Malik. I don't have any shit left. I sold it all. If I don't get this G, Noc and I are going to rumble on Friday."

Malik couldn't let King fight. *I need him to keep his nose clean. If he keeps getting in trouble, the cartel will be shut down before we have our first re-up. Hopefully, he'll use his brains and find a way to get this G.* "What about Rico and Jerome? Do they have something they can let you hold?"

"Man, Jerome, and I aren't cool anymore," King shared. "I picked him up earlier today and he was making comments again about Kristian. He thinks because he helped me with Darnell I should hook them up. Those were the wrong words to say to me. I left his ass downtown somewhere. Shit, my mother was down there, too. Hey, you know some light-skinned man with a scar on his face? I saw him eating lunch with my mom."

Malik blinked. Old Town Bistro was downtown, which is where Jay met Carmen for lunch. Unsure if he spoke to his father, Malik didn't comment on the encounter. "Don't you have a G you need to hustle? Maybe, we shouldn't be sitting here talking. I already told you, I don't pay another man's debt. You need to figure something out before Friday." Malik stood up from the couch about to head to his bedroom. Halfway there, he remembered what he needed to tell King. "Once you pay Lil' Noc, don't get another key from him. I mean that. All business deals with him are off."

"Why don't you give me the G?"

"If I give you the G, what do you learn? You took Lil' Noc's weight, gave some of it to Darnell, and he couldn't make good on the product. Now, you're struggling to pay the debt that is really his. I told you from day one, if you're going to hustle, you gotta hustle smart. You can't give your weight to a crackhead. You know Darnell smoked that shit up."

King jumped off the couch. "Man, fuck you," he spat. "I'm sitting up here, begging you for help. You're supposed to be looking out for me and all you're doing is biting me in the fuckin' ass."

"Sit the fuck down." Malik pushed him on the loveseat. "I was the one trying to get you an extension. I was the one who told you Lil' Noc was trying to get with Kristian. Your ass is hardheaded, and you don't listen. Now, I'm telling you right now, this man I'm trying to put you with doesn't play. You gotta come correct when you step to him. If you aren't coming correct now then you aren't ready to meet him on Saturday. I'm trying to get you more money than you could ever dream of. Your mama named you King for a reason and I'm trying to take you there, but you gotta listen. Right now, you need to get in those streets and hustle up that G. Pay Lil' Noc and cut your ties."

King stared at Malik in disappointment. Hatred was forming inside of him. He didn't know why Malik was pressuring him to hustle when he could toss him the cash. A G wasn't going to hurt Malik's pockets.

Since he couldn't stay in his house, King pushed his way past Malik. He didn't know how he was going to get the G and he was now desperate. King touched his neck, feeling the gold rope around it. Now in his car, he slapped the steering wheel out of anger. He couldn't pawn the necklace. It shouldn't have even crossed his mind. It wasn't even worth a G. He didn't have any more weight to sell, and he couldn't hustle with the two G's he did have. He couldn't risk losing one red cent. He touched his neck again, feeling the necklace. An idea came to mind, which he knew could work. His mother had done it and he could pull off the heist as well.

King left Malik's apartment complex, headed towards downtown Brookstone. There were a million and one jewelry stores in the area and all he had to do was take his pick. When he returned to Malik's apartment in the morning, he would be set. To ensure the feat, he opened his glove compartment and pulled out a black ski mask.

***

Several hours later, Kane woke up, hearing a door opening. He shielded his eyes from the sunlight, which was pouring through the doorway.

Once the door was shut, he dropped his hand at his side, seeing Carmen. She didn't speak to him, heading up the steps, two at a time. The silence forced him to follow her and automatically, he started shouting questions. "So you think this is funny? You think this whole little thing is cute? Where were you, Carmen?"

"Where were you last night?" she asked once they were standing in their bedroom. Kane closed the door behind him. She started to undress and in the middle of taking her top off, she noticed the red rose petals on their bedspread.

"I was here, where I was supposed to be. Where were you?"

"Where I was supposed to be," she answered, changing into a cami.

"I'm not playing with you, Carmen, where were you?"

"Where were you Tuesday night?"

Kane's rage was going from two to ten fast. "This is the last time I'm asking you. Where were you?"

"All is fair in love and war," Carmen stated. "You got yours, I got mine."

Kane grabbed her arm, pulling her towards him. "What did you say?" She tried to break his hold, but his grip was tight. He grabbed her other arm, holding her in place. "You said all is fair in love and war?"

"Let go of me," she told him, trying to break his hold.

Kane loosened his grip, but he didn't let go. "Who were you with? Let me know so I can kill this motherfucker right now."

"Let go," she yelled, trying to break free.

Kane held her even tighter, pulling her towards him. "Did you fuck someone? Is that what you meant by you got yours and I got mine?"

"I said let go," Carmen yelled.

Kane let her go, seeing her fall on the bed. She grabbed her wrist, rubbing the spot where he held her. Not the least bit concerned about her pain, he grabbed at her panties. He had to know if she did something. She pushed him away, but he only grabbed her again until he gave up. He didn't want to check her, he wanted her to be honest and tell him. "Were you with someone, Carm? I'm not playing any more fuckin' games. Tell me."

Carmen backed away from him. She had never seen Kane as aggressive as he was. She was only messing with his mind, but he was on some other shit. Still, she wasn't going to let up. "Fuck you," she retorted.

"Fuck you, fuck you, is that what you're saying to me now, Carm? Fuck you? You know what, Carmen, fuck you."

"Fuck you," she yelled back.

Kane got ready to charge at her, but instead he punched the wall. He heard the dent he made, but he didn't care. He needed to hit something. He couldn't hit her, so he hit it. "I'm tired of this shit, Carm. I'm fuckin' tired of this shit. I wish you would let another man climb inside you. I swear to God, Carmen, I will kill whoever touched you. You got yours so I got mine," he repeated. "What does that shit mean? You've been opening your legs? My mama said you would be the one to flaunt your pussy around."

Carmen stood on her feet. "Are you calling me a whore?"

"If the shoe fits," he replied. She walked up to him, and he knew what was coming. He could see it in her eyes. Before he could move, he felt the cold hard slap of her hand across his face. He then felt another slap. Before he knew it, he pushed her on the bed, holding her arms.

"You're going to fuckin' hit me? Fuck you, Carmen, fuck you," he shouted, shaking her. He climbed on top of her and that was when he felt hands on his shoulders.

"Stop, stop," he heard Kristian yelling. He ignored her, shaking Carmen even harder than before. He could feel resistance, but it didn't make him stop. It wasn't until he saw Kristian and Akaila's reflection in the bedroom window his conscience returned. He loosened his grip on Carmen, now seeing her tearstained face. Kristian held her mother in her arms. "I have to go," he blurted. "I have to go." Kane went to his closet, grabbing a duffle bag, and stuffed clothes inside. He had to get out the house if only for a couple of days. He had to let his rage die down.

"Daddy, wait," he heard Kristian yell.

He ignored her, coming out the closet and took one last look at Carmen. She was the woman he was supposed to love, the woman he would die for. Now, she was the woman he almost abused.

"Daddy, wait," Kristian yelled. "Daddy, please, stop, don't go," she shouted, following him.

Never one to walk out on his family; today marked a first. If he didn't leave, he would've hurt his wife. Certain of it, Kane left the house and headed to Malik's where he planned on staying for a few days. It wasn't far, but the distance was needed.

Meanwhile, Kristian sighed as she stared at the front door. Unsure of where her father was going, she decided to let him be. If anything, she needed to be seeing about her mother. She was the one who was shaken to death. She walked in the room and saw Akaila in the doorway. Her mother's back was to her, and Kristian wondered if Akaila introduced herself. "It's almost eight-fifteen," she heard Akaila whisper. Kristian nodded her head, knowing they needed to head to school. She didn't want to leave her mother's side so she figured she would let her make the decision for them. If her mother wanted her to stay, she would.

"Mama," she began.

"I heard her, Kristian," Carmen sniffled. "I know you gotta go to school. Get my purse from the dresser. You can drive my Lexus."

Kristian grabbed her mother's purse and handed it to her. Her mother pulled out her bill folder.

"It's a mad house this morning," her mother whimpered. "After school, you two need to go shopping. I don't want y'all around this tension until it calms down. Take Coco with you." Carmen handed over her Black Card, which she knew the girls would run wild with. Not the least bit concerned about the damage they could do; she gave them her back once Kristian had it in her hands. After that, the only thing she remembered was them leaving the room. Now alone, Carmen broke into tears.

***

Malik was awakened by the sound of his phone. When he opened his eyes, his gaze was centered on his alarm clock. It was almost eight-thirty. Not quite sure who could be calling him, he grabbed his phone to see Kane's name. "Yeah," he answered.

"I need to stay with you for a few days."

Malik cracked a smile. He knew Kane was joking because his friend wasn't the type to get put out his house. "Man, you don't need to come over here," he told him, pulling his covers back.

"I almost hurt Carmen this morning." Kane sped through traffic, trying to get to Malik's apartment. "I need to stay with you for about two or three days."

Malik wiped his face, trying to figure out if Kane was telling the truth. He wasn't known to have arguments with Carmen that required a leave of absence. Malik tried to figure out what they could've been arguing about. He then remembered the common denominator between them—Jay. While he hoped Kane didn't know about his friend's release, Jay could've been the issue. "Alright, alright," he told him. "Look, King is already here. You'll have to take the guestroom. It's the only space I have unless you want to sleep in Kristian's room. I still have those Strawberry Shortcake sheets on her bed from when she was little."

"I need someone to talk to. I could've sworn I was going to hurt her. I couldn't stop shaking her."

"Just calm down, it's going to be fine, y'all are going to be straight," Malik replied. He opened his bedroom door and peered in the direction of

King's room. He hadn't heard him come in, so he decided to see if he was there. When he opened the door to his room, all he saw was an untouched bed. He then went in the living room to see King's duffle bag in the same spot he left it in. King had been out all night.

"I'm outside; I'm on my way up."

Kane hung up the phone before Malik could reply. Less than a minute later, Malik heard his doorbell ring. When he answered the door, everything about Kane scared him. His clothes were wrinkled, he hadn't shaved, and he smelled musty. "You look like shit," Malik greeted, letting him inside. "Did you sleep last night? Shit, did you shower?"

"Barely," Kane responded. He dropped his bag on the floor and started pacing. He didn't know where to start.

"Sit down," Malik ordered. "I don't want you making a hole in my carpet. I just got the shit cleaned two days ago."

Kane did as he said. He sat on a loveseat opposite of Malik. His head went in his hands as he started the conversation by telling him about Tricia.

"Tricia?" Malik's eyes widened. He hadn't heard anything about her in a long time.

Kane gave him an update. "I couldn't leave her, so I stayed the entire night. I didn't tell Carmen and when I got in that morning, all hell broke loose. It carried over onto today because Carmen didn't come home last night. We got into it bad. I shook the hell out of her, man." Kane rubbed his temples, thinking back on what happened. "She tried to imply that she was with another man."

Malik stood on his feet. Carmen was playing a very dirty game if she slept with Jay. Not only would she ruin her marriage, but Jay wasn't mentally prepared to handle her quite yet. "Did she say who she was with?" Malik waited for him to answer and during that time, he noticed Kane's hand. "Shit," he screamed, running to the linen closet. Kane was out of it. His right hand was bleeding profusely, which told Malik he hit something. "You don't feel that shit?" He threw a towel at him and watched as Kane wrapped it around his hand. "Did you punch a mirror or something?"

"I punched the wall. I don't even know how many times. I need to stay here for a few days. I can't go back home right now. I need to chill out." Kane paused for a few seconds. "I wanted to kill Jay when he beat her. I never thought I would almost do the same. She took me there, Malik. I promise you."

"Unlike Jay," Malik countered, "you caught yourself in time."

"Do you think she was with someone?"

Malik didn't think so. "Carmen is very good at doing evil for evil. Personally, I don't believe she was with anyone. If anything, she was probably at Tiara's."

"I need to be certain. What hurt me the most out of everything is that Kristian and Akaila had to see that. My own daughter had to pull me off her. I will never forget the look on Kristian's face."

"Carmen is probably explaining everything to them right now. You don't need to...wait a minute, who is Akaila?" Malik asked.

Kane informed him about Tricia's kids.

A lightbulb went off in Malik's head. "Is that the same girl who use to run with Lil' Noc?"

"Is she who?" Kane didn't know what he was talking about.

"Oh, shit," Malik muttered, putting two and two together.

"What?" Kane probed.

"It's nothing, I got her mixed up with someone else," Malik lied.

Kane overlooked his statement. He couldn't believe how angry he'd gotten. He vowed right then and there to never let his anger get the best of him. He even prayed to God, asking for the Lord to restore him.

"You need to see a doctor; you're bleeding through the towel."

Kane moved his hand around. Nothing felt broken, but the pain was almost unbearable. It made him question how he drove to Malik's apartment. He figured his adrenaline numbed most of the pain. "Okay, I'm going to the ER," he told Malik, standing up. "I'll be back in a few, let King know I'm here."

"I will," Malik replied, "Do you want me to drive you?"

"Nah, I'll be good."

Malik closed the door behind Kane as he left. He picked up his phone to call Carmen and then placed it down. He didn't need to call her. She was going through something and questioning her about Jay would only put her over the top. It would work in both their interests if he waited until things calmed down. In the meantime, he needed to be checking on King.

12 | *Jesus Piece, Jesus Peace*

When there was money to be made, there was no time for sleep. King learned the lesson the hard way since he'd been up all night. While he was successful in his efforts, it was time to reap the reward.

A little after nine o'clock, he knocked on the door of Phase, a small-time hustler in West Brookstone, who used to work for Lil' Noc. A man who had a passion for jewels, Phase could help him come up with a G. All he had to show him was his new product.

After a couple seconds passed without a response, he knocked again. This time, he heard Phase's voice.

"I'm coming, I'm coming," Phase called from inside.

The door opened. Half a second later, it slammed in his face. King knew why when he remembered they shared a similar predicament. They both owed Lil' Noc a couple of Benjamins. Phase assumed he come to collect, but he was mistaken.

"I told Noc, I'm good for the ten G's. I only need a little bit more time," Phase yelled from inside. "I'm gonna get his cash."

"I'm not here for Noc. I need you to buy something from me," King yelled back. Phase didn't respond and his hesitation made King want to threaten him. "Open the door. My business is my own." King waited again, knowing his words weren't convincing. Certain he would have to show him his product; King checked his surroundings before taking out a diamond pendant. "Look, I need to sell this," he told him. "I have about six more, some rings, and some other shit. What do you say?"

Phase appeared in the doorway.

"Are you for real about this shit?" Phase asked.

"As real as I'm standing up here breathing," King snapped. He pushed his way past him. He went to the couch, spreading the jewelry on the coffee table.

"Man, I didn't want to take any chances. I have my baby girl in here," he explained.

King glanced at the playpen, seeing Phase's daughter. He then pointed at the jewelry. "Take a peek at this stuff. Let me know if you can work with it. I need a G before Friday."

"Damn, this some good shit," Phase whispered, inspecting the jewelry. He pulled out a jeweler's loupe and took a closer look at one of the pendants of Jesus. "What store did you rob?"

"It was a little spot about a block from Tiffany's."

"Did they have cameras?" Phase asked, picking up one of the rings.

"Of course, I was wearing a ski mask, though. I made sure I sprayed the cameras good. I robbed the place with a couple of older dudes when I was thirteen, so I knew where everything was. It was easy."

"This is some good shit, though; you want a G for all this?"

"Nah, I need to save some of it. That pendant and ring right there, I know is worth a G. I'll give that to you, and you can tell Lil' Noc its worth about two G's. He doesn't know shit about jewelry, so he'll believe you."

"I got about half his money right now. If I put it with these two pieces, I'll have seven G's for him."

"See, I'm trying to help you out," King told him. He looked at the playpen, hearing the baby coo. He asked Phase if he could hold her. Too busy inspecting the jewels, Phase didn't answer. Still, King reached in the playpen and picked the baby up. Her attention went to the table as she tried to grab some of the necklaces. To keep her entertained, King picked up a diamond necklace, allowing the baby to hold it. "Ain't it pretty? Ain't it pretty?" he repeated.

"I'm gonna take this," Phase told him, holding up the pendant and ring. "I'll give you a G for this," he said, reaching in his pocket.

"That'll work," King replied, keeping his eyes on the baby.

"Don't get too comfortable with my daughter," Phase joked. "If you want one, you know how to make 'em. Shit, now that I think about it, I don't see you with too many broads."

"I don't mess with none of these hoes," King admitted. "There is one, though, I'm looking at. Do you know Coco Masterson?" King waited for Phase's reply, watching as he rewrapped the jewelry. He then noticed the necklace was still in the baby's hands. He took it from her, admiring the piece. "Do you think she'll like this?"

Phase noticed the diamond and yellow gold necklace in King's hand. The piece contained about three carats. It was one of the necklaces he desperately wanted to buy, but he couldn't afford to give King all his cash. "Yeah, she's gonna like that," he told him. "Shit, any girl would, you must be serious about this chick."

King put the necklace in his jacket pocket. "Nah, it's nothing special, but she gave me some good advice. This is my way of saying thank you." King placed the baby back inside her playpen. He then grabbed the stack of hundreds on the table, stuffing the money in his pocket. "Good looking out, man."

They bumped fists and King made his way out the house. With his mission accomplished, it was now time to get some rest. He also had to show

Malik he found a way to get the money. Once he returned to his apartment, it would be time to flaunt.

In the meantime, Kane was also returning to Malik's apartment. With his hand now bandaged, he was ready to make amends with his wife. Malik agreed to be the mediator, but once Carmen was on speakerphone, she made it clear she wasn't ready to discuss the incident. Malik couldn't get her to change her mind before she hung up.

Somewhat disappointed, Kane decided to give her a little more space. Nevertheless, instead of moping around Malik's apartment, he announced he was going over to Tricia's.

Malik parted his lips to stop him, but Kane was out the door before he could voice his opinion. As if that wasn't enough, King was coming in the door. "Did you see your father?"

"Yeah," King replied, locking the door. "He was in a rush to get somewhere. He didn't even answer me when I asked why his hand was bandaged. What happened?"

"Kristian pulled him off your mother this morning. They got in a bad argument. Also, Akaila was at your house. Your father is supposed to be helping her mother. You know what that means, right?"

King wrinkled his face. Akaila wasn't the issue, but her mother was. He hadn't told anyone except Malik, but Tricia was the older woman who he paid for oral sex. He never thought they would cross paths again despite the friendship he had with her daughter. Now, based off Malik's words, they may run into each other sometime soon.

"I pray she doesn't say anything to him. Kane will beat your ass if he found out what happened between you two. On to other things, though, did you get the money? You've been out all night. You should have something."

"Shit, I got the money and a whole lot more," King said. He reached in his pockets, pulling out the necklaces, pendants, and rings he'd stolen. "I got some good shit," he marveled. "Take a peek."

King placed the jewelry on the coffee table. The sight of it told Malik he hadn't learned his lesson. He told him to keep his nose clean, but he went and committed another crime. While he was preparing him to become the underboss of a criminal enterprise, King's extracurricular activities could prevent him from taking the position. However, Malik's feelings were contradictory. King couldn't commit any crimes outside the Santiago cartel, however, inside; he would be praised for it. "Who did you sell this stuff to?"

"Phase," King answered, wrapping the jewelry up. "I have the money I need for Lil' Noc so on Friday I can cut my ties. Now I can sleep peacefully." King put the jewelry in the pockets of his jeans. Malik headed towards his room. His godfather hadn't said much, and it made him wonder what he was thinking. About to ask him, he remembered he hadn't questioned him again about the light-skinned man he saw with his mother. A part him wondered if he had something to do with his parents' argument.

"Does my mom have a new business partner?" he asked, following Malik into his bedroom.

"I don't know anything about that," Malik replied. "Your mother doesn't talk to me about Flame. Direct your questions to your godmother. Tiara is your best source."

"You've been around my mother for a long time. Y'all run in the same circle."

"I didn't hang with Carmen like that. My brother, Rakim, was the one who hung out with her. I was too busy running the streets."

King frowned, remembering the stories of Rakim. He decided not to press the issue since it was a sensitive subject for Malik. Instead of continuing the conversation, he headed inside his room. The second he laid on his bed, he was out like a light.

13 | *Baby Brother*

After leaving Malik's apartment, Kane drove to Tricia's house. He knocked on her door, knowing she was inside yet she wouldn't answer. When he knocked the fifth time, he heard someone moving. Less than five seconds later, Malachi opened the door. He was supposed to be in school, but he was at the house, which sent up a red flag. "What took you so long?" he barked, pushing his way inside. "Why are you even here?" Kane's eyes searched the house until he took notice of the solemn expression on Malachi's face. "Where's your mother?" he asked.

Malachi stammered. "I tried to stop her, but she had already shot up by the time I came home," he cried. "I didn't think she would steal from me. I tried to hide it."

Kane put two and two together. In his absence, Tricia managed to relapse. "Go pack your things," he ordered. "Whatever you need for school, clothes, shoes, pack it all." Kane did a slight jog to Tricia's room. While he expected to see the worse, she was standing in front of her mirror, trying to pull herself together.

"I'll be right there," she said, finger-combing her hair.

Kane could tell she had shot up. There were rings around her eyes, she was shaking, and her speech was slurred. No longer sympathetic, he showed her tough love. "You think this is a game, don't you? You keep doing what you're doing, and you won't be losing your kids, you'll be losing your life."

"I haven't done anything. I had a drink, that's all."

"A drink, you had a drink, look in the damn mirror, Tricia. Look at yourself. Look at your damn arms," he yelled. He pushed her head closer to the mirror. "Look at yourself. Is this what you want to be? I leave you for one night and this is what happens? I can't trust you. I told you, Tricia, I have a job to do, but I also have a family. I can't stay with you every night. When are you going to take responsibility? You know what, don't worry about it. I'm taking Akaila and Malachi. You can sit here and be in this shit by yourself." Kane took his hands off the back of her head, walking out the room.

"You can't take my kids. You can't take them from me."

"Watch me," he snapped, stepping in Malachi's room. The boy had packed most of his things and was stuffing his undergarments into a duffle bag. "Make sure you get everything you need," Kane reiterated. "You're gonna be staying with me for a while." Kane was about to pick up Malachi's book bag until he saw Tricia grab her son's arm. He moved in between the two, separating them. The move only sparked Tricia's anger as she tried to get control of the situation.

"He isn't going anywhere with you," she screamed, trying to get to Malachi. "He's my child, I'm his mother. You can't take him."

"I'm doing you a favor," Kane shot back. "I can either take them or call DSS. Believe me, Tricia; the outcome will be much better if they're living with me. If they get in the system, it will be hard getting them out."

"These are my kids," she yelled.

"You can't even feed your kids," Kane retorted. "You stole from your son to get high and now I have to come up with the difference, so he won't be short." Kane shifted his attention to Malachi who was continuing to pack. "Do you have everything?" Malachi told him no, zipping one of his duffle bags. "Finish packing, once you're done, get in my car." Tricia stood next to him in tears. "They don't deserve to be put through this. They've been through enough already."

"Don't do this, Kane, I'll do anything, don't do this," she said, grabbing his arm. "I need them."

"What do you need them for? Oh, you need to them to get high. Malachi is your supplier and Akaila sells herself so she can pay the rent and keep the lights on because you can't do it. Did you know your daughter was a prostitute? How do you feel about that, Tricia?"

"She doesn't have to do that anymore. I can go to work. I can make things good for them. I know a couple of places that are hiring. They're looking for new cashiers at Flame downtown."

"Do you really think my wife would let your application even...do you know what my wife would do if she knew you were applying at one of her stores?" Kane was being rough with Tricia, because she wouldn't change or get better if he continued to be empathetic. "Use this time to get yourself together." When he saw Malachi was ready, he told him to get in the car. Malachi did as he said, which only prompted another outburst from Tricia.

"I'll do anything, please don't take them," she begged.

Kane ignored her, about to follow Malachi until he felt Tricia's hands on his manhood. She had a firm grip, and he knew what she was implying.

"I'll do anything," she repeated, pressing her body up against his.

Kane was disgusted. He couldn't believe she stooped that low. Her actions didn't even deserve a verbal response. He pushed her away and walked out the bedroom. She followed him outside, screaming expletives even when he got in the car. The first thing he did was lock the doors because he thought she was going to pull Malachi from the car. When she didn't, Kane knew she accepted his decision. He hated to take her kids, but she needed a reality check.

Hopefully, Kane thought, *this will do it.*

"Where are we going?" he heard Malachi ask as he backed out the driveway. Kane remembered his current situation. Aware he couldn't explain his marital problems to Malachi, he told him, "Somewhere safe." When he pulled in front of Malik's complex, he told him their stay was only temporary. "My friend stays here," he told him. "We won't be here long, I promise."

Malachi appeared puzzled. Kane knew it was because he expected to be staying in a mansion. Although his house was big with an outdoor pool and pool house, it didn't match their annual household income. For some reason, Carmen preferred to stay in her parents' house versus acquiring a gated property. He didn't argue with her on the matter since the house was already paid in full.

"Well, it's better than where I was," Malachi responded, getting out the car. "Anything is better than that place."

"I just want you to be safe," Kane replied. He led the way to Malik's apartment, helping Malachi carry his things.

In the meantime, Malachi studied his surroundings. The apartment complex was in a posh section of East Brookstone, which told him Mr. Kane's friend had a lot of money. While he didn't expect to be staying at someone else's place, his curiosity was sparked. The emotion grew when the door to the apartment opened, and he saw Malik. He knew the man from around the way and felt honored to be in his presence. Every true hustler or gangster respected Malik. Malachi tried to contain his excitement while also trying to figure out how a cop like Kane formed a friendship with a gangster like Malik.

"What's going on?" Malik asked, noticing Akaila's little brother.

"This is Malachi," Kane told him. "He's staying with me for a while. Since I'm here, I had to bring him, too. Once I talk to Carmen, we'll both be out your hair."

Malik glanced at the boy, knowing he was working for Lil' Noc. If he hadn't sold his weight then there was a possibility he was bringing illegal drugs in his apartment. "Look, I don't know about this, Kane. I only have one room left, King is already here, and I have a feeling Kristian is coming, too," he joked. "He can stay, though, just let me change the sheets on Kristian's bed. He can sleep there." Malik allowed them to come inside and told Malachi to put his bags in the living room until the room was ready.

"Thanks," Malachi said, setting his bags on the floor. He was glad Malik let him stay, especially when he heard the name King. The only King he knew was the one who worked for Lil' Noc. He saw him in passing and admired him from afar. Though King was like him, a small-time dealer, he could see his potential from the respect he received in the streets. He thought to ask Kane about him, but when he looked at him, he had fallen asleep.

I don't even remember him sitting down.

Malachi decided to use his timely wisely and headed towards the back of the apartment. He found Malik in one of the bedrooms, pulling a pair of Strawberry Shortcake sheets off a bed. "Do you know where King is?"

Malik turned around, noticing Malachi in the doorway. "Do you have business with him," he responded. Malik became suspicious because he knew Malachi was still in good standing with Lil' Noc. If he came to send a message, he did it at the wrong place.

"I want to talk to him," Malachi admitted.

"Look, lil' man, I'm not scared to protect mine. If you got a message you need to send, this is the wrong place to do it. I'm trigger happy."

"Whatever, man, where is he at?" Malachi shot back.

Malik pointed down the hall. "He's in the room at the end. If he curses you out for waking him up, it's all on you."

"Thanks," Malachi muttered. He took another peek in the living room to make sure Kane was still asleep. When he saw he was, he continued to King's room. He listened for a few seconds to see if he heard any noise and then proceeded to open the door. He didn't want to wake him, but a part of him was hoping he could. He studied him for a bit until he noticed the Jesus piece hanging out King's pocket. The thief in him wanted to grab it, but he couldn't because of the respect he had for King.

"Standing over a person while they're sleeping is a death wish," he heard a voice say. Malachi focused his eyes on King and before he could say a word, King tackled him to the floor.

"What the fuck do you think you're doing?" King yelled.

"I wanted to say hi," Malachi voiced, trying to get out from underneath him. "I came here with your father."

"Hi? What the fuck do you want?" King put his body weight on him, inflicting even more pain. "Why were you standing over me?"

King recognized the boy as Akaila's little brother. He was also one of the younger dudes who worked for Lil' Noc. While he was surprised to see him at Malik's apartment, he shouldn't have been. Malik told him an hour ago his father was helping Tricia. Somehow, Malachi and Akaila were thrown in the mix as well. He realized the boy was harmless and moved away from him. In the process, he noticed his jewelry had fallen out of his pockets. In one swift motion, he picked up the pendants and slid the jewelry in a drawer. "What do you want?" he repeated.

"Rico told me you weren't going to work for Lil' Noc anymore."

"It hasn't been officially announced. Besides, you shouldn't be worried about me. Aren't you a little young to be hustling?"

"Don't try to play me; I've seen you with my sister."

King bit his lip. "Yeah, I know her," he admitted.

"Then you know our situation."

King remembered the time he spent with Akaila. They met one day when she approached him about a favor. He read between the lines, knowing Akaila was selling herself for money. She was rumored to have been with every major heavyweight in West Brookstone. When she started dating Lil' Noc, she calmed down, but the real trouble started. Every time he saw her, she was trying to cover up a pregnancy and was getting abortions. The worst part of it all was when she came to his car, bruised, and battered, accusing Lil' Noc of beating her. He took her to the hospital and even agreed to keep the incident a secret. It was because of the abuse; he would never allow Kristian to date Lil' Noc.

"Are you going to the block party on Friday?"

"No one is missing the block party," King told him. He laid down, hoping he could get back to sleep. He realized the chance was lost when Malachi continued to ask questions.

"So, what are your plans for today?"

Malachi was now sitting Indian-styled on the floor. The image made King respond with a fiery, "Shouldn't you be at school?"

"Shouldn't you?"

"I dropped out," King shared.

"Why do you hustle, King?"

King shrugged his shoulders. The reason he came up with didn't seem good enough anymore. He couldn't attribute his need for attention to his life of crime. "Who doesn't want to be on top? Who doesn't want to feel like they can't be touched?"

"Everyone wants power."

"Exactly," King told him. "Everyone wants power. My mother is one of the most influential black women in New York. How many women get out of prison and become a multi-millionaire? My mother has a self-made empire. She makes her own rules. My grandfather owns his own real estate company. He has power. He can move things for people. He can get people the buildings and houses they want. You know how important it is for people to own things."

Malachi understood his point. He glanced at the bedroom door. He figured Kane was still sleeping since he hadn't looked for him. When he turned back to King, he noticed his eyes were closing.

King hoped Malachi took the hint he didn't want to be bothered. He needed to get his rest because he planned on stopping by Brookstone High in a few hours to see Coco. He tricked Malachi into thinking he fell asleep so he would leave him alone. It worked, but the boy only curled up on the floor next to him. King realized he was stuck with him. If Malachi wasn't leaving his side now, he never would.

14 | *Explanations and Rewards*

Over at Brookstone High, Kristian waited in the school's parking lot for her friends to show. Although Akaila was riding home with her, she was hoping to spot her friends first so she could explain why they appeared to be so buddy-buddy. Coco dodged her all morning while she only saw Dijuan in passing. Now that school was over, she hoped to talk to them.

When she spotted Coco walking in the parking lot, she approached her with a smile. It wasn't returned so she knew her friend was heated. "Okay, Coco, I know you're upset."

"Kris, you drove to school without a license. It was okay for last night because we only went to church. Then, you had Akaila in the car. You know she doesn't like you. She is only playing nice because she wants to date King."

"Can you calm down for a moment? Akaila isn't rich," Kristian replied. "Her mother's a drug addict. My father is helping her family out. She's staying with us until her mother gets clean."

Coco's mouth dropped wide open.

"Everyone thinks she's some rich girl when it isn't like that. You know I don't like her, but I have no choice but to hang with her."

"Akaila DeGonzaza has a drug addict for a mother?"

"Don't tell anybody, please."

Coco folded her arms across her chest. Kristian's story sounded believable, but it was hard to digest. Akaila didn't have a perfect reputation, but she was known for always wearing the latest trends. Her style was the only reason she was popular. Of course, there were the girls who envied her because of the attention she received from their male peers.

"Do you forgive me?" Kristian asked.

Coco sighed. "Do I have a choice? We just talked about forgiveness in bible study. I gotta forgive you…and her, too. Speaking of Akaila, there she is." Coco frowned when she noticed Akaila was headed in their direction. Dijuan wasn't too far behind, which meant Kristian would have to break the news to him at another time.

"Hi," Akaila greeted, speaking just above a whisper. She was rather uncomfortable since she and Coco weren't necessarily the best of friends. She could already see the girl trying to read her. "I see that face you're giving me, Coco. I'm not trying to be bougie."

"I don't know what you're trying to be," Coco shot back.

"If you must know," Akaila snapped, "My mother needs some help right now. Kristian's father was nice enough to let me stay with them for a little while until she gets better. That is the only reason I'm hanging with Kristian. I'm not trying to come between you two. Besides, my own friends ditched me this morning because of her."

"Then they're not true friends, anyway," Kristian chimed in.

"I guess not," Akaila replied.

Dijuan joined them at the tail-end of the conversation. He wasn't quite sure what was going on though he noticed Akaila was standing with Kristian yet again. Before he could find out what they were discussing, Kristian announced she needed to get home to return her mother's car. She told him she would call him later. Once Kristian was in her car, he got ready to ask Coco about Akaila, but the conversation was interrupted before it began. Out of nowhere, King's black Mustang drove onto the school's property.

Dijuan was anxious to see what was about to happen, but his mother arrived. She honked the horn at him, sending him walking to her car. Before he was out of earshot, he gave Coco a sinister smile. "Take care of yourself, don't do anything I wouldn't do," he told her.

Coco winked at him before turning her attention to King. His eyes were locked on hers and he pointed at the passenger seat. Rather excited over the attention he was giving her, she got inside. "What's going on?"

King turned down the radio. "I got the money I needed for Lil' Noc. I talked to my mom, too."

"How did you get the money? Did Malik lend it to you?"

King shook his head. "Nah, I sold some stuff. Some stuff like this." He reached into his pocket and pulled out a small black bag. He opened it, taking out the diamond and yellow gold necklace.

"Where did you get that from?" she shrieked. "It's beautiful."

"Does it matter?"

"I guess not, but it looks expensive." Coco's excitement was fading as she thought the worst. She didn't want to accuse King of theft, but she had a feeling the necklace was stolen.

"Would you wear the necklace for me?"

"You want me to put it on? I can't go home with a necklace like that. My parents would know for sure I was running around with a knucklehead. My mother would take it from me."

"So I'm a knucklehead to you?" King dropped the necklace into his lap.

"No, that's not what I meant. I'm only fifteen. Where would I get a necklace like that?"

"From me," he replied. King unhooked the necklace and slid it around her neck. He then fastened it, admiring the piece up against her dark ebony skin. "I want you to wear it. I got it for you."

Coco was unsure if she could take the necklace. What made the decision hard was her genuine admiration for King. He was her first crush and the necklace confirmed he had feelings for her.

She traced the stones with her fingertips, not noticing his face as it moved closer to hers. Before she could back away, their lips connected. Unsure of what to do, she kept her mouth closed until her lips naturally opened. King then slipped his tongue inside. Coco didn't know how long they were kissing, but when he pulled away, she was out of breath.

"I swear you grew up overnight," he told her. "I thought you were my sister's annoying best friend, but you really have grown up."

Coco took his words as a compliment. Unfortunately, she had to tell him again she couldn't wear it. "My mom is going to be here soon. You wouldn't be upset if I slid the necklace into that bag, would you?" She pointed at the black bag on his lap and watched as he handed it to her. "I'll wear it when my parents aren't around." She unhooked the necklace and dropped it inside just as her mother's car came in the parking lot. "I have to go," she blurted.

As if he could sense her mother's presence, King watched as Mrs. Masterson parked next to his car. The woman was looking at him with an angry expression and he knew Coco was in trouble. To ease the tension, he waved, but Mrs. Masterson hesitated in waving back. He already knew what was going through her mind. Her little princess was sitting in the car of one of Brookstone's most well-known criminals. However, just like he saw it, her mother saw it, too. Coco wasn't a little girl anymore. Pretty soon, she would be doing more than sitting in his car. With Malik's plan for his future currently in the works, Coco had the potential to become the girlfriend of a New York underboss. Although he would never bring drug business around her, he was determined to take their relationship further than the short conversation in his car. He only had to make sure she was up for the challenge.

15 | *Hidden Agendas*

King was correct when it came to Malik's plan for his future. Nevertheless, before Malik could make King an underboss of the Santiago cartel, he had to deal with several issues at hand. One of the issues was the three people living under his roof. Then, there was Carmen's infidelity. Since he couldn't talk to Kane about it, he met up with Jay at Sapphire where they were sharing a bottle of Crown Royal. "Why do people run to my house when they have problems? I can't enjoy my place because the whole world is living with me. Kane is staying there because he got into it with Carmen and then he brought one of Tricia's kids."

Jay raised one of his eyebrows. "Tricia has kids?"

Malik didn't hesitate in elaborating because if it was a problem, Jay couldn't retaliate. "Yeah, she has two kids by Consuelo. They were fuckin' behind your back after you got with Carmen. I know that's a hard pill to swallow, but he's already dead. He committed suicide a couple of years ago."

Jay let out a chuckle because he could've cared less. It did bother him to learn Consuelo took his life, but his relationship with Tricia wasn't an issue.

Malik gave him an update on Tricia. "Kane is working with her, trying to help her get her shit together. If she doesn't straighten up, her kids are going straight in the system."

A rock sat in Jay's stomach. An addiction was the last thing he wanted for Tricia. He wasn't responsible for her habit, and it pained him to know she'd fallen on rough times. Their relationship wasn't perfect, because she was clingy and a gold-digger, but he wondered how things would've been if he hadn't dropped her for Carmen. Since he wouldn't ever find out, he steered the conversation in a different direction. "Oh, thanks for telling me the name of my son."

Malik became nervous. His palms started to sweat. He rubbed his hands on his jeans, knowing his plan to have King take over could be ruined. He wasn't quite sure how much Jay knew. "What's his name?" he asked.

"Jayceon Santiago," Jay replied. "Unfortunately, I also learned he has Kane's last name. His birth certificate reads, Jayceon Santiago Kane. You know, Malik, you're supposed to be in my corner, but you couldn't tell me what my son's name was. I never asked, but it wasn't because I didn't want to know. Why didn't you say something?"

Malik shrugged his shoulders. "What else did Carmen tell you about your son?"

"Not much," Jay replied, opening one of his drawers. He took out the business proposal and set it on his desk. "We talked about this." He pointed at the paper. "I'm a little apprehensive about this plan. I just came off this seventeen-year bid. I will kill myself before I go back. I don't know about this new guy you're bringing in. We might need to think about this a little more."

"It's too late to renege. I've already told him about the meeting."

"I'm not reneging. Maybe, we can use him for something else. For example, I lost the building for Iceland. Do you remember my jewelry store idea? Why can't we use him for that? I can go Carmen's route, steal a few diamonds, sell 'em at The Diamond Exchange and get me some quick cash."

Malik smiled. The idea was golden because his son just robbed one of Brookstone's biggest jewelry stores. "This new guy can handle that. I promise you. He's the best jewelry thief."

"Do you know who's even better? Carmen Davenport," Jay replied. "Tell me how a woman, managed to get to the Bahamas, steal a suitcase full of diamonds, leave the ship, and no one knows anything until she gets back to the states. Even then, it's only because Kane was wired. She would've been a free woman if he wasn't bugged. Carmen is our best choice."

"Carmen is thirty-nine years old, has two kids, a multi-million dollar business, a husband, and not to mention, a God-fearing heart. There is no way in the world you're going to convince her to do this."

"Do you know who you're talking to? I have Carmen wrapped around my finger. We both know how vulnerable Carmen can get. She may not admit it, but her mind goes crazy when I come around. She hasn't acted on those feelings yet, but she will."

Malik felt a wave of relief. His nerves were put at ease. Carmen hadn't slept with Jay. Now, he needed her to admit it to Kane. "I say leave Carmen out of it. Use her name for the restaurant and let the jewelry store idea go. It probably would've worked seventeen years ago, but now, it sounds like a dud. As far as this drug shit is concerned, King will bring in all the money you need."

"This drug shit is a dumb move. I spent seventeen years in hell for that shit," Jay fired back.

"No, you spent seventeen years in prison for murder and assault. They were willing to give you sixty years if you snitched. You refused so they gave you a life sentence. I know this shit because I was working with Gomez to try and get you out."

"I still don't know why you weren't arrested." Jay dimmed his eyes at the thought. "Where did you go, Malik? You were right there. You brought Carmen to me, and you jetted. Where were you?"

"How many fuckin' times do I have to tell this story? I hid. I was scared and I ran. I didn't do anything wrong. It's because of me; you have a place to lay your head."

"You've done a lot for me. I've done a lot for you. I put you and Rakim on so y'all could eat. Do you remember your brother?"

"What kind of question is that? Don't I look in the mirror?"

Jay backed down since Rakim was still a sensitive issue. "Let's change the subject," he said, standing up. "I'm set on this jewelry store thing. I know you're against it, but it's my call, right? Sapphire is my club. This restaurant is going to be mine, so I have the final say."

Malik nodded his head in agreement. "Everything is yours."

Jay paced the floor. "Kane can't have kids. I can tell from my conversation with Carmen she's bothered by it. I can't sleep with her because she's married, but I can flirt with the idea. If I get her weak enough, she'll do anything I say."

"Leave her alone, Jay."

An evil smile flew across Jay's face. "I can't, Malik. Carmen and I still have unfinished business."

***

In terms of unfinished business, Kane dropped Tricia all together. Only hours after their argument, he headed to the precinct to review her file again. He barely made it in his office before Harris spotted him. "Well, well, well, Kane finally has something to keep his attention. Give me an update," he demanded.

Kane needed to give him one, but he was in trouble. He couldn't tell the lieutenant Akaila and Malachi were living with him. Neither could he tell him Tricia shot up again.

"You know, Michael, I'm getting fed up with you. We both know that doesn't happen easily."

When Harris called him Michael, Kane knew it was time to talk. "She shot up again," he told him.

"I figured. Where are her kids now?"

Kane stared at the picture of Consuelo DeGonzaza on his desk. By telling Harris the truth, his badge was on the line, but he didn't want to lie. "They're living with me right now."

Harris slapped his hands on Kane's desk. "Who told you to play daddy?"

"I was trying to protect them."

"Protecting them is calling their social worker. Don't you know Tricia can file charges saying you kidnapped her kids?"

"She wouldn't do that," Kane replied. "Akaila asked to stay with me, and Malachi was willing to come."

"You know, I had this voice in the back of my head telling me this wasn't the case for you. I should've known your idea of protecting these kids was to take them and make them yours."

"I wasn't trying to do that," Kane fired back. "I didn't want them in the house with a woman who was shooting drugs in her arm. Do you want to take the case from me? Go ahead. Give it to a rookie cop. I promise you. The results won't be the same. I'm not trying to let these kids down. I'm trying to help them. I can try and work on Tricia when they're not around so when they're reunited, they can see her as something else besides a drug addict."

Harris wasn't buying his plan. The lieutenant was shaking his head and even left his office. He returned fifteen minutes later with a manila folder in his hands. At the sight of it, Kane knew he was taking him off the case. Harris opened the folder and laid it in front of him. Kane's eyes fell on a police report, which was dated for earlier that morning.

"Late last night, there was a robbery at a jewelry store downtown. A lot of jewelry was taken. However, the biggest loss was a diamond and yellow gold necklace, which was on its way to the Diamond Exchange. The jewelry store owners want it back and are willing to offer cold hard cash. Whoever robbed this place," the lieutenant continued, "was nothing short of a genius. Not only did he cover his entire face and body, he also painted all the cameras in the store jet black. The suspect is rumored to be a male, about 5'9, and either a light-skinned African-American or a darker skinned Hispanic. The so-called rookie cops can't find one trace of evidence to tell us who wiped out this jewelry store. I think you can, though."

"So who's taking Tricia's case?"

"No one," the lieutenant replied. "You're gonna do both."

Kane read the police report. He slid it aside, looking at the pictures of the damages. He would have to go downtown and look at the store. Something had to be there to give them more evidence.

"Michael, you're the best man we have. You're a good detective and an even better Triad agent. The last thing I want is to see you in court because you took Tricia's kids away. I don't know this woman from Eve, but

I know you do. If you say she's not going to press charges then I believe you. The minute she steps in here trying to start something, well, you're on your own."

"She won't. I promise you."

"Then continue doing your job. While you're at it, solve this case."

With those words, the lieutenant left his office. Kane read over the report some more, but he didn't ponder on the details. If anything, Harris made him want to change his focus. Instead of heading to Tricia's house or the jewelry store, he made his way to Bradford Court, the place he called home.

***

It wasn't until five o'clock that afternoon when Carmen found the energy and strength to get out of bed. She spent the last hour or so, tired of playing the depressed wife and decided to get back to her normal routine. Her plan was derailed when her cell phone rung on her way down the steps. She answered the call, seeing Jay's name on the home screen. "Hello, Mr. Santiago."

"I made reservations for Friday night at Cipriani's."

"Um, can I get a hello or what's up?" Carmen joked.

"Nah, I'm waiting on a yes. You need to be there at seven sharp. I want you to wear a dress with a nice stiletto."

Carmen declined the offer. "I'm not coming. I have some things going on. Until my issues are resolved, I need to focus on my family and not this restaurant. You can take Malik to Cipriani's, or you can invite your son."

"If I wanted to invite them, I would have," Jay replied. "I invited you because I have something you want. Be there at seven sharp and not a minute late."

Carmen listened as the phone hung up. Jay didn't allow her to say no twice. In addition, he mentioned he had something she wanted. Unsure of what it was, her curiosity was stirred. Instead of heading to her home office, she went to her closet to pick out a dress.

Carmen stared at a black and white dress she was given from another designer. The top part of it was mesh and displayed her cleavage while the bottom was tiered. She pulled it from the closet, remembering it was one of Kane's favorite dresses. *Would it be wrong of me to wear it to my dinner date with Jay?* The old Carmen would say no because it was only a dress while the new Carmen would say yes. There were memories in the dress and wearing it for Jay would be disrespectful. Nonetheless, it still was just a dress.

Although her mind wasn't made up, Carmen tried the dress on. Staring at herself in the bathroom mirror, Kane's reflection appeared. She hadn't heard him come in and she knew it was because she was engrossed in her thoughts.

"That's my favorite dress," he told her.

Carmen felt guilty. Kane was busy admiring the dress, but she wasn't wearing it for him. She tried it on to make sure it was presentable for Jay. To make her feel even worse, she could feel her husband's hands, caressing her shoulder blades. His presence reminded her of their argument. She needed to apologize to him.

"I need to say this, Carm," he said, beating her to the punch.

Carmen held up her hand to stop him. She was the one who needed to apologize. She tried, but he stopped her, pressing his finger on her lips. Then, he unzipped her dress. Before she knew it, the dress was lying in the doorway while she and Kane made love on the bathroom counter.

16 | *Head Shots*

When Friday came, everyone learned Carmen and Kane were back in each other's good graces. King expected for his father to come pick up Malachi, but the boy was far from his mind. Therefore, King spent most of the day with Malachi at his side. Now, they both were in Malik's bathroom, getting ready for the block party. To King, the event wasn't a fashion statement, so he slid on a pair of khaki shorts, a wifebeater, and a khaki jacket with a pair of white Air Forces. Malachi, who wasn't yet dressed, stood next to him in a white wifebeater and shorts. His focus was more on the diamond stud he'd given him than getting dressed.

"I look good," Malachi commented, interrupting King's thoughts. In response, King rolled his eyes. "Come on, you know I look fresh."

"Man, put your shirt on," King mumbled, walking out the bathroom. He headed into his room to look at some of the diamond pendants he'd stole. He planned on wearing one of them and figured it would be the Jesus piece. Footsteps sounded as he opened the drawer where he stashed the jewels under a stack of t-shirts. He pulled out the pendant and slid it around his neck.

"Do you remember what I told you?" Malik asked from the hallway.

"What was that?" King replied, being smart. Malik was dressed as if he was headed to bed. King closed the drawer before walking to the doorway where Malik was standing.

"I told you to keep your nose clean. You want this job, don't you?"

King caught an attitude. "I don't even know who he is. You keep making it seem like he's some big boss or something. Do you want me to work for him or not?"

"It isn't about what I want. It's about what he wants," Malik clarified.

"Then, I'm gonna do me. He can take it or leave it."

"Good choice," Malik replied, walking out the room.

"Whoa, watch it," Malachi yelled, coming in behind him.

Malik had almost run into Malachi. "You're going to the block party, too?" He watched as Malachi showed off the diamond stud in his ear. "You got that bling, huh?"

"I am bling," Malachi replied, popping his collar.

"Okay, whatever," Malik said, chuckling under his breath. He told King to keep an eye on him. The last thing he wanted was Kane coming home to find Malachi in trouble. He already had one troubled son and the last thing he needed was another.

Malik remembered he needed to talk to King. He signaled for King to come in the hall. "The meeting starts at six a.m. That means you need to be up at five, not six. You gotta be on time."

"I got this," King barked. "Matter of fact, give me his address and I'll meet him on my own. I'll handle everything."

Malik chuckled. "You can't handle this one, King. This one is out of your league. Trust me."

Malik walked down the hall. King wished Malik had more faith in him. If Malik felt he was ready to go work for a big timer than he needed to act like it. Instead, he was making him show and prove. *It ain't a problem*, King thought, *once I start bringing in that green paper, Malik will see more than my potential. I put my first thousand on it. All I need to do is end things with Lil' Noc. After this block party, I'm all in on whatever Malik wants me to do.*

***

Barricades had been set up at the top and bottom of the street. Kristian and Coco parked two blocks away due to the large number of people who showed up for the Harrisons' annual block party. A hot commodity in the neighborhood, the entire area was packed with people from their school, church, and the community.

"Dang, the whole state showed up," Coco said, seeing the large number of people. "Well, well, well, Lil' Noc decided to pay a visit," she muttered.

Kristian bit her lip, seeing Lil' Noc in front of his apple-red Cadillac. He was flanked by his crew who came in matching attire. They were all wearing dark denim jeans with forest green T-shirts while others wore white tees with forest green streaks in their shirts. Lil' Noc liked to flaunt his money and it showed in his cars and clothes.

"I know you want to stare at Lil' Noc, but that's no fun for me," Coco joked. "Come on, Kris." She poked her in the shoulder before pulling her towards a few of their classmates who had created a dance area in the middle of the street. Many of them were krumping and Coco joined right in. Kristian watched them for a few minutes before she noticed Dijuan walking through the crowd. His uncle wasn't too far behind him. Dijuan was busy keeping the party intact since his parents were out of town.

Still, she hoped he noticed her. Since her mother stayed in her bedroom for most of the day, Kristian took advantage of the situation. She purchased a strapless yellow cocktail dress for the party, which stopped about a good four to five inches above the knee. Rather buxom for her age, the dress hugged all her curves and displayed her cleavage. Her father would be ashamed to see her, but she hadn't seen him since his fight with her mother. If anything, the next time she saw her parents, she would be in her pajamas.

Kristian was so concerned over her parents' opinion of her dress, she allowed Dijuan to pass her without a word in her direction. She no longer spotted him in the crowd and the DJ was now playing a slow tempo song versus the crunk tracks he was spinning earlier. Her plan was to join Coco and the people she was dancing with until she felt someone grab her by the waist. The person pressed themselves against her and when Kristian saw the person's hands, she knew it was Dijuan. A smile formed on her face as he danced with her.

Their first time being close, Kristian was surprised at how freaky they were with each other. Dijuan was the son of a minister, and Kristian knew her parents would be outraged to know she was simulating anal sex in the middle of a neighborhood-friendly block party. Thankfully, her parents weren't there, and Kristian felt at ease to take things a bit further.

Kristian could feel his grip tighten on her hips as he pushed himself into her. Her dress was already short and when she bent over, she gave Dijuan more than he bargained for.

"Get it now," she heard a voice say close to them.

The comment made Kristian more aware of what she was doing, and she figured Dijuan had become uncomfortable as well. Before she knew it, he was pulling her towards his driveway where his father's Chrysler 500 was parked. He sat on the hood of the car before pulling her into his lap. Her dress was thin and skimpy, which allowed to her to feel every bit of his growing erection. Unsure of what to do, Kristian was glad when he asked if they could go inside his mother's Jeep. She obliged and they got inside, locking the doors.

"I didn't expect for that to happen," he told her after a few seconds.

Kristian stared at the bulge, which had formed in his pants. The first time she saw an erection, her mouth formed an O.

"Do you like it?" Dijuan asked.

"I've never seen it like that before. Well, I've never seen one…period," Kristian explained. "Does it hurt?"

Dijuan shook his head. "The dress did it. You look good tonight, Kris. You got everything out," he said with a chuckle, running his finger over her cleavage. "How come you never told me you were feeling me? Were you scared like I was?"

"Of course, I was. When your family moved here, all the girls wanted you. You were in the tenth grade, playing varsity basketball and you were the star of the team. Coco and I both thought you were going to be conceited until we met you at church. It was a coincidence that your father was the new minister. Before you knew it, we all clicked, and we became inseparable."

"Kris, your mother is a freakin' multi-millionaire. I never thought I could get with you. Then, I had to get over my fear of your brother. King ain't somebody you want to play with."

Kristian narrowed her eyes. "I'm going to say this one time and one time only. King doesn't choose who I like, who I date, or even who I kiss. I'm the one who chooses."

"Works for me," Dijuan replied, pressing his lips on top of hers.

Kristian engaged in her first kiss, leaving her mouth closed until their kiss was interrupted by the sound of commotion. People were running to one area of the block party and Kristian knew a fight had broken out. Dijuan jumped out the car and she followed behind him, hoping her brother wasn't involved. If he was, it would be his final strike and his free boarding pass to the county jail.

As Kristian and Dijuan ran to the crowd, King watched as Lil' Noc counted the money he handed him. Malachi turned in his money as well, trying to follow in his footsteps.

Though the block party wasn't necessarily the right place to handle business, Lil' Noc wasn't turning down any dough. "It's all here," he said, handing the money to Darnell. "Is this like a parting gift or something? You pay me my money and you call it quits?"

"That's what it looks like to me," King shot back. "Our business is over. In case you didn't know, I'm moving on to bigger and better things."

"So is your sister," Lil' Noc replied. "She took my eight inches without a problem."

Without warning, King swung, prompting Darnell to jump in front of Lil' Noc. He was on the receiving end of King's blow though he was no longer the source of his anger. Since Darnell wanted to jump in, King proceeded in finishing him off. The last thing Darnell would ever do is renege on someone who let him hold some weight.

King was on a roll until he felt someone jack him up. The person pushed him on his back, and he looked up to see Lil' Noc standing over him. For some reason, he broke up the fight. King shot a glance at Darnell. He appeared lifeless. King wanted to kill him, but he never thought he would. Perhaps, Darnell was only unconscious.

"You came to fight me, motherfucker," Lil' Noc taunted.

King didn't need the reminder. Lil' Noc said enough for him to go at him. He jumped on his feet, his fist connecting with Lil' Noc's face. He felt the same in return, but he was determined not to lose. Two minutes felt like ten and King was surprised when Lil' Noc broke away. He ran out of breath, his weight becoming a hindrance. Unsure of what to do, King watched as another one of Lil' Noc's hustlers stepped up to continue his so-called beatdown.

Continuously punched in his face, King didn't strike back. Instead, he grabbed the boy's neck, tightening his fingers around his windpipe. He got the reaction he wanted when the boy grabbed his arms, trying to loosen his grip. The boy's hands were now in a central location, which King used to his advantage when he kneed him in the groin. The pain sent the boy doubling over and since he was out, Lil' Noc went back in. He charged at King, forcing him on his back until someone cocked a gun. The sound prompted them to freeze as King realized he was staring down the barrel of a nine millimeter.

"What the fuck are you doing?" Lil' Noc yelled. He watched as the boy stammered as if he wasn't certain himself. "Put that shit away."

The gun was enough to send half the block party running from the scene. Kristian didn't know how long the fight had been going on, but judging from the commotion, it had been a long time. She ran as fast as she could to King while Dijuan gave up trying to find his uncle and called 911. "Excuse me, move," she said, repeatedly, as she fought her way through the crowd. She pushed people out her way, ignoring the expletives people spit at her. When she reached the front, she stopped, seeing Darnell's face. Her attention turned towards Lil' Noc who was jerking a gun out his friend's hand. He took notice of her, and Kristian shook her head in disgust. "You really are everything I thought you were."

"Bitch, who do you think you're talking to?"

Lil' Noc slid the gun in his waistband before grabbing her by her shoulders. The move prompted King to charge at him, separating Lil' Noc from Kristian. Kristian knew her brother was too far gone when she felt his blows. "Stop it," she yelled, pulling him away from Lil' Noc. King fell in her arms and for the first time, she noticed the blood, trickling from his face. She then noticed Darnell was regaining consciousness. "You almost killed him," she whimpered.

With over two hundred witnesses at the party, Kristian could see her brother's fate. The thought of him going to jail made tears form in her eyes. It didn't matter how much money her mother had; nothing could get him out. No one would overturn the charges for him either.

Kristian couldn't stomach her brother's image. Before she knew it, she took off. The disdain of watching him ruin his life made her do the one thing she always wanted to. She ran.

There was no thoughts of Coco or Dijuan as she took off in her mother's car. King came down the street behind her, Malachi in tow, but she didn't care. He could chase her if he wanted to. She pressed on the gas and didn't take a second look back.

17 | *Crash*

Cipriani's was one of Brookstone's most famous Italian eateries. Jay picked it for his dinner date with Carmen because it was memorable. It was the first restaurant he took her to at the beginning of their courtship. By bringing her back, he was hoping she would remember. On the flip side, his psychiatrist warned him about forming a new relationship with her. She reminded him to keep his feelings at bay so he wouldn't come between Carmen and her husband. Jay wanted to take heed to her advice, but his love for Carmen overshadowed anything Dr. Stuart said.

So far, Jay realized his next session would begin with, "You were right." It was going on eight o'clock and Carmen still hadn't showed. He remembered asking her to be there at seven sharp. A part of him wanted to believe she was caught in traffic, but she could've called. He checked the hostess stand for the third time and didn't see her there.

She stood me up. She fuckin' stood me up.

Jay tried his best to control his anger. He scrambled around in his pockets, trying to find his prescription. He was taking more dosages than allotted, but he didn't care. If he didn't take it he would have trouble on his hands. All he needed to do was control the urges.

She said she would help me. She said she was coming. I knew I couldn't trust her. She's not even good for a fuck nowadays. She's got money on her mind and Kane in her bed. I can't believe she married his ass. I should've killed him before hiding out. He would've been out my hair like the rest of them motherfuckers. Now, here I am, halfway broke, depending on her name to get me through. I could've finished her off it wasn't for Tiara's ass.

Jay got up from the table, hitting it with a bang, and rushed out the restaurant. He could hear the waiter calling his name, but he ignored him. He had too much adrenaline running through his veins to even care about the unpaid bill. The only item on there was a bottle of Alice White Chardonnay, her favorite wine.

Her favorite, her favorite, I was her favorite. I was her favorite seventeen years ago. It was my name she called out. It was me who she was willing to do anything for. What does Kane have to offer? I saw his ass. Black as midnight, bald head, only makes chump change compared to the millions I brought in. That's who she dipped out on me for. It's okay though, when I see her, I'm going to fuck her up. I'm going to fuck her up.

Jay hit the unlock button on his car, getting inside. He closed his eyes, hoping the medicine would take effect so he could get the evil thoughts out his mind. He needed something to calm him, but the pills weren't working fast enough.

He took the pills out his pocket and stared at them. He couldn't take another dose, but the thoughts were still coming.

You could've just come, and I wouldn't have to go through this. I wouldn't have to think these things. Why can't you do right by me? Why do you always have to fuck with me? I don't even want to hurt you. Why can't you treat me like you treat him?

Jay brought his head up from the steering wheel and stared out into the parking lot. He would give the medicine a few more minutes to take effect and then he would go home. He wouldn't dare tell Malik what happened. If he knew, he wouldn't allow him to meet with Carmen anymore.

She meant to come, she did, something major came up, and she's going to tell me about it tomorrow. I'm going to feel sorry for even thinking those things about her. I don't want her to die. I love her. I would die for her.

Jay slid his key into the ignition. He needed to get home and lie down. Once he did, he would be straight. The thoughts would be gone, and it would be another episode to share with Dr. Stuart. Certain of it, he pulled out the restaurant's parking lot.

In the meantime, Kristian made a sharp right turn, bypassing the street adjacent to downtown Brookstone. She slowed down, seeing she was going almost eighty. King was behind her, doing about the same. She peeked at him in her rearview mirror. In the process, she heard someone blowing their horn. When her eyes went back to the road, it was too late. She hadn't seen the Rolls Royce turning in front of her as she ran the red light. She slammed on the brakes, but she still managed to hit the car in the side.

King jumped out the car, seeing his mother's Lexus swerve to the right side of the road. Kristian hit the car in front of her, but his main concern was her safety. "Stay in the car," he ordered, hearing the passenger side door open.

"I want to help," Malachi yelled.

"Stay in the fuckin' car," King shouted. Kristian got out the car, running to the Rolls Royce. "Hold up, Kris," he yelled, not knowing who was inside. The door opened and a man got out. King stopped in his tracks, recognizing the man from Old Town Bistro.

"I am so sorry, sir," Kristian uttered.

"Girl, you fucked up my car," Jay yelled, checking the damage to his rear bumper. "Shit." He turned towards the girl who was freaking out. "Do you have insurance?"

"I got this," King interjected, pushing Kristian behind him. "You can direct all questions to me. What do you need to know?"

"Yeah, he got this," Malachi added, coming up behind him.

"What the fuck did I tell you?" King yelled, pushing Malachi away.

Malachi checked out the Rolls Royce's damage. "Damn, his shit is fucked up."

"Shut up," King told him. He addressed the man. "Look, we're sorry about all this, but we have a slight problem."

"I don't have a license," Kristian interrupted.

King bowed his head, not wanting her to say that. The man became puzzled. He looked at King before glancing at Kristian.

"How old are you?" the man asked her.

"None of your damn business," King replied.

"It is my damn business. Look at my Rolls Royce," Jay yelled. He pointed to the damage. "Who does the Lexus belong to? Did she steal it?"

"It's my mother's," Kristian replied, "I'm fifteen."

"Don't be giving him all that," King told her, grabbing her arm. Kristian got out his grasp, giving him an evil look. He was trying to help her, and she looked at him as if he was the enemy.

"You're about to be dead meat," Jay replied. "Your mother is going to kill you."

"I know, sir. I don't know how much it's going to cost, but I get an allowance, and I'll pay for your car to be fixed." Kristian watched as the man held his hands up.

"Nah, I'll help you," he told her.

"You're not doing shit," King walked in the man's vicinity. He took a long look at him, staring him in the eye. The man had a caramel complexion like his with bright hazel eyes. They stared each other down until King broke the gaze.

"Is this your sister?" the man asked.

King nodded his head. The man looked between him and Kristian. He raised his brow and King knew it was because he saw Kristian's dark complexion and his light one. He then took note of Malachi. "That's your little brother?" he asked.

"Might as well be, he follows me around like he is."

Malachi smiled in reply.

"I'll help y'all out," Jay offered. "I know somebody who can fix our cars. Follow me and I'll get it taken care of. We don't have to worry about cops or paperwork. I'll be nice on this one. Cool?"

"My sister ain't sleeping with you," King barked.

"What the fuck are you talking about?" Jay yelled. "I don't want a fuckin' fifteen-year-old. Get in the fuckin' car, follow me." Jay opened his car door but didn't get inside as the boy continued to be disrespectful.

"Nah, nah, I don't like this motherfucker," King voiced, walking closer to Jay. He stopped in his tracks when the man's right arm hit him hard in the chest. The blow sent him off his feet and onto the wet asphalt. It took him a second or two to catch his breath and even when he did, he didn't move.

"I'm trying to help you and you're gonna walk up on me. You don't know shit about respect or the game. Get your punk ass up."

King stood up. He signaled to Kristian to do as the man said. From the looks of things, he was her only hope. Now ready to comply, both he and Malachi got inside his Mustang.

"He knocked your ass down," Malachi whispered.

King muttered a few expletives. He followed behind the Rolls Royce as they hit the interstate for the city limits of Brookstone.

18 | *Good Deeds*

"Man, I don't know about this one, you got a tough one this time," Dante said, looking at the damage done to both cars. One of Jay's personal mechanics, he called him up to see if he could save the day. "I know I can finish this one, but yours is an older model. Your bumper will probably take a couple of days to get," Dante continued.

Jay dimmed his eyes, knowing he couldn't afford to get a brand new car. "You can fix the Lexus though?"

"I can fix it before the sun comes up. I'll call my men in and get them to open shop."

"Fix the Lexus and I'll get the money. Try and get the part for the Rolls Royce, too." Jay watched as Dante nodded his head, taking out his cell phone. Jay left him alone in his garage and headed in the house where he left the kids. He walked in his living room, seeing Malachi asleep on the couch. Kristian was asleep as well while the older kid was wide awake. For some reason, he refused to give him his name. "I got some blankets upstairs I'm gonna get for them." He headed up the steps.

Jay went in his closet and searched the shelves. The kids would be there until morning, and he figured he would cook breakfast for them before they left. Jay knew he was helping them because he would want someone to help his son if he got into that kind of trouble. He would rather someone help him than let him come home with a messed up car.

Glad his son wasn't involved, Jay grabbed the blankets and headed down the steps. Nothing had changed.

"He can fix it?" King asked, standing up.

"Yeah, he can fix your mother's car, but it's up in the air on mine," Jay told him. He unfolded one of the blankets, laying it on Malachi. The boy came over, grabbed a blanket, and placed it on his sister. Jay noticed the blood on his face.

"Why are you doing this shit?" King asked.

Jay peered at the two kids who were sleeping. "You don't want me to help you? You want me to let you go home with a fucked up car?"

"No, but, you don't know us."

"So, you don't know me," Jay snapped. They met eyes, searching each other faces. Jay broke the gaze to look at the two kids who were sleeping. When he saw they were resting well, he headed in the kitchen to figure out what he was going to cook.

"Why are you dressed like that?" King asked, sitting on one of the bar stools. "Are you some kind of businessman?"

"I am a businessman. My meeting was canceled," he replied.

"I'm a businessman."

"Yeah, whatever," Jay told him. He heard the boy suck his teeth, but he didn't care. The boy had a lot of growing up to do.

"I want to get out of here," he heard the boy say.

Jay pulled a bag of grits from the cabinet although it wasn't time for him to start cooking. "Do you want to get out this house or out of Brookstone? One is a whole lot easier than the other."

"I don't even know."

Jay got an idea in his mind. The boy didn't trust him, but he knew his good nature would eventually rub off on him. "There's a bar open downtown. Why don't we go get a couple of drinks and play some pool? You need to take a load off."

"I'm not old enough," King replied. "Besides, I don't feel comfortable leaving Kristian and Malachi here."

"I'll lock the doors, they'll be straight. Dante and his crew can't get in through the garage. The door is locked. They'll be fine. I'll leave them some milk and cookies if they get hungry, too." The boy gave him a smile, but Jay considered it minimal improvement. He opened another cabinet and pulled out a first aid kit, which he slid towards him. The boy opened it and started cleaning the scratches on his face. Once he was finished, he hopped off the stool, ready to go.

Jay closed the cabinets and grabbed a sheet of paper where he was writing a grocery list. He scribbled a quick note, telling the kids where they were going and what time to expect them back. He left it on the coffee table before leaving the house. An old Benz was in the garage, which he hardly drove. It was last of his cars, which wasn't impounded or wrecked. He got inside and headed towards the bar.

"What's your name?" King asked. "I tell mine. You tell yours."

Jay decided against the idea. "I don't want to know you and you don't want to know me."

"Fine, then," King replied.

Jay kept quiet as they neared the downtown area. A feeling of queasiness came over him as they passed Cipriani's. A part of him wanted to look to see if Carmen's car was there, but it was stupid of him to think so. They were supposed to have met at seven and it was way past that time. He pushed the thought aside as he pulled into a parking space in front of the Blue Lagoon. "Come on," he told King, getting out the car.

King followed his lead, heading inside the bar. He had never been in the Blue Lagoon, but he could tell the bar and pool hall were for a more mature crowd. The man went straight to the bar, ordering a drink, and he sat down beside him.

"Now, you know you ain't getting nothing, but a Pepsi," the bartender joked.

"That's all I want," King told her, recognizing her as Ms. Rita. She placed a drink in front of the man. He then placed a fifty on the counter before grabbing his drink and heading towards the pool tables. Seconds later, Ms. Rita set a glass in front of him.

"So you're a gangster now?" she asked, leaning on the counter.

"Ms. Rita, what are you talking about?"

"Why are you hanging with a man like him?"

"Mind your business," King told her, taking a sip of his Pepsi.

"I'll tell your probation officer you're out here rolling with snakes."

"Snakes, what do you have against my friend?"

Ms. Rita checked the bar to make sure she didn't have any customers waiting. "Your friend was one of the biggest drug dealers in America. He's been locked up for some time. He's senile and heartbroken. He killed a man when he was fifteen. You better watch out."

King didn't look in the man's direction.

"I was working here when he started his businesses," Ms. Rita continued. "He owned a club not too far from here, a couple of laundromats. He was sitting on money. Then he got caught, went to prison for a long time and is now back in Brookstone. If I was him; I wouldn't have come back. What did he have to come back for?"

Her words had King curious. "You have a problem with him or something?"

"Nah, I don't have any problems with him," Ms. Rita admitted, "maybe scared of him a little bit, but that's about it. He's killed so many men I don't see how the cops let him walk around freely. Word on the street is that he tried to kill his baby mama."

King eyed Ms. Rita, trying to decide whether to believe her or not. The man sounded like a cross between a gangster and a serial killer. He lived in a house bigger than his parents, which made King suspicious. Ms. Rita wasn't known to lie, but there had to be more to what she said.

"Look, I don't know who his baby mama is," she lied, "but I heard he messed her up bad. They said she almost lost the baby. He had a lot of men working for him, though. I heard he had a real team."

"Why don't you stop telling me things you heard and tell me things you know," King told her, getting agitated. "I don't like this rumor shit."

Ms. Rita giggled and set a bowl of nuts on the counter. "All the news around here is some he said/she said. We haven't seen him in a long time."

King observed the man, seeing him win the first round of pool. He didn't want to believe the man was dangerous, but he knew Ms. Rita. She gossiped, but her gossip was like the Bible. It was the truth. When they met eyes, King knew he had to find out the man's name. If he was as dangerous as Ms. Rita said his mother didn't need to be near him. He would protect her at all costs even if it meant losing his life.

***

The idea of Jay and King being in the same room was far from Kane's mind. He was currently staring at Carmen who was asleep on his chest. They made amends, but "the conversation," still hadn't taken place. He needed to apologize for putting his hands on her while also telling her about Akaila and Malachi. If he didn't get a move on, the conversation would never happen. "Baby, wake up," he whispered, smoothing his hands over her back. "Come on, Carm, we need to talk." She opened her eyes, letting out a slight moan. She signaled she was ready, and Kane whispered he was sorry.

"I'm sorry, too," she repeated. "What happened that morning?"

Kane took a deep breath. "You insinuated the wrong thing. You know how bad I want a baby. The thought of you being with another man and getting pregnant, made me go to another place. You know how bad I want another child."

"It was a bad move. I was wrong. I just wanted to fuck your head up." Carmen sat up so they could be face to face. "I'm sorry," she told him, "I love you. I got caught up in my feelings. You forgive me, don't you?"

"You know I do," he replied, kissing her lips.

"So, where did you go after the argument?"

"I went straight to Malik's."

"Well, you're never going back. This is your home."

Kane nibbled on her neck. After dipping back inside her, she showed him what he missed while he was away. He needed to feel a soft body and relieve some tension after leaving the precinct. While his intention was to start round two, the thought of the precinct prompted him to ask her about Akaila. When he saw her facial expression, he knew an argument was coming or a genuine concern.

"Akaila being in our house is not a problem. I want to know about her mother who you spent the night with." Carmen had almost forgotten about Kane's dirt until he brought up Akaila.

"Her mother's name is Theresa," he lied. "She's a drug addict. Harris put me on the case because her kids are in danger of being put into the system. They arrested her, but released her, hoping she could get some help. Long story short, I left her alone for one night, and she went and shot up. Now, I have her kids."

"You took her kids?" Carmen was shocked.

"Akaila wanted to stay here, and Malachi didn't need to be there."

"So who is watching Theresa and making sure she's not overdosing?"

"I can't be in two places, Carm."

Carmen swallowed. "I haven't met Malachi."

"He's with King."

"You let her son be with King?" She was even more shocked.

"He's very fond of him. He's the little brother King never had. With that being said, I want you to fight with me on this. I want to adopt them."

Carmen's eyes got big. "You want to adopt them?"

"I want us to become their guardians."

"Okay, Kane, you've went too far on this one."

"Carmen, they need a good home, and..."

"Their mother needs help. You're trying to save these kids, what about her? They could've been the only thing keeping her from shooting up. A social worker should be working with this family, not a Triad agent."

"Listen to me, Carm," Kane stressed. "Akaila was prostituting herself to keep the bills paid. Malachi works for the same guy who put King in the game. They support themselves and Theresa doesn't work to put food on the table, pay the rent, or anything. My main goal was to get them out the house and into a better situation. If their social worker knew Akaila was sleeping with every Tom, Jack, and Harry, do you know how quickly they would rush her to a treatment center? They would say she couldn't control her sexual urges when she can. She performs sex acts for money. Malachi, on the other hand, is in danger of getting caught with narcotics. He's two feet from juvenile detention."

His words did something to Carmen and before long, her eyes became full. "If they want to stay then my answer is yes."

Kane nodded his head. It was a done deal. He knew Carmen would come around when she heard the complete story. It was enough to make any person want to reach out and lend a helping hand. He would talk to Akaila and Malachi about it and then bring the issue to King and Kristian. He would still look after Tricia, but at least Akaila and Malachi were protected. He closed his eyes but reopened them when he felt Carmen's hands wrap around his package. "You want it again?" he mumbled. Carmen nodded her head in reply. Without hesitation, Kane slid inside her.

19 | 6 O'clock Blues

It was five o'clock on the dot when Malik's alarm sounded. He stumbled out of bed, cursing Jay in his head although it was his idea to hold the meeting at six. About to open his bedroom door, he listened for any sounds in his apartment. Not hearing any, he opened the door and walked in the living room. King and Malachi were both asleep on the couch as if they were too tired to go in their rooms. Since he didn't want to wake Malachi, he walked over to King and tapped him on the shoulder.

"Get up," he ordered, looking at King. Fresh scars were on his godson's face, which meant he had been rumbling. "Get up." He shook him.

King opened his eyes. "Dang, I'm up, I'm up," he said. "Stop shaking me."

"Good, now get dressed. We have business to take care of."

Malik walked to his room until he heard a squeaky voice.

"Can I come?" Malachi asked.

"No," Malik replied. "Go back to sleep."

"This is big boy stuff," he heard King tell him. "You'll shine in due time."

Malik stepped in the shower as he thought about the thin ice he was walking on. If Jay didn't accept King; he didn't know who could get the Santiago cartel back on its feet. They both had tried. King was their last hope. Their future was in his hands. After dressing, he walked in King's room to see him wearing a pair of baggy jeans and a wifebeater. White Air Forces were also on his feet. "You must be out your damn mind." Malik pushed his way past King, opening his closet door. He threw around a few clothes until he found King's Christmas gift, which he'd been holding for Carmen. "You're not about to walk up in this meeting with that shit on." He handed over the suit, which was specifically designed for him.

King grabbed it and read the tag, *King by Carmen Davenport*. "My mama designed this?"

"Surprise, surprise, it debuts in December, now put the shit on."

King glared at the suit as Malik walked out the room. He remembered complaining to his mother about the favoritism she showed Kristian, not knowing she had something for him in the works. The new line was supposed to be a secret, but it was the best gift Malik gave him. Unable to hide his excitement, he tore off his clothes so he could put on the suit. Minutes later, he joined Malik in the living room only to see him picking up

Malachi. He carried him to his bedroom and when he returned, King watched as he admired his new look.

"Now you're a G," he told him. "Let's go."

King followed him out the apartment and into his car. Not quite sure where they were going, he was surprised when Malik pulled up in front of an abandoned building in the downtown area. Formerly known as Sapphire, the building was empty most of his life.

"Do what I say when I say it, okay?"

King nodded his head. Once Malik unlocked the door, he followed him up the steps to the second floor.

"Stay here, Scarface," Malik ordered.

Malik went inside and the door was closed. Seconds later, he heard voices. He tried to make out their words, but it was pointless. When Malik opened the door, he walked inside and paused in his tracks. In front of him was the man he spent the last few hours with. He paid for his mother's car to be fixed, and even gave him a first aid kit to clean his wounds. King was beyond shocked, and he could tell the man was, too.

"This is King," Malik introduced.

King watched as the man rose to his feet. He remembered Ms. Rita's words and he realized the connection Malik and the man had. They were involved in the same drug ring. Now, they wanted him to join.

"No time for feelings to get involved," the man began.

King became irritated. Questions were being hurled at him, yet he didn't know who he was talking to. Malik said his name, but the man never said his. "Who are you?" King asked, interrupting him. He felt Malik's eyes on him, but he wasn't backing down. "You know my name, now tell me yours."

"Jigga," the man said.

Malik held in his laughter.

"Your mama named you Jigga?" King asked.

"Your mama named you King?" Jay shot back.

"It's not my real name," King told him.

"It's not my real name," Jay repeated.

King saw they were getting nowhere. He dropped the issue since he now had a way to address him. With a name, he could start talking business. They were standing inside an abandoned club, which needed to be open. It took money and time, but he figured Jigga, and Malik had the loot while he had the time.

"I'm going to tell you what I need and you're going to tell me if you can get it. This position requires brain, skills, and the ability to network and connect. You're representing an empire much larger than you think. If you fuck me over, I'll kill you, no questions asked. Do you understand?"

King smiled. "Basically, if I double cross you, I'm a dead man."

"Exactly, and I don't give a fuck about you being younger than twenty-one. If you can't handle the sight of blood then I suggest you run now. The door is less than three feet away."

"I'll kill, too," King replied. Jigga's eyes darted towards Malik and then at him. King wanted to show him he was just as bad as he was. He also wasn't easily intimidated. However, he was proven wrong when he noticed Jigga's suit was one of his mother's designs. It was a clear reminder of the connection Jigga had to the woman he loved the most.

"I like you," Jay admitted. "Now, for part two; I need men, lots of 'em. If any of them fuck up, please believe; they can be eliminated in a matter of seconds. I will bury a narc alive." Jay took a second to catch his breath. "You will take the fall for whatever they do so choose them wisely. Did Malik tell you about my jewelry store? You like to steal, right?"

"Whoa," Malik said, hearing Jay mention Iceland. "I don't know about that one."

Jay ignored him. "You like to steal?" he repeated to King.

"When it calls for it," King replied.

"I need someone who likes to steal, someone who likes to rob. I can't afford diamonds, rubies, gold, so I need a thief in the night. First thing first, though, get the men, bring them back to me, and we'll issue assignments. Anytime you're conducting business, you wear a suit. If I see you in anything less, you're fired."

"What are you going to pay me?"

"Right now, I'm gonna let you live with the shit I told you. When you get the men, you'll see a check. Work comes before pay."

King chuckled at how Jigga tried to scare him. Ms. Rita warned him about the man yet for some reason he believed he was harmless. "Is there anything else?" King asked. "Let me know what you need."

"If you have ear to the streets, find out who has the best crack and heroin in this city. They're our competition. We beat them, we take over Brookstone. We take over Brookstone, we capture New York. Then, we control America. Got it?"

"Everything is crystal clear."

"Good, you're dismissed."

Jay sat in his seat and listened as Malik told King to wait outside. Once they were alone, Malik bowled over laughing. He didn't know what he found funny, but he knew Malik was going to tell him. After a few seconds, he did.

"Why did you tell him your name was Jigga?"

"Did you really think I was going to say Jay Santiago? Jigga was the closest thing to Jay. I thought Jay-Z and the word Jigga came out."

"You know you didn't scare him, right?"

"Yeah, he's a tough one. I like him, though. You did well." Jay slid a check across the table. It was written to Malik, a small price for his services. "I know it isn't much, but at least you can pay your rent."

Malik tried to slide the check back, but Jay wouldn't let him. It was written for a small amount, only ten thousand dollars, which was rather large compared to how much money Jay had. For everything he wanted to do, every penny had to be spent wisely. "So he has your stamp?" Malik asked, deciding to take the check.

"I approve. I just don't know if it's because I like his answers or because he looks like my grandfather."

Malik almost choked. "He reminds you of your grandfather?"

"Yeah, my father was short and fat, but my grandfather, Vincent, was skinny. My grandfather, of course, is Puerto Rican, but King looks a lot like him. I don't know. I haven't seen a photo of my grandfather in seventeen years." Jay thought on it some more, but eventually gave up. Ready to head back to bed, he picked up his keys, deciding to head home. Malik did the same, the two of them going their separate ways.

***

Malik made good on his promise to help Jay rebuild the Santiago cartel. Unfortunately, Carmen hadn't done the same with the restaurant and the guilt plagued her in the form of a nightmare. Saturday morning, she woke up, to find her husband leaning over her. His eyes were filled with concern and worry, which scared her.

"Baby, not again," he told her, stroking her cheek.

Carmen blinked several times. Sweat beads were on her face and the smell of sex was in the air.

"I heard you. You said his name. You dreamt about him again."

Carmen tried to gather her thoughts. She remembered Cipriani's and a second later, she remembered Jay. *Shit, I stood him up. I fuckin' stood him up.*

Carmen had to get to him. She pushed Kane away, but he only grabbed her arms, trying to keep her in bed.

"You have to tell me what brought this on," he demanded.

Carmen ignored him, pushing him away. "I need to get to work. I'm going to be late."

"Baby, its Saturday. Besides, did you even hear what Kristian said? She got into a car accident. Some man helped her get your car fixed. She said she wanted to be honest about the situation."

"Yeah, baby, I heard her," she lied, trying to slide from underneath him. "I could care less about the car. Material objects can be replaced. She can't."

Carmen gave him another quick shove and this time, Kane allowed her to get out of bed. She rushed in the bathroom, quickly showering before getting dressed. She hardly worked on Saturdays, which meant she needed to think of a better excuse than the one she gave him. "You know about Kristian modeling for Flame," she said, putting on a pair of hoop earrings. "If I want to promote this line the right way, I gotta put in the work. Our personal time may be limited for a while."

"I know. You've been talking about the *Peaches* line for months. If you say you gotta work you gotta work."

"Thanks for understanding."

Now dressed, Carmen ran to him and gave him a quick kiss on the lips. He tried to pull her back in bed, but she managed to break his grasp. After another quick kiss, she grabbed her purse and headed out the house. She took the long way to Jay's house in case Kane decided to follow her. The route forced her to drive downtown and as if it was meant to be, she spotted Jay walking out of Flame. Several clothing bags were in his hand, and she pulled over so she could talk to him.

When she first called out to him, he ignored her. She tried again, which garnered a reaction. He didn't speak yet he looked in her direction. "I already know," she told him, aware of his feelings. "Kane and I had a big falling out. We were trying to work through our problems, and I lost track of time. I'm sorry. I know how much this restaurant means to you. Let me make it up."

"No," Jay declined. "I want to end this. I'll find someone else to help with the restaurant. I thought I would give you the chance to expand your brand, but I see you were too busy expanding something else."

Instead of stooping to his level, Carmen maintained her stance. "I want to help you."

"Have you talked to your father about the building?"

Carmen was about to give feed him another excuse. He could tell because he sucked his teeth.

"I thought so," he admitted. "Of course, you haven't." Jay hung the suits he purchased in the backseat and closed the door. Carmen was still standing there as if he was going to change his mind. "Don't make promises you can't keep. I'm barely making ends meet and I need someone to cut me a deal. Right now, you're holding me back."

Carmen exhaled, but she was determined not to give up. "I'm sorry, Jay. I'm here now and we should be using this time wisely. I know you don't have money like you used to. To be honest, our roles have switched. I'm the multi-millionaire and you're the one struggling to make it. I know that feeling. It's because I do I want to help you. I also owe you. I can't give you back moments with your son or your freedom. What I can do is give you my time, starting today, right now. All I need you to do is take it. Or you in?"

Jay cursed under his breath. He was heated, but he needed Carmen more than she needed him. "Don't let me down," he told her. "I need your help."

"You have me at your disposal."

"Get in, then. I want to go to Lucky's. I have a taste for Asian."

20 | *A Little Secret*

Jay wasn't the only one who had a taste for Asian cuisine. For the past six minutes, Tiara had been waiting outside of Lucky's Restaurant for Malik to show. A regular lunch date for them, Malik wanted to discuss the direction of their relationship. They had been secretly dating for the past ten years and he was ready to make it known.

Tiara was against the idea because she didn't believe Carmen would accept their relationship. Her friend had non-platonic relationships with almost all of Jay's closest friends. She kissed Rakim, Malik's twin brother, and even slept with her ex-boyfriend, Carlos. Although Malik made it clear he and Carmen never had any inappropriate interactions, Tiara didn't believe him. She didn't bring up the issue after their initial discussion, but she always watched him whenever he was around her friend. He didn't do anything out the ordinary and eventually she started to feel guilty.

Tiara knew she couldn't hold on to Malik forever. Every time they would make love, he would remind her they were living in sin. Then, the discussion would turn to marriage and babies.

Even now, she suspected how their lunch date would go. Nervous about it, she checked the parking lot to see if he was there. While she didn't see him, she spotted Jay and Carmen, heading inside the restaurant. Since their presence was unexpected, she got out the car to follow them inside. Almost to the door, she watched as Malik pulled up to the restaurant.

"We have company," she told him once he was in earshot.

Malik ignored her statement, grabbing her waist. "I haven't seen you in two days. I've been busy with Jay." Malik gave her a small kiss before pulling away. "Who's our company?"

"Well, it's the lovely Jay Santiago and Carmen Davenport-Kane. I guess they're on a lunch date, too. I say we give them some privacy."

"I say we don't." Malik grabbed Tiara's hand and led her into the restaurant. She tried to coax him into leaving, but he ignored her. She didn't let up until they were standing in front of Jay and Carmen's table. Their hands were intertwined, a shock to both Jay and Carmen. Malik overlooked their stares, inviting himself and Tiara to the table. "We came to get a bite to eat and saw y'all two walk in. I hope we're not interrupting anything." Malik noticed the papers, which were strewn across the table. He recognized the documents to be Jay's proposal.

"We were talking about the restaurant," Jay replied. "Y'all should join us. We have enough space." Jay slid further in the booth and Malik sat next to him. Meanwhile, Tiara sat next to Carmen. The two exchange words. When Jay heard Carmen ask Tiara why she kept the relationship from her, he put an end to the conversation. "Not here, not now," he told her.

Carmen set her menu on the table. She found it hard to believe that Tiara and Malik had suddenly started dating. She hadn't known for them to be with anyone for several years and now she knew why. They couldn't date other people because they were dating each other. Why they kept it from her, she didn't know. Tiara had been her friend for over twenty years and should've known she would have supported her. She may have been hesitant about it, but in the end, Tiara would get her full support.

"Do you have a problem with this?" Malik asked, directing the question to Carmen. "I can smell the tension."

"Why would I have a problem? I'm married," Carmen replied. "What I have a problem with is you two sneaking and doing this behind my back. What does that say about our friendship?"

Malik gave her a reminder. "Carm, we know how you've been in the past. For example, the shit that went down between Rakim and Monifah."

"How I've been, what are you talking about, Malik?"

"I'm talking about how you broke them up," he clarified.

Carmen became defensive. "I didn't break them up. I never told Monifah about my kiss with Rakim. I also didn't tell her he was in love with me. Your brother did that shit. He broke them up."

"Damn, can you calm down?" Jay grabbed her hand, seeing her anger. "All Malik is saying that—"

"Malik doesn't need to say shit. If anything, he needs to keep his mouth closed."

"Tiara and I have been dating for ten years," Malik announced. "I want to marry her. I think it's time we start our family."

"Good luck," Carmen shot back. "Tiara doesn't want kids."

"I don't expect for you to be happy, Carm," Tiara began. "You're acting the exact way I thought you would. Malik and I aren't engaged, but if we were, you wouldn't be happy. A wedding would only mean you would have one day without glory. Well, unless you design my dress."

"Did I do something to y'all?" Carmen yelled. She peered at Jay who appeared to be just as confused as she was. "Fuck this shit," she muttered, pushing Tiara out the booth. She heard Jay call her name, but she ignored him. She wasn't going to sit there and allow Malik and Tiara to wrongly accuse her.

"Carmen," she heard a voice call.

Now, outside of Lucky's, Carmen turned to see Malik behind her. She didn't know why he followed her when she was only going to jump down his throat. "I can't believe your fuckin' ass. We've been down for I don't how long, and you're going to sit up there and play me. I'm not upset because y'all are together. I'm upset because you hid it for ten years. What reason do I have to sabotage anything y'all want to do?"

"Carmen, calm down."

"No, you calm down, Malik. I have every right to be angry."

"Look at it from Tiara's point of view. You slept with Carlos. He was her ex-boyfriend. She has trust issues. It took me a while to get her to even consider dating me. She still isn't over that shit."

Carmen huffed, heading towards Jay's car. "Carlos is dead. She needs to let him and what we did rest in peace. I've moved past it, and she needs to do the same. If she doesn't, she won't walk down the aisle to anyone."

Carmen tried to open the passenger side door and discovered it was locked. Now forced to stay at Lucky's, she breathed a sigh of relief when Jay walked out the restaurant. Tiara wasn't with him, which meant she and Malik were possibly staying. Sure enough, like she thought, they were parting ways. Malik and Tiara were staying at Lucky's while she and Jay were heading to his house. Carmen didn't complain about the move because it put her out the public eye. She didn't know Kane's plans for the day, and she didn't need to be any place where he could see her.

21 | NYPD *Blue*

Staying in the house while his wife slaved at Flame was not Kane's intention for a Saturday afternoon. Since his marital problems were under control and Tricia's kids seemed to be adapting to his household well, he decided to work on his second case.

He stepped in Westland & Co., the site of the jewelry store robbery, as a cop snapped photos of the damages. Upon entry, the man waved for him to come over. Kane played catch up by asking him a question. "When was this place robbed again?"

"Late Wednesday night," the cop said.

Kane looked around the store. It wasn't entirely in shambles, but a number had been done on the glass cases. "So, what are we looking at?" He peered at the cop and apologized for not introducing himself. "I'm Kane," he said, extending his hand. "I'm the Brookstone PD's resident Triad agent. Harris put me on the case. What have you found so far?"

"I'm Sanders. Right now, we don't have much. We found one tape that shows a guy in a mask. You can't see his face, but you can see a little bit of his arm before the screen goes black. It's the only decent visual we have."

"Do they have a list of every item stolen?"

"Yeah, I have it right here," Sanders replied, handing him a sheet of paper. Kane took it from his hands and scanned the price list of the missing items. Most of the pieces weren't too expensive except for a diamond and yellow gold necklace. It was worth a decent amount. He hoped the owners had insurance in case he couldn't get it back. He handed the list to Sanders and asked to see the videotapes. A television was set up on one of the counters, which he figured Sanders had been using.

The officer did as he asked. From reading the police report, he could tell the man's description was accurate. The guy had to be about 5'9 and was light-skinned. Black shades and a ski mask covered his face, which Kane could see before the guy sprayed the entire camera black.

"Pause it," he ordered. Sanders did as he was told, and Kane put his finger on the screen. "He's wearing a watch."

"Yeah," Sanders said, having noticed it as well. "He's wearing a watch because he needs to keep up with the time. He needs to be in and out."

"Rewind the tape."

Sanders did as he was told and pressed play. Kane put his head closer to the screen and he wondered what he was looking at.

"I can't make it out with the naked eye," Kane shared, "but it looks like one of those new Rolexes. I know for a fact they only made five of those bad boys. It was a test watch. It's so expensive; you can't find it in a jewelry store like this."

"So what should we do?" Sanders was curious.

"Take the tape to the lab, have them magnify the footage, see what kind of watch it is, and we'll find out which stores in New York carried it. We'll see when they were sold, review the tapes from those stores, and hopefully find our guy."

"What if he's wearing a knock off?" Sanders asked the question prematurely.

"Why would a jewelry thief wear a knock off? He's a jewelry thief."

"True," Sanders said, ejecting the tape. "Well, that's the most we've got. It won't hurt to try." He grabbed his notes and headed to the precinct to fulfill Kane's request.

Meanwhile, Kane continued snooping around the jewelry store. He looked at the front door of the place, noticing it was perfectly intact. The chances of the thief coming through the front entrance were slim to none unless he used a lock pick. Still, Kane knew he entered somewhere. He scratched his chin, peering up at the tiled ceiling. All the tiles appeared to be in place at first glance. The tiles weren't that big and the chances of the thief being able to slide into one seemed farfetched. However, it wasn't impossible.

After spotting a broom, he picked it up and attempted to move each of the tiles. The broom wasn't long enough to hit the tiles, so he scoured the area again until he located a ladder in the far right corner of the room.

"Hey, are you the owner?" he asked a man who was busy fixing a display case. The man told him he was, and Kane proceeded to question him about the ladder. "When you came in the store after it was robbed, was the ladder where you remembered leaving it?"

"It was over here, I think," the man responded. He pointed at a different area. "I don't really remember."

"Does your alarm detect movement," was Kane's next question.

"Why do you want to know that? The alarm never went off. I came Thursday morning and found the place like this. He messed with the wiring."

"If he messed with the wiring then he knows this place in and out." Kane moved the ladder back to where the owner said it was. He took the broom with him and once he had the ladder in place, he climbed it and hit the tiles with the broom. When the tiles didn't move, Kane tried his next idea. He moved the ladder back to where he found it, climbed it again, and hit the tiles there. This time, the tiles moved easily. Without much force, he moved all the tiles until he had a clear passage to the roof. It took a lot of maneuvering to fit inside the small space, but he made it on the roof. He could hear the owner underneath him, asking what he was doing, but Kane didn't reply. He was looking for another ladder. As expected, he found one on the right side of the building. Kane was ready to share his findings until his phone rung. The number came up unknown, yet he still answered.

"We got the watch," Sanders began, after Kane said hello. "It's a Rolex Pearl-DateJust. According to news reports, they made a total of six of them. One is kept at the Rolex company while five were shipped across the United States. Two were in Cali, two were here in New York, and the other one was sold to Bill Gates."

"I need you to contact the stores that sold the watches. We need receipts, video footage, anything they can give us. I've already figured out how the suspect got in. Now, we need to find out who he is."

"I'm on it, sir," Sanders replied.

Kane listened as the phone hung up. He couldn't help but smile at how quickly he was going to solve the case. Once he had a new inmate at the county jail, he would prove to Harris he hadn't lost his fire.

***

While Kane made headway with his new case, Carmen sat at home, making developments on Jay's restaurant. Despite the drama at Lucky's, once they returned to his house, they were able to put the nonsense aside and get to work. Now, a new business proposal was in motion, which featured a soul food restaurant they agreed to name Blue Magic.

Currently working in her home office, Carmen called her father to handle a major part of the plan: location. As usual, she dialed her father's cell to keep from having to speak to her mother, Patricia. He answered on the first ring. "That was quick," she greeted. "You were waiting on my call, weren't you? Well, I'm here now."

"I see," her father responded. "Give me an update, Peaches."

"Well, I decided to invest some of my money and attention into a new business. This one, you might like. I want to open a restaurant."

"I already know where this is going. Go ahead and give it to me."

Carmen didn't hesitate to voice her request. Her father was the best person to get a building from since she was putting it in her name. He wouldn't question where the money was coming from because he knew she had millions in the bank. "I've already checked your listings online. There's a building downtown in your company's listings. I want to buy it."

"This is a big investment, Carm. Do you have a partner?"

Carmen parted her lips as the front door opened. A ball of guilt dropped in her stomach when she saw Kane. She changed the subject. "I have the money together. I need you to set up an appointment with the realtor. I want to look at it. More than likely, I'm going to buy it so start on the paperwork, too. You can fax it to me at Flame."

"When did you start ignoring me?" her father asked with a chuckle. "Okay, okay, you want to keep your partners a secret. I understand. Ahh, tell me where this building is, I need to see who else might be trying to get it."

Carmen gave him the address and seconds later she heard a sigh.

"Are you sure about this, Peaches? A restaurant is a very big project. When did serving food spark your interest?"

"Daddy, I love you and I can't wait to have you eating in my establishment. Thanks for everything." Those were her final words before she hung up. If things worked in her favor, she would inspect the building on Monday and have it in her name by Friday. Certain her father could pull it off, Carmen reminded herself she only needed a mustard seed of faith.

22 | *Deception*

Monday morning was filled with expectations. Kane was waiting for the exact moment when he would narrow down the suspect in the Westland & Co. robbery while Carmen waited for an agent to call her regarding the building for Blue Magic. Neither of them was making progress. Carmen was forced to deal with her duties at Flame and Kane strolled into the Brookstone City Bank to make a few changes to the savings account he shared with Carmen. With Akaila and Malachi now under his roof, he decided to move eighty thousand dollars out their savings and into two separate accounts for the DeGonzazas. Although he hadn't discussed it with his wife, she had too much money to notice eighty thousand dollars was missing.

"This line isn't moving," a woman said behind him. "I'm not about to stand here for forty-five minutes."

Kane shot her a look before looking at the people in front of him. Only three tellers were on duty, which made the line longer than usual. Aware he was going to be there for a while, he searched the place, looking for anything he could use to occupy his time. The detective in him looked for surveillance cameras. Within the first minute or so, he noticed three of them in various places on the ceiling. Most of the cameras were pointed towards the offices of the bank's representatives, which is where Kane looked next. Two men were stepping out an office, both dressed casually. They were shaking hands as if they finished sealing a deal. One of the men, light-skinned with a shaven head, carried a briefcase and folder. The other man was empty-handed. Kane figured the man had come for a business loan and was successful in the meeting. About to turn away, Kane stared in shock horror as he recognized the man.

Never in a million years did Kane think he would lay eyes on Jay Santiago. *When did he get out? Who granted him an appeal?*

So many questions bounced around Kane's mind he missed seeing Jay walk out the bank. When he headed outside, it appeared as if Jay disappeared. As if on cue, a black car drove passed him. One look at the license plate and he knew it was Jay. It was never his intention to follow him, but the car was confirmation his eyes hadn't played tricks on him. Now, he needed answers. Forgetting about the transfer, he headed towards the precinct. He ran in the Narcotics division and into Harris' office.

"Let me call you back. A lunatic just ran in here," the lieutenant said, hanging up the phone. "The door was closed for a reason. You can't come barging in here. I was on a very important call with the DEA."

"Did you know Jay was out of prison?" Kane asked. Harris squirmed in his seat. "Did you?" he barked. "I saw him downtown at the bank."

"Yeah, I knew," Harris admitted. "He's been out for about a week. You're not late on the news."

"So when were you going to tell me? You have me walking around here with the dumb face while my biggest bust is cruising the streets?"

"I wanted you to concentrate on doing your job," Harris explained. "Your job is to help Tricia and find out who robbed Westland & Co. I didn't want your hatred for Jay to interfere with your work."

Kane's volume increased at Harris' words. "You don't want my hatred to interfere with my work? We're talking about my family, Harris. This motherfucker has ties to my family. What if he tries to hurt Carmen?"

"We've been keeping a close eye on him," Harris explained. "He sees a psychiatrist once a week. From what we've seen, he's trying to open a few businesses. He's going about things the right way."

Kane shook his head. The whole thing sounded iffy. Harris should've told him about Jay. He had a right to know. He raised Jay's son and married his ex-girlfriend. "Where's the footage? The pictures, the videos; I want everything you have on him."

"Right now I think it would be good if you focused on—" Kane didn't wait for him to finish. He went straight for the lieutenant's file cabinet where the precinct's most publicized cases were kept. The cabinet wasn't locked and when Harris saw he was able to get inside, he tried to push him away. Kane didn't let him and soon they were tussling with each other until Kane overturned every item on the lieutenant's desk. A direct reflection of his rage, he wasn't surprised when Harris handed him the folder.

The folder contained a copy of Jay's release papers and several black and white photographs. Each photo was dated and in chronological order. The first picture was of Jay, and he was sitting outside a restaurant, which appeared to be Old Town Bistro. He was dressed in a suit, somewhat like the one he was wearing at the bank. Kane went to the next photo. It was a picture of his wife. Same day, same location. The next photo was of her and Jay. His jaw tightened as he looked through the rest of the pictures. There were shots of them at the park, walking inside Lucky's and even getting in Jay's Benz.

"I didn't want you to know." Harris offered a heartfelt apology. Kane didn't want to hear it. He stuffed the pictures in his jacket pocket. Then, as quickly as he rushed in, he was out the door.

Before he questioned Carmen, he was going to get an update on the robbery. He approached Sanders' desk where the officer was watching surveillance footage.

"Good morning," Sanders greeted. "I tried to get your attention when you walked in, but you were on a mission. Only two stores carried the Rolex here in New York. However, none of the stores were in Brookstone." Sanders changed tapes and pressed play so Kane could see the footage. "I had the tapes cut so we only see the footage of the people who purchased the watch. The other stuff isn't important. This man..." Kane shushed him.

"Stop the tape," Kane ordered. "He's not our culprit. He works for Ivanka Trump. Play the next tape."

Sanders did as he was told. Once the second tape played, he pointed at the screen where a woman was walking inside a jewelry store. "I don't know what to think when it comes to her."

Kane watched as a blond-haired beauty approached the service counter. An associate came to her aid before disappearing from the tape. When she returned, she had a box in her hand, which she opened and showed the woman. "Zoom in." The footage was magnified by about fifty percent. Kane stared at the woman, making Sanders rewind and fast forward almost six times. The longer he stared at her, the more familiar she became. "I've seen her somewhere. I'm not sure where, but I've seen her."

"Do you want me to see if I can find her?"

"No, I got this one, I'll remember in a second or two."

"Where are you going?" Sanders asked when he saw Kane walk away. He wanted to finish the case and he needed him to do it.

"I have business to take care of," Kane replied. He hurried out the precinct and to his car. He made it to Flame in less than six minutes. He looked crazy running inside, but he had to see Carmen. Once he made it on her floor, his speed decreased when he took notice of her receptionist. The woman from the videotape, he took a minute to go back to his case. "Good morning, Cathy," he greeted.

"Good morning, Mr. Kane. Carmen is available. You can go inside."

"Oh, I know, I had a question for you. Have you seen one of those new Rolexes, it was a limited edition?"

Cathy nodded her head. "I had to pick one up for Carmen last year. It was a Christmas gift for King."

Kane took a step back from her desk. *How did I forget? She bought it for our son.* Kane muttered thanks before heading towards Carmen's office. He never expected King to be a thief, but his son pulled a fast one. Still, King's criminal behavior couldn't keep him from the task at hand. With Jay in Brookstone, his focused needed to be on his wife.

When Kane strolled into her office, Carmen was reviewing one of her newest designs with Tiara and Jerry. He didn't speak when he walked in, listening to their conversation as they stared at a mannequin.

"I swear, you two are racking my nerves over this dress," Carmen was saying. "I don't know whether to put it in the women's collection or with *Peaches*. I employ you two to help me, but you only want to fuss."

"It's her fault," Jerry said, pointing at Tiara.

Carmen rolled her eyes, but only because the disagreement was Tiara's fault. There was still tension from their conversation at Lucky's and Tiara was taking it out at work. Ready to dismiss her from the room, she turned around to see Kane standing in her office.

"I need to talk to you," he voiced.

"Okay, let me finish up here, and I'll be with you."

"No, I need to talk to you now." Kane walked towards her but paused in his step when Carmen raised her hand to him.

"Give me one second to finish up, okay?" Carmen turned towards Tiara and Jerry, but before she could speak, Kane cut her off.

"Carmen, we need to talk," he pressed.

"I heard you," Carmen shot back. "Give me one second. I promise. You'll have my undivided attention."

Kane listened as Carmen pointed out errors in the design. He let her continue for a minute longer until he saw Jerry walk towards the door. Although Tiara was still standing there, he grabbed Carmen's arm and pulled her into the bathroom. He then locked the door. "Did you know Jay was out of prison?"

Carmen wanted to run from the question. If she said yes, one word could take Kane to a dangerous place. If she said no, she could make it through the day without putting another wound in her marriage. "What are you talking about?" she shrieked. "Who let him out?" She put on a good act to hide everything she'd been doing. "Look, if he tries to contact me, I'll let you know. I promise."

"So, you haven't seen him?"

"No, Kane," Carmen told him, raising her voice. "That's what I just said."

Kane wondered why she was lying to him. He had pictures in his jacket pocket to prove she'd been meeting with Jay behind his back. Now, he had no choice, but to put her on blast. He reached in his jacket pocket, pulling out one of the pictures. "The Brookstone PD has been watching him since his release. From the looks of it, they've been watching you, too."

Carmen stared at the photograph, seeing a shot of her and Jay outside Old Town Bistro. About to reach for it, Kane threw it at her, allowing the photo to hit her in the chest. He then showed her another one, this one taken on Saturday when they were headed inside Lucky's. He threw it at her as well.

"You have the nerve to look me in the eye and lie to me?"

Carmen didn't say anything. She couldn't. Kane caught her in a bold face lie and all she could do was face the music. "I didn't want to hurt you. It happened so fast. It was just last week when Malik called and gave me the news. Then, Jay came here, and one thing led to another. We reconnected and we're trying to build a friendship. In fact, we're opening a restaurant."

"Wait a minute, I didn't hear right. You're opening a restaurant?"

"Jay owns the restaurant," she explained. "You know the drama his name brings. I agreed to let him use my name for the paperwork. My father is going to let us buy a building, Malik is helping find a chef, we're all in this together."

"You're fuckin' crazy," Kane yelled, losing it. "This motherfucker is a fuckin' schizophrenic and he has you putting your name on his business?"

Carmen backed away at Kane's rage. Her bathroom was small, so she only managed to take two or three steps. "Baby, listen to me. Jay has been nothing but a gentleman. I owe this to him. It's because of me he spent seventeen years in prison. The least I can do is help him rebuild his life. Think about what he came home to. He doesn't know his son, he lost—" Carmen's voice trailed off. She was getting ready to say Jay lost his girlfriend, yet she decided not to.

"Are you sleeping with him?"

Carmen's eyes became outstretched. "Did you seriously ask me that?"

"You've been sneaking around with him behind my back. You didn't come home Wednesday night. You claimed you were with someone then, but you said you lied to try and fuck my head up. Were you really telling the truth? Did you fuck him?"

"Hell no," Carmen yelled, reaching for his arm. She expected Kane to back away, yet he pushed her against the wall.

"Don't put your hands on me."

Carmen held her hands up in defense and watched as Kane reached inside his jacket pocket. He pulled out more photos to use against her. "Baby," she began, "my relationship with Jay is platonic. I didn't sleep with him. We didn't kiss. Nothing happened. He knows we're married."

The pictures in Kane's hand told a different story. "This one is at a lake. Y'all went to the park together? Why do you need to go to the park to talk about a damn restaurant? You're going out with him in public, but you didn't think I deserved to know he was out of prison? I don't get this shit, Carm. What the fuck are you doing?"

Kane wanted a response, but all he got was Tiara's loud voice on the other side of the door. She was asking if everything was okay. Kane was seconds away from telling her to fuck off.

"I never slept with him," Carmen cried. "We didn't do anything."

Carmen came towards him again, wrapping her arms around Kane's neck. He allowed her to get close, but it was a ploy to degrade her even more. He pulled her close to him, and even lifted her off her feet until she was seated on top of the bathroom sink.

"I can smell him on you," he whispered. "I know his fuckin' scent. I followed it for months until I got him in prison. I smell him again." Kane backed away from his wife, shaking his head. "You told me seventeen years ago you couldn't let him go. You said he would always be around. I didn't believe you, but now I do. He came back, you fell for him, and you gave him the same gift you gave me. You're weak when it comes to him. Just tell me, say you fucked him."

"I didn't do shit with him," Carmen screamed. "I'm only helping him with his business. He doesn't have shit because I took it from him."

"Stop fuckin' lying to me, Carm. Stop fuckin−" Kane punched the bathroom mirror. The glass made a crackling sound, which was followed by someone banging on the bathroom door. Tiara was on the other side, demanding to be let in. As if that wasn't enough, Jerry joined in.

Carmen didn't know what to do. Kane was out of control, and she couldn't say anything to make him believe she hadn't been with Jay. Desperate to save her marriage, she offered herself. "I'll prove it," she told him, unbuckling her pants. "Go ahead," she cried, "try me."

Kane studied her as she pulled down her pants. When her panties dropped to her ankles, he didn't know where to turn. His adrenaline was running, he was getting the itch and his blood was also smeared on her bathroom mirror. When he felt her hands on his pants, he knew where they were headed. In one swift move, his manhood was freed, and he slid it inside her kitty box. "Try me," she urged. Kane closed his eyes at the feel of her walls. The fit was perfect. She didn't feel any different than the night before. If anything, she felt better.

"See baby, this is yours," she moaned. Kane pushed her up against the bathroom sink, giving her every inch he could. "It's yours," she told him again. Kane had no choice, but to believe her. She was giving him her absolute best. He tried to contain his vocals as he began to climax. It was hard to do, and he knew Tiara and Jerry could hear their lovemaking.

"I love you," he whispered as he came inside her. "I love you," he repeated. A few seconds later, he came again. His eyes closed as he listened to Carmen climax. He held his position for a minute or so before pulling out of her. When he did, his eyes opened. He stared at his blood on the mirror. The sight of it brought him back to reality.

This is my wife. This is the woman I stood before God with and promised to love and care for till death. She told me she didn't do anything with him, and I didn't believe her. She slept with me to prove she hadn't been with him. How could I do this to her? It's my fault this whole thing happened. I was the one who stole her from him. I got us in this shit.

Kane became disgusted with himself. He didn't bother to clean himself off as he pulled his pants back up. Carmen dressed as well, but Kane couldn't bear to watch. Too disgusted, he unlocked the door, and ran out the bathroom. The move was the wrong one because Tiara and Jerry were both in the office, screaming at the top of their lungs when they saw the blood. Kane didn't care, though. He needed to get away from the scene. He didn't know what was happening, but for some reason he was turning into a monster. If he didn't get help now, he would become trapped.

***

For the first time, Kane wanted to call his mother and tell her about his marital problems. He hardly ever argued with his wife and none of their arguments had been as serious as the ones in the past week or so. Most of their arguments would last a couple of seconds and would never escalate to the point where they were cursing. Now, Kane didn't know what was happening. Although distraught over the issue, he decided not to call his mother. She didn't fancy Carmen all that well and if he told her the story, she would demand he get a divorce. His mother was against their union from the beginning. The only time she came around was when Carmen gave birth to Kristian. His baby girl was the gem, which created a cordial relationship between her and Carmen.

Since he wasn't seeking his mother's advice, he sat in his car outside the precinct, plotting his next move. The Triad requested for him to return to the agency to work on another narcotics case. He refused. Now, he needed to go. He couldn't stomach looking at his wife remembering what he did to her. She never should've been put in a situation where she had to sleep with him to prove her innocence. If they sexed again, he wondered if she would remember. Not wanting her pain on his conscience, Kane made up his mind.

He got out his car and headed to Sanders' desk. He picked up the videotapes from the jewelry store and returned to his office where he played each one. He knew his son was on the tape, but he had to watch it again. As he played the video, he watched the way the guy moved and without a doubt; he knew it was King. His son had a swagger all his own. The charge wasn't one King needed, but Kane had to turn him in. If he didn't, another officer would.

Kane stopped the tape once the cameras went black and listened as someone opened his office door. Harris walked inside despite not having an invitation.

"Are you okay?" the lieutenant asked. "I was trying to look out for you. Yes, Jay is free, but he's not the same man he was seventeen years ago. He's been attending his sessions and taking his medicine. We've been watching him. He wants to get better."

"I want to go to Cali," was Kane's reply. The lieutenant appeared shock. Kane knew it was because his answer had been no for weeks. "Go ahead and put me on the case. I'm ready to go."

"Are you sure? Have you talked to Carmen about this?" Harris was surprised at how Kane's decision changed. Still, he wasn't going to talk him out of it. "If that's what you want, it's a done deal. You can start training now. You've got six months to solve this thing."

"What about Tricia?" Kane asked.

"You have two months of training, meaning you have two months to secure her case and the robbery at Westland & Co. I'll make Sanders your partner, so you won't have too much on your plate."

Kane liked the idea. He would have to keep the trip to himself, but he had enough work to keep him away from the house. The case would hurt his wife, but he was doing what was best for them. When he returned, things would be better. He would even ask her if she wanted to renew their vows. A little time apart was all they needed. Once they reconnected, the spark would return. Certain of it, Kane made the call to the captain of the Triad. He told him; he was back.

The incident in her office was far from Carmen's mind. Even her husband wasn't on her brain. If anything, she was calling King back to back, trying to get him on the phone. With Kane aware of Jay's presence in Brookstone, it was a matter of time before the news hit. She had to tell her son the truth before the media did. She should've done it years ago, but she thought it was pointless. Jay was in prison and Kane was the perfect father to her son.

Little did she know; her son was trespassing on the property of Brookstone High. Clad in another unreleased design from the *King* collection, he stepped in the school's library where Coco claimed to spend third period. Taking a small break from his cartel duties, he spotted her at one of the computers in the back of the room. She didn't notice him until he sat next to her. "I think I may be lost," he joked.

Coco's eyes widened. "What are you doing here?"

King winked. "I'm a substitute teacher. The suit fooled them."

Coco smiled, seeing how devilish King was. "You're going to get in trouble, you know. Your mama can't bail you out of everything. How are things going with you two? Are y'all talking?"

"We have an understanding of each other," King expressed. "I told her I was trying to find out who I was, and she told me I needed to Google myself. I know she was joking because the only thing I'm going to find is a bunch of news articles about my arrests."

"True, but you should still try. There's a reason she told you to do it. Maybe, there was something she wanted you to see. Even if it is all your arrests, you can see your past and determine your future."

"You're right, let me stop playing."

King clicked Internet Explorer and once the webpage was up, he headed straight to Google. He first typed Jayceon Kane, but the only entry to come up was an article about his fight with Darnell. He proceeded to type in Jayceon Santiago Kane. He didn't think his middle name would make a big difference until he saw the numerous results. "Did you mean Jay Santiago? Who's that?" he asked, clicking one of the links.

Coco watched as images of a man came up. "Do you know him?" Coco had never seen the man, but his name was like King's. Her mouth formed an O when a picture of King's mother was displayed. She was in an orange jumpsuit and her hands were handcuffed behind her back. "Who is he?" He was ignoring her. He clicked on a picture of Jay and read the news article.

"After disappearing from the spotlight, Jay Santiago, the son of acclaimed New York politician, Hector Santiago, has finally emerged out the shadows. The Triad will speak on the investigation on tomorrow's edition of the *Today Show*. Santiago has been given a life sentence in prison without parole for murder, attempted murder, and the illegal possession and distribution of narcotics and weapons," King read.

He slid his chair back as he stared at Jigga. Jigga was Jay Santiago. There was more to the story, though. He swallowed. His light skin matched Jay's. They shared a similar name, yet his last name was Kane. *It doesn't make sense, though. Jay is supposed to be in jail for life. Why is he out? How the fuck is he out?*

King put the pieces together. He was lighter than Kristian because Kane wasn't his father. Jay Santiago was his father. He could look at him and make the comparison. Still, he wanted more. He went to another search result and learned Jay Santiago had been in a full-fledged relationship with his mother. In addition, the man was Puerto Rican, and once owned Sapphire, the abandoned building where he met with him and Malik. "I got to go," he said, standing up.

"King, wait, what's going on?" Coco exclaimed. She stood up as well ready to follow him to his next destination.

"I have to go," he repeated.

He placed a quick kiss on her cheek and left the library. Coco watched him as he left before turning to the computer screen. The article was no longer on the screen, but she didn't need to read it. She could tell from King's behavior the article was disturbing. She may not have known who Jay Santiago was, but it was obvious he was someone from Mrs. Kane's past. In addition, he was also someone connected to King.

23 | *A Time to Unveil*

King sped through the streets of Brookstone unsure of where to find Jay. He didn't remember the exit to get to his mansion, but he did know how to get to Sapphire. When he pulled in front of the building, he wasn't shocked to see Jay's Benz out front. The only person there, he was surprised to find the door unlocked. He let himself in, hearing Jay's voice from the second floor.

"We've locked in the building?" he heard him ask as he crept up the steps. "I have the suitcase ready whenever you need me to hand it over."

King stepped in the room. Jay pointed to his cell as if he was telling him not to interrupt. King could have cared less about the call. He let him know when he approached his desk. "Hang up," he ordered. Jay's face became tight, yet he didn't end the conversation. Instead, he finished it. From listening in, King learned he was on the phone with his mother. "So, you know Carmen Davenport-Kane?"

"You don't know who the fuck you're dealing with, do you?" Jay barked, no longer on the phone. He rose from his chair and came around the desk. "Maybe, you don't quite understand who I am. I don't tolerate disrespect from no one. You see me on the phone; you keep your ass at the door until I tell you to come in. You don't demand shit of me. The streets didn't teach you that?"

"A father's job is to teach his son."

Jay was taken aback. "What the fuck does that mean?"

"Yesterday, you invited me to your house to school me on the game. You told me everything about the cartel except for the biggest piece. You never told me why you let it fall. You never said why you needed me."

Jay swallowed before pulling out his wallet. He took out his license, handing it to King so he could see his real name. "Is that the lesson you felt you didn't get? Do you want to know who Jigga is? There you go. The answer is right there. Everything else is out there for you to read."

King stared at his license, receiving confirmation he didn't need. He knew Jigga was Jay Santiago. The man's looks hadn't changed in seventeen years. He handed the license back to Jay and pulled out his own. He handed it to him, but Jay didn't take it. "Here," he yelled, throwing it at him. It hit Jay in the chest. The license fell on the floor. Jay didn't pick it up, but he looked down to read the name. King was certain Jay saw his name inside his own.

King spoke first since Jay was tongue-tied. "Did you know my mother was pregnant? Am I a surprise to you like you are to me?"

It took Jay a few seconds to get each word out. "She...told me...the day... my warehouse...was raided."

"I saw you with her. Y'all were downtown. I knew something was up. You don't look like any of the guys who work at Flame. That scar," King ran his hand down the left side of his face, "told me something wasn't right. My mother doesn't hang with people like you."

Jay didn't want to focus on Carmen. The moment in front of him would only come once in his lifetime. When it was gone, he could never get it back. "I waited seventeen years to meet you," he expressed. "I dreamt about you. I always wondered what you were doing, when you took your first step, I wanted to know what you looked like."

Jay walked to his desk and opened the top drawer. After King left his house on Sunday, he went on a hunt for a picture of his grandfather. He was anxious to see if there was a resemblance and he learned there was. Now, he wanted King to see. He brought the 8x10 frame to him and put it beside his face. When King caught a glimpse, his son jumped. "It's like looking in a mirror, isn't it? I bet you went all your life, trying to figure out who you were. No more searching, King." He handed him the picture. "Vincent Santiago, he's your great-grandfather. That's who you look like."

King stared at the photo. "This is where I belong?" He bit his lip to keep from crying yet the tears still came. "I didn't look like anyone, act like anyone. I was the fuckin' black sheep of my family. Do you know how that shit felt? I could've had you, though. Why didn't you reach out to me?"

"I wasn't always like this, King. Is that what they call you?"

"Yeah, they always call me King. My mama only says Jayceon when she's angry or being sentimental. My father never says it." He wiped the tears off his face. "I'm sorry, Jay, this is...this is new to me. I don't even know what to do."

"You do what you've been doing," Jay replied. "You continue to learn the game and chase this paper. In the meantime, we learn each other. Kane may have raised you, but you're still my son. No one can teach you how to be a Santiago better than me. Right now, we're the last two standing."

"What about my mom?"

"What about her?" Jay asked. "Carmen and I have our own agreement. You probably heard a little bit of it."

"I want her to own up to what she did. She lied to me. I want to confront her."

"There's a reason for everything. You'll find out in due time."

Jay held out his hand for the picture of Vincent. When King gave it to him, he set it on his desk. The room went quiet for a few seconds until he heard King's footsteps. His son placed his hand on his shoulder and Jay tried to control his tears. He lost the battle when King embraced him. While he didn't know where their relationship was going, he made a promise to himself. From that day forward, he was going to make up for every single year of King's life. Today was only the beginning of what was to come.

***

Jay remembered King's request to speak to his mother when Carmen telephoned him Tuesday morning. She had finished checking out the building for Blue Magic and was ready to collect the money for the down payment. Jay agreed to meet with her and when he finally saw her, he asked her to join him for dinner. He just didn't tell her King would be there. She seemed a little hesitant, but after a bit of coaxing, she agreed.

Now, they were sitting across from each other at Cipriani's while King waited in the lobby. With a champagne flute in their hands, they toasted to their latest victory.

Carmen told him she wanted to discuss an issue. "Kane knows you're here," she announced. "He also knows we've been meeting. I want to help you, but this friendship is ruining my marriage. I feel like, one day I'm going to have to decide."

Jay set his glass on the table. "I ran into him at the bank. To tell you the truth, I knew this conversation was coming."

Carmen closed her eyes for a brief second. Kane never told her he saw Jay at the bank. If she was honest with herself, Kane hadn't told her anything since he left her office. He came in late Monday night and today, she was out the door before he woke. "I guess he saw you and did some digging. That's the detective in him."

"So, what are you saying? You give me the restaurant and leave me hanging? I know you don't want to do that. You're excited about Blue Magic like I am."

"It's like I gotta choose between this restaurant and my marriage. What good is it to have a successful career if I don't have my husband?"

Jay lowered his eyes only because he could hear the concern in Carmen's voice. It also pained him to hear her love for Kane. His feelings for her were still there and he had plans to win her back. "I need you, Peaches," he whispered. "I only have three people in my corner right now; you, Malik, and my new protégé."

The words slipped from Jay's mouth. While he wasn't ready for King to make his entrance, the time had come.

Carmen became curious. "Who is your protégé?"

"Forget I said anything," Jay replied. He picked up his fork, eating more of his food. "If you gotta bow out, you gotta bow out. I have the building. I can handle the renovations. We'll be good."

"Okay, and what if I choose to stay on, I still want to know who the third person is. My name is the only one on this paperwork. Is it another female? I can't expect you to be single forever. One of these days, I will be attending your wedding."

Jay was certain he wasn't getting married. If he did, it would be to her, and the probability was lower than he could count. "Do you want to meet him?" he asked, revealing his partner's gender. "I can get him here." Carmen nodded. "I'll get him, Peaches, hold on." Jay stood up from the table and headed towards the lobby. He motioned for King to come, and his son followed him to the table.

Carmen was sipping her champagne when she saw a figure in white move beside her. She turned to see King. His facial expression was deadly. Not quite sure what to think, she looked at Jay. When her eyes went back to King, she swore she saw steam, flowing from his pores. Tears streamed down her face as she shook her head. "It wasn't supposed to be like this," she told him. "I tried to tell you…I called you…like fifty times yesterday. I left messages."

Jay intercepted only because King wasn't talking. His son's expression spoke volumes. "We talked about this last night," he explained. "I told King everything. He knows how we met, he knows about Pierre, Carlos, and the pink diamond. You've hid enough stuff from him, and I didn't want to do the same. If I didn't tell him, the streets would. The news broke today of my release. I've already had a few reporters outside my house."

Carmen's lip trembled as she stared at her firstborn. "He said he didn't want you. I was twenty-two, fresh out of prison. I was scared. Kane was there and he offered to give you the life I wanted you to have."

"Fuck you," King growled. "All these years I contemplated who I was, and you lied to me? Fuck you."

"What do you want from me?" Carmen yelled. "Kane loved you like you were his. He took care of you. He taught you everything you know."

"I have nothing but respect for him," King admitted, "but he's still at fault. Why deny me the chance to have a relationship with my father? Who are you to make that decision?"

Carmen wiped her face as the conversation attracted attention from other guests. Things were getting heated, and she dreaded ever coming to Cipriani's. "I did what I thought was right. I was young, I was pregnant, and Kane was ready for marriage. Who else was going to take me?"

"Tell him about the money."

Carmen was in complete shock. She was so used to getting his checks on the regular, she had forgotten about King's trust fund. Even with them both in her face, she hadn't thought about the money.

"What money?" King's eyes darted back and forth between his parents. "I have money. How much do I have?"

"I gave your mother ten thousand every week. This is the first week I haven't paid," Jay explained. "Do I still owe you, Carm?"

Carmen wiped her face although it was useless. The trust fund held a rather large amount and King would be shocked to learn he could afford a mansion. "You have a little over eight million dollars. You can't touch the money until you turn eighteen and even then, I can make it unavailable until you're twenty-one."

King jumped from his seat. "You mean to tell me; I was stressed as hell about paying Lil' Noc three grand and I'm a fuckin' multi-millionaire? I should fuck your ass up."

Jay grabbed King's neck the second he heard the threat. He nearly put his son in a headlock trying to get him in his seat. When King was calm enough for him to let go, he watched as he knocked over Carmen's champagne flute. As if that wasn't enough, King started another tirade until Carmen got up from the table. Without another word, she grabbed her purse and ran out the restaurant.

"It was not supposed to go down like this," Jay said through gritted teeth. "We talked about this. What you did tonight was not acceptable."

King didn't utter a single word. His anger wouldn't let him. He hadn't found closure and his pain rested in the middle of his chest, heavy like a boulder. When he would get over it, he didn't know. Time held all wounds yet his was only growing deeper.

***

All Carmen's emotions could easily be read as she stumbled through the parking lot of Cipriani's. Her heart was broken, and she knew who was to blame. It was her plan to tell King about Jay, but someone had beaten her to it. That someone was Malik. He had to be the one who set the whole thing up. Certain of it, she was ready to unleash the second she could get in his presence.

The second she was in her car; she dialed his number. He answered on the third ring. She told him they needed to meet. Ten minutes later, they were staring each other down in one of the parking decks of Flame. Her tears had dried, but her urge to rip him apart was stronger than before.

"I'm going to fuckin' kill you," she threatened.

Malik took a step back. "What?"

"I had every intention to tell King about Jay. Somehow, you thought it was your job and did it before I could. You had to go behind my back. Was this my payback for what happened at Lucky's?"

"I may have put them in the same room together," Malik admitted, "but that doesn't mean I told King about Jay. If you want to know the truth, I didn't even know King knew about him. They must've pulled a fast one."

"You meant to do it, Malik. I know you. You're sneaky."

"Don't give me the bullshit tonight. I'm not sneaky. Jay needed someone to run his businesses and you needed help keeping King out the streets. Jay wanted to give his businesses to his son, so I set it up. How did you find out?"

"We were having dinner at Cipriani's and Jay mentioned he had a protégé. I demanded to know who it was and lo and behold, King walks in. I promise you, Malik, he deserves an Oscar for the best cursing scene *not* in a movie."

"How did you expect him to react?" Malik wiped his face as he saw the deeper issue. "You're so concerned about King, but you have a bigger problem on your hands. Jay is fuckin' bipolar. Dr. Stuart also diagnosed him with schizophrenia. Although he has medicine to control his behavior and mood swings; guess what, he's still a fuckin' schizophrenic. Any day now he can flip on all of us."

"Fuck you, Malik," Carmen shot back. "You played me at Lucky's, and you did it again with my son. I'm warning you, Malik, stay away."

Malik blinked his eyes. "What did you say to me?"

"You heard me. Stay away from my family. I don't want anything to do with you. Since you wanted to scheme, trying to make sure Jay's legacy continued through his son, you ruined the relationship King, and I, were trying to build. Now lose your relationship with my family. Pretend you've never met us. We go our way; you go yours."

"Are you out your fuckin' mind?"

"Bitch, I might be."

Malik walked up to Carmen, his face less than a millimeter away from hers. "I can't believe your ungrateful ass. After all the shit I've done for you; you feed me this. Who do you think was working with Kane to get your ass out of prison? Who took care of your kids when you wanted to fly overseas and across the damn country to promote your little fashion designs? I signed the paperwork to be their godfather. This is how you repay me?"

"Yeah, motherfucker, this is how I repay you."

Malik felt so much rage it was only natural for him to hit below the belt. "How could Rakim love you so goddamn much? Then, Kane had the nerve to marry you. If that wasn't bad enough, Jay went crazy over you. Shit, the devil doesn't wear Prada. It wears Flame."

"You'll never know, will you, Malik? You were never given the chance to love me. Your brother ruined that for you."

"I never wanted to," he told her. "Why have everyone's leftovers?"

"Because you would've proved you were worthy to have me, too."

Carmen knew how to mess with his head. Like any man, Malik was weak when it came to a woman. Every female was sitting on a goldmine, which men couldn't resist.

"I am more than—" Malik stopped. "I could've gotten you any day of the week, Carm. I didn't try because I'm loyal. I'm not my brother, Kane, or Carlos. I don't need to steal anyone's girl."

"Come on, Malik, we both know you didn't have the chance. I never could have fallen in love with you. You were Jay's sidekick. You didn't stand on your own like Rakim and you always let Jay intimidate you. Carlos, on the other hand, wasn't scared to break out on his own. I knew you wanted to, though. You wanted everything they had."

Carmen took a step closer to him. She could see the struggle in Malik's eyes. His mind was telling him he was being fucked while his body was telling him he had a one-time opportunity in front of him. Her body was pressing down on his, her hand was cupping his face while his arm slowly wrapped around her waist. Seconds away from kissing, Carmen spoke just above a whisper. "Didn't Tiara warn you about me? She knows I'm manipulative. You know I don't want you. You never would've been able to get with me. It's obvious, though, the thought ran through your mind."

She noticed the change in his facial expression when he realized he'd been played. "Have a good day, Malik. Do what I said, too. Stay away from my family. If you don't, I'll tell Kane and Tiara about that." Carmen pointed at the bulge, which had formed in his pants. She chuckled to herself as she walked back to her car. Seconds later, her phone vibrated in her purse. By the time she retrieved it, she had already missed Kane's call. Glad he left her a voicemail message; she listened to it as she started her car.

"Baby, I hate to tell you like this, but I don't have a choice. I'm looking for King right now. I don't know if you heard about it on the news, but he's responsible for the robbery at Westland & Co. I'm going to be out all night until I find him. If you know where he is, tell him to turn himself in. It'll be a much easier process for me."

24 | *Battlefield*

It was no surprise to Kane when Carmen called him. The robbery at Westland & Co. hadn't reached her ears so he had the pleasure of explaining everything. The drama with King kept them from discussing their own problems. Carmen accepted what he had to do, and Kane spent most of the night searching Brookstone for his son. He didn't find him until Wednesday afternoon when he spotted him near the Blue Lagoon. It took him a second or two to recognize him because his son was dressed in a solid gray suit versus his regular jeans and Timbs. Unsure of what sparked the change, his intention was to have a one on one conversation before the arrest.

King didn't appear nervous and agreed to chat with him inside the bar. Neither of them ordered drinks although Kane needed one when King questioned him about Jay. Before he could answer, King dispelled everything he knew. He even told him he was staying at Jay's house. For two minutes, Kane was unable to speak. Then, he admitted he wasn't King's biological father and offered a heartfelt apology. The blow wasn't as bad as he expected. However, he did notice the tension in King's face when he told him he was aware of his involvement with the robbery downtown. His son didn't become irate, but his voice shook as he realized he was staring at another charge.

"I can't be in jail right now," King told him. "I have too much going on. What are my options? Is there sufficient evidence?"

Kane nodded his head. All the evidence was in his possession and had been viewed by Sanders and the lieutenant. They both were expecting him to return to the precinct with his son in handcuffs. "You don't have any options. If you turn yourself in, you have a shot at bail. It might help if you return everything you stole."

King wiped the sweat off his face. According to his mother and Jay, he had plenty of money to pay the bail. He just couldn't touch the money until he was eighteen. If he got one of them to pay it, he could give them their money back on his eighteenth birthday. Nonetheless, he would only be free for a few months before the case went to court. Then, he would receive a prison sentence, which would ultimately keep him from his duties with the Santiago cartel. Not the route he wanted to take, he was stuck between a rock and a hard place. In his opinion, his father made the decision for him when he pulled out a set of handcuffs. His time was up. King made the stance he knew well. He stood up and put his hands behind his back. 'Don't mess up my suit," he mumbled. "I paid too much for it."

Kane handcuffed his son and led him out the bar. He could feel everyone's eyes on him including Ms. Rita. His Jeep was parked about a block or two away, so the walk allowed any passers-by to see the arrest. King didn't appear embarrassed. If anything, he was apologetic.

Once in the backseat, King asked, "Do you think Mama will lend me the money for bail? I can pay her back with the money in my trust fund. I can pay the lawyer fees, too. I know Clement is expensive." He spoke of his mother's attorney.

Kane looked in the rearview mirror at his son. "When has your mother ever said no? I've said it plenty of times, but she still comes to your rescue. Today shouldn't be any different."

King remembered the incident at Cipriani's. "I hope she pays it," he replied. "I pray she does."

Kane started up the car as the word pray echoed in his mind. *When had King ever prayed?* He wondered what kind of influence Jay was having on him. *Maybe, Carmen is right. Maybe, Jay has changed.*

"Tell Kristian and Malachi, I'm sorry," King said, interrupting his thoughts. "I know they were counting on me."

"I'll let 'em know. No worries."

***

The news of King's arrest hit the local news around three o'clock that afternoon. Far away from a television or the Internet, the news hadn't reached Kristian and Coco's ears. Too busy shopping at the Brookstone Galleria, the only thing on their minds was the money they were spending. Since Akaila wasn't with them, Coco wanted to take advantage of the time she had with her friend. She also was debating about telling her about Jay. King hadn't spoken to her since Monday, which put her nerves on edge. The only thing calming her was the diamond and gold necklace around her neck. It was the only thing she had to represent their relationship. Nevertheless, a part of her questioned if it was a relationship. Only a few days had gone by since their kiss and King never said he was her boyfriend. She also never claimed to be his girlfriend.

"Why do you keep playing with it?" Kristian asked as they headed out of H&M. "I know you like it, but dang, leave it alone. Where did you get it from, anyway? I know your mother's job at *XXL* doesn't pay for a necklace like that. That piece is exquisite."

Coco wasn't going to tell her the piece was from King because the situation was uncomfortable enough. If Kristian knew she kissed her brother, it would probably create tension in their friendship. It also put Kristian in the middle if things didn't go as planned. Still, Kristian didn't let up. The necklace captivated her, and Kristian kept talking about it even when they decided to head home. Almost to the exit, they passed a police officer who stopped in his tracks at the sight of her. Coco knew it was because of the necklace. He was the second person in a row who glared at her.

The cop put her in the mindset of Toni Childs' husband on *Girlfriends*. She smiled at him, but the look he gave her wasn't one of admiration.

"Hi, ladies," he greeted, his eyes still on Coco's neck. "I couldn't help but notice your necklace. Ma'am, that's a real expensive piece."

"I know," Coco mumbled, running her fingers along the necklace.

"You know, a jewelry store was robbed a couple of days ago. It was Westland & Co. downtown. I'm not saying you were involved, but you need to come down to the station with me. A necklace like the one you're wearing was stolen. Let us look at it and you'll be free to go. I'm Officer Sanders by the way. Can you tell me your name?"

"Look, Officer Sanders, I didn't steal this necklace. I'm not going anywhere with you because I haven't done anything." Coco raised her voice at his accusation.

"Ma'am, I'm asking you in a polite manner to comply with a direct order. The last thing I want is for anyone to go to jail over this. I only need to see if the necklace matches up with the one that was stolen. I mean, it may not even be real."

"It is real," Coco yelled in response.

Kristian grabbed her arm aware of the seriousness of the situation. "Look, let's just go with him and we'll call my father," she whispered.

"I'm not going anywhere," Coco yelled. "My necklace isn't stolen." She jerked her arm out Kristian's grasp, watching as the officer pulled out handcuffs.

"Ma'am, you leave me no choice," he told her.

Coco became frantic over the idea of being arrested. She tried to back away, yet the cop grabbed her, pushing her against a store window. He pulled her hands behind her back, and she listened as Kristian made a quick phone call to her father. Tears of embarrassment flew down her face. She knew in her heart the necklace wasn't stolen. King respected her enough to not give her a piece of stolen merchandise. If he didn't, their relationship was over before it began.

"My parents are on their way," Kristian announced after the officer read Coco her rights. "Everything is going to be okay." Kristian wasn't worried because she knew her father was going to take care of everything. He told her to follow the officer's orders and to make sure Coco remained calm. Kristian trusted him despite the look of horror on her friend's face. She told Coco to calm down, but the words went in one ear and out the other.

***

Carmen rushed to the police station six minutes after Kristian's phone call. She didn't tell her daughter about King's arrest, but she knew the story would reach her ears soon. Kane told her they were in an interrogation room, and he ordered an officer to escort her there once she reached the station. While she should've called Coco's parents, it was best to keep them at bay until Coco was released. The plan was to have all charges dropped against Coco within the next ten minutes.

Upon entry, she noticed Coco sitting at a table, tissue in hand. Kristian was beside her while Officer Sanders stood in the middle of the room. She was only there for a few seconds before Kane walked in with King behind him. The first time she had seen her son since the incident at Cipriani's, Carmen turned away. Although she wasn't looking at him, she could hear him questioning why Coco was there. Obviously unaware, King fired question after question, yet Coco didn't speak.

"King has already confessed to the crime," Kane announced. "I've met with Harris on the matter and all we need is a confession from Miss Masterson to let her go. Hopefully, we can get a bail hearing in the morning. If we don't get a confession," Kane pointed at Coco, "she'll be joining him. Right now, she can take the fall."

"She didn't steal it," King barked. "I gave it to her. You arrested her?" King noticed the handcuffs around Coco's wrists. "Why the fuck did you do that shit? You know she didn't steal it." King glared at Coco, trying to get her attention. "You know I owed Lil' Noc money. I was desperate and I slipped. You weren't supposed to take the fall. I never would put you in that situation. I gave you the necklace because you were there for me. Remember when I came to your house? The necklace was my way of saying thank you."

Carmen rolled her eyes when she realized her son had done one of Jay's old tricks. King hadn't known his father long and he was already rubbing off on him. Jay did the same thing to her at the beginning of their courtship. She grunted at the thought and excused herself from the room. The situation was severe, and she was ready to give Jay his first experience with parenting. While everyone remained inside, she called him. By the time she hung up, Kane was at her side, asking her about bail. She was quick in her response because of Coco's current predicament. "I'm through with his mess," she told Kane. "I'm not paying one red cent. King needs to lie in the shit he creates."

Carmen didn't feel the least bit guilty about what she said. Kane was shocked, but he shouldn't have been. If he wanted his son back on the streets, he could use his money to make it happen. She knew what was in his personal account and while it didn't compare to hers, his money could get the job done. If he didn't want to pay the bail then there was Jay, who was walking towards them with two officers beside him. The moment was awkward, and Carmen moved in between him and Kane.

"We all are King's parents," she began. "We're going to deal with this as adults and leave the past where it is. I'm not paying to get him out. If you two want to cough up the money, go ahead. It just won't come from me."

Jay snuck a glance at Kane before heading in the interrogation room. Kane didn't deserve anything more than that. Whatever devilment King had gotten into, he would clear up. Money may have been low since he was paying out the fees for his restaurant, but he would work something out. If he had to, the restaurant would be put on hold until the New Year.

When he walked in the room, Kristian waved at him. He gave her a smile before approaching King. He started with his questions.

In the meantime, all eyes were on King and Jay's conversation. Carmen and Kane returned to the room while Kristian tried to figure out if Jigga put him up to the robbery. She pushed the thought aside when she remembered the robbery occurred prior to them meeting. Certain Jigga wasn't a part of it, she turned to her parents.

"Why did you call him?" she heard her father ask.

"He needs to be here just as much as you do," Carmen stated. "We are all in this together." Carmen glanced at her husband. His temple was throbbing, and his right hand was balled into a fist.

"I'm a part of his life now," Jay shot back, having heard Kane's question. "You may not want me to be, but I'm here."

"Not for long," Kane replied.

He headed in his direction, which forced Jay to stand up. When they squared off, Carmen moved in between them again, placing her hand on Jay's chest. She knew what he could do, but she couldn't let him get a murder charge. "Both of you need to sit down. We are not about to do this here. We have a bigger situation to deal with."

"He thinks he can walk in here and try to take over," Kane yelled. "He hasn't done shit for King for seventeen years. He doesn't get that luxury. You shouldn't have called him. We should've handled this."

Carmen closed her eyes for a split second. When her eyes opened again, Kristian and Coco wore indescribable expressions. While she wanted to explain the situation, both Jay and Kane were barking insults left and right at each other.

"I don't even want to bury the hatchet with you," Jay replied. "For seventeen years, I wondered what I would say to you if we ever met again. To be honest, I don't want to say shit. I want to slit your fuckin' throat."

The threat was enough to set Kane off. Carmen tried her best to hold him back. Sanders ran to her aid, so she went to Jay who attempted to throw a punch in her husband's direction. He was too strong for her and before she knew it, Kristian was at her side, trying to keep Jay from striking her father.

"You don't have to hold me back," Jay barked, pushing Carmen away. "Let him go. We can handle this as men since he wants a challenge. I've been waiting on this day since they let me out confinement. Let me go, Peaches."

The sound of her nickname set something off in Kane. He charged at Jay. It only made the situation worse because she was in the middle. Blows were exchanged until Sanders managed to pull Kane away. Jay was quick on his feet, but she managed to block him from going at her husband.

"Move the fuck out my way, Carm. You're not going to stop me from killing him," Jay yelled.

"You're not killing shit," Kane retorted, spitting blood out his mouth. A direct result of a blow, he was ready for round two.

Jay fired back. "You still can't stand that I fucked your wife. I didn't kill your sperm, Kane. God did."

Jay's comment hit the nail on the head. Kane charged at him, pushing Kristian down in the process. She tried to grab him, but it was no use. Jay returned the force until King stood up, moving in between them. Both Jay and Kane crashed into him, all three of them collapsing on the floor where Kristian was. Ready to get the situation under control, she grabbed Kristian while Sanders pulled Kane away. The tension was leveling off until a startling scream sounded from Coco's mouth.

A nine millimeter pistol was in her husband's hand. The gun was pointed at Jay.

Jay pulled a gold Desert Eagle pistol out his waistband. The room became filled with police officers. Carmen ordered them not to shoot because she knew they would fire at Jay first. Before she could get to him, King moved in front of him, shielding Jay from any bullets. The move silenced the room. Kane then dropped his gun. A look of disappointment was on his face from seeing his son protect Jay. Without another word, Kane left the room.

25 | *Breakthrough*

The effect of the afternoon weighed heavily on Carmen's heart. Although she and Jay discussed everything in vivid detail, she couldn't sleep. To add to her nervousness, Kane hadn't returned home. She was forced to sit Kristian down alone and tell her the truth about her brother's paternity. Her daughter had more questions than she could stomach, but she got through all of them.

Early Thursday morning, she got up, and headed to the precinct where King was held. Harris was the only person in the Narcotics division and granted her access to her son. She met with him in one of the interrogation rooms and she could tell the night hadn't been easy for him. "I had to come here," she told him. "I couldn't sleep with everything going on. I knew you were the only comfort I was going to find."

"You don't need to be here," King replied. "I was the one who fucked up. You tried to help me, but I didn't want to change. This is my last straw, though. I'm tired."

"What made you realize you ran your course?"

"My father." King realized he needed to clarify. "Jay told me you weren't going to pay bail. I was upset at first, but then I understood. Why should you pay it? You've been covering my ass for years. Maybe, I need to sit down for a while. If I wasn't looking for fast cash, Coco wouldn't have been arrested. Everything falls in my hands. I ruined our relationship before it started."

"I know it hurts, baby." Carmen grabbed his hands, holding them in her own. "You're going to get her back. It just takes some time."

"I know I am. Jay already told me he's going to get me out. He doesn't want me to be like him. He gave me the same spiel you did." King paused. "I promise you. Whenever I get out; I'm leaving this shit behind. I'm gonna help Jay with his businesses, but that's it. I can't do this anymore. There's no point."

"It sounds like a plan." Carmen parted her lips to say more until Harris came in the room. He told her their time was up and offered to escort her back to the lobby while another officer took King to his cell.

Not quite finished with the conversation, Carmen hated to leave on that note. It was a privilege to be granted access to her son, so she didn't put up an argument. She simply told King she loved him and followed Harris to the lobby. Her son said Jay planned on getting him out, but she wasn't certain how he was going to do it. The building for Blue Magic almost put him in the red, which was why he was forced to apply for a business loan. Carmen wasn't going to bend on her decision, so she was eager to see what Jay came up with.

***

Only nine o'clock, Jay hadn't come up with a solution to paying his son's bail. His checking account was almost maxed out and his savings had experienced a drought. To add to the madness, a bail hearing hadn't been scheduled. He didn't know how much he needed, which meant, he didn't know where to start. Carmen already said no, but he didn't know if Kane had the money to put up.

Unsure of what he was going to do, Jay listened as someone rung his doorbell. He thought for sure Carmen had stopped by until he found Malik on the other side. His best friend held up a copy of *The Brookstone Times*.

"I know you're heated with me," Malik began. "I knew about the robbery, but I didn't think they would catch him. Hopefully, we can keep the men we did get. Now—" Jay interrupted him as he let him into the house.

"Carmen isn't paying his bail," Jay told him, "so everything is on me. I don't know how much I need, but I gotta find this money fast."

Malik stuffed his hands in his pocket. "I was going tell you about King. I was waiting for the right time."

"I can't worry about that shit right now. My son is looking at a couple of years in prison. He agreed to give everything back, well, what he has, so hopefully the judge won't hurt him too bad. I just need to get this money without setting us back. If the cartel was a go, this wouldn't be a problem. We would have the money."

Malik debated about voicing his thoughts. Jay didn't want to sit down with Kane, but if they talked one and one, they could come to a compromise. "King has three parents, not two. If you ask me, you and Kane need to come up with the money. Carmen has been bailing him out for years. She's paid for him to be in treatment centers, therapy, she's done it all. Maybe, Kane needs to step to the plate. I know he got a good million off you. That money gotta be sitting around somewhere."

Jay was against the idea until he thought about it further. If he could control his anger for at least twenty minutes, he could get the money King needed. It would stop him from going in the hole and protect everything he was trying to do. "That could work," he voiced, thinking aloud. "Kane gotta be open to the idea. Maybe, I can try and talk to him. It's worth a shot."

"I agree," Malik replied. "It's best to catch him now before another case gets thrown his way. Don't let me hold you up."

Jay's face broke into a smile. He took Malik's advice and headed to the Brookstone PD. While he wasn't fearful of meeting with Kane, he did have a gut of nervousness. Police officers followed him the moment he pulled up and even now, they had him trapped. He came in peace, yet they were ready to gun him down the second they saw him. Instead of causing a scene, he knocked on Kane's door. Then, he tried the doorknob. The office was unlocked, and he went inside, seeing Kane at his desk. "I need to talk to you."

"Get out."

His words were stern, but Jay didn't back down. He closed the door behind him and took a seat across from Kane. "I need your help. If King's bail is over a hundred thousand dollars, he will be in jail until he's sentenced. I think we both will agree we don't want to see him there."

"I stand behind my wife's decision. If she says no, I say no. If you're lucky, the judge will only require ten percent. If so, you should be able to afford it. I know you have a briefcase or two hidden somewhere."

"There you go again, taking another cheap shot," Jay muttered. "We both know a judge isn't going to grant that. King has already made headlines and my release has, too. Pretty soon, the story is going to break that he's my son. When it does, all hope for him is gone. Every law enforcement agency in New York hates the name Santiago. You know that. You work for the Triad. He deserves another chance."

"Is this what this is about? Does he deserve another chance, or do you want one? You can't be a father if he's in prison."

"I do want a second chance. I want to help raise my son."

For the first time since Jay walked in the room, Kane met eyes with him. "Don't give me that sappy shit. I know your intentions. You don't want King. You could care less about him. The only thing you want is Carmen. I've studied you, Jay. I know your intentions."

Jay chuckled, expecting his response. "You will never let that shit slide, will you? Must I remind you that you stole my girlfriend? It wasn't the other way around. Carmen and I never broke up. You came, took her, and married her. You signed King's birth certificate, showing the world how you were born without a heart. Unlike you, I have one. You seem to know me so well, but you don't know your wife. I'm not the one you need to be concerned about. Did you forget I was Carmen's first? I taught her everything she knows and now you're reaping the benefits. Make her mad and you're fucked. See, I knew Carmen when she was innocent. She was a virgin, untouched, wouldn't harm a fly. Then, her ambition got the best of her, and she turned into a manipulator. She's a charmer who knows she can get anything she wants. It's what you love and hate about her."

Jay swallowed before he continued. "Unfortunately, I was too weak to handle her. She got the best of me, and I ended up trying to kill her in my own house. If you've ever seen that side of her then you've probably jumped on her your damn self. No one likes to have their brain fucked with. Carmen's good at that. She can make you think she loves you and in the same breath say you don't mean shit to her. She did that to me. She fucked me one day and the next day she was fuckin' my best friend. That's enough to make any person go off the deep end. Don't you agree?"

Kane didn't want to admit he was right. Carmen was a manipulator. "I've been married to her for seventeen years. I know more about her than you ever could. Your little eight months of dating doesn't compare to our marriage."

"We only needed eight months," Jay shot back. "Like I said, I'm not the one you need to be concerned about. I respect your marriage. My problem is with King, don't get it twisted."

Kane stood from his desk, wanting the conversation to be over. "I gave you my answer. You're free to go."

"Fine then." He gotten nowhere. "I'll wait until the bail hearing to see what I need. Hopefully, Carmen will change her mind."

"She won't and neither will I."

"We'll see," Jay told him, unlocking the door. He stepped outside of Kane's office and noticed the large number of cops who were standing there. He counted fifteen and the number made him shake his head. Instead of taunting them, he only winked in their direction before leaving the precinct.

26 | *Transition*

December

Four weeks after Jay's meeting with Kane, the bail hearing was set. When the judge read the amount needed for King to make bail, Jay knew he couldn't pull the amount on his own. He couldn't ask Malik to help because he offered to use his funds to keep their operation going. Tiara wasn't an option, and neither was Carmen. The only other choice he had was to give up something he loved. He decided to get a change of scenery. He called his realtor and put his house up for sale. A week later, he had a potential buyer. The sale would give him the money for King, help fund his businesses, and buy him a new place to stay with incentives.

Jay felt it was time to let the memories go. He even spoke to Dr. Stuart about the move. She was proud of his progress, but Jay knew something was missing. For a while, he thought it was the holiday season until he realized the issue was much deeper.

The lack of companionship put a burden on his fresh start. For seventeen years, he was forced to be celibate. His actions landed him in confinement and his rights were stripped of him. While he heard the rumors of how the female guards were giving out extra loving, none of them approached him. He was the black Hannibal, the man they were afraid of despite his beautiful hazel eyes. He tried to seduce them through his mask, yet it never worked. When he made progress and a judge granted his release from confinement, he started to get advances from other inmates. Each one he ignored and eventually, he resorted to fantasy. Carmen came to him every time he needed her, his own hand, relieving him of years of torture and pain. Still, it wasn't the same.

He needed more than sex. He needed a wife. What pained him was that he couldn't find one woman who wanted to be with him. His rap sheet scared women away. The only woman who could handle him was Carmen and she pledged her love to Kane. Despite the growth in their friendship, Carmen never gave him the idea she wanted to get back together. If anything, she made it clear she only wanted to see him win.

The decision to choose celibacy was a hard one and Dr. Stuart wasn't ready for him to give up. When she asked him if he felt like Carmen was it for him, Jay said yes. He told her it was either Carmen or no woman at all. Not because she was the only woman he ever truly loved, but because she was the only woman who could handle him. It would be too dangerous to bring in anyone new. Certain of it, Jay made his decision. He would spend his life alone.

***

The holiday season wasn't any easier for Kane. He had thrown himself into preparing for the case in California, an assignment he still hadn't told his wife about. He was now in his final month of training and ignored all problems in his household. His relationship with Carmen was nonexistent because of Jay and he still hadn't adopted Akaila and Malachi. Carmen already viewed them as hers, but they weren't. To make matters worse, he didn't know anything about Tricia. His home life was falling apart while his career was booming.

He felt guilty about the situation and enlisted Minister Harrison to help him make sense of his demons. His relationship with his wife was going down the drain because she continued to help Jay with his restaurant. His anger over the issue even made him consult a lawyer for a divorce. He didn't go through with it because he couldn't live without Carmen. She created a lifestyle for him, which he wasn't ready to walk away from. Therefore, he sought spiritual counseling to help him stay in the marriage. It was hard for him to admit his faults, but once he started talking, he felt like bricks were coming off his chest.

"I'm glad you're finally saying something," Minister Harrison told him. "We all have problems in our marriage, but we're afraid to admit it. Admittance is the first step in solving the problem."

"I wanted to get some help," Kane responded. He went on to tell him about Tricia and the incident at her house. He then shared the story of what happened when he came home. He wanted to make sure he gave both sides of the story. In the end, Minister Harrison asked if he confronted his daughter about the incident. She was, however, the one who pulled him off Carmen. The conversation had never taken place. Kane assumed Kristian knew he made mistake.

"You need to talk to your daughter about what happened. You need to tell her that kind of behavior is unacceptable. You don't want her husband to do the same thing to her, do you? Carmen may have forgiven you, but you don't know what your child is thinking."

His minister was right. He didn't know when he could talk to Kristian because they were both busy. The next day he was leaving for Cali so the conversation would have to take place once he returned. A six month gap, he wondered if it was worth bringing up.

"You did a good thing," his minister told him. "Coming in here and trying to make sense of it all helped you. You understand yourself a little better. You're human, Kane, and you're going to make mistakes. The important part is learning from your mistakes. Now, I want to see your wife in here. Your marriage needs help. Saying I'm sorry and jumping in the bed is only going to last for a short amount of time. Talk to her about it."

Kane agreed to do so because he needed to voice his concerns to his wife. He was willing to go to counseling, but the only drawback was his flight to California. Their issues would be pushed aside until he returned. Hopefully, when he did, everything would return to normal.

***

There was no such a thing as normalcy in the Kane household. If anyone was experiencing just the slightest bit of it then it was Kristian. A witness to the tension between her parents, she ignored their problems. To her advantage, she started working on the *Peaches* campaign which kept her busy. When she wasn't working, she was spending time with Dijuan. Their relationship blossomed overnight, and he was officially her boyfriend. The change was a positive one although she was scared to share the news with Coco. Her friend was still in the dumps over King and the Mastersons refused to let her talk to him. Eventually, though, Kristian did.

As for her brother, he spent most of his days with Jay and Malik. She wasn't quite sure what he was doing, but his duties kept him occupied. The only time she saw him was when he came to the house to move out. Malachi was moving into his old room while Akaila redecorated the guestroom to her liking.

Kristian grew accustomed to having Akaila and Malachi around. In fact, she now referred to them as her brother and sister. They were treated as such and were held to the same rules and chores as her. Even now, Akaila joined her at the mall, and they were busy shopping for Christmas gifts for their parents. Coco was with them in another store looking at cookware. By the time it reached nine o'clock, they met up at the food court so they could head home.

Almost at the exit, Kristian was surprised to see Lil' Noc. He wasn't alone, flanked by his posse, and she realized she hadn't seen him since the block party in September. The situation between him and King was nonexistent, and she never knew what happened to Darnell. She hadn't seen him at school, so she figured he either dropped out or transferred.

"Don't be looking over here," he growled. "Y'all can keep it moving."

Kristian did as he said. Coco said something smart under her breath, but Kristian didn't respond. She left the mall and tried to forget she saw him. She thought her plan was working until she heard Lil' Noc behind her.

"Let me holler at you, Kris."

The request made Kristian stop in her tracks. Akaila did the same and she watched as Lil' Noc looked at her sister. They had a quick exchange of glances and Kristian knew it was because Akaila had slept with him. "What do you want, Noc?" she asked, catching his attention. "I need to get home."

"I'll drive you," he offered. "Can you spare five minutes?"

"Um, hello," Coco interrupted. "We don't have licenses. You can drive her, but how are we gonna get home?"

Lil' Noc chuckled. "Give them your keys, Kris. My car is right outside. I only want five minutes of your time, I promise." Lil' Noc exchanged a quick glance with Akaila. His request made her uncomfortable and it showed when she walked away.

"She has a boyfriend, you know," Coco hissed.

Lil' Noc repeated her words in a whiney voice. "Who gives a fuck?" he yelled, returning to his natural voice. He turned towards Kristian. "Are you coming or what?"

Kristian bit her lip. "It's only five minutes," she told Coco.

"Are you sure, Kris?"

Kristian nodded. When Coco accepted her decision, she handed over her keys. In the process, Lil' Noc grabbed her hand, pulling her towards his Cadillac. They passed Akaila who was standing outside, her hands across her chest. Kristian knew she was upset, but she planned on dealing with her sister later. If anything, she needed to find out what was going on with Lil' Noc. They were alone in his car when he spoke.

"Look at you," he whispered, opening her jacket.

Kristian pushed his hand away. He hadn't changed. "I didn't forget about the block party. I remember you calling me a bitch."

"I haven't forgotten about that shit either. I saw you and Dijuan dancing together. Is that when you started dating A-I?"

"I told you from the beginning how I felt about Dijuan. I never lied about my feelings. Are you jealous?" she asked.

"I don't have a reason to be jealous," he replied. "You may like him, but you're not going to turn me down. I can see it in your eyes. You like me, Kris. Why do you keep trying to fight it?"

Kristian allowed a few seconds of silence to pass. She made a mistake when she got in his car. He was still trying to get with her despite everything that went down between him and King. As if that wasn't enough, she could feel his fingers once again on her chest. He was squeezing her left nipple, giving her a sensation she never knew existed.

"Why do you let me do this? You know you have a man. This doesn't belong to him?" Lil' Noc grabbed her breast, giving it a tight squeeze.

"It does," Kristian told him, smacking his hand. "Just take me home. I should've known you only wanted to feel me up." Kristian looked around the parking lot. Coco had already left. She was stuck with Lil' Noc unless she caught a cab.

"You're a fuckin' tease. You don't really want to be with Dijuan. If you did, you wouldn't have gotten in my car. Admit it." Lil' Noc leaned in closer to her. "Are you fuckin' him? I saw the way y'all were dancing at the block party. You can't be a virgin."

Kristian became disgusted. He wasn't worthy of a reply, so she unlocked the door and got out. He tried his best to get her to come back, shouting apologies, but she was already on her phone, calling Coco. Before the phone even rung, her mother's Lexus pulled up next to her. Coco was at the wheel while Akaila was in the passenger seat.

"You know I wasn't leaving you without supervision," Coco joked.

Kristian breathed a sigh of relief. She got inside and told Coco to get as far away from the mall as she could.

While Kristian expected her friend to question her, Coco didn't. Akaila didn't either until they got home. Instead of Akaila going to her room, she went in hers.

"What is it?" Kristian asked, noticing the silence.

Akaila contemplated whether she should tell Kristian about her relationship with Lil' Noc. Her sister knew they dated, but she didn't know everything she'd gone through. "Why are you messing with him?"

"I'm not messing with him," Kristian yelled. "Who told you that?"

"Why did you get in his car? You know I was with him. I know everything about him. I know the kind of person he is."

"And I know what kind of girl you are," Kristian told her.

Akaila wasn't even shocked at Kristian's words. "Say it," she told her. "Go ahead. I'm waiting. You want to tell me I'm a slut, whore, prostitute, fast, hoodrat. Need I say more?"

"Whatever, Akaila," Kristian replied. "I'm not trying to get with him. Even if I was, your relationship was over a long time ago. He's free game. Get over it."

Akaila tried to hold back her frustration. She failed to do so, and she vented right there in Kristian's room. She gave her a quick rundown of her life story. "The responsibilities fell on my shoulder. I had to make ends meet so I hustled. I just chose to use my pussy instead of drugs." She caught her breath. "Do you know what I hate about girls like you? Y'all only look on the surface of things. You always judge what you see and not what you know.

I loved Lil' Noc," Akaila continued. "Not only was he supplying my family with lots of money, he was my boyfriend. He was the only person I was messing with. Girls hated on me because I had him."

Kristian motioned for her to get to the point.

"I got pregnant," Akaila barked. "I got pregnant, and I had abortions. Then, the abortions turned to miscarriages because I had too many abortions. I couldn't afford a baby. I was taking care of a family. Everything was good until Noc found out about the abortions."

"What did he do?" Kristian asked.

"He beat the shit out of me. Yeah, Kris, it was me. I'm the girl who Lil' Noc beat up. I'm the rumor." Akaila took off her shirt, showing Kristian the scar tissue on her back from where Noc stomped her. She didn't wait for a verbal reaction, sliding her shirt back on. "King saved me. I ran to him barely alive, and he took me to the hospital. He never told anyone what he did for me. He tried to help me, but without Noc, I had no choice, but to go back to the streets. Now, I'm safe again. I don't have to turn tricks."

Kristian was beyond speechless. She was certain Lil' Noc had a crush on her, but it seemed he was only flirting with her to get back at Akaila. He knew what he had done to her sister. Now, she knew as well.

"Do you still think you should be with him? He only wants you for sex. Did he try and feel you up? That's how it started with me."

Kristian didn't want to continue the conversation. "Let it go, please," she begged. "We are two different people. Just because he treated you one way, doesn't mean he'll do the same to me. Besides, I think you're jealous. I have an amazing relationship with Dijuan, supportive parents, a good image, and your ex-boyfriend on my trail."

Akaila stared at her sister in disbelief. She couldn't believe how she took her story. She thought she was jealous of her when she was trying to protect her from being hurt. "I don't want Noc. My time with him is over and yours should be, too. Dijuan is a good guy, and you shouldn't be messing around on him."

"Why are you putting words in my mouth? I'm not messing around on Dijuan. I haven't done anything with Noc."

"I don't believe you." Akaila folded her arms across her chest. She didn't believe one word Kristian said. There was a reason Lil' Noc approached her at the mall. He obviously believed he had a chance.

"You don't have to," Kristian argued. "I will say this, though. If you even think about telling Dijuan I did something with Noc, you will come home to your shit on the sidewalk."

Akaila giggled. "One, you are messing with Lil' Noc, and two, your parents aren't going to kick me out. We're sisters."

Kristian dimmed her eyes. As much as she wanted to curse, she couldn't utter a four-letter word out her mouth. "Get out," she screamed.

Akaila chuckled until she realized a wall was wedged between them. They had become close over the last few months and the argument was no longer funny. In fact, she was now uncomfortable. There was already enough tension in the house, and she added to it. To keep from starting another argument, she left Kristian's room. She headed downstairs where she found Kane in the kitchen with a jar of peanut butter and a box of Ritz Crackers. "Hey," she greeted, grabbing a cracker from him.

"Hey," he repeated. "Did you finish your Christmas shopping?"

Akaila gave him a half smile, thinking about the shopping bags upstairs. "I didn't buy anything for my mother. I didn't know if I should."

Kane felt a stab of guilt. "You know things have been crazy around here. There's the situation with King, Jay, and everything is kind of falling apart. I don't know what's going on with your mother. To be honest, the only thing I do know is that she's alive. Where she's living, if she's working, I can't give those answers to you. I hope she's in treatment somewhere."

"So, where does that leave us? It's almost January."

"Carmen and I have talked about adopting you and Malachi. We know we can't take the place of your parents, but we want y'all to give us a chance. What do you say, do you want to be a Kane? You and Kristian are close. Malachi adores King."

Akaila bit her lip. Kane didn't know about her disagreement with Kristian. She didn't want the argument to hold her back from having a real family. She made the decision to make up with her. "I want to stay here," she told him.

"Great," Kane replied. "Carmen and I will work on the adoption. In the meantime, I'll check on your mother. She can't be too far." Kane gave her a slight smile although he told her a lie. He didn't have any intention of finding Tricia. California was calling his name and it would be six months before he could look for her. If he was lucky, the case would be handed to a person more worthy to have it: a social worker.

27 | *Abandonment*

Thursday afternoon, Kane was in his office, finalizing the details of his trip to California. He was going undercover as a chef at an Italian restaurant, which was rumored to be the sight of numerous drug deals. If things went his way, the case would be solved in a matter of three months. If not, six months of his life would be spent in Cali. Carmen was still unaware of the trip, but he planned to tell her once he came home. The Triad was ready for him to report, and he was scheduled to board a plane tomorrow morning. If he was successful in the feat, his payday would be huge.

"Good evening," a male voice said, interrupting his thoughts.

Jay was standing in the doorway of his office. Surprised to see him, Kane watched as Jay sat in front of him. He wasn't quite sure why he was there, assuming Jay came to boast. He knew all about Jay selling his house to bail King out. The move earned him extra points with Carmen. If the man came to rub it in his face, the visit would be short.

"We're making progress on Blue Magic."

Kane cursed under his breath. The restaurant was a clear reminder of the large amounts of time his wife was spending with him. He was still against her involvement, yet she wasn't backing down from her position as partner.

"King is doing well," Jay continued. "I know y'all don't speak that much. He's helping me with Sapphire now. Maybe, next year, we can open the—"

"What the fuck do you want?" Kane yelled.

Jay wasn't trying to argue. If anything, he wanted to thank Kane for keeping his distance. "I wanted to let you know you did the right thing. You took a step back so I could have a relationship with my son. Yesterday, King called me Pops. It made me feel a certain way. Maybe, we can work this out. I've proven I'm only here for my son."

Kane didn't give him any glory. "Why do you want praise for the stuff you're supposed to be doing? I'm not giving you milk and cookies for being a father. I didn't get any and I don't need any. I did what I was supposed to do. He can tell you that."

Kane saw disappointment on Jay's face. His words cut him, which wasn't his intention. "Look, I'm sorry. I gotta be real with you on this one. You can't be his father. I played that role. I was there at the most critical part in his life. He's never going to look at you the way he looks at me because you weren't there. I'm sorry if you feel I took those moments away from you. When he thinks of daddy, he will always think of me. You can try all you want, but at the end of the day, you will only be Jay, the biological father he learned of when he was seventeen years old. You'll never be daddy. Once you accept it, you'll stop trying so hard."

His words stung. The delivery may have been wrong, but the message was clear. Jay made progress, but he would never be King's father. At the end of the day, the role belonged to him. Not even time could change it. Kane took a deep breath when Jay rose from his seat. There was nothing left to be said and Jay proved it when he walked out the door.

***

Carmen knew all about the growth in King's relationship with Jay. She spoke to her ex daily while King checked in every week. Things were coming together for them, and she wished she could say the same for everything else. Her relationship with Kane was declining and they were merely going through the motions. Even now, when he walked into their bedroom, he gave her a kiss on the cheek, yet he didn't utter a word in her direction. When he went in their closet, she noticed the large duffle bag in his hand. He was making a lot of noise and her curiosity was growing. "What are you doing?" she yelled. She headed in the closet where he appeared to be packing. "What's going on?"

Kane dropped the duffle bag at his feet. "We need to talk," he began. He walked out the closet, grabbing Carmen's hand so they could sit down. He brought her to their bed and sat her in his lap. "The Triad offered me a case. They offered it a long time ago, but I declined. Now, I've decided to take it."

Carmen remembered a previous conversation with Kristian. "Is this the California thing? Don't even answer. It isn't important. Tell me, how long?"

"The whole thing could take three to six months."

"Six months, are you out your damn mind?"

"The kids are grown now. They're doing their own thing. King is keeping his nose clean. Kristian is modeling. Akaila and Malachi are doing well. They're both on the honor roll. Everyone will be fine."

"What about me, Kane?"

Goodbye wasn't an easy thing to say. He hadn't even dropped the real bomb. She didn't know he was leaving in the morning. "I need this right now, Carm. You know we've been having problems. I've been talking to

Minister Harrison, and he thinks this case is a good thing. I need to get away."

"You've been going to counseling behind my back? You've been telling him our business?"

"I needed help. I was depressed. I needed someone to talk to before I shot my damn brains out. I need this."

"What about me, Kane, what am I supposed to do?"

Kane didn't have an answer. "Please understand. I'm not doing this to hurt you. It's supposed to help us."

"Why do you think running away from your problems is helping us?" Carmen stood up so they could be face to face. "You always run away. When we got into it over Akaila's mother, you ran away. When we got into it at the office, you ran out. You always run out."

"I'm not running out," he yelled. Kane took a deep breath. "I can't stay here. I've made up my mind. I'm leaving tomorrow morning."

Carmen glared at him. "How long have you known about this?"

"I told you, a long time ago."

"No, when did you get your reporting date?"

"I started training after I arrested King."

Carmen was furious. "So you knew for months and you're just now telling me?"

"I had to find a way to tell you. This isn't easy for me either."

"You're right, it's not easy. What if I told you I was going away for six months? What if I told you I was leaving you here with four kids? You know what? Don't bother answering the question. I've never done that to you. I've never left. I've always been here."

Kane rose to his feet. "We need this, Carm. I know things will be better when I get back."

"What if you don't come back? What if they find out who you are and kill you? Kane, I'm scared," Carmen cried.

"There are people in place for situations like that. If a problem arises, I know how to handle it." Kane moved towards her, but she only moved away. "Can I hold you?"

Carmen covered her face, not believing what he was telling her. For six long months, once again, she would have to go without him. He did it to her in the past and she thought she would be okay, but she wasn't. She was scared out her mind. Her husband was gone, she had two children to look after, and any day she could get a phone call that something went wrong. When he returned, he promised he wouldn't go undercover again. Now, he was breaking his promise.

"I want to hold you, baby," he told her, coming closer.

Carmen allowed him to hold her as she continued to coax him into staying. "If you love me, you'll tell them you're not going," she whimpered.

"I can't do that. My mind is made up. I'm going."

"Tell them, Kane. Tell them you can't go." Carmen broke his grasp and grabbed her cell phone. She handed it to him so he could make the call. "Tell them," she repeated. She handed him the phone and when he didn't take it, she cried harder. "How could you leave me?" Carmen fell on the bed, bursting into tears. "You don't love me."

Kane watched in pain as his wife cried. Her tears forced him to lay beside her, pulling her in his arms. "I love you, but we need this. We've been faking long enough. When I get back, our heads will be clear. We can go to counseling. Right now, we need time to breathe. We've been going strong for seventeen years, baby. These little six months are not going to break us." He kissed her lips. His hands then removed her clothes. It was their last night together before his six-month stint in California. He would be forced to fantasize about her to get through the lonely nights. "Don't ever say I don't love you," he told her as they made love. "It's a lie."

Carmen listened to his words as he penetrated her. She couldn't stop her tears as she thought more and more about the separation. They were having problems, but she didn't understand how being miles apart would make their relationship better. He wasn't even gone, but the thought of abandonment kept her from appreciating the love he was giving. Ten minutes in, he climaxed. The first time she hadn't reached her peak, he noticed.

"Carm," he whimpered. "Don't hurt me like this."

"Don't hurt me," she told him. She pushed him off her and turned towards the door. He wanted to spend the rest of the evening in bed, leave in the morning, and then return six months later to pretend everything was okay. That was his plan, but it wasn't hers. She burst out crying again and something told her to give up. He would have to see his mistake on his own.

While those were her initial thoughts, her mind changed again when she heard him calling to her. Her anger tripled and she left the bed, running in the bathroom. He followed her, bringing her back in their bedroom. She let him make love to her again until he forced her to scream his name. Carmen didn't know how many times they made love, but it was one right after the other.

She didn't know if they slept at all that night. When she saw the sun come up, she knew it was their last time making love. Once they were done, he went in the bathroom, showering. She got up as well, sliding on a pair of boy shorts, a cami, and her robe. Their sheets were soaked so she pulled them from the bed. She put a fresh pair of sheets on the bed and sprayed the room down with air freshener and Febreze. When Kane came back in the room, she watched him as he dressed. He then went in their closet. A door opened. One she never knew existed. Guns, grenades, and other tactical equipment were hidden in her bedroom without her knowledge. He got the things he wanted, and the door was closed back.

"Kane, please don't do this," she cried. "Just tell me what you want. Is it Jay? Do you want me to stop working on the restaurant?"

"We've already had that argument. You said no, remember?"

"I'll get on my knees." Carmen dropped to the floor, showing him how serious she was. It was useless because he only stood her on her feet. When he headed for the door, she tightened her robe around her and followed him down the steps. Her sadness was turning to anger, and she wanted him to know it.

"I guess I don't need you as much as I thought I did," she told him once he was at the front door. "I guess I don't need you at all."

"Don't start this right now," he whispered, setting his duffle bag on the floor. "The kids are waking up. They don't need to hear this."

"I have every right to be upset. You fuck me and then you leave me. The kids deserve to know where you're going. Did you tell them? Do they know you're abandoning them?"

"I'm not—" Kane stopped when Kristian and Akaila appeared at the top of the stairwell. He couldn't bear to see the hurt on their face. He chose to not say anything. Instead, he picked up his duffle bag and opened the front door. The move triggered Carmen's anger.

"There you go again, running away. That's all you're good for." Carmen wanted to hurt him. She wanted him to feel the pain she was feeling. "I can't promise you I'm going to be here when you get home."

The threat didn't garner a reaction. Kane only slammed the door closed not saying a word. His silence made Carmen drop to her knees. She cursed him, wanting revenge for what she was forced to endure. When she cursed again, another cry joined hers. Carmen opened her eyes to see her kids now at the bottom of the steps. Kristian's face was wet while looks of disappointment were on the faces of Akaila and Malachi.

"He was going to adopt us," Akaila cried. "Why did he leave?"

"I'm gonna do it," Carmen whispered. "I'll start the process today, I promise." Carmen hugged her before grabbing the other two in her arms. For minutes on end, they sat there crying as Kane made his way to California.

28 | *Beautiful Betrayal*

Three hours after Kane left, Carmen stood in front of the eggshell-colored building Jay called home. After paging him, the doorman let her in, and she made the trek to his penthouse apartment. He put his money to good use because he lived in one of the most lavish apartment buildings in East Brookstone. His new home contained three bedrooms, two baths, and overlooked one of the busiest parts of the city. Very much impressed, Carmen pressed the doorbell, hoping to see inside.

"Ready for the tour?" he asked once he opened the door.

"I have my ticket," Carmen joked. She walked inside and gave the living room the once-over. An antique loveseat was in the middle of the room while an oil painting of King overlooked the fireplace. Their son had to be no older than six months in the portrait. She assumed King gave him the picture. "Who made this for you?"

"A friend in France I recently connected with. He called it my housewarming gift. I sent over the picture, and he worked his magic." Jay grabbed her hand, leading her closer to the fireplace. He showed her pictures of him and King, which had been taken within the last few months. "We're together every day. He would be here now if you hadn't asked for privacy. What's going on?"

"I needed a friend. It seems I've pushed them all away. Tiara and I still haven't discussed what happened at Lucky's. It's like we decided to simply ignore the issue. It's pretty much the same with Malik. I can't talk to my kids about my problems so you're the only person I have."

Jay headed to the couch and patted the space next to him. "Tell, Dr. Santiago, all about it."

Carmen let out a small smile. "Kane left for California this morning. The Triad called him back in for a case. He knew about it for months but didn't tell me until last night."

"He didn't tell you on purpose. If you ask me, he wants to see you hurt. He did a good job because you're sitting here crying on my couch." Jay tapped Carmen's leg. "Come on, I made breakfast."

He grabbed her hand, this time, leading her in the kitchen. The table was already set. Two plates were filled with French toast, scrambled eggs, and sausage patties. The meal was prepared especially for her. Jay encouraged her to eat. "What kind of syrup do you want?" he asked, reaching in a cabinet. When he didn't get a response, he looked at her.

Her expression gave away her true intention. She was biting her lip as if he could easily be devoured. While it would be easy to give in to her, it was all a game. "What bullshit are you on? Are you really trying to do this? You're fuckin' married." Jay put distance between them. When he reached his bedroom door, he realized he headed in the wrong direction.

"We've fought it long enough," he heard her say.

Jay didn't dare turn around. He closed his eyes, contemplating whether to give into her manipulation. Carmen knew he was weak. He went seventeen years without the touch of a woman and there she was, ready to give it up to him. He was going to let her, too. He hadn't touched her in years and was curious to know how she felt. "Come here," he said, not turning around. He didn't hear her footsteps, so he repeated his words. This time his tone was harsh. She took a few steps forward, but it only forced him to tell her to come closer. Once she was behind him, he turned around. He planted a soft kiss on her lips. The connection was electrical, transporting them back in time.

Carmen saw herself at the diner in West Brookstone, exchanging glances with him. She remembered the first time they made love and even their first argument. More memories flooded in her mind until she was forced back to reality. She realized they were overdue when they both fell on the bed, stripping each other of their clothes. He undid her pants, the image reminding her how desperate she was to see him. She remembered when she stumbled upon him in the shower. His nude body tempted her to get undressed with him. She wanted to feel him inside her even then. Now, the anticipation was stronger.

Both nude on the bed, Jay's eyes outlined her body. "Come on," she told him, touching his shoulder. He followed her order and Carmen spread her legs, wrapping each one around his waist. She told him to go slow. Above average in size, she wasn't quite sure if she could still handle him. Jay was delicate, entering her until they both were satisfied. Then, the slow grind began. Her eyes were forced closed from the intense sensation.

When she bedded Carlos, she dreamt it was Kane, but this time she cheated, her mind was focused on Jay. As of right now, Kane was the enemy. Although she prayed he never found out, the possibility of him walking in and catching her, turned her on. She could see her husband's face when he walked in the room and saw her pleasuring Jay. Her ex was getting everything she gave him plus more. Certain of it, Carmen opened her eyes so she could see her latest victim. Jay's face was scrunched up as he concentrated on giving her the best stroke. He was enjoying the connection and Carmen longed for Kane to see it.

Don't do this to me, she imagined her husband saying.

It was too late, though. She started the deed, and she was going to finish it. It felt too good for her not to.

Carmen felt Jay thrusting faster inside her. He moved his hips at a rapid pace, and she touched his shoulders, not wanting him to climax. She wanted something else from him. She pushed his shoulder, signaling she wanted him to stop. He pulled out and Carmen used the time to flip over. Not one to normally engage in anal sex, it was part two of her experience with Jay. She closed her eyes, waiting for him to enter her and when he didn't, Carmen looked to see what he was doing. He opened one of his drawers and pulled out a condom. "No," she screamed.

"Carm," he said, appearing shocked.

"Do you want this or not?" She let him know he had a choice. He dropped the condom on the floor. He then pulled out a bottle of lubricant. *He knew this was gonna happen. He planned for it.* Jay took his finger, massaging and lubricating her asshole. Seconds later, he pushed himself inside her. Carmen moaned, not knowing it was going to be as painful as it was. She closed her eyes and after a while, the pain ceased. He pumped faster every time and Carmen felt him as he fell out of her.

"Turn over," he ordered. "I know you remember." He put his hand underneath her stomach as if he was going to flip her over. She moved, allowing him to lie down and then mounted him like a bull. When he slipped back inside her, she rode him the best way she knew how. In response, he grabbed her hips, forcing her to go faster over his erection. Much bigger than his regular nine inches, his thickness excited and pained her at the same time. She tried to overlook it, focusing her mind on his heavy pants and moans. Seventeen years had passed since he'd experienced a woman and Carmen wanted him to remember every second of the experience. The best she ever had; Carmen cried out in excitement as Jay moaned her name.

She tried to hold back, but his hard-on was directly on her spot. She was only a minute away from cumming. To make the mood even better, Jay's moans were now at an all-time high. Carmen used everything he taught her, bringing all the skills into remembrance.

"Fuck," he yelled. "Fuck."

Carmen felt him release, his juices flowing down her legs. The wetness only heightened her pleasure, and she rode him even faster, screaming his name as her walls contracted around his meat. The timing was perfect and two seconds later, she experienced the greatest orgasm of her existence. Her body shook with pleasure and a single tear fell down her face from how good he felt. Carmen hated to admit it, but no man had ever brought a tear to her face. Kane hadn't done it and she slept with him on a regular basis for the past seventeen years. She looked at Jay. He noticed the tear. She could never let him know he pleased her more than her husband. Still, she had to tell him something. The words I love you fell from her mouth. He then repeated the words. Minutes later, they were in a deep sleep.

It was ten o'clock when Carmen came to his house and when they woke up, it was going on almost four. Unsure of what Jay was thinking, she peered at him, hoping he would share.

"I have a feeling this isn't going any further than what it has."

"Why do you say that?" Carmen sat up.

"Because I know you love your husband. You're upset with him right now, which is why you did this. I've been going back and forth with this whole thing in my head. You've had every opportunity to fuck me before he left, but you waited 'til he was gone to do it. It's cool, though, I needed to get off, and you needed the revenge."

"What are you saying?"

"I'm saying it's time for you to put your clothes on," he told her. "We go back to doing us. You know, keeping our relationship strictly platonic. Don't get me wrong, I love you. I enjoyed this. I'm not saying I don't want to do it again, but let's be real. You love Kane, not me."

Carmen's lips trembled because Jay saw through her scheme. She did use him for revenge, but her feelings for him were also real.

"But since you used me," he continued, "there is one thing I want."

Carmen raised her brow. "What is that?"

A smile flew across his face. "How about a little oral fixation before you leave?"

***

Carmen returned home that evening as if nothing occurred. Not the least bit guilty, she grabbed the mail and went inside like the day was as normal as the others. Kristian was in the kitchen, a cookbook in front of her and Carmen assumed she was about to start on dinner.

In the meantime, she reviewed the mail, telling Kristian everything that was received. "Fashion show invitations, letter from Chanel's people, bank statements, letter from *Girl*–" Carmen tore into the envelope and pulled out the letter. "Dear, Mrs. Davenport-Kane, we wrote to you earlier, requesting your participation in our November issue of *Girlfriend Magazine*, but we failed to receive a response back. However, we are still interested in your story and would love to set up a time where we can discuss your career achievements, family, fashion sense, and plans for our March issue. We would also love to set up a photoshoot at your home. Please contact our Senior Editor if you wish to comply. We hope to hear from you soon." Carmen thought long and hard. "I never got the first letter."

"Daddy got it," Kristian told her as Akaila walked in the kitchen. "He forgot to give it to you. So, are you going to do it?"

Carmen shrugged her shoulders. "It's a family thing. Do y'all want to do it?"

"It sounds like fun," Akaila chimed in. "It'll be like pulling teeth to get Malachi to do it. You know he doesn't want to soften his image."

Carmen rolled her eyes. "He's gonna do it. I want all my kids in the spread. Hopefully, King won't be in prison when it's set up." Carmen frowned at the thought and slid the letter back inside the envelope. She finished distributing the mail before retiring to her room. While it was her plan to take a nap, she got a surprise phone call from Jay. He requested her presence again, this time at a local restaurant named Papi Chulo. Her desire to see him made her say yes. Not quite sure what was up his sleeve, she left her house unsure if she would come back.

The evening started off one way and ended another. She met him at the restaurant, but they never went inside. Jay had other plans, which she learned when they went to his car. He drove to a nearby alley and round two started before he had the car in park. Just as good as the first, the only difference was the guilt, which now stabbed Carmen's heart. She created a problem, which she wouldn't be able to control. She could try, but in the end, she knew where she belonged. She was ready to disclose her thoughts to him until he gave her the same message as earlier.

"I know this isn't what you want. You're confused and so am I. We never had any closure with our relationship. We were pulled apart. If this continues, we'll only be pulled apart again. Let's not wait for that to happen. You got what you needed, I got what I needed. Let's just let it go."

His words reflected his own guilty conscience. Still, she agreed to end things and left the car. The dynamics of the relationship wasn't fair to either one of them, which led to its demise.

As she headed home, Carmen made the decision to never sleep with him again.

29 | *A Surprise Guest*

Carmen was on her way back home while her kids were in the kitchen baking homemade cookies. One of their evening pastimes, the plan was to perfect the recipe so they could give the cookies away as gifts. They were too busy sampling and baking, the doorbell rung twice before anyone noticed.

"Who is that?" Malachi asked, sticking his finger in the cookie batter. "Do you think it's Malik?"

Kristian shrugged her shoulders. "I don't know. It could be Tiara. I don't think Mama went to work today." Kristian headed to the foyer and yelled for Malachi to watch the cookies. Akaila was in the kitchen with him, but her sister was too busy reading *New Moon* to pay attention to what her brother was doing. Or so she thought. Akaila joined her in the foyer and stood there as Kristian checked the peephole. "Uh oh," Kristian murmured when she saw her grandmother.

It had been a full year since her grandparents visited. They only came to New York for the holidays, which didn't give her much time to get to know them. From what she did see, her grandmother was full of attitude and sass, which her mother couldn't stand. "She's feisty," Kristian warned. She answered the door, giving her grandmother a fake smile.

"What took you so long to answer?" Patricia greeted, coming inside. "Oh, I see you have company. Is this one of your friends from school?"

Kristian shook her head. "Well, we were baking cookies. This is, um, Akaila, she's your granddaughter, too. My parents are adopting her and her brother. Malachi is in the kitchen."

Patricia gave Kristian a strange look. "Did I miss something? I talked to your mother recently when King got sentenced. She didn't tell me anything about an adoption. What's going on here?"

"The cookies are ready," Malachi yelled from the kitchen.

"I'll get the cookies," Kristian offered. She was desperate to get away from her grandmother and hurried to the kitchen.

Meanwhile, Akaila was left standing there. Patricia's eyes were frozen on hers. Patricia looked the girl up and down. Her olive skin was lightly tanned and paired with long, silky black hair and big almond-shaped brown eyes. Too beautiful to describe, she watched as a young boy joined them, his appearance identical to Akaila's. About to inquire about their presence, she didn't get the chance when Kristian came back in the foyer with a plate of cookies.

"This is Malachi," Kristian introduced, pointing to her younger brother. "You've met Akaila. I guess you're wondering where Mama is. I'm not quite sure, but I think she went out to dinner with Jay."

"Who?" Patricia questioned. She hadn't heard the name in years, but she was certain Kristian was referencing Jay Santiago.

"He's King's father," Malachi explained, biting into a cookie. "They go out a lot because Mama is helping him with his restaurant. He owns a club, too. King's been working with him, and he said if I stayed on the honor roll, he'll let me come for an hour on opening night."

Patricia took a seat in the dining room. She closed her eyes, not believing what she heard. When her eyes reopened, she grabbed a cookie, sticking half of it in her mouth. She came to Brookstone to surprise them only to find out the entire household changed overnight. "Where is your father? I know he has something to say about this."

Kristian answered her. "He left this morning. He went to Cali. He took a case with the Triad."

Patricia put her head down. The entire house was in disarray. "How could he leave—" Her words were cut short when she heard a familiar voice.

"I don't smell any burnt cookies this time," Carmen yelled. "Finally, y'all make some that are edible." She stopped in her tracks when she saw her mother seated at the table. She knew her mother better than anyone and an argument was about to take place. Therefore, she excused the kids from the room.

"Your husband went back to the Triad," Patricia stated once the room was clear. "You're going out with Jay? What kind of game are you playing? Are you out your damn mind?"

"Jay isn't who you think he is. Right now, he's the best thing in my life. As you can see, my husband left me, and I have four kids and a business to look after. Not to mention, your grandson will be in prison soon."

"This is too much, Carmen. You're adopting two kids?"

"Don't touch that one," Carmen told her. "Don't say anything about them."

Patricia didn't press the issue because she could see the kids were a sensitive issue. "I won't say anything about them, but I will say you have outdone yourself. I mean, this is shocking. Your father would have a heart attack if he knew you allowed Jay Santiago, of all people, to come back in your life. Did you not get enough when he tried to kill you?"

"I don't give a flying fuck what you think," Carmen yelled in response. "Matter of fact, you can get out my damn house."

Patricia glared at her daughter. "Fine, when he beats you in the head with a baseball bat, don't say I didn't warn you. Keep hanging with the crazy and deranged. You're going to end up the same way you were before; a bruised and pregnant woman, lying in a hospital bed. So much for this trip, I'm going back home."

Carmen narrowed her eyes as her mother left the house. She was glad she was gone and hoped her negative energy wouldn't linger. After experiencing another rendezvous with Jay, the last thing she needed was stress. She needed only positive energy in her circle. Everything else, could take a tip from her husband, and leave.

30 | *Unexpected*

Carmen tried to keep her lunch down as Cathy stepped in her office. Her receptionist handed her an envelope from the law offices of Clement & Winkle. It had been nearly three months since she started working on adopting Akaila and Malachi. The process was one headache after another. She tried not to involve the kids, but they saw her frustration when she had setbacks. Add it to her stomach bug; she was surprised she made it into work.

"So, what is it this time?" Cathy asked, aware of the situation.

Carmen glanced at the letter. "Theresa DeGonzaza isn't in the database. They say the adoption can't go through if she hasn't given up her parental rights."

"Oh," Cathy mouthed. "Do the kids know where she is?"

"They haven't seen her since September. They're not even looking for her. Akaila never had a good relationship with her. I don't know about Malachi. He stays under King these days."

"So I guess you're back to square one, huh?"

"I guess so," Carmen told her, getting up from her desk. "Can you excuse me? I'm getting sick again."

"Sure," Cathy replied. "Are you going to be okay?" Cathy turned away when she saw Carmen fall over the toilet. She then covered her ears when she heard her vomiting. There was a small bug going around the city, but Carmen was the only one at Flame who caught it. "Do you have a fever? What about a runny nose?"

Carmen flushed the toilet, thinking the spell was over. "I used to sneeze a lot," she told her. "I probably need to go to the doctor."

Cathy walked in the bathroom just as Carmen started to brush her teeth. "You're the only who caught this bug. We work in close quarters so someone else should've gotten it. Do you want to know what was wrong with my sister the last time she got sick?"

"What was wrong with her?" Carmen asked, brushing her teeth.

"She was pregnant."

Carmen took the toothbrush out her mouth. "I'm not pregnant."

"I'm not saying you are. I go in and out your office all day. I've never heard you sneeze; wipe your nose, cough, or none of that. You don't seem to have any signs of mucus."

"I'm not pregnant, Cathy, but thank you for your observations."

"You're welcome," Cathy joked. "Come on, Carm, you and Kane haven't been doing the wild thing? I know you've talked about wanting another baby."

"Kane went undercover. I've been celibate since December."

"Well, if we do a test, you'll fail," Cathy said. "I'm going to the drug store. Stay near the toilet. I'm your receptionist, but you don't pay me to clean up vomit. I'll be back in a few minutes."

Carmen pondered on what Cathy said. Since she had unprotected sex with Jay twice, it was a possibility. Her period was late. If she was, she had to be close to four months since she slept with him in December. Carmen looked in the mirror and lifted her shirt. Her stomach had slightly protruded outward. "Cathy jinxed me," she said aloud. She couldn't be certain until Cathy returned with the pregnancy test.

If she was pregnant, Carmen knew she was keeping the baby. She would have to tell Jay, her kids, and then face the hardest part of it all, telling Kane. Her parents would have a field day with the news, and she could see her father's disappointment. Of course, this would all occur if she truly was pregnant.

"Here we are," Cathy yelled, coming in her office. "Tiara just came back in from lunch. Do you want me to get her?"

"Please," Carmen begged. She grabbed the test from Cathy's hands. Although their friendship was still on the rocks, Carmen needed Tiara's support. If the test came back positive, her entire world would come crashing down. She opened the box, pulled out the test, and undid her pants. Once she was done, she set the test on the counter as footsteps neared the bathroom door.

"I can't even work because Cathy is going nuts in my office," Tiara yelled. "Carm, what have you gotten yourself into?"

Carmen washed her hands, seeing the results hadn't come up. "I don't know," she replied. "What did Cathy say?"

"Are you pregnant?"

Carmen dried her hands off and opened the door. "The results aren't up. It probably needs another minute or two." She knew her friend wanted to ask the million dollar question. They stared each other down until Carmen broke the gaze. She went back in the bathroom and picked up the pregnancy test. Two lines appeared and she picked up the box to see what it meant. When she realized she was pregnant, she dropped the box in the sink.

"Two lines, Carmen. Your ass is fuckin' pregnant."

Carmen tried to stay calm although she really wanted to scream and fall to the floor. "The baby is Jay's," she admitted, covering her mouth. Tiara's face was indescribable. "I was mad at Kane for going undercover and I slept with him. We did it twice. The first time, I wanted revenge. The second time," Carmen brought her hand down from her mouth. "I was in love. I think working on Blue Magic opened doors we thought were closed. We said it wouldn't happen again and it hasn't. With the baby coming, I don't know what we're going to do. I don't know where my marriage stands."

Tiara closed the bathroom door. "I'm not surprised this happened. I told you about yourself at Lucky's. I just didn't think Jay would fall victim to your advances. I guess he fooled me on that one. Well, your marriage is officially over. I know you're not on speaking terms with Malik, but he can at least give you the heads up on Jay's reaction. He probably wasn't expecting to get a baby out the deal. He's just getting to know King."

Carmen wiped her face, hearing her best friend's advice. Her words were harsh, but she understood her thinking. "Thank you for listening."

Tiara opened the bathroom door, but she didn't leave. "I'm still your best friend, Carm. I may be upset with you, but I'm always here for you even if you are cheating on your husband. Besides, I was the one holding you down when you were getting your hair braided in D-Block."

Carmen giggled as she heard Tiara's catchphrase.

"Go talk to Malik. When you're done, you need to talk to Jay. The quicker he knows, the quicker y'all can figure out what to do."

Carmen followed her out the bathroom. She called Malik and in less than twenty minutes, she was meeting him at the Brookstone City Park. His face was rather blank, and she could tell he was uncomfortable. "I have something to tell you," she told him.

"Can we talk about what happened the last time we met?"

Carmen's eyes became outstretched. "Is that still on your mind? Malik, I don't want you. Get over it. What I came to tell you is that I'm pregnant. Jay and I are having another baby."

Malik broke into a loud cackle, learning of her current predicament. "Damn, Carmen, you're finally going to get what's coming to you. Call it evil of me, but I hope Kane drags your ass in court."

"I came to you because I needed a friend. I still haven't told Jay."

Malik was still chuckling. "Now you want a friend. Where was our friendship when you told me to stay away from your family? Where was the friendship when you were leading me on?"

"Come on, Malik, you know I've never had feelings for you."

"Can't a man dream?"

"Don't you love Tiara, anyway?" Carmen asked.

"I do love her, but she won't marry me."

"Neither will I," Carmen told him, rolling her neck.

Malik sucked his teeth. "You do your dirt and then you want people to feel sorry for you. When Kane hands you those divorce papers, you're going to want us all around, telling you everything's going to be okay. It isn't going to happen. We're on his side. He needs to divorce your whorish ass. You're so damn grimy. When you do your dirt, you do it where it hurts. You know Kane can't have kids. You gave up seventeen years of marriage for eight minutes of pleasure?"

"Twenty," Carmen corrected him. "It was twenty minutes of pleasure, and I enjoyed every bit of it. Jay knows how to keep a hard-on."

Malik spat. "Go to hell."

"I've been there," Carmen retorted.

"Go back," he yelled, walking away. He headed to his car until he heard her behind him.

"Malik, listen to me," she begged. "I need your help. I don't know how to tell Jay. I don't know what this means for us."

"Jay isn't your problem. Your husband in California is. You should be concerned about how you're gonna tell him." Malik continued walking towards his car. He stopped in his tracks when he felt her hand on his arm. "What do you want from me, Carm?"

"Tell me it's going to be okay," she cried. "Tell me you're going to be there for me like you've always been."

Malik let out a loud grunt. "You are one sad woman. You're one of the richest women in America, but you've got to be the dumbest. I'll ride with you, but if you pull anymore bullshit, I'm through. You hear me?"

Carmen told him yes. She gave him a quick hug before he ordered her to go see Jay. She took his advice, but instead of heading to Jay's apartment, she asked him to come to the park. He accepted the invitation and now she was watching him as he got out his car. He greeted her with a warm smile while all she gave him in return was a blank stare.

"You can't speak?" he asked, opening his arms for a hug.

Carmen embraced him and whispered a low hello. She didn't give any kind of warning, telling him in his ear she was pregnant. He pulled away from her, his eyes searching every part of her body. "I'm pregnant," she said louder. "It's yours. I did sleep with Kane before he left, but he can't have kids. I've never used a condom with him, and I didn't use one with you."

Jay gave her a blank stare. "I should've put that condom on, Carm. I just...I wanted you so bad." Jay pulled her towards him, wrapping his arms around her. "I know this isn't what either of us wanted. This baby has changed things for you and me. I promise you this, though. I don't care what Kane tries to do. I'm going to be there for my child." He thought of his firstborn. "We need to tell King. Before you know it, you're going to be showing and the baby will be here. He needs to know before he goes away."

Carmen exhaled. She wasn't quite sure how King was going to take the news. He would be disappointed, but she prayed he forgave her. If he didn't, all the hard work they put into their relationship would go down the drain. Only time would heal the wound and her son would have plenty of it in the coming months.

***

King wasn't expecting to see anyone at Sapphire. His father had already left for the day while Malik was supposed to be over at Blue Magic, checking up on the renovations. When he heard footsteps, he pulled out his glock, setting it in his lap. He didn't put it away until he heard his parents' voices on the stairwell. When they came in, his father went straight to the mini bar. He took out a bottle of Crown Royal. He poured the liquor in two glasses then handed him one.

"You're going to need this," Jay told him.

His mother gave him a nod of approval. They knew he was underage but was offering him a drink. He took it from Jay's hands, but he didn't drink it. He set it on his desk, eyeing them. "What is it up with you two? Did something happen in Cali?"

Carmen shook her head. She sat in front of King and slid the drink to him. "We're having a baby."

King grabbed the glass of alcohol, taking it down. Once it was gone, he set the glass back on the table. "Okay, tell me again, I didn't hear right. What did you say?"

Carmen exchanged glances with Jay before her eyes went back on King. "I'm pregnant. You're gonna have a little sister or brother."

King laughed in her face, thinking she was pulling his leg. "She's kidding, right? Please tell me you're kidding."

"No, baby, I'm not. I'm almost four months."

King felt betrayed. Jay was adamant about spending time with him and getting to know him, but he wondered if it was real. From the information presented, Jay was getting on his good side to get closer to his mother. "Is this what you got out of prison for? You wanted my mother, right? You were trying to play daddy with me because you wanted her. Fuck you, Jay. I thought you were trying to get to know me. At what point in time were you creeping with my mom? I live with you. Were y'all fuckin' when I was sleep?"

Jay didn't entertain most of King's questions. "I have a history with your mother, which I've explained to you in detail. I've never lied to you about being in love with her. I told you the truth. When it comes to my sex life, I don't have to tell you shit. That's none of your business."

"It is my business if you're in my face, telling me she's pregnant by you." King was beyond appalled. "I was better off without you."

"Is that how you feel?" Jay asked. "You don't need me?"

"Get the fuck out my face."

Carmen was unsure of what to say. She remained silent until she found her words. "Jay didn't do this by himself. It takes two to make a baby. We were wrong, but the deed is done. Now, as a family, we're going to get through this. I know it won't be easy. If you want to blame anyone, blame me. I'm married."

"Then you can get the fuck out, too," King replied.

Carmen reached for the bottle of Crown Royal, but Jay picked it up before she could throw it. Glad he had, Carmen got up and left the room. Jay followed behind her a minute or so later, leaving King by himself. The second they were outside the club; their son twisted the cap off the bottle and finished it off. He then grabbed his car keys to start the search for Kristian. If anybody was going to understand his anger, it would be her.

***

Ever since her relationship with Dijuan had taken off, Kristian started bending the rules. She would tell her mother she was going to the movies when in actuality; she and Dijuan were finding deserted areas to make out. Currently parked at a dead end road, Kristian prayed no one stumbled upon them. Dijuan was driving his mother's Jeep, and despite the tinted windows, the car could still attract attention. Even now, as Dijuan kissed her neck, the idea of getting caught made her nervous.

"How did you find this spot?" she asked him. His reply came out muffled and she pinched his arm to get his attention. When he leaned up, she repeated her question. "You always find these dead end roads."

"I just keep driving until I find something. Calm down, no one has caught us yet. How many times have we've been doing this?"

"What would your parents say?"

Dijuan sighed out of frustration. He felt they were doing more talking than kissing. During the week, their time together was limited so all they did was talk on the phone. The weekend was their time for intimacy, but Kristian wanted to talk then, too. "My father has an idea," he replied.

"Your father knows? He's my minister. Why would you tell him?"

Dijuan looked at her sideways. "Every boy talks to his father about sex. He knows I'm not a kid anymore. I have hormones just like he does. Of course, he's teaching me to wait for marriage, but I'm human."

"Well, I think—" Kristian didn't finish her response when she saw a set of car lights. "I see some lights, D. Pull your pants up."

"They'll see it's a dead end street and turn around," he responded.

Kristian closed her eyes, seeing the lights go away. Dijuan's hands were now massaging her breasts and she could feel him undoing her bra. She tried to get back in the moment, but it was hard when she thought she heard a door closing. "Wait a minute, D, I heard something."

Dijuan pretended to look out the window. "It's nothing, baby. Can you play with it again?" Dijuan closed his eyes, feeling her hands wrap around his manhood. It took only a minute before she had him rock hard. Then, right when he thought he was going to release, she ruined the groove again.

"Dijuan, I hear something," he heard her say.

"One second, baby, and I'll check it out," he moaned. "Don't stop, though." The sensation grew stronger, and he bit his lip as he felt the effects of an orgasm.

"Dijuan, I'm serious," Kristian yelled.

"Kris—" He didn't finish saying her name when the sound of glass breaking echoed throughout the car. Kristian screamed, forcing him to sit up. One of his mother's windows was cracked.

"So you're the one trying to get the panties," King yelled.

Kristian screamed in embarrassment as King reached inside the car and unlocked the door. Both she and Dijuan were trying to get presentable, but King moved fast. Before she knew it, he grabbed Dijuan by his leg and pulled him out the Jeep. The second she was decent, she was at her brother's side, trying to talk sense into him as he beat Dijuan to a pulp.

"Do you think my sister's a hoe?" King was yelling.

Kristian pushed her brother away. She could smell alcohol on his breath, and something told her he was drunk. "Stop it," she yelled, trying to hold him in place. She held him for a good five seconds, which was enough time for Dijuan to get on his feet and pull up his pants. She wanted him to stay where he was, but he shocked her when he ran to King and punched him in the face. The move set King off and he charged at Dijuan, throwing him to the ground.

"Oh, I'm about to kill your ass now," King barked.

Kristian jumped on her brother, smacking him in his head, but he only pushed her away. She kept trying until his fist flew down hard on her face. He sent her entire world black.

In the meantime, Dijuan scrambled to his feet, praying she was okay. King was busy pacing the ground as if he couldn't believe what he'd done. "Baby, wake up," Dijuan cried, shaking her. It took a few seconds, but Kristian's eyes opened. Dijuan picked her up, carrying her to the car. King was trying to apologize, but Dijuan wasn't having it. He told Kristian to ignore him as he wiped the glass from the passenger seat. He already knew he was in big trouble, and he contemplated telling his mother the truth. If she knew he wasn't at the movies, it would be the last time he got to use the car. Still, he had to tell her something to explain the damage.

"Let me talk to her," King ordered. "I need to tell her something."

"Stay back," Dijuan yelled. "You've done enough."

King ignored him, trying his best to get Kristian's attention. "Mama is pregnant, Kris. She's having a baby by Jay. They told me today."

Dijuan froze, hearing King's news. He looked at Kristian whose face was stained with tears. His plan was to take her straight home, but now, he wasn't so sure if it was a good idea.

"She can't be," Kristian cried. "She didn't cheat on Daddy." Kristian covered her face as she realized her family situation was going from bad to worse. Her father was still in California and would return to find her mother pregnant or a newborn in his house. "I can't believe this."

"Oh, shit," King was saying as he took notice of the damage done to the Jeep. "Oh, shit, man, I'm sorry. I can take care of this for you," he said, turning towards Dijuan. "I know a man named Dante. He can fix this shit right up. He probably can do it tonight."

Kristian looked at her brother and told him with her eyes to get in the car. He was drunk and he didn't need to be on the road. It was the only excuse for why he attacked Dijuan. She instructed her brother to direct them to Dante and she prayed he was sober by the time the car was fixed. If not, his Mustang would be left at the dead end road where they agreed to leave the fight.

31 | *Intermission*

Kane pulled the white toque off his head, walking towards a newsstand. He stopped at the stand once a month, looking for any magazines that featured his wife or an ad from the *Peaches* collection. He never purchased anything, and the owner asked him the same question at every visit.

"Is there anything in particular you're looking for?"

"Just trying to keep up with the times," he lied. He walked around the newsstand until he saw the latest issue of *Girlfriend Magazine*. He blinked twice when he recognized his wife on the front cover. He picked up the issue, reading the headline three times in his head. "Carmen Davenport-Kane is really something, isn't she?"

"Oh, Carmen Davenport, I've heard of her. That woman is loaded."

"She does have a lot of money. I'll take two," he told him, sliding him a ten.

"What cha need two for?"

Kane shrugged his shoulders and grabbed the magazines. In a rush to get back to his apartment, he sprinted down the street. Once inside, he went straight to his bedroom, kicking off his shoes. He read the entire article, noticing Akaila and Malachi had been featured in the pictorial as well. He felt a little closer to home seeing his kids, but it was Carmen's quote about him, which made him question his decision to go undercover.

The man I love is strong. He's the love of my life. He's the man who makes me happy, the man who makes me cry. The one who has always protected me. I'm forever indebted to him.

Kane flipped the page to see a picture of his wife. "You're so beautiful," he said, running his index finger along the photo. "Damn, I miss you. I promise. Give me another month or so. I'll be there. Just hold on."

32 | *Fury*

Carmen stopped in the doorway of the kitchen, feeling an immense amount of pressure in her lower abdomen. The second occurrence that morning, she made the right decision staying home from work. She sat on a stool to get off her feet. Kristian was at the sink, preparing a salad and while she thought to share her concerns, she remembered her feelings regarding the pregnancy. Kristian was hurt by it and even limited their communication. Though it hurt her to see her unhappy, Carmen prayed her attitude changed once the baby arrived. As for her other kids, they accepted the pregnancy. When it came to Jay, he was excited about the baby, but questioned the future of their relationship. Carmen knew she was in love with him, but it wasn't easy to walk away from a seventeen-year marriage. Therefore, their future hadn't been decided.

"Kristian," she called, getting her daughter's attention. The pressure was joined by a sharp pain. It showed in her face because Kristian rushed to her side. She shouted questions at her, but Carmen wasn't quite sure what to say. She didn't know what was wrong until she felt a sudden gush.

"Mama, what's wrong? Talk to me."

Carmen tried to come to grips with what was happening. She was only twenty-three weeks along, but her water had broken. "We need to go to the hospital," she murmured. "My water broke."

"It's coming?" Kristian rushed to her phone. "Let me call Grandma."

"Hell no," Carmen barked, hearing her reference her mother. "She hasn't known about this pregnancy for six months and she's not going to find out now. If you're calling anyone, call Jay." She tried to gather herself. Tears streamed down her face as her worst fears came to light. If she gave birth that night, her baby would be premature and the chances of it living were slim. Aware she had been stressed during the pregnancy; Carmen assumed her depression affected the baby.

"I have your purse," Kristian said, handing it to her. "I also grabbed a towel for the car. I don't want you peeing all over the seat."

Carmen cracked a small smile despite the tears on her face. She tried not to show her nervousness, which seemed to work until she heard her daughter break the news to Jay. She could tell from Kristian's responses he was concerned like she was. She feared for her baby's life and each second that passed, she prayed to God for strength and favor.

"Is it coming?" Kristian asked, helping her out the house.

Carmen mumbled a low no and encouraged Kristian to move faster.

"What are you going to name it if it's a girl?"

"Can we talk about that later?" Kristian opened the car door. Despite the wetness in her underwear, Carmen tried her best to get comfortable. It was hard to do yet she managed when Kristian backed out the driveway. She kept her eyes closed for the duration of the ride until Kristian announced they were at the hospital. Then, she gave her a few orders. "I need you to call your sister and brothers. Akaila and Malachi are probably still with Malik. He took them to a game. Hopefully, he'll bring them to the hospital."

Kristian pulled out her cell phone so she could make the necessary calls. In the meantime, she followed behind her mother as they entered the emergency room. Her mother signed in and a short while later she was called back. She wasn't quite sure about her mother's condition, but the nurse made it clear she was being admitted. Kristian waited until the nurse excused himself from the room before she rushed to her mother's side. "Is the baby going to be okay?"

Carmen wiped her face again. "I hope so," she whispered. "The baby is definitely coming." Carmen took a deep breath before handing Kristian a sheet of paper. "I need you to get these things from the house. I'll text you my room number once I'm admitted."

Kristian took the list and left the room. She started a prayer, which she didn't finish until she turned on Bradford Court.

***

When Kane pulled in his driveway, he wasn't quite sure what to expect. From first glance, the first change he noticed was the fuchsia peonies in the garden. Carmen's Lexus was parked in the driveway, a clear sign she was home. Anxious to see her, he ran his hand along the beard he'd grown, hoping she liked it. If not, he would shave it off the moment she expressed her displeasure. About to unlock the door, he was surprised when it opened for him, and Kristian walked out.

"Daddy," she yelped. She threw a duffle bag down on the floor.

"Dang, Kris," he yelled, about to fall. He pushed her away so he could look at her. "Yep, you're my daughter," he exclaimed. "Everything about you looks the same."

"What are you doing here?"

"Baby, it's been six months. I—" He stopped, remembering the way he left. "I am so sorry," he said. "I was wrong at how I handled thing. I'm sorry. I want to make it up to you. To you, your mother; I want to make it up to everybody."

"I would be lying if I told you I wasn't pissed. I was heated," she told him, putting her hands on her hips. "But you're here now."

"I am, and I'm ready to see everyone. Where's everybody, anyway? I see your mother is in the house."

Kristian looked at her mother's Lexus. The sight of it made her recall the current crisis. Her father was back in town and her mother was about to give birth to Jay's baby. "I bet you're wondering what you came home to, huh?"

"Is your mother doing okay? I know she's hurt."

Kristian responded quickly with, "I'll take you to her. You drive since you have her car blocked in."

"No problem," Kane replied, taking out his keys. He unlocked the doors and got inside. Kristian joined him and he started up a conversation on the article in *Girlfriend Magazine*. "So, the whole family became celebrities while I was gone. Y'all did a good job. I was glad Akaila and Malachi were a part of it. Those two really took a liking to your mother. They even called her mom in the interview."

"It happens like that when you're around someone all the time. Mama does everything for them. Cooks, buys, and washes their clothes, checks their homework, she does it all. Like Mama said, they're my new sister and brother."

"I needed that interview," Kane admitted. "It's so hard being someone you're not so when you see a part of you, it makes you appreciate what you had." Kane pointed at the stop sign and asked Kristian where to go. She pointed left and he turned off their street. "The case was hard. I know you probably heard about the bust on the news. The money was great, but I don't ever want to be in a gun battle like that again. Luckily, only one agent was shot when we did the raid."

"Oh," Kristian muttered, spotting the Hospital sign. She told her father to head to Brookstone General. She saw the questionable look on face, yet she didn't give him any kind of explanation. He started to say something, but then stopped as if he didn't want to know. When he turned in the hospital's parking lot, he spoke.

"Who's here, Kris?" Kane asked. "Is everyone okay? I checked the prison system. King hasn't turned himself in yet."

Kristian remained mum. She told him to follow her, which he did. It wasn't until they reached the sixth floor of the hospital he spoke.

"This is the Maternity ward," he stated, not leaving the elevator.

"This is the Maternity ward," she reiterated. "You might as well see who's pregnant."

Kane did as she asked not quite sure what to think. So many thoughts were running rampant in his mind. His first thought was that Carmen was pregnant. The second was that Tiara was pregnant. Then, he had a feeling it was Coco. Although she wasn't dating his son, he had a feeling King impregnated her. If so, he was going to spend the evening kicking his ass. They had talked about condoms and King knew to use one if he wanted to have sex. Certain that was it, he was taken by surprise when Kristian opened the door to a hospital room, and he saw Jay. His mouth dropped open when he noticed his wife in the bed. Then, he noticed Jay's hands wrapped around her stomach.

Kane walked inside, seeing the look of astonishment on Carmen's face. She was just as shocked as he was. When he glanced at Jay, he noticed he was backing away. Tension entered the room, which they all could feel. "I'm going to excuse y'all," he heard Jay say. Kane looked at him out the corner of his eye. He didn't speak, trying to piece things together. He wanted to believe his wife was pregnant by him, yet he couldn't play dumb. He left his wife alone for six months with her ex-boyfriend and now she was pregnant. "Did you cheat on me?" he asked, facing her. "Is he the father?"

Carmen nodded her head. In response, he let out a slight chuckle. "You couldn't wait until I got back to get a good fuck?" He walked towards her and stopped in his tracks. He remembered the charge he would get for putting his hands on a pregnant woman. "Okay, okay, okay, it's okay, this is what I came home to, okay," he said, trying to be nonchalant. "So you know the baby is his?"

"I don't know."

"You don't know?" he asked. "How many men did you sleep with?"

"I think we need to have this conversation in private."

"How many fuckin' men did you sleep with?" he repeated. "If you slept with both of us then we can assume the baby is his because I can't make a baby. I tried, Carm. I can't do it. Don't sit up here and tell me you don't know when you fuckin' do."

"Daddy, can you refrain from cursing?" Kristian asked.

Kane's chest moved up and down as if he ran a marathon. "So, you know I want a divorce. You also need to find some place to stay. I don't care where you go, but you're not coming back in my house. Make sure you take the bastard with you."

Carmen grimaced at how he referenced the baby.

Kane was on ten. "Did you really think I was going to raise another baby by this motherfucker? I took King because I wanted him. I knew he wasn't mine from the beginning. This baby, though, this baby isn't getting shit out of me. I don't care if Jay dies or rots in prison."

"Daddy," Kristian began, catching his attention.

"Baby, you're going to have to deal with it," he told her, shooting a quick glance in her direction. He turned towards Carmen, asking the most important question of all. "Why are you here?"

"My water broke. I'm only six months."

Kane's eyes narrowed. "You're only six months. Bitch, I've been gone for six months. When did you sleep with him?"

"Daddy can you—" Kane cut his daughter off.

"Get the fuck out the room."

Kristian frowned unsure if she should leave her mother alone.

"Don't talk to her like that," Carmen ordered. "You're mad at me, not her. She has every right to want us to have an adult conversation."

"Don't tell me how to talk to my daughter when your ass is sitting up here fuckin' other men. Answer my damn question. When did you sleep with him? Was it before I left? I know for damn sure I fucked you like nine times in one night so when did you fuck him?"

"Kristian is in the room," Carmen yelled.

"Is he bigger than me?"

"Kristian is in the room," Carmen yelled louder. "Get out, Kristian, just get out," she shouted, knowing Kane's language wasn't going to change. Kristian followed her order and once she was gone, they resumed the conversation.

"I want a fuckin' answer," Kane stressed. "Believe me, Carm, if your ass wasn't pregnant, I would've slit your throat by now."

"You are a monster."

"And you are a whore."

Carmen couldn't help but cry. "How can you stand there and call me a bitch in front of our daughter? I'm a whore to you?"

"How can you sit there and act like I'm not supposed to be upset when you're having a baby by another man? We've been through this. I struggled for fifteen years to have another baby and you do this to me."

"I got confused. I was mad, I wanted revenge, and then… you know how I feel about Jay. From day one, when we put our cards on the table, I told you, I had feelings. Over the years, the feelings went away because I fell in love with you but working on the restaurant...I guess the feelings came back. I tried to ignore it, but the feelings were there."

"How long did you wait before you slept with him?"

Carmen swallowed. "Three hours after you left, I went over to his place, and it happened."

Kane's eyes got big. "I wasn't even in the fuckin' air yet. I was still downtown at the Triad. Your ass couldn't wait to run to him. Tell me, Carm, was it good?"

The question wasn't one Carmen wanted to answer. She didn't respond yet Kane pressed the issue. "It was good. I enjoyed it. Perhaps, subconsciously, a part of me wanted to get pregnant."

"Well, I can tell it was good for him, too. He shot a good load in you and made a baby. Kudos to him and all the other men in the world who can make a baby. I'm sorry I wasn't blessed with the skill."

Carmen wiped away a tear. "I'm sorry. I know this is hurting you. Right now, I only want to do what's right. That means, asking you for forgiveness and going to counseling to get over this. With God, I know we can do it."

"With God, I'll be getting a divorce. Just answer this question, did I not please you? Is he bigger than me? I want to know."

"Those questions are personal."

"Personal goes out the window when you're pregnant by another man. Just answer the question. What could I have done better? Is it because I didn't go down on you? I mean, you never asked me to. You never did it to me. You said you never did it to him. You were uncomfortable with it. Did you do it with him this time?"

"Why does it matter if you're going to divorce me?"

Kane sat in the chair where Jay had been sitting. "Because it does, now answer the damn question."

Carmen exhaled. "You've always pleased me. I've always enjoyed making love to you. When it comes to Jay, he is bigger than you. He's probably bigger than a lot of men. What you need to remember is that he was my first. He taught me everything. He trained me on how to please him. Right now, I only want to do what's right. You can divorce me, but I'm not ready to walk away. Seventeen years is an investment."

Carmen stared at the tears, falling from her husband's face. She thought her words were making him look at things differently, but he fooled her. He only picked up where he left off.

"You didn't answer my question. Was he better than me and did you go down on him? I want to know."

"The answer is yes. That is the answer for both questions."

"Thank you for your honesty. Now, to let you know, I didn't cheat on you in California. I jerked off on your *Girlfriend* cover every second I could. It's all good, though. According to the Word, I can divorce you, remarry, and live my life with someone else. All I need to do is take care of my kids." Kane headed for the door, ready to be out her presence. "I'm gonna get your shit together. I don't care where you go or what you do. I don't give a fuck anymore."

Carmen's mouth parted yet the door slammed before she could speak. Since she couldn't respond, she closed her eyes, crying herself to sleep. When she did finally wake, the result of a small contraction, the first thing she saw was her husband. Kane was asleep in the recliner and a blanket was thrown over him. Unsure of what his presence meant; she didn't get her hopes up. She simply laid there until her eyes were forced back closed.

33 | *Special Delivery*

Carmen woke up to the sound of nurses outside her door. She could feel the baby moving inside her and she rubbed her stomach, trying to soothe whatever was bothering it. Kane was still in the recliner, fast asleep, and his presence was still a shock. After the way he'd left, she didn't expect to see him again unless their paths crossed when she moved out.

"Morning," an older lady greeted, coming in her room with a tray. The dietician set her breakfast on the meal counter.

"Morning," Carmen replied. She gazed over her plate as the lady left the room. About to dig in, she heard a knock at the door. A man was standing in the doorway, holding a large envelope in his hands.

"I didn't know he was here," he told her, pointing at Kane.

Carmen smiled. "Yeah, he's in fantasyland. Can I help you?"

The man walked in the room, handing her the envelope. She took it from him, and he uttered three simple words: You've been served. Her mouth dropped open in surprise only because she wasn't expecting the paperwork that soon. With everything they owned it wasn't possible for him to have divorce papers drawn up in less than twenty-four hours. Curious to know what the papers entailed; she tore open the envelope. "Michael Antonio Kane vs. Carmen Denise Davenport-Kane," she read. She scanned most of the pages already aware he was divorcing her on grounds of adultery. When she came to the section regarding spousal support, she nearly screamed. Kane was requesting a total of ten million dollars. The number shocked her to the point she tossed the papers at him, allowing the documents to hit him in the face. He woke up, grabbing the papers which were now resting in his lap.

"I told you I was gonna do it."

"How do you get divorce papers drawn up in one day?"

"I started them a while ago. When we first started arguing, I didn't know what was going on with us. I got confused so I went to a lawyer and had the papers drawn up. I decided to stick with the marriage and never filed the papers. Yesterday, things changed."

"Do you really think you're getting ten million dollars out of me? I don't remember you drawing any one of my designs. I worked my ass off for my company and now you want a big chunk of the pie?"

Kane chuckled in disbelief. "I supported you for seventeen years. I was always here for you. I never did you wrong. I never cheated on you. You did that shit to me. I deserve something for my pain and suffering."

"Yeah, yeah, yeah, Mr. Perfect Husband, you should get an award."

Carmen turned her head, not wanting to look at him. He continued talking about the divorce and she tried her best to block out his voice. It was hard and she managed to catch a few things he was saying. He figured out how they would divide their property, each of them keeping their cars, him keeping the house, and splitting their stock down the middle. He didn't want a custody battle for the sake of the kids and demanded they both changed their wills. Carmen grunted at his words until a slight pain ran through her body. It lasted for a couple of seconds, and she repositioned herself. When it occurred again, it was much sharper, forcing her to close her eyes.

In addition, the baby monitor was making a weird noise.

"I never asked anything of you. I never asked you for money, lavish trips..." she heard Kane say.

Carmen ignored him, feeling the onslaught of pain. Normal contractions usually started out slow, but this time around, her contractions were quick and sharp. She wasn't ready to go into labor, although she was about to. She pressed the nurse's call button and when a lady answered, she couldn't say anything. It hurt too much. She closed her eyes, feeling another contraction, and tried to count the seconds in between each one. By the time she got to two, she could hear a nurse coming in the room. The lady turned her over, pulling the covers off her body. Then, she heard someone running away.

"Is the baby coming?" Kane asked.

The room became filled with different voices. Someone moved her onto her back while her legs were spread open. She then heard someone instruct Kane to put on a set of scrubs.

"Your baby is coming," the doctor said, "and it's coming fast. When I instruct you, I'm going to need you to push, okay?"

Carmen nodded as someone placed their hand on her right shoulder. When she turned to see who it was, she moaned at the sight of Kane. He served her divorce papers and now he wanted to be sympathetic.

"Baby, I'm right here," he told her.

"Carmen, I need you to start pushing," a nurse said. "There's blood from the sac on the sheets. You were bleeding throughout the night."

Carmen felt another contraction, which made her face scrunch up. Once again, the nurse gave her a directive, which she didn't follow.

"Carmen, I need you to start pushing, you can do it, come on."

Carmen did as she was told; following each directive the nurse gave her. She wasn't quite sure how many times she pushed, but she felt like she was getting nowhere. If the baby's head was out, she didn't know, because they didn't announce it. Sweat droplets were on her face and she was almost out of breath. To make matters worse, Kane was kissing her forehead, encouraging her to give one more good push.

"This is it, baby, they say this is it. The baby only needs one more good push, okay? I know you have it in you. I love you, okay? Just give us one good push."

"I got the head," the doctor yelled. "I only need one small push this time. Just one small push," he repeated.

Carmen listened to Kane's voice, hearing him tell her he loved her. He kissed her repeatedly until she heard claps around the room. She could hear the baby crying and her arms reached out, longing to hold the gift she'd received from God.

"It's a boy, baby," Kane whispered. He wandered to the foot of her bed. He conversed with the doctor for a few seconds before he was handed a pair of surgical scissors. Carmen closed her eyes as her baby was detached from her. When her eyes reopened, Kane was holding the baby in the palm of his hand. Her son's skin was pale, his frame tremendously small, and the width of his fingers no bigger than a sheet of paper.

"What's his name?" she heard someone ask.

Carmen looked at her son. "Rakim," she replied. She rubbed her fingers along his face until the doctor told her they needed to take him. Kane handed the baby over and Carmen closed her eyes, feeling the afterbirth. Once it passed, she grabbed her phone and called Jay.

By the time he arrived, Kane had left, and they were alone in her room. He was upset and the look on his face was worse than his tone. She tried to soften the tension. "I named him Rakim," she told him. "I hope that's okay."

"He did that shit on purpose, Carm."

She knew what Jay was getting at. Instead of pretending she didn't, she dealt with the situation head-on. "Everything happened so fast. I was in so much pain, I couldn't call anyone. Why didn't you stay?"

"I stayed the entire time y'all were arguing. I left for about ten minutes and when I came back, he was sitting in the room. I asked him to leave, he refused, and we started an argument right there in the hallway. The nurses threatened to call security so I left because I couldn't risk being banned from the hospital. This happened at two o'clock in the morning. My plan was to come back at eight, but before I could, you gave birth."

Carmen further understood his pain. He was trying his best to keep the tension down while it backfired on him. It upset her to know he missed the birth by twenty minutes.

"I'm glad you named him Rakim, though," he said, commenting on her initial statement. "We never talked about middle names."

"I decided on Rakim Antonio Davenport. Before you say anything, let me explain. I'm not one hundred percent sure this baby is yours. The baby should be, but until I find out for sure, I want his last name to be Davenport. As far as Antonio goes, I've always loved the name and—"

"That's your husband's fuckin' middle name. Do you really think I'm going to be down for that shit?"

"Jay, it has nothing to do with Kane. I promise you. He served me divorce papers today so the last thing I want is to name anything after him."

"Are you looking for some sort of sympathy from me? I spent seventeen years in prison because of his fuckin' ass. I don't care about him divorcing you. You shouldn't have been with him in the first place. Now, back to his middle name, if it has nothing to do with Kane then why is Rakim's middle name Antonio?"

"Jay, it's not important. Our son is upstairs fighting for his life. He's barely over a pound."

"I know what he looks like. I went to see him before I came to see you. I know he might not make it up there. That's the reason I'm putting my foot down. You're not going to play me on this one. I want a relationship with my son. I also want you to move in with me. If we need to get a bigger space, we can. Until then, you and Rakim will be living with me until we can put a down payment on a house."

"Whoa, whoa, whoa," Carmen yelled. "We talked about this. We agreed we would co-parent, not start a relationship. Did you forget that conversation? It was your idea."

"I know what I said," Jay shot back. "I said it because we didn't how your marriage was gonna turn out. Now that he's given you divorce papers, you shouldn't have a problem living with me. Your marriage is over and now our agreement is out the window. If I gotta live with a son named Rakim Antonio then you gotta live with me."

"You don't have to live with anything," Carmen replied. "His birth certificate hasn't been filled out. If you want to argue with me on Antonio, fine, argue with me. The name isn't official. In terms of my divorce, I don't think Kane is going through with it. He was very compassionate when I was giving birth and I think he had a change of heart."

Jay got up from his seat, not bothering to say goodbye. Carmen's words were cutting him like a knife. He was partly to blame because he didn't fight for her when he had her. He agreed to co-parent only because Kane was unaware of the baby. Now that divorce papers had been served, he wanted to reclaim what was rightfully his. Carmen, on the other hand, wanted to hang on to her marriage.

Carmen knew Jay didn't understand. All he saw was her while she saw two men she was undeniably in love with. Carmen wasn't giving up on having a relationship with him, but she wanted to give her marriage a fair chance. All she wanted from Jay was a little bit of time.

Speaking of time, Carmen thought, *I haven't even called my kids. They don't even know Rakim is here.* Carmen sighed as she pulled her phone off the meal counter. She called Kristian's cell, praying her daughter answered. When she didn't, she left her a voicemail, informing her of the news. She tried to reach King, but she didn't get a response from him either. Giving up, she set her phone back on the meal counter. In due time, she would hear from them. Until then, she needed to be resting. The day had already been long, and something told her, it was only getting longer.

34 | *Sidetracked*

Kristian watched as her mother's name disappeared off her phone. She didn't answer on purpose because she was standing in front of Lil' Noc's house. After leaving the hospital with her father the day before, she drove to the park to clear her head. Her plan was to have time to herself, but somehow, Lil' Noc showed up, and the afternoon took a turn. There was something different about him. For the first time, he admitted to attacking Akaila. He even said he felt guilty about it. He wanted to apologize, but it wasn't possible. Akaila wouldn't talk to him. Therefore, he asked her to do it for him. Kristian agreed and accepted an invitation to his house.

He answered the door, wearing a pair of jeans and a black wifebeater. "Come on in," he said. The house was old-fashioned, and Kristian realized he still lived with his parents.

"They're not here," he told her, reading her mind.

"Oh," she mouthed. "Did you want to talk to me about something?"

"Maybe," he whispered. "Why don't you come upstairs?"

Kristian was trying to be a big girl, but it was obvious, she entered an arena she didn't know anything about it. "Why can't we talk down here?" she asked as he neared the staircase.

Lil' Noc smirked at her question. "Why talk down here when we can have privacy upstairs? My folks aren't here, but they can always come back. Do you have a problem being in my room?"

Kristian couldn't hide her nerves. "Look, Noc, I thought you wanted to—" Lil' Noc interrupted her.

"Why do you keep fighting it? Is it your brother or Akaila? Is it your boyfriend?"

"It's all of it," she told him. "It's the fear of the unknown. It's the walk on the wild side. I've always played it safe, Noc. Even right now, coming over here," Kristian felt Lil' Noc's finger on her lips.

"I didn't invite you over here to talk."

Kristian knew what his words meant. She told herself she was a big girl, and she could handle what he was throwing, but she was lying. If her mother knew what she was about to get into, she would ground her for life. Then, there was her sister, the person who warned her about getting close to him. However, Lil' Noc had her intrigued. He represented the bad boy in every good girl's dream.

Despite the concerns of her sister, Kristian followed him up the steps. Once the door to his bedroom was closed, she allowed him to kiss her.

This time, they didn't stop, and they took things a step further. More experienced than she or Dijuan, Lil' Noc moved faster than what she was accustomed to. While Dijuan would only squeeze her breasts, Noc put his mouth on her nipples, sucking each one until she squirmed from the sensation. Too enthralled in his affection, she forgot to please him.

"Don't be greedy," he mumbled, "grab my shit."

Kristian did as he said, sliding her hand around his meat. His length wasn't long like Dijuan's although he was slightly thicker. She was only playing with him for a minute before he moved her hand.

"How far are you trying to go?"

Kristian shrugged her shoulders. "I don't know. I didn't expect to go this far. I just became curious. How far are you trying to go?"

"Well, you can give me some, but I don't wear condoms."

Kristian knew unprotected sex was not what she was going for. In addition, she was a virgin. She planned on keeping her virginity until she was married. *Well, that is the plan,* Kristian thought. "I can't have sex without a condom. I'm only fifteen. I'm too young for a baby. My parents would kill me."

Lil' Noc smirked, yet he didn't respond to her words. Instead, he changed the subject. "Let me show you something," he said, pulling his boxers off. He grabbed her hand, wrapping her fingers around his dick. He moved her fingers up and down his shaft, slowly at first until she caught on. "This is the money right here."

Kristian continued to please him as his fingers slid inside of her.

"Do you like it?" he asked.

Kristian muttered a low yes only to feel him pull his fingers out. Somewhat shocked, she looked at him, quizzically.

"Can I put it in now?"

Kristian was shocked "You said you weren't gonna wear a condom."

"It'll only be for a minute. I won't leave it in for long."

"I can't get pregnant, Noc."

"It'll only be—stop calling me, Noc. I don't go by that anymore. My name is Nicholas."

Kristian raised her brow. "Nicholas? Your real name is Nicholas?"

"Yeah, it's Nicholas Powers. Don't call me Noc."

Kristian felt his hands spread her legs apart. She told him no yet her actions contradicted her words. She needed to stop him, but she didn't. When the tip of his penis went inside her, the feeling wasn't bad. When he pushed it in further, she screamed at the top of her lungs. He jerked away and Kristian covered her mouth in embarrassment.

"I thought you slept with Dijuan," he yelled, shocked as well.

"I'm sorry, I didn't mean to scream."

Nicholas moved to the other side of the bed. "I didn't know you were a virgin. I know you told me at the mall, but I thought you were lying."

"I guess I should've reiterated," Kristian mumbled. "What do you want to do? I mean, we could always try again."

"Nah, there won't be any sticking going down. We'll go back to where we left off." He moved closer to her, sticking his fingers inside her.

Meanwhile, Kristian grabbed his penis back in her hands. She didn't know how long they went at it, but it was only a few minutes before they were both moaning. Nicholas came first, exploding in her hand while a minute later, she lost all control. A feeling she couldn't describe, the sensation was exquisite and put her in a deep sleep.

35 | *Changes*

Kristian still hadn't listened to her voicemails when she snuck back in the house. Now ashamed over what she'd done, she tried to sneak to her room, but her father noticed her before she could get inside. His voice made her stop in her tracks. She peered into his bedroom. Three large boxes were in front of him. He was dropping items inside. "What is that?" She pointed to the boxes.

"Your mother is moving out."

Kristian stared at her mother's designer labels. "Are you serious about this? Daddy, where is she going to go? This is where she lives."

"She's a multi-millionaire. She'll have a house in no time. Besides, she'll be living at the hospital. Your baby brother was born this morning. She named him Rakim. You haven't heard from your mom?"

"I have," Kristian replied, remembering the missed call. "You don't even know if the baby is Jay's. Weren't you the one talking about how many times y'all slept with each other? What if the baby is yours? You would feel guilty for packing her things."

"The baby isn't mine," Kane growled. "Even if it was, she still cheated on me. I don't trust her. If you can't trust a person, you can't be with them. Remember that."

"I will, but you're gonna throw her out before doing a paternity test? I know you can get a kit online. What if Rakim is yours?"

"The baby isn't mine. Don't say that again."

"You don't know until you do a paternity test."

Kristian left Kane with an idea that was farfetched. Rakim wasn't his son yet there was a possibility. Unsure if he should do a test or not, he dropped one of Carmen's dresses in a box and grabbed his car keys.

It was the middle of the afternoon, and he was certain he could find Malik at his apartment. If not, he would head to Sapphire. Lucky for him, Malik was home and let him inside. "Did you hear the news?"

"Straight from the source," Malik replied. "Jay left a few minutes ago. He brought over some pictures of the baby. I'll tell you this; Rakim needs a lot of prayer. I've never seen a baby that small."

Kane remembered how he held Rakim in his palm. He hadn't seen the baby since that morning. He prayed everything was going well. "This whole thing has been an experience. I've been gone for six months, and I came home to a whole lot more than I bargained for."

"You sure did. You're a good one, though. I was shocked when Jay told me you were at the hospital. I guess you're trying to stick in there, huh?"

Kane shook his head. "We're getting a divorce, which isn't what I came to talk about. Kristian thinks I should do a paternity test on the baby."

Malik's eyes grew. "Why would you put yourself through that? I know Jay said she slept with y'all back to back, but you know your situation. I understand you wanting to know, but after fifteen years, do you really think you fathered a child?"

"With God all things are possible."

"True. I can't debate on you that one. If the baby is yours, are you still going to divorce Carmen?"

The question was the same one Kristian posed. He didn't have an answer to give. "I'll take it a day at a time. First thing, first, I need to get this test done." Kane pulled out his cell phone. "I'm gonna go handle this. I'll check in with you later."

Malik tried to change his mind because Kane was making the wrong decision. The DNA test was only going to further reiterate what he already knew. "You're only setting yourself up for failure," he told him. His friend refused to listen and left his apartment with his mind made up. Malik told himself to let it go. Once Kane got the results, he was going to wish he listened.

***

Two weeks was the turnaround time for the DNA test. Within that timeframe, Carmen moved out the house and was living in her two-bedroom apartment. Most of her time was spent at the hospital, which Kane frequented on a regular basis. They would make small talk during his visits, yet he never told her about the test. On the day he received the results, he directly to Brookstone High instead of the hospital.

School hadn't let out for the summer, and he walked in the attendance office, hoping he wasn't interrupting one of his daughter's exams. "I need to get Kristian Kane an early dismissal," he told the attendance clerk. "I'm her father. Is there anything I need to sign?"

"There is a small form," the lady told him, handing him a clipboard. Kane filled out all the details as the lady instructed for one of the students in the office to get Kristian. Anxious to see the results, his plan was to have Kristian do the honor since she was his only biological child.

If the results were in his favor, their new baby could potentially change the course of their marriage. While it was obvious he still loved Carmen, the wound of her betrayal hadn't healed.

"Daddy, what are you doing here?" he heard Kristian ask. "Is everything okay? You know I drove this morning."

"We'll see," he replied, pulling the envelope out his pocket. His daughter's eyes grew. They left the office and headed to the school's courtyard. He never told her about the test so she would be shocked to learn of the envelope's contents. "Will you do the honor?"

Kristian ran her fingers through her hair because she was unsure of what she was opening. "What is this?" She took the envelope out his hands. "I hope this isn't divorce papers."

"It's the results of the DNA test."

Kristian's mouth dropped open. She tore the envelope open and scanned the document. "Ninety-nine point nine percent," Kristian screamed, shoving the paper in his face. "Daddy, he's yours."

Kane grabbed the papers from her hands. "He can't be. It's not possible."

"It is possible," Kristian yelled, hugging him. "You gotta tell Mama. She can move back in. You gotta tell her now."

Kane stared at the results in disbelief. God had finally answered his prayer. "I'm gonna tell her now. There's no point in putting it off. Do you want to come with me?"

Kristian declined. "No, you need to do this alone. I'm gonna stay here and go back to class. We're reviewing for exams."

"You're right," he agreed. "I'm gonna find your mother. You take care and I'll see you when I get home." Kane kissed her cheek, giving her another quick hug. Once she was out his grasp, he waited until she was back in the building before he left. He wasn't quite sure where Carmen was, but he checked the hospital first. It was only a little after twelve and he knew she spent her lunch hour there. If he missed her, his next stop was Flame.

He found her at the hospital, standing over Rakim's incubator. Her eyes grew big when he pulled out the envelope.

"Are you really going to do this here?" she asked him. "Kane, I agreed to meet with your lawyer. We don't have to discuss the divorce around Rakim. I want to keep positive energy around him."

"This isn't about the divorce," Kane whispered. He opened the envelope and slid out the results. When he handed the papers to her, she didn't take them. "You need to look at this, Carm."

"What is this about? You're scaring me."

"Do you remember the last time we made love? We did it over and over, not knowing if it would be our last time. We didn't know it then, but that moment was special."

"Kane, look," Carmen began, "You don't have to do this. The deed is done, the cards have fallen. Let's just try our best to get through this divorce. Seventeen years is a lot to be throwing away, but we're moving on. Right now, my focus is Rakim. He's much better than when he was born, but he's still fighting. We need to be strong for him."

Kane handed the results to her again. This time Carmen took the papers. Her eyes grew big when she saw Rakim was his. Then, she threw the papers down in disgust.

"What is this, Kane? Why are you doing this?"

"He's mine, Carm. I don't know what happened, but I got you pregnant. It was me. Jay didn't have anything to do with it."

"I didn't have anything to do with what?"

Jay was standing behind him. Kane hadn't heard any footsteps and he figured it was because he was too engrossed in Carmen. The moment became surreal, and he chose not to reply to Jay's question. Instead, he picked up the papers.

Carmen moved past her husband, pulling Jay aside. She rubbed her hands along his arms to calm him. "He did a paternity test on Rakim. The results say the baby is his."

A blank stare fell over Jay's face. Once content, his demeanor turned to anger and then to rage. "He's lying. He did this shit because he started seeing a declining bank account. He knows Rakim isn't his." Jay slid past Carmen, headed straight for Kane who was holding the papers in his hands. "Who did you get to alter the results? I know you got connects."

Jay's voice was thunderous. Carmen tried to calm him, but Jay was ready for battle. "He did this shit on purpose. He knows Rakim is my son. What would make you do a fuckin' paternity test? You've never given her a child. You know you can't have kids."

"Sir, I'm going to have to ask you to leave," a nurse interrupted. "We can't have this commotion in here. It's not healthy for the babies."

Carmen grabbed Jay's hand, but he pushed her away.

"Don't tell me you believe him, Carm. You know he's lying. He got these papers drawn up to make it look like Rakim is his." Jay grabbed the papers from Kane's hands, looking the documents over. While the papers looked legit, Kane had pull at the Triad. "Do you believe him?" he asked Carmen.

She parted her lips almost scared to reply. "I don't know, Jay. The documents are certified. I can only believe what I see. If it's true, we can make this work. I know you love Rakim and—" Jay ripped the papers in two before walking out the NICU. Carmen followed behind him, but every word she fed him went ignored. Once they were in the hospital's parking lot, the conversation was over. With her car keys still in the NICU, she was forced to let him leave. Cursing under her breath, she jumped when she felt someone's hand on her shoulder.

She turned to find Kane beside her, holding the remains of the test in his hands. Carmen didn't know what he was trying to do, but he wedged a wall between her and Jay. Not ready to deal with the issue, she headed back in the hospital. Kane followed her, but she didn't speak one word to him. Once back in the NICU, she tried calling Jay to apologize, and as expected, he didn't answer. Still, she kept calling. She didn't give up until her phone went dead.

36 | *Runaway*

King woke in the middle of the night to the sound of something heavy hitting the hardwood floor. He looked underneath his door to see a shadow moving back and forth. The sound only grew louder as he got out of bed. Still somewhat asleep, he got out of bed. He opened the door to see his father with several suitcases in front of him. "What are you doing?" He rubbed the sleep out his eyes.

"I'm packing," Jay replied. "I'm going back to San Juan."

"You're going back to San Juan? Why are you going to Puerto Rico?"

"The baby isn't mine," Jay announced.

King pulled up his sweatpants, which had fallen below the rim of his boxers. "What are you talking about? Rakim is yours. I went and visited him two days ago. His eyes are hazel."

"Kane got a paternity test. The papers say the baby is his."

"Oh, shit," King muttered. "Well, how long are you gonna be gone? You know I only have two weeks left before I turn myself in."

"I don't know yet. You can stay here. You don't have to leave. I'm getting out of here, though. I already have a pilot to fly my plane."

King's eyes widened. "You have a private plane? When were you going to tell me you had a private plane?"

"I don't have to tell you everything," Jay roared. "Some things you need to keep private."

"Do you have other kids, too?" King shot back. "Is that private?"

Jay dropped the suitcase in his hand. "You're the only child I have. Sometimes you act like you're not mine."

"How do I do that? I've always respected you. I'm here, aren't I? I'm helping you with these businesses, I got the cartel poppin'. I still haven't dealt with my own shit. I lost the only girl who gave a damn about me. We're both hurt. What happened to us riding this shit out together?"

"You want to ride this shit out?" Jay pointed inside the room. "Pack you fuckin' bags. We're going to Puerto Rico."

37 | *Breakup to Makeup*

It wasn't Jay's intention to tell Carmen about his trip to San Juan. In fact, he wasn't going to tell her anything.

King did it for him, calling her before he got on the plane. King told her he would be back in two weeks although he couldn't give an answer for his father. He didn't know if Jay would return to Brookstone. From the way he was acting, San Juan was home.

The news was upsetting for Carmen, yet she hid her emotions. She didn't want Kane to know there was a problem although he was the cause of it. In his mind, they needed to be rejoicing. Carmen couldn't share in the joy not when she knew the pain Jay was feeling. He was looking forward to being a father to Rakim. Like his freedom, the opportunity was snatched. Carmen was searching for a way to make it right, yet Kane was trying to keep her mind off everything involving Rakim's paternity.

"What are you doing Saturday night?" he asked. They were standing in the parking lot of the hospital about to part ways.

"I'll probably be here with Rakim."

"Do you wanna see a movie? We could get Akaila and Kristian to sit with him for the night. I mean, he's making excellent progress. The nurse said he probably could go home next month."

"Why do you want to go to the movies? We're going through a divorce. Now that Rakim is your son, you don't want to divorce me? Is that it?" Carmen unlocked her car doors, ready for the night to be over. It was going on almost two and she was ready for her pajamas and a warm bed.

"I'm willing to work on our relationship if you are. We need to do this for the sake of our kids. So, will you come with me?"

Carmen didn't agree to the date. "Do you remember how you were when you found out I was pregnant? You called me a whore, a bitch. You cursed me to hell. Now, it's like, you're willing to forget everything."

"I'm willing to try. You can try, too."

Carmen exhaled. "You want me to try? Okay, Kane, I'll try. Pick the movie and call me tomorrow, okay?"

Kane told her he would before giving her a quick kiss on the cheek. Carmen wasn't quite sure what to make of the affection or the date. The last two weeks was tumultuous. First, she moved out their house then she received a nasty phone call from his mother. To top it off, her pregnancy leaked to the blogs. Kane didn't give her any kind of sympathy, not that she expected it, but it made it hard for her to believe he wanted to reconcile. He went from hating her to wanting to work things out almost overnight.

If they were able to work through their differences, they would stay out of court, and she would keep ten million in her pocket. If not, she would be signing a check and walking away from the longest relationship of her life.

***

Saturday afternoon, Carmen wasn't faring too much better. Jay still wasn't returning her calls, and the update on Rakim's paternity had reached her parents' ears. Her mother gave her a mouthful, which ended with her hanging up the phone while she was in mid-rant. The day didn't improve until Kane picked her up for their movie date. They made small talk on the way there whereas the real conversation didn't start until after the movie was over.

"I should've known you were going to pick a detective flick," she said, getting inside his Jeep. "You talked through the whole movie."

"Well, you shouldn't have let me choose," he replied. "I wasn't too bad, was I? I didn't give away the ending this time."

"Did you not hear those people talking about us? They were like, 'why doesn't she tell him to shut up,' I was so embarrassed."

"Hey, that's what happens when you let me choose," Kane laughed. "You could've picked the other movie. It was a comedy, I think."

"I know, but I wanted to see this movie," Carmen replied. "The lead actress is in talks right now to do some modeling for Flame. I mentioned it in my interview with *Girlfriend*. You read the article, right?"

"I told you what I did with that magazine." Kane's mind went in the gutter. "Do you want me to show you? I demonstrate better than I can tell."

Carmen rolled her eyes. "I'll pass."

Kane chuckled for a bit as he started up the car. He wasn't in a rush to get to her apartment, but he could tell Carmen was worn out. If anything, she was probably ready for the night to be over.

"I talked to King earlier today," she shared. "He's enjoying San Juan."

"That's good to hear," he replied. "He has a week left, right?"

"Yep. He won't even get to see Rakim before he goes in. I was hoping he would come back early."

Kane drove in silence until he reached her apartment complex. About to start another conversation, Carmen was taking off her seatbelt as if she was rushing out the car. "Can we at least chat for a little while? We have plenty to talk about."

"You're right, we do."

Kane turned on some music to set the mood. "Did you enjoy yourself tonight?" He slid his hand in her lap, giving her thigh a small squeeze. She replied with only a glance. "I miss you. I was gone for six months and when I came back, you know, we were pulled apart again."

"I know—" Carmen was taken aback when Kane's lips smashed into hers. Rather unexpected, the kiss turned sensual until she remembered the pending divorce. The thought of it made her push him away. She even wiped off his kiss. "We're not doing this," she told him, unlocking her door. "I'm not going back and forth with you."

"I didn't mean any harm. I wanted to…"

"Do you remember our divorce? I haven't seen any signs of you trying to stop it. If you are, let me know, because right now, there is ten million dollars on the table. You also don't have any rights to Rakim because your name is not on the birth certificate. Those are two major issues we need to deal with before we start kissing each other."

Kane got silent, hearing her words. He didn't know what to say so he allowed her to get out the car. Once she was inside her apartment, he punched the steering wheel hard, blowing the horn. The divorce was in limbo because of him. He hadn't stopped it because he wanted to make the right choice. Not quite sure if he could trust her, he wanted to take things slow. Carmen, on the other hand, wanted a decision that very second. He could give her what she wanted, but he was taking a risk. If anything, he needed to show her he was serious about working on their marriage. Therefore, he resorted to their most common form of communication.

This isn't easy for either of us, he texted. *We both don't want to be led on. I'm not ready to jump in full throttle because we need to rebuild. Once I see we're ready, I'll put an end to the divorce. We still have plenty of time. Can you give me some time?*

Kane sent the text, telling himself he wasn't going home until he got a response. While it seemed like forever, he finally got one.

Yes.

Carmen's reply was the start of a shift in their relationship. What Kane initially called rebuilding, he now viewed as courting. After that night, they dove headfirst. Only a week had passed, but the change was intense. He even started spending the night at her apartment.

Currently next to her in bed, he was watching her sleep. Carmen hadn't brought it up, but their first scheduled mediation with their lawyers was coming up in a few days. Afterwards, they would be meeting with a judge. Since he was unsure of Carmen's thoughts on the matter, he couldn't sleep. The past several days had been great for them, yet he still wasn't ready to commit to her. Although she hadn't brought it up, she would soon. In fact, when she turned to face him, he knew she was about to bring it up.

"Why are you still awake?" she whispered.

"You're awake, too," he replied. "I thought you were sleep. You fooled me. What has you up?"

"Our mediation is coming up soon," she told him. "Are you going to stop the divorce?"

Kane sighed, knowing he hadn't decided. "I don't know."

Carmen didn't understand why it was taking him so long. Their relationship was stronger, and they were even sleeping in the same bed again. Jay wasn't in the picture, so she didn't understand his hesitance. "What do I need to do to make you see I'm serious about us?"

"I don't know how to please you." He spoke honestly.

"You don't know how to please me? What are you talking about?"

"I want to make you lose control. Show me what I need to do. Tell me what you need. You said Jay was better than me. I need to be better than him. If I am, you won't have a reason to seek him for anything."

Carmen could tell from his tone how serious he was. Her husband always pleased her, yet she couldn't teach him Jay's skills. She wasn't quite sure what her ex did, she only knew he did it well.

"Teach me," he told her, kissing her neck.

How was she going to teach him how to bring a tear to her eye? Carmen couldn't come up with a solution until she realized the difference between Kane and Jay.

"I need you to be aggressive. If it's yours act like it's yours," she told him. She peeled off his clothes. Kane did the same to her and once he entered her, she wrapped her legs around his waist. He was already using her advice, tugging on her hair as he thrusted inside her. Something he'd never done, he made her feel powerless and weak.

They hadn't changed positions, but there was something different about the connection. Maybe, their sex life did need more spice. In need of a change, Carmen mounted him. His body now between her legs, she rode him until he was rock hard. In return, he guided her hips back and forth over his manhood. The sensation was more than she could handle. She grabbed the wall for support as she came quicker than she imagined. A loud moan echoed from her lips, followed by a stream of tears down her face. Then, as if on cue, Kane came inside her, his voice louder than hers. Despite his volume, he ended their lovemaking with three simple words she longed to hear from him.

"I love you."

38 | *Taking Chances*

The following morning, Carmen woke, feeling refreshed. Kane left an hour earlier, telling her he would see her at church. A few hours before morning worship service, Carmen stopped at the grocery store with plans to head to the hospital afterward. She only planned to pick up a few snacks, but she got more than she bargained for.

Malik was standing in the canned fruit aisle. "Malik Yoba," she joked, catching his attention.

"Carmen Jones," he greeted, picking up a can of mixed fruit. "How are you? Oh, let me ask this, how are you and Kane?"

Carmen rubbed her lips together before forming her mouth into a smile. "We're working on things," she admitted. "How are you?"

Malik let out a small chuckle. "I'm stuck in the same spot. To be honest, I'm ready to put my foot down. You know I've been hanging out a lot with Malachi since King has been gone. The experience tells me what I already know. I want a baby. I also want to get married. When it comes to Tiara, I'm at the point where I'm not taking no for an answer. It's either we make it right or we split."

"I hate it's come to that. You both deserve to be happy."

"I know she loves me," Malik stated. "I don't understand why she's so scared."

"I hope I'm not the reason." Carmen remembered the incident at Lucky's. An incident she and Tiara still hadn't discussed, she wondered if it was still an issue.

"Nah," Malik disagreed. "I think she's passed that. Right now, she thinks no one respects marriage. She used to look up to you and Kane. Now, after learning of the affair, she's more fearful of marriage."

Carmen didn't want her marriage to be the reason Tiara didn't give Malik what he deserved. Ten years of dating would go down the drain if her friend allowed Malik to walk away. "I don't know if this is going to work, Malik, but you can try this. Tell Tiara what you want and how you feel. The choice is hers. She can comply or you'll have to move on. You've instilled ten years in this relationship. That's a marriage right there."

"I don't want to lose her, Carm."

Carmen gave him more advice. "I know my friend. She likes aggression. You got to be firm with her. Tell her how you feel and until you do, you can't be Rakim's godfather. You also need to tell Tiara the same thing. If she doesn't marry you, she can't be Rakim's godmother. That should make her comply."

Malik chuckled at the thought, deciding to make his request known. Until he gave Tiara an ultimatum, they would continue down the same path. A journey which wasn't meant for him, he decided to go after what he wanted.

***

It was no surprise to Carmen when Tiara called her later that evening. Her friend wanted to talk, and Carmen told her to meet her at the hospital. After her discussion with Malik, she expected Tiara's phone call. Whether the conversation would be brutal or joyful, she didn't know.

When Tiara arrived, her friend appeared to be in good spirits. They made small talk about Rakim's progress before Tiara switched the conversation to one about relationships. It was the only hint Carmen needed. Anxious to know Tiara's response, she sat there on pins and needles.

"I've realized over these last few months that it's time to face my fears. As you know, I haven't always been in the best relationships. I've been degraded, humiliated, cheated on, and whatever else you can remember. The only time I've ever felt somewhat safe is with Malik. When he came to me today, I thought I had. He poured his heart out to me, Carm. He demanded I marry him."

"What did you say?" Carmen asked, her anxiety growing.

Tiara held up her hand to display a bright green diamond ring. Two white stones were on both sides of the green diamond, creating an intricate look. "I said yes," Tiara screamed. She covered her mouth when she remembered where she was. "I didn't want him to leave me," she whispered.

Carmen jumped up, grabbing her friend's hand. "Oh, Tee, look at it. Dang, Malik shelved out some dough for this one. I bet he was saving for years. This is a beauty. It's also different. The stone is green." Carmen fanned herself, feeling an onslaught of tears. "Now, it's time to plan the wedding."

"Yes, we are going to start immediately. Malik wants it to be soon. I told him he should've given me the ultimatum earlier. I know King's time is winding down, so he won't be a part of the wedding."

"I'm still not ready for him to go in." Carmen sighed. "It also doesn't help that he's in Puerto Rico. I can't even spend time with him."

"I know," Tiara agreed. "At least he and Jay are getting along. I know that's what you wanted." Tiara glanced at Rakim, realizing the baby was staring in their direction. His eyes were opening and closing as if he was fighting sleep. "We also are going to start trying for a baby. You know they say it's harder the older you get so we're going to start now."

"Wow, Tee, this is a lot. You're going to have a marriage and a baby all in the same year? What did Malik say to you?" Carmen joked.

"I told you, he poured out his heart." Tiara stood up to get a closer look at Rakim. His eyes were now closed, but she had already seen what she needed to see. Kane may have been Rakim's father, but the baby clearly had Jay's eyes. She didn't mention it to Carmen, deciding to change the subject to one of work. "I know it's important for you to be here with Rakim. However, I was hoping that maybe you could take next weekend off and come with me to a fashion show in the City. It's for Mantra Designs. I think you need to get away."

Carmen didn't want to spend a day without Rakim yet alone a weekend. If she did take a break, she would have to use her breast pump double time to make sure he had enough food. "I could get Kane to watch him. He hasn't been working on any major cases lately. I could get the girls to come with us."

"See, there we go, it could be like a trip celebrating my engagement."

"Now you're talking." Carmen gave her friend a large smile before grabbing her into a hug. "I'm happy for you, Tee. You and Malik deserve this. Not only will your marriage be successful, but y'all are going to make the best parents. I can see you two now."

"Do you really mean that, Carm?"

"Of course," Carmen replied. "Just think; you've had plenty of practice with my Brady Bunch. You and Malik will be just fine."

39 | *The Beginning of the End*

By Monday morning, the news of Tiara's engagement spread like wildfire. The offices of Flame were abuzz with the news while it was the hot topic of the day on the streets. The only person who was unaware of the engagement was Kane who was busy searching for his next case. He was searching through local police reports when his last case walked through his door. Not quite sure what to think, Kane stared at Tricia's curvaceous frame in awe.

"Good afternoon," she greeted, smoothing her hair behind her ear.

"Tricia," Kane stammered. "Look at you."

"It's a long shot from the last time you saw me, huh? It's been what, almost a year? I've been clean for a while now. I got my weight back up, got a job. Some girls even helped me get an apartment on the Eastside. I'm doing a whole lot better than you probably imagined."

"I see," he said, admiring her new look. "You look great."

"Thank you. How are my babies?"

"Excellent, excellent," he replied. "You know, Malachi will be starting the eighth grade soon. He's not hustling anymore. Akaila is on the high honor roll. We're struggling with her and this whole driver's license thing, but she's working on it. You should be proud."

"I am," she told him, "you and your wife have been doing good with them. It wasn't easy getting clean, but once I saw that spread in *Girlfriend Magazine*, I had to do something. Carmen was claiming my kids like I was dead or something. They were even calling her mom. I know I haven't been the best parent, but they're still my kids. I don't want to cause any drama, but I want to see them. I know I'm not Carmen's favorite person."

Kane's hand flew up. "Carmen and I are separated. We had another baby, but I haven't decided on whether I want to stay in the marriage."

"Oh," Tricia said under her breath. "What happened?"

Kane exhaled. "She slept with Jay."

"She was a whore from the start. You should've known that was going to happen." Tricia covered her mouth once she realized how insensitive she was being. "I'm sorry. I know that hurt."

"Enough about me," Kane told her, clapping his hands. "Why don't I take you out for a little celebration? You can even choose the restaurant. We can have a bite to eat and then I can take you to see your kids."

Tricia accepted his invitation. She didn't think twice about seeing Carmen. In her opinion, Carmen should be fearful of her. Now that Jay was back in town, she needed to make her move. Once she laid eyes on him, she wanted to remind him of what he left.

"Where do you want to eat?" Kane asked once they were in his Jeep.

"It doesn't matter, I'll eat anything."

"Ahh, come on," Kane urged. "I know you have a little spot you want to go to."

"Why don't we go to the Blue Lagoon for a few drinks?"

"I promised you a dinner, not a bar," he joked.

"How about we eat at Lucky's then?"

"Lucky's it is," Kane agreed, "one of the best eateries in town."

Tricia smiled at the progress she made. This time around, she was able to share her success with not only her kids, but Kane as well. No longer in danger of losing them, her plan was to reclaim what was rightfully hers. Now, all she needed was Jay.

***

So far, the evening had been normal at the Kane household. Malachi was in his room playing video games, Kristian was on the phone with Dijuan while Akaila was studying for a Government exam. Almost eight o'clock, Akaila decided to take a break and crept down the steps to the kitchen. Once at the bottom, she paused when the front door opened. Kane announced his arrival for the entire house to hear. She smiled at his presence until she saw he wasn't alone.

"You won't believe who I found," Kane yelled, pointing at her mom.

"I got an A on my—" Akaila looked behind her, seeing Malachi on the steps. "Where have you been?"

Kane noticed the disgruntled expressions on the kids' faces. Unsure of what they were thinking, he decided to give them some privacy. "Tricia, I'll let you take over. I'll be in the office, okay?"

Tricia nodded her head. Her kids had changed tremendously. "Well, don't just stand there," she cried, holding her arms out. "Come here." Malachi was the first to move. He gave her a hug while Akaila stood frozen on the steps. "Aren't you going to give your mama a hug? I'm clean now."

"That's good, Mama," Malachi interjected. "I've missed you."

"I've missed you, too, baby." Tricia ran her hands over his face. "I got an apartment, too. Y'all can come spend the night. It's a two-bedroom."

"Our rooms are here," Akaila replied. "This is where we live. The Kanes are going to adopt us."

"Baby, I'm back. They can't adopt you."

"Why not," Akaila shot back.

Tricia straightened up, hearing her tone. "I'm not giving up my parental rights. I—" Tricia watched as Akaila went upstairs. She looked at Malachi, who only did the same, following his sister. Their reactions weren't what she expected yet it was what she thought she deserved. She hadn't been the best mother and it showed in how they treated her. Instead of forcing them to accept her return, she headed in the home office. Her face was tearstained, which prompted Kane to console her.

"Are you okay? What happened out there?"

Kane closed the door and motioned for her to sit down.

"She looks at me like I'm nothing," Tricia cried. I've been doing so well, and I want her to see that. She won't even give me a chance."

"It's going to take some time. They've been through so much. It won't happen overnight. Why don't we go in the kitchen and whip up some chocolate chip cookies? The kids love those."

Tricia frowned. The last thing she wanted to do was bake cookies. She didn't respond to him, leading Kane to massage her shoulders. The affection turned her on, and she changed her mind about going after Jay. Kane's voice was soothing, and his hands caressed her skin like he was asking for more. With everything he did for her, it was time to repay him. When she faced him, she knew what she wanted to do. Despite his resistance, she managed to undo his pants.

They tussled for a bit, but she squeezed him enough times to make him erect. She then tugged at his boxers until his manhood became visible. It was then he stopped resisting. Kane was a perfect size and Tricia didn't hesitate to slide his penis in her mouth. She took as much of him as she could, pleasuring him until she longed for more. She then pulled her pants down and felt him as he slid the seat of her panties to the side. Her thighs became centered on his as he entered pink heaven.

"This is what I needed," she moaned. To make it even more pleasurable, she moved off his lap and bent over in front of the couch. "Come on," she urged. His dick was rock hard, and she pointed to her ass, directing him to their next position. He did as she commanded, trying his best to enter her. When he pushed his way inside, he laid on top of her, his dick exploring her region. A few minutes later, Tricia had taken all she could. Kane gave one final thrust before she came on the couch and his seed splattered inside her.

***

Everything happened so fast; Kane wasn't quite sure what he'd done. He even went in the bathroom to wash her off him. He committed the same sin as his wife. He turned away from Tricia, who was sleeping on the office floor beside him. He wished he could take it back.

When Tricia wrapped her arms around him, he moved away. In due time, he would tell her the truth. The moment they shared was just that, a moment. Their relationship wasn't going any further. She would never equal up to his wife. It was best not to lead her on. He would thank her for the experience and then send her on her way.

40 | *Coming Home*

The drama back in Brookstone was far from King's mind. Currently looking over the balcony in his room, he watched as two new employees of his father's loaded a limousine with their luggage. During the night, his father had a change of heart and was ready to head back to Brookstone. While he wasn't ready to face his problems, King didn't have a choice. He only had a few days before he was scheduled to turn himself in. Then, it would be a year and some months before he saw Brookstone again. If he didn't head home now, he wouldn't get to see his family before he was locked up.

"Time to go," his father said, coming in his room. "Are you ready?"

"I'm never gonna be ready," King told him. "Only half our work is done."

"It's a good half, though," Jay retorted. "You did a lot in a short amount of time. The cartel is booming, Sapphire will be opening soon, and the renovations are almost complete on the building for Blue Magic. The only thing left is Iceland and I have that on lock. You should be proud of yourself."

"I still don't have Coco," King replied, leaving the balcony.

"Then, I suggest you use your time wisely. Spend some time with your family and try to find her. It'll work out in the end."

King huffed. "You make it sound so easy. What are you going to do about your problem?" King glanced in his father's direction. "I heard your conversation with Silvas." He spoke of his father's butler. "You really love my mother, don't you?"

Jay chose not to answer. Instead, he made his exit. "Get your stuff together. The plane leaves in five minutes."

King knew his father hadn't dealt with the situation. He was still hurt over Rakim's paternity. King wasn't going to press the issue because he already knew his father's thoughts. However, he didn't know his plans.

***

Based off what occurred the night before, Carmen was no longer the only person in the center of Kane and Jay's triangle. The only difference between her and Tricia was Jay's nonexistent feelings for his ex-girlfriend. In addition, Kane had no knowledge of Tricia's sexual tryst with King. Kane was confident in his decision to end things, yet Tricia thought differently. She left his house only minutes ago, but somehow she found her way back inside.

"Malachi let me up," she explained. "You're not upset, are you? I thought we could chat for a bit."

Kane gripped the towel around his waist, keeping his distance. Tricia was a predator who was likely to pounce at any given time.

"I've already locked the door. I'm ready when you are."

Kane declined. "We can't do this. I told you this morning. Carmen and I are still together. We may be separated, but we are still together."

"Then why are you divorcing her?" Tricia shot back. "I read the newspapers and blogs. You're headed to court soon. You requested the fastest divorce in New York history. Word on the street is that you want ten million. That's a lot of money to take from the woman you love."

"Everyone wants to focus on the money. What about what she did to me? She cheated on me and got pregnant."

Tricia gave him a quick reminder. "She cheated on you, but she had your son. Did you forget about that? You also forgot you slept with me. We made love, Kane."

Kane grabbed his clothes from the bed. "We fucked. We didn't make love. There's a difference." He pulled the towel off and slid on his boxers. As he did it, he noticed Tricia when she took her right thumb and sucked on it. The temptation grew like his manhood.

"Does Carmen do this for you?" she asked.

Kane would never admit the truth. His wife didn't. That was why he allowed Tricia to please him. Right then and there, he came in her mouth. He then pushed her away, going inside the bathroom to clean off.

This is just a sexual thing, he thought. *It won't ever happen again.*

Kane told himself the rendezvous would be their last. He was certain of it when he walked in the kitchen and saw King. The last person he expected to see, he walked out the kitchen and came back inside to make sure he was seeing right. "When did you get in?"

"Two minutes ago."

"Oh," Kane muttered. He walked up to him, about to give him a hug until he noticed the look on King's face. He wore a malicious scowl. "Is there something you want to say?"

King's eyebrows furrowed. "How are you going to have that bitch in your bedroom?"

"Oh, I see the problem," Kane replied. "You saw Tricia here and you want some sort of explanation. I don't have to give you one."

"Fuck you," King yelled, jumping off his stool. "You're supposed to be with my mom and you're running behind her like this? Does this shit make you feel better or something? How long have you been banging her?"

They were standing face to face. "You don't have the right to ask me about anything I do. I suggest you watch your mouth."

"Nah, you need to watch your mouth," King shouted. "Matter of fact, you need to wash your mouth. That hoe sucked my dick."

Kane shot a right hook in King's face. He had done it so quick; he didn't feel King's retaliation. His son grabbed him at the waist, and they were wrestling on the floor when Kristian and Akaila barged in. They pulled King away from him, yet Kane managed to punch his son again.

"How could you leave my mama for her? She's fuckin' dirty, man. You need to wash your mouth out with soap."

Kane's chest heaved up and down. He was ready for round two, yet King ran from the kitchen before he could jump on him. Meanwhile, Akaila and Kristian were staring at him in disbelief.

"He's only been here five minutes. What happened?" Kristian screamed. "Who is he talking about?"

"No one," Kane replied. "He doesn't know what he's talking about."

Kane grabbed a dishtowel from the island and wiped the sweat from his face. He then left the kitchen only to see King's Mustang disappearing from the driveway. He didn't know where his son was going, but he prayed he kept his relationship with Tricia a secret. The moment Carmen found out; he could kiss her and the ten million dollars goodbye.

***

King pressed his foot harder on the gas, speeding into Coco's neighborhood. He hadn't spoken or seen her since their eventful day at the Brookstone Police Department. After the fight with his father, he had to see someone. His heart longed for her.

Once in her driveway, he got out his car, hollering her name. It was early and if he was lucky, he would catch her before she went to school. "Coco, Coco," he yelled, hoping she heard him. He banged his fist on her door until it opened. Mrs. Masterson looked at him like he was deranged. He took a step back as she came on the porch. The last person he wanted to see, he stood there speechless.

"Jayceon Santiago. Well, you're the last person I thought I'd see on a Tuesday morning. What's wrong with you? Your lip is bleeding."

"I need to see her," he said. "I have to talk to her."

"Jayceon," Mrs. Masterson said, "Coco, and I made a mutual decision for her not to see you. Now, I can tell her you're here, but she's not going to talk to you."

"Yes, she will, she's just scared of you."

"No, she's not scared of me. She doesn't want to talk to you."

"I need to talk to her," King yelled, starting to lose it.

"Okay, now you can get off my porch with that one."

Mrs. Masterson closed the door in his face. King stood there in denial, waiting for someone to come. When no one did, he left the porch, going back to his car. He looked at Coco's window, only to see her staring back at him. Before he could do anything, she moved away. Unsure of where to turn or what to do, he got back inside his Mustang. He drove around the city until he ran out of gas.

41 | *Cleaning Out My Closet*

Kristian turned to Akaila as she pieced together what they witnessed. Based off what King said, there was another woman in the picture. If King suspected it to be Akaila's mother, he was confused. The woman had been at their house, but it wasn't because she was in a relationship with their father. She came to see about Akaila and Malachi. "What do you think?" she asked Akaila.

Akaila shrugged her shoulders. "Who knows? There's always something going on. They'll make up by dinner."

Kristian didn't reply. The idea of her father cheating on her mother didn't sit well with her. It did more than hit home because it reminded her of her tryst with Nicholas. So far, it was a onetime thing, but it was one time too many. She didn't want to be like her mother, and something told her to end things with Nicholas before she cheated again. If she didn't, Dijuan would find out and she would lose him.

"I have a stop to make," she told Akaila when they got in the car. "I'm going to drop you off and I'll be back in a few minutes."

Akaila waited for an explanation. Kristian didn't give her one, so she decided not to pry. Her sister had been steering clear of Lil' Noc so she figured she was sneaking around with Dijuan. It was something she was known to do since she got her license.

Little did she know, Kristian was going to see her ex-boyfriend. On terms different than before, Kristian was certain she was making the best decision. Not the least bit afraid to speak her mind, she drove to Nicholas' house unannounced. Thankfully, his Cadillac was in the driveway. He answered the door after the second knock. He let her inside; however, he didn't let her go past the foyer. She understood why when she noticed his father sitting in the living room.

"I didn't expect this," he admitted. "What's going on?"

"I wanted to talk to you about something."

"Look, I know those words," he stated. "You don't have to beat around the bush. If you're concerned over what we did, I understand. I'm not going to pressure you."

"It's that, but there's a little bit more to it," Kristian began. "I feel guilty about it. You know, I'm with Dijuan, and I'm certain, you know about the issues going on with my parents. I don't want to be that girl. I want to stay faithful to my boyfriend. To do that, I can't be with you."

Nicholas chuckled although a part of him was hurt. "I knew you were sprung on him. I also know you're not up to my speed. We got a good four years between us. Maybe we'll get together another time. Who knows? Do you really think you can resist me?"

Kristian put her hands on her hips. "Hey, I can do anything if I put my mind to it. Besides, it's about being loyal. It's also about finding a way to deal with this guilt. I guess you should know I'm planning on telling him about us. It may seem like the wrong move, but in the end, I gotta live with this. I'm not one of those people who can cheat and just brush it off their shoulder. That's not me. I want to do what I feel is right. Hopefully, he'll forgive me, and we can move on."

Nicholas folded his arms across his chest. "It takes a real woman to sit up here and bare her heart. I wouldn't recommend that, but if you must, go ahead. I mean, we both know Dijuan ain't gonna press me. If anything, you'll catch all the heat."

"Maybe so," Kristian replied. "So, we're cool?"

Nicholas opened his arms for a hug. Once Kristian was in his embrace, he kissed her cheek. "We're always going to be cool. I knew from the beginning how you felt about him. I know one thing, though. He better take care of you. I'll fuck him up if he does you dirty."

Kristian chuckled although he was serious. "Thank you, Nicholas, for understanding and everything."

"Yeah, well, you know, I'm making a lot of changes this month. For one, I enrolled at Brookstone University. I'm starting school in August. Since that new guy entered town, the streets aren't paying the same. I need a new hustle. Well, a legit hustle."

Kristian broke away from him. "So, first your name is Nicholas and now you're going to college. What else is new?"

"That's it, ma. I'm making a change. You see that man in there," Nicholas pointed at his father, "he wants me to be better than him. He told me it was time to hang it up, so I did. I got enough for tuition so I'm good."

"You've done a major change from when I first met you. I gotta give it to you, I'm proud." Kristian gave him another quick hug, which he returned. If time was on her side, she would've said more. Since it wasn't, she whispered goodbye and headed to school. The day went by quicker than expected. Before long, she was meeting Dijuan on the basketball court at their local rec center. She didn't want to interrupt his game, so she waited until he was done to speak to him.

When he dribbled the ball her way, she headed over to him. "Was that a warm-up for the championship game?"

"Yeah, something like that," he said with a smile. "I would hug you, but I'm all sweaty now." Dijuan sniffed his armpits, which only made Kristian laugh.

"I want to talk to you about something," she began. "You know what I'm going through with my parents. I was disappointed in my mom, but I'm no different than her."

Dijuan wrinkled his face. In his mind, Kristian wasn't anything like her mother. She was the exact opposite, which was why he was drawn to her. "You and your mother are two different people. You won't ever be like her. Why are you comparing yourself to her?"

"Because I'm just like her," Kristian told him. She moved closer to him. "You asked me before if I liked Lil' Noc and I told you no. I said we didn't have anything going on because we didn't. One day, though, something happened."

Dijuan dropped the basketball. "What do you mean something happened? Did you kiss him?"

"It was a one-time thing. It won't happen again. We agreed on it."

Dijuan's face turned bright red. He looked around the gym to see if anyone was eavesdropping. She was admitting to him in public that she cheated. "You mean I've been walking around here with the dumb face while he's been messing with you. He probably told everybody."

"He didn't tell anyone anything. I didn't either."

"Then, why are you telling me, Kris? It's obvious you're guilty. What happened besides the kiss? Did you do something else with him?"

Kristian's lip trembled. She was on the verge of tears, and she could tell he was as well. He was trying to hold it together. "We messed around," she told him. "We didn't have sex, but we did things."

Dijuan's mouth dropped open. "You touched him, like, you played with him?" As the thought settled further in Dijuan's mind, his volume increased. "You had to do more than that. He's not a virgin, Kris. Everyone knows that. I know you had sex with him."

"I didn't have sex with him," Kristian cried. "We messed around, but it was eating me up inside. It only happened once, and I felt bad about it. It won't happen again, but I felt like, if I didn't tell you, I wouldn't be able to breathe. I love you. I only wanted to be honest about the situation."

"Well, I appreciate your honesty, but I don't date cheaters."

Dijuan picked up the basketball, taking a step away from her. "If you really loved me, you would've had self-control. What you loved was having your chance of being with a thug. I guess you wanted recognition. I don't need that, though. I didn't date you because you were a model or because you had a famous mother. I dated you because you were someone special. I only wished it was the same."

"It is the same, Dijuan. You mean the world to me. I'm sorry."

Dijuan shook his head, not wanting to hear her apology. "It's all good, Kris. We'll go back to being friends and you can tell Lil' Noc you're single. I know that's what he wants."

"I don't—" Dijuan turned on his heel and went back to his teammates. Kristian cried as she went, her heart breaking into two. To make her feel worse, he started up another game as if he hadn't dumped her. Not quite sure what to do, she left the gym, crying the whole way home.

42 | *One Becomes Two*

Torn was an emotion both Kristian and Carmen could identify with. While her daughter longed not to follow in her footsteps, she had, and was now reaping the consequences. As for Carmen, the consequences of her actions had already come. Now, her patience was dwindling. The mediation between her and Kane was scheduled for tomorrow morning, yet her husband hadn't said anything about canceling it.

Not quite sure why she allowed him in her bed, she moved away from him. They stayed in that position until the alarm clock woke them both. Kane was the first one up while she remained in bed. He still didn't mention the meeting although they were both scheduled to be there at nine o'clock. He simply showered, dressed, kissed her forehead, and left. Two hours later, she was sitting across from him in a meeting. He didn't back down from the ten million, which shocked both her and Clement. He even stated he wanted to move forward with the divorce. Halfway through the meeting, Carmen walked out.

In Carmen's mind, there was nowhere to turn. Kane wanted a divorce, which she had no choice, but to grant him. Before she agreed, she called King to tell him how his father was acting. For some reason, her son didn't act surprised. In fact, he encouraged her to divorce him. King's words were shocking until he reminded her she didn't need the extra stress.

With Rakim in the hospital and her eldest son on his way to prison, Carmen needed to eliminate as much headache as possible. Therefore, she returned to the meeting and told Clement her decision. She was ready to move forward with the divorce.

43 | *Caught Out There*

The first step to Carmen moving on was joining the girls and Tiara in the City for Mantra Designs' fashion show. Before she could, she had to drop off a few things for Rakim at Kane's house. She didn't necessarily want to go to there, but she was running late and the drive there was shorter than the one to the hospital. "Are y'all excited?" Carmen asked the girls. "This is one of the biggest fashion shows of the summer. Y'all have an all access pass."

"I'm excited about meeting Misa," Coco said from the backseat. "She designed a new line of dresses, which I'm hoping to get. What about you, Miss Flame?" She tapped Kristian's shoulder, noticing she had been quiet for most of the ride. "Are you alive up there?" she joked.

Kristian gave her a small smile. She hadn't been listening to the conversation, her mind centered on Dijuan and their break-up. "I guess I'm sort of nervous," she said, unsure if her answer was correct for the question. "I want to see what's trending."

"Well, you will see plenty of that," Carmen replied. She pulled in Kane's driveway and asked Akaila to hand her the bag filled with breast milk. Once Carmen had it in her hands, she got out the car, and walked towards the house. She looked at it totally different because of the current state of her marriage. Since the mediation, Kane hadn't come over or visited her. They stopped all contact.

Not quite at the door, Carmen noticed a light-skinned woman emerging from the house with her husband. They were holding hands, causing her to drop the bag of milk. She stared at the woman, trying to figure out who she was. She looked familiar, but she couldn't put a name to her face. Kane appeared shocked as well, although he knew she was coming over.

He dropped the woman's hands. He walked towards her, yet Carmen backed away, picking up the bag of milk. She now remembered who the woman was. An ex-girlfriend of Jay's who she hadn't seen in over seventeen years.

"Carm, wait a minute," Kane yelled. "I need that bag."

Carmen ignored him as she got inside and locked the doors. She backed out the driveway, screaming questions at her daughters and Coco. "Who knew about her? Is she the reason he decided to move forward with the divorce?"

Kristian covered her face, sighing at the image of her father and Tricia. "No one knew about them, Mama."

"Well, I kind of knew," Akaila admitted. "She is my mother."

Carmen's foot slammed hard on the brakes. "She's your what? I thought your mother's name was Theresa. That isn't her name?"

Akaila bit her lip because she was spilling more details than she would have liked. "My mother's name isn't Theresa. I'm not quite sure why you thought that, but her name is Tricia DeGonzaza. I didn't know they were dating, but I kind of assumed something was going on."

Carmen put her head on the steering wheel, starting to cry. She now knew the reason why Kane hadn't stopped the divorce. He was seeing another woman and couldn't decide who he wanted to be with. "I can't believe this," she whimpered. "How could he do this to me? He said he wanted to…" Carmen's voice trailed off. The conversation wasn't one she should be having in front of the girls. She dried her tears, telling herself to get it together. "This is what we're going to do," she told him. "Y'all are going to take the car and meet up with Tiara. I'm going to stay behind and take care of Rakim. Call Tee and let her know I'm not coming. Y'all can ride with her since she's making the trip alone."

"We're not going to the fashion show without you," Kristian shrieked. "This is for Tiara's engagement."

"Baby, I can't go. I need to wrap my mind around this. I'll make it up to Tiara. Tell her what happened."

Carmen pressed her foot on the gas before handing her phone to Kristian. Her daughter didn't take it at first, but after a few seconds she did. She made the phone call to Tiara, breaking the news of her father's infidelity.

A pill Carmen couldn't swallow; she forced it down. She even confronted Kane about it when he came to her apartment. Her husband appeared to be relieved and embarrassed all at the same time. She was anxious to hear his explanation especially since he'd been put on blast in front of their daughters and Coco.

"I'm waiting," she told him, tapping her foot.

"Can I come inside so we can talk like two adults?"

Carmen narrowed her eyes. "Not after what I witnessed. You were the one telling me how you wanted to work on our marriage. How we needed to get the trust back. How long have you been sleeping with her? Was it before I slept with Jay? Were you the one who was cheating this whole time?"

Kane knew Carmen would try to spin the whole thing. "I wasn't with her. To be honest, I'm not with her now. It's just something going on I'm trying to figure out."

"What do you need to figure out? Is that why you're divorcing me? Our court hearing is in a month, Kane. Our divorce will be final then. So, are you giving yourself a month to choose between us? Please believe me when I tell you, you don't need it. The decision was made when I saw you with her."

Kane rested his back on the door as he gathered his thoughts. He wanted Carmen and Tricia, but for different reasons. Sexually, Tricia was more open than his wife, but his wife was more stable. While Carmen had all the financial means in the world, she also had Jay Santiago who he learned was back in Brookstone. He could never trust her if he was in the picture. "We weren't ready yet, Carm. Things were good, but I wasn't ready to make another commitment."

"You didn't want to make a commitment, but you sure as hell wanted to come and fuck me. Well, Kane, it's my turn to ask the questions. Did you sleep with Tricia? I already know you did. I can see it in your eyes."

"I am sleeping with her. I didn't do it for revenge, and I didn't do it to hurt you. The opportunity was there, I got weak, lost control, and it happened. Now, I gotta live with it."

A tear fell down Carmen's face. "I'm done, Michael. I am. I tried to work this out, I tried to save our marriage, but I can't do this anymore. I give up. If you want to be with Tricia, be with her. I'll see you in court." She started to close the door, yet Kane's arm stopped her.

"I need some time, Carm. I need some time to see where this is going to go."

"Then, you can take your time. I'm not waiting on you anymore. Our relationship is over. You go your way, I go mine." Carmen pushed him in the hall and closed the door. Symbolic of their relationship, she broke down crying, realizing she officially ended their relationship. Seventeen years of her life was down the drain. Karma had taken a bite once again.

To make matters worse, she was ready to get her revenge. Jay was back in Brookstone and the idea of devouring him was tantalizing and tempting. She found enough strength to get off the floor and grabbed her phone from the kitchen. She started to dial his number until the guilt hit. She may have loved him but running to him because she was hurt wasn't fair to either of them. Jay deserved more than a one night stand. Therefore, she put the phone back down. In the process, her fingers accidentally dialed his number. She wasn't aware of the error until she heard a deep voice say hello.

"Jay," she called.

When the line went silent, Carmen was unsure of what to think. The last few weeks were hard for him, and he probably had second thoughts about talking to her. "I guess this phone call was in the cards," she told him. "I dialed your number accidentally."

"So you didn't want to speak to me?"

Carmen sighed at his question. "There's been so much going on. I was so used to you being around that when you left—" Jay saw through her scheme.

"The blogs can tell the story faster than you can. I know about your divorce, Peaches. I know Kane is still moving forward with it. I also know he wants ten million dollars. Is that what he calls working on a marriage?"

"Did you hear about Tricia? He's sleeping with her."

Jay let out a chuckle. "That doesn't surprise me. I could've told you all this. Well, the Tricia part surprises me. I knew from the beginning Kane was a snake. Now, you can see it for yourself."

Carmen broke down crying. "This is who I married?" she cried. "Seventeen years of my fuckin' life is gone. I lost my husband to a fuckin' drug addict."

Jay listened to her until he decided it was time to put an end to her tears. "Some people come in your life for a season. Sometimes you don't find out until the season is over. They also say, if you love something, let it go, if it comes back to you, it's yours. Do you believe that?" Jay didn't give her a chance to answer. "I let you go, Peaches. When I went to San Juan, that was me letting you go. You wanted to work on your marriage, I let you. Now, I'm back. All you gotta do is give me a chance."

Carmen wiped her face at the sound of his words. "I didn't want to do this with you, Jay. I don't want you to think I'm running to you because of what happened with Kane."

"I don't think that. I think you wanted to do the right thing and work on your marriage. When you saw it wasn't going to work, you realized you didn't have any fight left. We don't know what can happen down the line. I say we stop putting it off and do it now. So what if the timing isn't right? Has it ever been? I say, let's do it. Let's put aside everyone's opinions and do what we want to do. You've forgiven me, right?"

"Of course I have."

"And I've forgiven you. What else is holding us back?"

Carmen looked at her phone, staring at his name. *What is holding me back*, she asked herself. *I'm about to be divorced. I already know I'm in love with him. What else do I possibly have to lose?* Carmen exhaled. "You're right. Nothing is holding us back. I say we take it slow and see where we end up."

A smile formed on Jay's face although Carmen couldn't see. "You're all I need in this world, Peaches. Starting today, right now, I'm gonna make you the happiest woman alive. All I need you to do is watch."

44 | *The Other Side of the Game*

August

Within two months, the dynamics of Carmen's life changed. She divorced Kane, started a relationship with Jay, and Rakim was now at home full-time with her. In addition, King turned himself in and was currently at a state prison about two hours from Brookstone. Although the technicalities of her divorce were hard to work through, she was glad the judge only ordered her to pay two million of the ten Kane requested. In the end, she was able to move on and apparently Kane had as well.

For the past month or so, Kane had been allowing Tricia to stay with him. He thought the move would improve the relationship she had with her kids, but nothing changed. The only difference he saw was how he felt about her. In the beginning, their relationship was something new and fresh. She showed him a side of sex he'd never experienced. The pleasure soon ran dry. Even now, he could only give her a slight grunt when he came. Every part of him was in misery.

"That was good, baby," she whispered, giving him a small kiss.

Kane held her in place, wanting her to sleep on his chest like his wife used to. Tricia didn't seem up for it because she pulled away. When he grabbed her, she made it known she didn't want to be bothered.

"It's hot," she complained. "Playtime is over."

Kane didn't want to hear those words. He needed something to let him know she cared. The little things, like waking up to her asleep on his chest, and running his fingers through her hair, were the things he missed. Tricia never gave him the affection he needed. If anything, she simply wanted him to cum so she could go to sleep. Their relationship was one big sexual fantasy. It was satisfying in the beginning, but now Kane missed having a companion. With Tricia, he was her bank, and she paid him with her body. When it came to his wife, they were more of a team.

He proved himself to be right when Tricia woke him up an hour later to discuss an unpaid credit card bill. The conversation set him off, causing him to yell about her inability to be responsible. "Things aren't the same around here. I don't have Carmen helping with things anymore. You can't go out and buy expensive clothes and put them on a credit card you can't pay. Your waitressing gig doesn't support a bill like that. Not when you have two kids to feed. You're lucky Carmen is still taking care of them. If she wasn't, none of us would have a pot to piss in."

"Why do you have an attitude all of a sudden?" Tricia barked.

Kane jumped from the bed anxious to get away from her. "I have a whole lot more to think about than that bill. Both Kristian and Akaila are graduating from high school next year. Are you thinking about college? Carmen takes care of the kids, but when it comes to this house, she doesn't pay me a dime. You live here so you need to help with the bills. You can't do that because your chump change goes to a stupid credit card bill."

"Whatever," Tricia told him. "You knew my financial situation before you got with me."

Kane went inside the bathroom and slammed the door closed. He wanted to punch the glass, but if he did, it would only be another bill. Still, he needed to do something to calm himself. He was seething and could die from a heatstroke at any given moment.

"Kane," he heard her call from the bedroom. He opened the door. "I'm sorry," she said. "It's my bill. I'll work a double tomorrow to pay it."

"Fine," he replied. He slammed the door back only to stare at himself in the mirror. Every single day, she tested him. It was almost making him resent her. To add to his frustration, she turned on the television. The volume, much louder than his thoughts, poked at his temper. "I can't do this," he said aloud. He showered and dressed before heading for his bedroom door.

"Where are you going?" she asked as he grabbed the doorknob.

"Out," he told her. He slammed the door shut, leaving the house without another word. He got in his car and drove to Carmen's apartment. There was no set way to say he was wrong except to say it. Then, he would get on his knees and make her take him back.

Meanwhile, Tricia stared at the bedroom door, which was shut in her face. All the signs were there, which told her, he was fed up. He was barely speaking to her and when he did; his attitude was as fierce as a lion. The only reason she was still there was because of her kids. Although they held resentment towards her, Tricia felt whole being in their presence.

She tried every day to please them. She would always fail, but the next day she would try again. If she was ever going to give up then it would be now. However, she would only give up on Kane. She had seen and heard enough to know he wanted his wife back. The first initial sign was when he called Carmen's name in his sleep. It hurt her to her core, but nothing compared to that morning. It wasn't even about the credit card bill. What hurt the most was seeing his wedding ring on his hand. At that moment, their relationship was over. Therefore, she packed her things and moved back to her apartment.

45 | *The Woman You Love*

Jay kept the door to Rakim's room open although the baby monitor was on. In case Rakim needed their immediate attention, he wanted to be accessible. For the most part, Rakim had been sleeping throughout the night, but occasionally he would wake up crying and they would put him in their bed. "He's down for the night," he announced, walking in the living room. Carmen was flipping through channels while he tended to Rakim. He picked up her legs, putting them over his as he sat beside her. "I turned the monitor on, so we'll know if he needs us."

"Thank you, baby. Did y'all have fun feeding the ducks today?"

"Did we? He had more fun than me and he didn't throw in any bread. For him to be so small, he didn't cry or anything when the ducks came near us. Rakim might be a soldier."

"Well, we do want him to be all he can be," Carmen joked. She gave Jay a quick kiss on the cheek and felt him as he slipped the remote out her hand. He turned the television off as if he was setting the mood.

She smiled. "So, you think you're going to get it that easy?"

"I can go without sex, Carm. I was trying to help you out."

"Trying to help me? Okay, I'll take that one."

Carmen watched as he stood up only to drop to his knees. She raised her eyebrow. "Wow, Jay, are you really going to beg?" She giggled at the thought until she noticed the change in his expression. "You are, aren't you?"

"I'm not about to beg," he stated.

He changed his position to where he was only on one knee. When he dug in his pocket, Carmen closed her eyes. When she reopened them, she screamed, seeing the diamond ring. Her hands became clasped over her mouth as she studied everything about it. Way over ten carats, the ring had a sapphire stone, which had been paired with an emerald cut. The word yes came out her mouth three times before he posed the question.

"You know you're out of order, right?"

"My answer is yes, put it on," she yelled. She held out her hand.

"Can I do my part, please?"

Carmen tried to control her emotions, yet she was beaming with excitement.

"Carmen Denise Davenport, will you marry me?"

"Yes," she yelled, throwing her hand in his face.

Jay chuckled at her antics as he pulled the ring from the box. He slid it on her finger, engaging in a kiss at the same time. Before things got too heavy, he pulled away. "I want something else from you," he told her. "You've been good to me, allowing me to take care of Rakim, but I need something else. I want a baby."

Carmen remembered his face when he found out Rakim wasn't his. An expression she didn't want to see again, she told him yes. "Whatever you want," she replied. She leaned in to kiss him until she heard the doorbell. She watched as Jay stood up to answer it. She remained on the couch.

"It's almost one o'clock in the morning," she heard Jay yell.

Carmen jumped from the couch, pulling Jay away from the door. She figured Kane was in front of him and she needed to put space between them. "Go check on Rakim," she told Jay, grabbing his arm. "Give me five minutes, okay?" She gave him a quick kiss on the cheek and waited for him to head to Rakim's bedroom. Once he was gone, she turned to her ex, not expecting him to show up after Jay's proposal. "What are you doing?" she asked. "Rakim is asleep. We just put him down."

"I'm sorry," Kane said, going straight into his spiel. "I love you and I made a mistake. I can't do this without you. I'm living in hell right now. This Tricia thing was a mistake. I don't want her."

"Your timing is way off. I'm engaged."

Carmen held up her hand to show him her ring. His face turned upside down. "I'm helping Tiara plan her wedding and now I'm going to be planning my own. I'm not sure of the day, but I want to tie the knot after Malik and Tiara come back from their honeymoon."

"You're fuckin' kidding me."

Kane went ballistic, pacing the floor as if he couldn't believe the news. "You can't marry him. Look at me," he shouted, pointing at his chest. "I'm your soulmate."

"You were my soulmate. We moved on. I'm marrying Jay. That's the end of it."

Kane wasn't backing down. "I'm not going to let you."

"You don't have a choice. Things are different now. I'm serious about marrying Jay. There's more to this whole thing than this marriage."

"Then what is it?" He stared at her, searching for any kind of hint.

"We're going to have another baby." Carmen took a deep breath. "He doesn't know yet. I was about to tell him when we heard the doorbell. I'm four weeks pregnant. There's no question this time. The baby is his."

Kane backed away from the door, shaking his head. She couldn't marry Jay. He couldn't stop her from having the baby, but he could stop her from getting married.

46 | *Deal or No Deal*

It was never Carmen's plan to tell Kane about the pregnancy before Jay. When she did finally tell Jay, it was perfect timing. A full eight hours before Sapphire's opening night, the news took him over the top. While he wanted to stay and celebrate, he had to get to Sapphire to put the finishing touches on the club.

Currently standing in the middle of the dance floor, Jay listened as the DJ spun a few tracks. He signaled to Malice, his in-house electrician to test the lights. Seconds later, the whole entire room turned royal blue. Add in the well-stocked bar and bouncers, Sapphire was back in business. "Four hours until showtime," he shouted. He looked towards the window of his office where Malik was sitting. His friend looked down, giving him a fistpump regarding their latest feat. Everything was coming together, but there was still a missing piece. The main person responsible for getting the club together wasn't even present to see the dream come alive. Right then and there, Jay made a promise. Once King was out, he was having another grand opening in honor of him. About to voice the thought to Phase, he was interrupted.

"I need to talk to you," someone said beside him.

Jay looked to his left to see Kane. Certain he knew about the engagement and pregnancy, he wanted Kane to say the wrong thing so he could pounce on him. "The club opens at ten. You can get in line like everyone else."

"I need you to call off the engagement."

Out of all the people in the world, Kane had the nerve to make a request of him. "Don't come with that bullshit, Kane. Get out my fuckin' club."

"I'm serious. I need you to call off the wedding. Tell Carmen you made a mistake."

Jay stepped inside Kane's body space. "Do you really think I'm about to let her go when she's about to have a baby by me? Your words are as stupid as your face."

"I'm giving you until the end of the week to call it off."

"I know you aren't giving me a deadline."

"You have until the end of this week," Kane repeated.

"I have until the end of the week and what? Are you going to try and send me to prison? Guess what, Carmen will bail me out because after tonight, I'm going to tell her about this conversation. I'm going to tell her you came here trying to threaten me."

Kane made his wants clear. "I want my wife back."

"You don't have a wife," Jay told him. "You divorced her. You don't remember? Nah, you forgot. Do me a favor, Kane, take your ass off my property."

Kane spat on the dance floor. Under normal circumstances, Jay would've punched him. Something told him to remain calm. He was too close to being on top to let Carmen's ex-husband ruin things for him.

Jay knew it to be true when he saw the large stacks of money left on his desk after the club closed. The moment felt surreal, and he shared it with Malik once he answered his call.

"We had to stop letting people in because things got packed," Jay told him. "If we can do this every night, we'll be set." Jay got inside his car. "Man, I'm going to—" Jay stopped, hearing his passenger side door open. A gun cocked in his ear.

"Hang up the fuckin' phone."

Jay hung up on Malik. The barrel of the gun was pressed at his temple.

"Don't say a fuckin' word."

Jay stared out the corner of his eye as the barrel came down. The voice belonged to Kane. He waited for him to give a directive.

"I'm going to tell you one more fuckin' time—"

"You're about to die in this motherfucker," Jay yelled. The barrel went back to his temple.

"I got a gun to your head and you're still talking shit. Shut the fuck up and listen," Kane spat. "You're gonna call off this engagement. I'll let you keep your baby, but this wedding ain't gonna happen."

"What bullshit are you on? Go ahead and pull the trigger. I'm not calling off the engagement."

Kane pistol-whipped him to show he was serious. The move only made Jay reach for his nine, but Kane was quick. He placed a pistol at Jay's chest, which he felt. "Put the fuckin' gun down, bitch."

Jay's temper flared, hearing the same words Kane said to him when he brought down his cartel. The situation was much deeper than the one seventeen years ago. He allowed his nine to fall from his hands. A gun was at his temple and chest, which he knew Kane would use. Therefore, he had to think fast. "Listen up," Jay shouted. "I have a proposition for you." He waited for Kane to respond and when he didn't, he kept talking. "I got something you want, and I need you to get something I want."

"Spit," Kane told him, wanting to know the plan.

"Do you remember the Pink Sunrise?"

"Is that what you want?" Kane asked. "Good luck getting it."

"We both know it's mine. You give me the pink diamond; I'll give you your wife back. The minute you put it in my hand, I'll call off the engagement. No questions asked. There is a catch, though."

"I already know the catch. No one knows where it is."

"Shit, you're a fuckin' Triad agent. Find it. I'm giving you three days." Jay looked in his rearview mirror and watched as Kane moved the guns away from him. "If you don't find it in three days, the deal is off. I'll marry Carmen as planned. I'll be honest. I know you're not going to find it."

"Where is she now?"

"She's at home with Rakim."

"It's probably in the safe deposit boxes at the bank," Kane replied. "It doesn't matter. I'll find it in three days. Count me in."

47 | *Dead Presidents*

The following morning, Kane left his house. The only thing on his agenda was to find the pink diamond. With only three days to cough it up, he had limited time to search various places. His initial plan was to use his Triad pull to gain access to Carmen's safe deposit boxes. When he arrived at the bank, he went straight to one of the tellers, requesting permission to enter the safe depository room.

"I need you to sign in," the lady told him, pointing at a clipboard.

Kane did as she said and then followed her to a long corridor. The teller unlocked the door for him and went inside, grabbing a clipboard.

"Okay, Agent Kane, what safe deposit boxes need to be open?"

"I need to see the safe deposit box for Carmen Davenport."

The woman looked at the list and then checked a few boxes. She then turned the page, checking more boxes.

"Okay, there are a total of six boxes. I'll unlock them for you. You're not allowed to take anything because you didn't bring in the formal documentation from a judge. However, since you have a warrant I'll let you be. I will have to let the security guard check you to ensure you didn't take anything. We also have a security system."

Kane watched as she opened the boxes. He waited until she was gone before he ran to the first one. He opened it and pulled out a bunch of papers. It was useless information, so he closed it back and moved on to the second box. He opened it, seeing a slip inside. It was a note for the status of an account she had. He stared at it seeing King's name on it and read the amount. For the first time in seventeen years, he learned his son had a trust fund in the amount of eight million dollars. He made a mental note and threw the slip back inside.

"I'm getting nowhere," he mumbled, bending down to the third box. He stared inside of it, seeing a bunch of documents. He recognized them as Carmen's release papers as well as court documentation of her trial. He didn't bother taking the documents out, closing the door to the box. When he went to the next one, he discovered more documentation. She owned stock in several companies including Baby Phat, Versace, and even in her mother's store in Texas. From what he was reading, Carmen was sitting on more than twenty million dollars. While the number was shocking, his main concern was the two boxes, which were left. The next one contained the certificate of ownership for the Rolex she bought King.

When he got to the last box, he was certain the pink diamond was inside. However, when he opened it, all he saw was a slip of paper with seven different numbers written on it. He didn't know what the numbers meant so he wrote them down on an old receipt in his wallet. If he was lucky, it would give him another lead. He closed the box and took the receipt to the teller. He slid the paper to her, hoping she could be of service. "Do you know what these numbers mean?"

"Bank accounts," she told him. "There are sixteen digits."

"Can you pull up these accounts for me?" he asked.

"I can. Do these accounts belong to the same woman from earlier?"

"Yeah, does she have seven bank accounts?"

The woman told him yes, starting to type in the numbers. "These numbers represent savings accounts. The first account is listed under Carmen Davenport and the balance is forty million dollars. The second account is under Carmen Davenport and Jayceon Santiago. It's for ten million. The third account is under Carmen Davenport and Kristian Kane. It's for ten million. This fourth account is for Carmen Davenport and Akaila DeGonzaza. It's for ten million. The fifth account is for Carmen Davenport and Malachi DeGonzaza. It's for ten million. The sixth account is for Carmen Davenport and Rakim Davenport for ten million. This last account is for Carmen Davenport and Baby Santiago for ten million."

"Baby Santiago," Kane questioned. He stared in the lady's eyes, realizing his ex-wife was already saving for her new baby. He shouldn't have been surprised since his wife's success was readily known. Instead of asking further questions, he told the teller thank you and left the bank. The visit had gotten him nowhere, but he now knew his wife was sitting on more than a hundred million dollars.

48 | *Overdose*

Back at her apartment, Tricia moaned as her body soaked in the warm water. A needle slipped from her fingertips, landing on the side of the tub. Her eyes dimmed from the sensations as the drug ran its course through her body. Moments later, Kane appeared in front of her. She could hear him telling her how sorry he was. Then, as if she accepted his apology, he slid in the tub with her. "I love you," she murmured as the hallucination continued. Her legs kicked at the water over the excitement of him being there. The enthusiasm was short-lived as reality sunk in. The last couple of days had been hell. Envious of his ex-wife, Tricia threw punches at his image, hitting nothing, but air. "Your wife doesn't even do what I do," she yelled at no one in particular.

Tricia laughed to herself and picked up the bottle of liquor she had brought in the bathroom with her. She took a large gulp before pouring the rest in the tub, the brown liquid mixing in with the clear water. A tingling sensation formed in her legs. "Stay calm," she whispered, feeling the effects of the heroin, "you're a big girl." The words were barely out her mouth before she started convulsing. Her body shook violently, foam pouring out her mouth until she eventually blacked out.

***

Tricia's apartment was only a few blocks away from the bank, which was why Kane decided to go there next. He had a key to her apartment, which he retrieved once he was at her door. Upon entering, he called her name several times only to never receive an answer. The silence prompted him to check her room where he found the clothes she wore earlier. He walked to the bathroom door and listened for any sounds. He could hear dripping water. He opened the door.

Then, he saw her. White foam covered her mouth, and her arm was hanging out the tub as if she tried to pull herself out. Long black lines were down her arm. He stood there frozen as he stared at Tricia's lifeless body. Kane knew he pushed her over the edge. He pushed her so far she went to a place of no return. Responsible for her demise, Kane stood there in disbelief before he dialed 911. Minutes later, a detective appeared on the scene as well as two paramedics. After giving a statement, she was declared dead, and he left the scene. While his next move should've been to Carmen since Akaila and Malachi were now their responsibility, he bypassed her all together. Time was of the essence, and he had less than sixty hours to find the pink diamond. If he didn't, his chances of ever being with Carmen again were lost.

***

The news of Tricia's death was headline news on all the major stations in Brookstone. Far away from a TV, Jay poured himself a glass of Cîroc and lemonade as he waited for Malik to arrive at Sapphire. The only one there, he paced the dance floor until he heard the front door open. When Kane walked inside, he noticed he was empty-handed.

"I can't find it," Kane stated, stopping in front of him.

"I know you can't find it. That's why I made the deal."

"I need an extension," Kane barked.

Jay replied with a chuckle. "That was never part of the deal. If you ask me, you're wasting your time. You should accept our engagement and stop the search. If you really loved her, you never would've let her go."

"I searched her safe deposit boxes, her house, every location of Flame, and even the corporate office. I can't find anything."

"Then the deal is over."

Jay walked away, hearing the door open again. This time, Malik walked inside. Jay pointed towards his office, hoping Kane would see himself out.

"Tricia is dead. She overdosed this morning."

That was the last thing Jay expected to hear. "God bless her soul," he whispered. With those words, he headed up the steps.

49 | *All Falls Down*

Sunday afternoon, Jay took Rakim off Carmen's hands so she could tend to Akaila and Malachi. He spent most of the day with her son at the park, not returning until later that night.

"Aww, look at you," she squealed, seeing Rakim asleep on Jay's shoulder. "My little Superman is out." She followed Jay into Rakim's room where he changed his diaper and put him in a new set of pajamas.

"Do you have some energy for me?" Jay asked as he placed a blanket over Rakim. "I know today was rough for you. How are Akaila and Malachi holding up?"

"Akaila really isn't showing any emotion. Malachi is staying to himself." Carmen placed her hands on her baby bump. "To answer your question, though, I do have some energy."

"Go ahead and get in bed. I'll be there shortly."

"I'll be waiting." She left Rakim's room, going in her own, and stripped herself of her clothes. She left on her bra and panties, staring at her growing stomach in the mirror. Jay's reflection appeared minutes later. He wrapped his hands around her. Not wanting to prolong their lovemaking, she brought her face to his, kissing him. "I love you," she told him, taking a breath.

Jay repeated the words before leading her to the bed. He pulled the covers back so they could get underneath. She undressed him in the process. Once he was completely naked, he did the same to her. Ready to devour, he pulled her legs apart, sliding himself inside. His body tensed up as he thrusted. Smiling amidst his moans, he told her he wasn't showing her any mercy.

Carmen didn't respond to his comment. She pushed him on his back, a devilish grin on her face until she was eye level with his manhood. In one quick second her hand was around his shaft while his head disappeared in her mouth.

"You learn quick," he moaned. "You're taking all that shit." Jay ran his fingers through Carmen's hair. He gave it a slight tug as more of his meat disappeared in her mouth. "Damn, Carm, you're taking all that shit," he repeated.

Carmen sucked him harder until the only sounds he made were moans. Not wanting him to climax too soon, she stopped before pulling him inside her yummy. She grinded her hips over his manhood, only pausing when she thought she heard something from the baby monitor. Realizing her error, she continued riding him, moaning as loud as she could.

Carmen knew he was close to climaxing when he pushed every single inch of himself inside her. "You're going to hurt the baby," she giggled. He thrusted harder and she threw her head back in orgasmic bliss. A loud moan sounded from her lips but was cut short when she heard a gun cocking. "What," she asked, opening her eyes. She peered at Jay only to see a gold-plated Desert Eagle in his hand. "What are you doing?" His eyes were bright red, and he was giving her a look she hadn't seen in years. *No one can have you,* she remembered. "Jay," she whispered. About to say more, she jumped at the sound of a loud creak.

Carmen watched as her closet door opened. When Kane stepped out, she covered herself. In the meantime, Jay stood from the bed, continuing to point the gun in Kane's direction.

"What the fuck are you doing?" Jay barked, holding the gun towards Kane's head. "Answer me, motherfucker."

Kane's face was distraught from watching his wife's performance. Still, he had to get her away from Jay. "I lost," he told her with an apologetic expression. "I tried, but I couldn't find it."

Jay draped his arm at his side, taking the gun away from Kane's head. The deal was never supposed to reach Carmen's ears.

"What are you talking about? What were you looking for?" she asked.

Jay gritted his teeth, not wanting Kane to disclose their secret. "Shut the fuck up," he yelled, pointing the gun at his head. "You don't even know what you're talking about."

"No," Carmen replied, "I think he does. What were you trying to find?"

Jay responded before Kane had the chance. "He's fuckin' crazy. Tricia's death made him a lunatic."

"Carmen, I love you," Kane began. "I made the deal because I needed to get you back. He wasn't gonna call off the engagement."

"What is he talking about, Jay? Tell me," she begged.

Jay didn't respond. When he saw Kane's lips move, he almost fired.

Kane revealed the secret. "He told me if I found the pink diamond, he would let me have you. I had three days to get it, but I couldn't find it. I didn't even find it here."

Carmen stood on her feet. "Is this true?" she asked Jay. She walked over to where he was, looking him square in the eye.

Jay swallowed. "He didn't find it."

"You fuckin' son of a bitch."

Carmen hit him with a cold hard slap. "You fuckin' son of a bitch. Is that what this shit is about? You want the fuckin' Pink Sunrise?"

Jay told his side of the story. "He put a fuckin' gun to my head. He threatened to kill me if I didn't call off the engagement. I had to think on my feet. I don't give a fuck about the diamond. I only want you."

"You dirty ass motherfucker." Carmen grabbed her hand, pulling the engagement ring off. She charged at Jay, pulling his mouth apart, forcing the ring inside. "Choke on it," she yelled.

Jay grabbed her shoulders, pushing her back as he spit the ring out.

"I can't believe you," Carmen whimpered. She backed away from him, tightening her robe around her. "How do you go and make a deal with my heart? What makes you think I want to be with him? Why would you trade me for a diamond?"

"I knew he wasn't going to find it. No one knows where the Pink Sunrise is."

"I know where it is, Jay," she screamed. "He could have asked me. If I told him, our relationship would've been over. We wouldn't be getting married. Do you understand that?"

"Would you have told him?" Jay asked. "Would you?"

Carmen threw a book at him, which missed his head. "I told him when he asked me the first time seventeen years ago. I just didn't know Tiara had it. If I told him then, guess what, I would tell him now."

Jay balled up his fists but relaxed his hands. His chest heaved up and down. He tried to maintain control. "I love you, Carm. I made the deal knowing he wouldn't find the diamond. I wasn't trying to play with your heart. If anything, I made the deal to keep him from putting a bullet in my damn head."

"Well, you lost. Pick up your ring."

Jay stared at Kane. His facial expression hadn't changed. He was staring into space not saying a word. "Tell her," he ordered. "You know what you did. You know I don't give a fuck about that diamond."

Kane didn't reply. Carmen called off the engagement and anything he said could make her change her mind. Therefore, he kept quiet.

Deep down, Jay knew Kane wasn't coming to his aid. He wanted their engagement to end. He found a way to do it without even finding the Pink Sunrise. "It's not about winning or losing," he told Carmen, grabbing his shirt. "It's about finding a way out. I was looking for a way out, so I made the deal. If you end things with me, you were only looking for a way out."

Carmen disagreed with him. "I never looked for anything. You gave me a way out. You and Kane made the decision for me."

Jay swallowed, making the decision to give her some time and space. The news of the deal was fresh, which meant she could potentially come around once she thought things over. He dressed and gathered his things, preparing to leave. Before he could, he turned to face her one last time. "I don't want to be alone, Peaches."

Carmen didn't reply and her lack of words prompted Jay to leave. She listened as he let himself out and she followed behind him so she could lock the door. In the meantime, Kane joined her in the living room. When she noticed he was there, she dismissed him as well. "You can leave, too," she told him. She opened the door and pointed to the hall.

"Where is the pink diamond?" he asked, not moving.

Carmen let out a small sigh before closing the door. "After everything that's happened, you're gonna ask me that? Why didn't you ask me when you made the deal with him? You were the one who had to find it. I swear, Kane, to be the highest paid Triad agent, you gotta be the dumbest. Maybe, you didn't want me as much as you thought you did."

Carmen walked up to him and grabbed his hand. She was surprised to see him wearing his wedding ring, yet she didn't ask why he had it on. She lifted his hand to his face so he could see the band. Two spectrums of color appeared, but as she continued to move the ring, pink became the only visible color. "There's your answer," she told him, dropping his hand.

"You put it in my ring?"

Kane's eyes grew large, realizing the diamond was right under his nose. He became confused, stuttering his words, which only went ignored. Carmen had gone back to the door and was holding it open like she was ready for him to leave. "Why did you give it to me?"

Carmen was ready for the night to be over. "Why don't you tell me?" She pointed to the hallway and waited for him to make his move. Once he did, she closed the door. He rung her doorbell, but Carmen ignored him. Upon entering her bedroom, she noticed her engagement ring on the floor. Not wanting to look at it, she got inside her bed, crying herself to sleep.

50 | *Making Peace*

The events of that night never faded from Carmen's mind but were put on the backburner. Her focus turned to Akaila and Malachi. Even now, as they walked to Tricia's grave, she studied Akaila's face. She still wasn't showing emotion towards her mother's death.

Akaila followed behind her mother's casket, still hearing the bittersweet voice of the woman from their church. Her brother's hand was in hers and she couldn't help but let the words of the song slip silently through her lips.

The battle is not yours, it's the Lord's, was a lesson Akaila learned early on. From dealing with her father's suicide, her mother's addiction, and her days of turning tricks, she survived it all by the grace of God.

Malachi cried on her shoulder, and she tried her best to comfort him. He wanted their mother to overcome her battle and it hurt him to see she failed. Akaila reminded him that things happened for a reason, yet she knew those weren't the words he wanted to hear. To soothe his mind, she told him they were in a much better place than before. With both of their parents deceased, there wasn't anything in place to stop Carmen and Kane from adopting them. In a month or so, the paperwork for their adoption would be complete.

Akaila took a deep breath as a tear slid down her face. She wiped it away like it was never there.

Kristian noticed the tear although she had her own. A few hours earlier, she met with Dijuan who wanted to make peace. While he wasn't ready to be in a relationship, they were now on speaking terms. No one knew of the conversation until the repast.

The news made quite an impact and led Coco to visit King at his prison facility. The first time she spoke to him since her arrest, the visit made her nervous. King spent most of the time talking about his family, ignoring the issues between them. Based off what he told her, his father was now living in Puerto Rico because of his failed engagement. In addition, he was set to inherit eight million dollars when he turned eighteen. King spoke proudly of his plans until she interrupted him.

"I had to take some time away from you," she told him. "I thought things would be different with me. I never expected to get caught up in anything you were doing. After seeing Dijuan and Kristian make up, I realized how importance forgiveness is. I decided to forgive you. I even told my parents I wanted to give you another chance. Of course, my mother isn't pleased, but she knows I want you back in my life."

"I never left," King replied.

Coco rubbed her lips together, staring at him. She touched the window with her right hand, showing him he had. "This is what's separating us. It's trying to keep us from finishing what we started, but I won't let it. I'm willing to make this work if you're willing to as well."

King pressed his left hand on the window. "I won't let anything stop us," he told her. "I'm all in." King meant every word he said. He made a promise to himself. Upon his release, he would never see the walls of a prison again.

Epilogue | *Diamonds Are Forever*

Carmen watched as Tiara stuffed a huge slice of cake in Malik's mouth. Only a few feet away from them, numerous photographers stepped in front of her, snapping photos of the new couple. A camera was in her hand as well, yet she hadn't snapped one single photo. She was reminded of it when Kane pulled it from her hand.

Their relationship had taken another turn, this time ending in a ceremony where they renewed their vows. The decision wasn't an easy one especially after learning she was giving birth to Jay's first daughter, Nyla Jaslene Santiago. The marriage wasn't necessarily what Jay wanted to hear yet the deed was done. While Carmen's initial plan was to still marry him, the communication lines became blurred once he left for Puerto Rico. Now, they hardly spoke unless it was about Blue Magic or their kids.

Everything about her life was changing. For one, she purchased a multi-million dollar estate on the outskirts of East Brookstone. In addition, she employed a new maid to assist with the household. Kane also found a buyer for their old house, deciding to sell it to King who was set to receive a lump sum from his trust fund. The house would be a new start for him once he was released and would also remain in the family.

Carmen's attention shifted back to Tiara and Malik. They were engrossed in a full-on kiss, which garnered more flashing lights from the cameras. To add to the moment, Malik had his hands wrapped around Tiara's waist, showing the world she was five months' pregnant with their first child. The perfect ending to their wedding, Carmen looked at her own husband. She remembered the question he'd posed when they were at her apartment.

Why did she give him the pink diamond? Why did she put it in his wedding ring?

Carmen wondered if he ever discovered the answer. Certain it was the last thing on his mind; she touched his leg to get his attention. When he looked at her, she gave him a quick kiss on the lips. She now had an answer to share. "Do you remember when you asked me about your ring?" She didn't wait for his response, deciding to give him her answer. "It's always been said that a diamond is forever. Well—" Carmen was interrupted by a round of applause. She turned her attention towards Tiara and Malik who were both holding flutes of sparkling cider. Then, her eyes fell on Malik's best man. His eyes were frozen on hers as if she was speaking directly to him. "Just like that diamond," she said, as she stared at Jay, "my love is forever."

www.ingramcontent.com/pod-product-compliance
Lightning Source LLC
Chambersburg PA
CBHW02074225062 6
47155CB00003B/872